Penumbra

Dan Ackerman

Supposed Crimes LLC • Matthews, North Carolina

This book is a work of fiction. Names, characters, places, and incidents are products of the author's imagination or are used fictitiously. Any resemblance to actual events or locales or persons, living or dead, is entirely coincidental.

Published in the United States.

ISBN: 978-1-952150-14-2

Cover Art by Vincent Pesce

www.supposedcrimes.com

This book is typeset in Goudy Old Style.

For David

PENUMBRA

For generations, *Eden* had watched, motionless, as the planet died below it.

Although, Arden supposed, he only thought of the planet as *below* because the gravity made by the space station oriented them so that the north pole of the planet was beneath the floors they walked. In space, above and below didn't really exist.

Built to house several million people comfortably, most of *Eden* sat unused, cleaned and serviced every so often by the thralls. Arden's great-great-great-grandmother had built *Eden* with room for the population to grow, a haven for humanity.

It hadn't gone exactly to plan.

Most people couldn't afford a place on *Eden*.

No one new had come aboard since before Arden had been born.

"Your Eminence?"

Arden peeled his eyes away from the dying planet to look at the thrall who addressed him. A plain, unremarkable man, one of the thousands of generationally indentured people that served the peerage.

Rhys kept his eyes demurely lowered and his hands folded over his abdomen.

"What could have you disturbing me at this hour?"

"I beg your forgiveness, Your Eminence. I thought you might want to review this quarter's numbers."

The slightest bit of defiance.

No other thrall would have dared to approach Arden in his private viewing room, let alone suggest he might need a thrall to remind him of anything, let alone something as important as *Eden*'s quarterly reports.

No one would have allowed a thrall to get away with something like that, but Arden let Rhys do so with disturbing regularity.

Arden stared down Rhys, who peeked up with a hint of a smile curling one corner of his mouth. "Is there any difference from last quarter?"

"I regret to inform you there's no improvement."

Arden grunted.

The same problems as always: not enough people to do all the jobs *Eden* required. The limited number of thralls couldn't produce enough goods or crops. Oh, no one starved, of course. Not even the thralls.

"Did you wish to see the numbers?"

"No, I trust you, Rhys." Arden moved over to one of the lounging couches and reclined against the arm. His robe spilled open to reveal a pallid expanse of scrawny chest, all bones. All of him looked like that, too thin and too pale.

Even the most sycophantic peers had never managed to convince Arden that they wanted to fuck him for anything but status and favors.

None of the thralls had ever dared to so much as look at him, let alone touch him. Plenty of thralls came on to the peers; it was an effective way to get something special, a nice treat or an hour or so off from work. None of them came on to Arden. Not a hint of that flirtatious defiance that thralls used to show interest in a peer.

"Does Your Eminence need anything?" Rhys offered. "Breakfast?"

Arden stretched and twisted a length of auburn hair over his shoulder. "How about a little bit of Twelve?"

Rhys bowed his head and withdrew from the viewing room. He returned a quarter of an hour later with a tray bearing a shot of Twelve, as well as a small bowl of oatmeal and strawberries.

Arden downed the shot and closed his eyes as the familiar warmth and numbness rolled through him, toes to teeth. He sunk lower into the couch and ran his fingers over the smooth, soft fabric of his robe.

He smiled.

"Any appetite?" Rhys asked.

Arden opened his eyes. He took the oatmeal. He wasn't hungry but he liked strawberries.

By the time he finished eating, the Twelve had settled over him, smoothed him out.

Rhys casually reminded him of a Council meeting and Arden consented to be bathed and dressed.

A few more thralls came in, their eyes so downcast Arden thought they would have gotten more done blindfolded.

But that *was* their place.

How would Arden have behaved toward someone to whom he owed more money than ten lifetimes could ever repay?

Every thrall on *Eden* had indentured themselves to the Torre family.

Even the debts of those who had come aboard with the first wave of citizens had not yet diminished by half. Arden's children and his children's children, and likely even their children, would still hold indentures.

If he ever had children.

Some peers his age had taken a spouse and started a family, but many more waited. A thrall of thirty-five would have a brood, as many as they could have by biology or adoption. More children spread the debt around and made it somewhat more likely that it might ever get paid.

But Arden, well. He'd never had occasion to know any children and couldn't say whether he liked them or not.

As for a spouse, he could have had anyone he wanted, even if they had already wed another.

A thrall pulled a long jacket over his arms and onto his shoulders. It glittered, the thick black fabric studded with black beads.

Another helped him into silver shoes, the only color in his ensemble that day.

The thralls departed.

Rhys followed him to the Public Chamber, which, funnily enough, only became available to the public twice a year: Founder's Day and Giving Day. Except for those days, only Council members and the head of the Torre family could enter.

And Rhys.

But he never said anything that anyone else could hear. He stood behind Arden, a shadow clad in the plain garments of a thrall. He would, rarely, lean forward and whisper something.

For the most part, no one noticed him. Just another thrall, his dark hair in a small bun, his skin pale brown, and his eyes as black as the void outside. Unobtrusive, unremarkable.

Half the time Arden forgot he was there. Sometimes even when Rhys was talking to him.

Eleven Council members took their seats around the long table of the Public Chamber. They chattered among each other, grumbled about the earliness of the hour, the incompetence of the thralls they rented, the surliness of their partners or children.

Arden soaked in the calm of the Twelve he'd taken.

He listened, half-heartedly, to the usual discussions about shortages, especially on items deemed luxe. At the direction of the Council and the distress of the peers, the Work Committee had moved most artisans from their crafts to different trades. Farming, maintenance, those more necessary things.

The Council had resisted Arden's suggestions to do so for about a year.

Arden had ignored Rhys's advice to do so for longer than that. Rhys had bought Arden's confidence with quiet bits of good advice for a decade.

"My daughter hasn't had new shoes in months," Burton Riley said. "The poor thing is heartbroken."

Arden blinked slowly and examined the beading of his jacket. "Are her feet still growing?"

"I'm sorry, Your Eminence?" Riley asked.

"She's close to thirty, now, isn't she? She can't still be outgrowing shoes."

"I...Your Eminence...For a young woman of the peerage, you must understand the importance of staying relevant."

"I have three pairs of shoes," Arden pointed out. "Am I irrelevant?"

"Of course not, Your Eminence, I didn't mean to imply any such thing. Only that my poor Esme, she doesn't have the same advantages..." Riley trailed off.

"Councilmembers, shall we weigh the merits of food against silk?" Arden asked.

"It is only that the peerage is accustomed to a certain lifestyle—" began Madge Yarrow.

"Then they shall become accustomed to a different one," Arden cut her off. He didn't snap. He didn't have to. Others stopped speaking as soon as he opened his mouth. "There are not enough workers for new shoes or dresses or jewels every few months. Even with the thralls breeding as they do, it takes *time* to grow a thrall to working age."

Behind him, Rhys shifted.

It was so unusual that Arden noticed. He ignored it, but he noticed. "Three years ago, we nearly had to put in place rations. I would not revisit that. Bex Torre didn't build this place so it could fail because we've become too indulgent to understand the value of a meal."

The Council members stared, some angry, some cowed.

Arden stood. "Reconsider your priorities before I reconsider my Council."

He left the Public Chamber.

Rhys trailed behind him and stood quietly nearby as Arden leaned against a railing and looked over Curie's Esplanade.

A young man of the peerage dropped his cup in front of a thrall cleaning the floor. A few drops spilled onto the floor. "Pick it up," he told the thrall, his voice carrying.

She dutifully mopped it up without a word.

He made a face but left her alone.

Another thrall intentionally bumped into the young man. She barely brushed his elbow.

"Watch where you're going," he warned.

She didn't drop her eyes. "Pardon me, sir," she answered shortly.

They looked at each other for a moment longer, long enough to confirm the thrall's consent to what happened next.

The peer took the woman by the upper arm and led her away.

Arden had lived among the game between classes his whole life but still didn't fully understand why anyone bothered with it. Oh, he understood sex and he understood the exchange of favors for pleasure, but the game itself seemed silly.

Easier to say, "I'll blow you for an apple tart," or "I'll give you bracelet if you let me cum on your tits."

People didn't take well to that kind of forwardness, though, now that he thought about it.

They tolerated it from Arden, but they would have tolerated outright assault from him.

His uncle Morris certainly got away with a lot of that and he wasn't even the Autarch.

"You didn't like what I said in there," Arden said to Rhys.

"You spoke admirably, Your Eminence. Some changes must be accepted for the sake of survival."

Arden glanced at him. Eyes lowered, hands folded. Not in the mood to speak his mind, subtle as that could be.

"Go, Rhys, I know there's work to be done elsewhere and I don't need a shadow today."

"Yes, Your Eminence."

As Rhys left, Arden said, "You do bore me sometimes, you know."

Rhys kept walking.

The wiser course.

Rhys always walked the wiser course. Arden didn't know anyone smarter than Rhys. He saw things Arden couldn't, that the Council couldn't. He knew exactly how to shift around numbers to keep *Eden* alive for another year.

Arden walked Curie's Esplanade, bored by every peer he came across. The same simpers and praise from every mouth.

He shouldn't have left the Council early, but he hated to hear them whine.

Maybe he did need a new Council.

Fresher minds.

All eleven members were remnants from his mother's days, nominated and elected by the peerage, then confirmed by the Autarch.

New Council members.

The idea rolled around in Arden's head. It could be better. It would, at least, be different. Maybe even interesting.

Hadn't Rhys suggested something like this a while ago?

Oh, he never would have outright said it. He had probably said something like, "The Public Chamber hasn't seen a new face since your mother's time," or, "This is the longest-serving Council, did you know? Such loyalty to the position." Spoken with quiet appreciation but meant to spark a thought in Arden's mind.

Arden lunched with a few old schoolmates. He didn't strictly enjoy their company, but he had once upon a time. That had to count for something.

Zira, just as pale and thin as Arden, picked at a salad and sighed wistfully half a dozen times.

Arden knew that trick. She wanted him to ask what was wrong. He didn't bother. He peeled apart his edamame pods and fished out the beans.

Cole and Mace chattered about their latest game of handball and teased Arden about never playing anymore.

"Ardi's *too busy* to play games," Cole said. "He's the Autarch, don't you know?"

"But we miss him. Don't we miss him?" Mace asked.

The two of them leaned together and tittered.

"Leave him alone," Cathie scolded them. She put a hand on Arden's forearm. Her hand warmed his skin instantly, gorgeous bronze against his watery paleness.

She always felt so warm. She always had.

Arden had loved her in the worst way as a child. He'd liked her since the first day of school. Another child had yanked a toy out of his hand and Cathie had snatched it right back and returned it to Arden. She'd been a roly-poly little girl and she'd grown into a beautiful, gloriously large woman. She swallowed up people with her hugs and Arden, even now, felt that old familiar urge to bury himself in her arms.

He'd thought that urge outgrown, or at least, fully suppressed.

He twisted his fingers into her hand.

"Bull and I walk the Solar Deck every morning. I know you're up, so you might as well join us."

Arden and Bull shared a mutual dislike, not over Cathie, of course. Over other things, ugly things that had started long before Cathie and Bull had gotten together.

"Maybe."

She made a face.

"I'd take it, Cath. A maybe is more than any of us have gotten out of him in years," Cole advised.

Arden scowled at Cole. "Some of us do have responsibilities greater than handball, poetry, and fucking."

"My poems get very good reviews," Cole sniffed.

"Critics are still out about the fucking, though," Mace teased.

Cole smacked him.

Arden smirked out of reflex rather than amusement.

Cathie kept her hand around his for the rest of lunch. She insisted on walking him to his next location.

Once out of earshot of the others, he said, "So you and Bull are fighting?"

She protested, "No."

"You only want to spend time on me when you two are on the outs."

"Ardi! That's not true," she scolded.

He raised an eyebrow.

"I'm hurt, honestly," she said.

He didn't apologize. He didn't say anything.

"Bull is a little grumpy these days, though."

"And why's that?"

"He wants us to move in together."

"And..."

"And I like having my own place! There's nothing wrong with that."

Arden hummed a non-answer. He had no answer to give, no opinion on the matter.

"Is there?"

"No. Do what you want, Cath. Who cares what Bull wants?"

"I do! I love that man but...I like my apartment. I like having..."

"Breathing room?" Arden guessed.

She rolled her eyes. "I told him a thousand times I don't want a wedding or kids. He doesn't listen."

"He never has."

She gave Arden's arm a light smack. "I thought I was walking you to Hydroponics Three."

"You are."

"We walked by four lifts."

"But not past the stairs," he said.

She smiled. "And here I was thinking you just liked to walk with me."

They walked down to Hydroponics Three together, down at least a dozen flights of stairs.

Arden had given his first handjob in a stairwell. Maybe not this exact one, but the stairs went almost entirely unused, even by thralls. He'd been...fourteen. He didn't remember exactly who it had been with. One of the Han triplets. They were identical, so he thought it forgivable to get Wei and Li confused. Ai had turned out to be a girl, which made things a little easier when it came to telling her apart from her brothers.

In Hydroponics Three, Arden stopped thinking about which Han sibling he had fondled and started to frown at the plants.

He glowered at the unsown rows.

Thralls hustled around the bay, their arms laden and their heads bowed. They gave him an extra-wide berth, either due to the look on his face or the rarity of his visits to their work areas.

Charles Raleigh, the supervisor of this bay and Hydroponics Four, made a big show of telling off a few thralls for their sloppy work, then greeted Arden with a false smile. "How are we today, Your Eminence?" he asked.

"We're well, Charles."

"Honored to have you visit, of course. Is there something you needed from H-Three?"

Arden glanced around the bay. So many unsown rows. "Numbers are down."

Raleigh glowered at the nearest thrall. "Unfortunate, I know. A lot of bad things piling up down here. Four on maternity, a few home sick, and *six* passed this quarter. We do have an unusually high number of aged thralls in H-Three."

"Hmm."

"We make do as best we can."

"It's a little warm in here!" Cathie noted.

"The plants here like it warm. Eggplants and peppers. Things like that," Raleigh told her.

Cathie let her wrap shimmy down her shoulders a little. "I wonder if this is what a beach felt like."

"I've read that beaches were windy," Arden noted.

"This place could use a bit of a breeze!" she said. "Are you going to be down here long?"

He nodded.

She fanned herself and looked around. "Not much to see," she pointed out somewhat sulkily.

"Go, then, Cath."

She blinked several times and her mouth sagged.

"Thank you for walking me down," he said, both to soothe his previous curtness and to make sure she left.

She gave a warily happy smile. She put her hand on his back and kissed his cheek. "I meant it about those morning walks."

"Maybe."

Once she'd left, he turned to Raleigh and said, "I want to see your daily logs."

A quizzical look passed over Raleigh's face, surely to ask, "Why?" but he thought better of it and said, "Of course, Your Eminence."

A thrall struggled past with an overladen crate of produce.

Arden dismissed Raleigh to return to his actual work. As he skimmed through the bay's daily logs for the past few months, he came to realize that Raleigh's job consisted mostly of interrupting the thralls to tell them to do more.

Arden hoped the show was for his benefit and not the usual way of things in Hydroponics Three. It seemed to disturb the flow of things in the worst way.

The daily logs illuminated nothing.

Arden drummed his fingers against the tablet, then closed the logs and flicked through the wider work logs to see where Rhys had been stationed today. When he wasn't with Arden, he floated in and out of other jobs to supplement their current crew or as a substitute for someone sick or injured.

Some thralls couldn't hack it as a floater, but Rhys had the wits to pick up about any job that wasn't highly specialized.

Ah, there he was, cleaning the kitchens.

Arden tapped in his password and had Rhys reassigned to Hydroponics Three for the rest of the week.

He closed everything out and returned the tablet to Raleigh. "I sent you a bit of help. A floater. He's got good reviews from his other assignments."

"Thank you, I appreciate that."

Arden gave a small nod, then left.

The Twelve he'd taken with breakfast had started to wear off, bringing back the world's jagged edges.

He retreated to his chambers to go over a few other things.

He itched for another shot of Twelve, but he knew better than to risk too much of that formula too close together. He'd spent almost all his later teens steeped in Twelve. Thralls had needed to literally carry him from place to place and prop him up in his chair. He didn't think he'd learned a single thing for the last two years of school.

Well.

No.

He'd learned a few very important things that had nothing to do with literature or mathematics.

He read a few letters from Terra Four. Their planet thrived, their population happy and healthy. Supposedly, too far away to send aid of any sort to Terra One, the planet that died below *Eden*, the global leaders of Terra Four sometimes sent letters to Arden. They offered condolences, advice, and relevant bits of technological advancement.

Arden thought they had to be disappointed with how Terra One had ended up. An asteroid had wiped out Terra Prime a thousand years ago, which made Terra One the oldest confirmed human settlement left.

Some said that humans still lived on Earth, but most level-headed people knew Earth had never existed any more than *Eden*'s namesake had. One more ancient human myth, same as magic and monsters.

This letter contained a few helpful hints about making a hyperspace engine. Apparently, different companies owned different parts of the actual engine design, which made it hard to get the actual schematics.

Arden didn't have an interest in space travel. *Eden* needed people to leave like Arden needed another hole in his head.

He skipped dinner in favor of an early bedtime, aided by a bit of Nine mixed with a nutritional shake. Nine didn't have the same warmth and calmness of Twelve, but it also had no risks or side effects. Nine provided sleep, instant, cold, and empty.

Because of the Nine, he got a late start the next morning, which didn't matter.

He did get a pouty message from Cathie about walking the Solar Deck. He tapped out a meaningless apology, then wandered through his closet.

He pulled on the first shirt and pair of slacks he could find. Everything he owned was black or gray, or something that might as well be black or gray. Dark, muted teal, or deep, dusted rose, colors like that.

He shrugged on his favorite coat, a subtly shimmery silk smoking jacket.

Not what a thrall would have picked out for him to wear. They always dressed him like the Autarch, regal, sumptuous, and imposing.

Arden, though, in this jacket, just felt like Arden.

He wiggled his feet into gray ankle boots and frowned at the laces. His fingers struggled with the slippery strings, but he managed.

He walked through the nearly empty Goshawk Alley. Only a handful of shops remained open. A few tailors, one jeweler, a cobbler or two.

Ten years ago, this street had bustled.

It had positively *swarmed* when he'd come to find an outfit for his inauguration.

He'd nearly shit his pants just looking at all those people. He'd spent just over two decades avoiding the peerage and he'd been thrust into it all at once.

Mama had spoiled him. She had kept him safe and coddled in their private chambers. He'd cry then get to stay home, snuggled in her lap. She'd passed when he'd been thirteen and Mother hadn't let things slide the way she had.

Mama had balanced out the Autarch, warm and sweet where Mother had been different. Not unloving, but strict.

She had wanted so much for him.

He passed by the windows, peering at old displays. The shop he'd visited for his inaugural outfit had closed, one of the victims of redistributing thralls.

Mother had dressed a lot like Arden, simple garments of quality in a limited variety of colors. She'd gravitated towards warmer tones, earthy neutrals.

Mama, though, she had loved to dress up. She'd loved to glitter and shine, to drip with jewels and satin. She had dressed Arden like a little doll for years, matching outfits for the two of them. She'd been a lot younger than Mother, forty years or so. She'd only been a surrogate at first, just a means to the end of making an heir for the Autarch. Arden didn't know when they'd fallen in love, but he remembered them that way his entire childhood.

Maybe Arden could do that. Find a sweet, silly person who'd agree to raise his child. Someone who'd become something more to him.

Except Arden suspected he'd need a lot more than familiarity and playing house to ever feel something about another person these days.

He left the empty shop window. He visited the handful of remaining shops, offered encouragement to the managers.

The shop keepers made their usual subtle complaints about being short-staffed.

A lot of the peerage had lost money in the restructuring, but it was better to lose a little capital than go hungry. Everyone had more than one venture under their belt, anyway.

Arden passed through the days.

He scheduled for Rhys to come to his chambers after his last shift in Hydroponics Three. He reclined on the couch with a tablet in his hand. He flicked through a few reports, then indulged in a few episodes of *This Endless Life*, an old soap opera from Terra One.

He glanced at the time halfway through the episode where Trisha revealed the father of her baby.

Rhys was almost half an hour late.

Unlike him.

Arden closed the episode and doublechecked that he had scheduled the appointment and that Rhys had acknowledged it. Thralls didn't, as a rule, have tablets, so Rhys would have had to used one of the consoles mounted to the walls in the Quarters. Sometimes those got crowded and messages went unseen.

Rhys had responded to this summons in the affirmative, though.

Arden went to the door and peered down the corridor. He spied a slow-moving figure in olive and brown. He almost didn't recognize the figure as Rhys. It lacked his usual upright posture and self-assured stride.

He watched for a bit, then got tired of waiting. He tied his robe and went out to meet Rhys.

The thrall had a sizeable cut on his temple, already sealed with surgical glue.

Rhys glanced up. He tottered unevenly and braced himself against the wall with one hand. "I'm sorry, Your Eminence," he breathed before Arden could say anything.

He looked like shit, his skin sallow under its usual brown.

Arden watched, uncomfortable, as Rhys struggled to right himself. A weird, twisting discomfort settled into his gut. He put an arm around Rhys and shouldered the other man's weight.

Rhys stiffened.

Arden's stomach twisted even more. He practically had to drag Rhys for the first few steps until he got over himself and started to walk, letting Arden support him.

In his room, Arden deposited Rhys on a couch. He sat on the far end of the couch and pulled up one leg. He rested his chin on his knee. "You look terrible."

Rhys pushed himself more upright. "It's not so bad." He pressed his lips together and swallowed.

Arden preemptively forgave him for throwing up. It seemed inevitable. "It's not like you to be late."

"I am sorry, Your Eminence—"

Arden rolled his eyes. "How'd you get hurt?"

"H-Three. It's..." Rhys closed his eyes and slowed his breathing. He swallowed. "The way Raleigh runs things..."

Arden shook his head. "Tell me in the morning. You went to a med center? What did they say?" He reached out and titled Rhys's head to the side. Not exactly perfect work; he still had a bit of blood crusted in his hair.

Rhys didn't pull away from his touch, but he remained motionless until Arden withdrew his fingers. "No."

"No? Why not?"

"The med center costs too much."

Arden frowned. "Didn't you get hurt on shift?"

"Yes."

"The cost is covered under worker's compensation," Arden reminded.

"Under what?"

"Worker's compensation. Haven't you ever gotten hurt at work before?"

"A few times. I've never heard of that before. It covers med center bills?" Rhys asked.

Arden smiled. "Yeah. You just tell your supervisor and they'll write you up a little slip to take to the med center."

"There's no way that's real."

Arden covered his mouth to stifle a giggle. He'd never seen Rhys like this before, unpoised. He must have been too out of it to be careful with his words. Arden dragged over the tablet and went to the worker's compensation reports for the month.

Only four had been filed on all of *Eden* and all of them had been issued to peers. He checked a few months back. He checked a year back, and then three, and then four. Similarly low numbers came up for every month he checked. The only time a thrall filed for worker's compensation was if they'd been badly injured, something that couldn't go without medical attention. A broken arm, outright unconsciousness, and one grisly report of a thrall who'd fallen on a broken beam and skewered herself. "Hmm."

"What?"

"Hmm, hmm, hmm," Arden fussed as he scrolled through the reports.

"What?" Rhys asked again.

"We'll talk about it in the morning." Arden stood and called for a shot of Nine and one of Three.

While he waited for them to arrive, he took some of the blankets and pillows from his bed and brought them out to Rhys.

"I'd offer you the guest bed, but I haven't had a guest since I was nineteen, so it's not exactly set up. Everything in that room is under a sheet."

He dropped the blankets on Rhys's lap and placed the pillows against the armrest.

"I should go back to Walker's Rest."

"Where?"

"Oh, it's...it's what we call Quarter Two."

"Mmm. Well. I've already made a gracious host of myself, so it's a little rude that you've decided to spurn my hospitality."

"Oh, no, Your Eminence, I just, I don't want—"

"I do make jokes, Rhys. You know that. Sometimes you even laugh at them."

Rhys barely smiled. "Sometimes you're funny."

Arden grinned. His stomach fluttered, a pleasant warm flutter, not at all like the hideous way it had twisted before. "Is that sass?"

Rhys dropped his eyes. "Sass or not, I couldn't give you anything in my present state."

Arden sighed. He wished Rhys would act a little less like a thrall sometimes. Holding a conversation got difficult if the other person kept deferring to him and dropping their eyes as soon as things got interesting.

This was why Arden didn't fuck thralls. They were either spineless or defiant. Stupid game. How had it even started?

A thrall brought in the shots Arden had ordered.

Arden presented them to Rhys. "You'll be out like a light."

"I don't know if I should."

"Your eyes look fine and you can hold a conversation. You'll be okay to sleep. Take the shots."

Rhys took them, though Arden didn't think it was because he trusted Arden's medical advice.

Within minutes, he fell asleep.

Arden flicked the blanket over him, then went to bed.

In the morning, he puttered around until Rhys woke and got the details of his head injury out of him.

Apparently, Raleigh didn't just boss around his thralls, he pushed the limits with safety regulations. Rhys had gotten hurt because Raleigh had ordered him to do a two-man job on his own.

"If I were looking into things, as Your Eminence already is, I'd look into how the workers in Hydroponics Three died," Rhys suggested mildly from beneath the blankets. "They were older but not old enough for that many to pass away so close together."

He looked sort of adorable nestled liked that.

Arden smiled at him. "What else would you look into?"

"Why I've never heard of worker's compensation."

Arden did think that was fishy. "I'll walk you to the med center. How is your head?"

"I feel better, thank you, Your Eminence."

"Three is good like that, isn't it? Still, the doctors will at least prescribe a few days' rest."

Rhys straightened up. "I don't think that's necessary, Your Eminence. I'm alright to work." A bruise had come up around the cut on his head, making it look worse than it had last night. He pushed his way out from beneath the borrowed blankets and straightened his clothing. "I'll call for—"

"I didn't ask you to do that."

Rhys winced at Arden's tone. Maybe because his head still hurt, or maybe because he worried that he'd displeased Arden.

Arden took out his tablet and fiddled around to find a worker's compensation form. He started to fill it out. "Go to a med center. Take the rest they give you. It's not up for debate, Rhys."

His eyes trained on the floor, Rhys said, "Yes, Your Eminence, of course. I apologize, I...I only meant that you don't need to concern yourself with things like this. You have so many other things—"

"Don't start simpering now. I have work for you to do but I need your mind to be sharp for it." Arden printed the slip on a thin film of algae paper and handed it to Rhys.

Rhys took it, eyes still downcast.

"I'll check in, too, to make sure you went."

"Yes, Your Eminence." Rhys hesitated at the door. "Would you like me to send for someone?"

Rhys sounded so sad and unsure of himself that Arden said, "Yes," just so Rhys could feel like he'd accomplished something.

The thralls who came might have well been animated washcloths and clothes hangers for all they said.

Fuck. Maybe he did need to start walking with Cathie in the morning if he had started expecting the thralls to entertain him.

Maybe Bull would get too pushy and she'd end things with him. He briefly entertained the idea of pursuing a relationship with Cathie if she became single. She had, in the nicest and subtlest ways over their long friendship, made it clear she would have sex with him if he made her, but felt no attraction towards him and that it would end their friendship.

He didn't know how she'd managed to say all that to his face without hurting his feelings. He'd certainly had feelings to hurt back then.

Maybe her feelings had changed since then. He had certainly changed, maybe Cathie had too.

Unlikely.

He called for a shot of Twelve before he started to think about it too much.

People milled around the Solar Deck in various states of undress. That was, after all, the point of going there. To feel the light of a star on your skin, to soak in the necessary vitamins, to get a bit of color.

Arden shucked off his charcoal jacket, necessary for the constant coolness in other parts of *Eden*. He tossed it on a bench and rolled up his sleeves.

Cathie bustled over and hugged him when she saw him. "Ardi! You made it."

He wanted to linger in her embrace but pulled back. "I was already awake when I got your message."

He'd been lying in bed watching *This Endless Life*, to be perfectly honest, but Cathie would tease him about watching it, so he kept that to himself.

Bull gave an unnecessarily stoic nod and said, "Morning."

"Good morning, Jon."

Bull frowned at the use of his given name. Named after his father, who had regularly battered his mother, Bull had taken his mother's maiden name as his main moniker as a child.

A low blow on Arden's part for sure, but he did what he could to hurt Bull.

Even with Twelve to smooth things, Arden still felt uneasy with the man's presence.

Cathie put a hand on both of their arms, an attempt at peacemaking. "Let's walk."

They walked in uncomfortable silence sometimes punctuated by Cathie's comments or a greeting from another peer.

Arden's mouth grew dry and not just from the heat.

He loosened the buttons at his throat.

Years later and he remembered the night as if it had just happened.

Like it was happening now.

Arden scrambled for an excuse. Any excuse.

He spied the lift to the gymnasium and headed towards it. "Nice to see you, Cath. I've got a...I promised the other two I'd stop by and watch their match."

She pouted at him. "Alright, well, I wish—"

"Next time," he promised and practically ran onto the lift.

He hated lifts but not as much as he hated Bull.

The other peers in the lift made nice with him and he made it through the conversations on autopilot.

He exited on the floor for the handball courts. He didn't know if Cole or Mace would be here today, but they didn't do much, so the odds likely tipped in his favor.

He spotted a familiar shock of dark reddish-brown hair that had to be one of them. Only a year apart, most people didn't believe they weren't twins.

He watched Cole sprint and jump around the handball court.

People kept trying to talk to him, old teammates of his, reminiscing about when he'd played. He'd never been good, but he'd managed to avoid being bad. A bit of Six before practice and games had snapped him out of the mellow of Twelve. He might have been better if he'd put his heart into it, but handball had only been a way to have an automatic group of friends.

He fumbled his way through those conversations. After a while, though, he found the banality of it soothing.

When the match ended, Cole ran over with a grin. "Hey! Ardi, I didn't expect to ever see you here again."

He licked his lips and considered what to say. Cole knew what Bull had done, one of the four people who'd stayed late at that party. "I. Breakfast? I didn't eat yet."

"Oh. Sure. I'm a mess, though. Let me wash up. I'll be right out."

It took less than fifteen minutes for Cole to reappear, freshly scrubbed and smelling like citrus.

He wore casual, athletic clothing and asked, "Did you want me to dress up? I'll have to stop by my room if you do."

"You're fine as you are."

They headed toward Crumbs, a teenage haunt of theirs, and requested a table in the corner. The manager, Zira's uncle on her father's side, hugged Cole and bowed to Arden. Once upon a time, he would have hugged Arden, too, but Arden had made himself unavailable to people.

Once they sat and received their food, Cole tucked in and Arden ripped apart the oat biscuits he'd ordered. Every so often, he dredged a piece through a bit of strawberry compote.

"So," Cole said.

"Hmm?"

"You seem out of sorts."

Arden shrugged. He didn't want to talk about it, but he couldn't stop the memories from playing in his head. Practically too drunk to move, lying next to Mace, woken up by Bull's quiet, awful grunts, jostled by his thrusts.

Bull still had a mark on his arm where Arden had bitten him, too panicked and drunk to do anything else.

Mace said he didn't remember anything. He'd laughed about it afterward and said, "Well, it's probably the only way an idiot like him could get someone as pretty as me."

He had broken up with Arden a few weeks later, though. He'd promised it was unrelated. He had been upfront about not being sure if he even liked boys prior to the thing with Bull and Arden hadn't been a particularly good boyfriend.

But Mace hadn't dated much after that.

Poor fucking thing.

Arden shoved a piece of biscuit in his mouth. "I think I'm bad at this."

"At what? Eating?"

"Being Autarch."

"Oh." Cole went quiet. He sipped his water. "I wouldn't know anything about stuff like that."

"You just write poems," Arden supplied for him. He usually used that excuse when it came to anything that required an opinion.

Cole smiled. "The critics like them."

"The critics are vapid."

Cole's olive skin darkened. He looked crushed. He tried to smile but didn't manage it convincingly. "Well, uh." He let out a wounded chuckle. "Not for everyone, I guess."

"They think they're reading love poems or sad little things about heartbreak. If they knew what they were really reading, they'd hate them."

"Ardi, uh, Your Eminence, I, just. They're really just nonsense poems, that's...there's nothing to them."

"It's not a reprimand, Cole. I like your poems."

He flushed again. "I didn't know you'd read them."

"You send me copies."

Cole shrugged. "Still."

"You shouldn't pretend to be stupid."

"I am stupid. Being sensitive and scribbling about it doesn't mean I've got any brains."

Arden pushed a biscuit towards him. "The compote's good."

Cole tried a bite. "My father always said Angie got all the brains in the family. This still tastes exactly the same! I haven't been here in years."

"Me neither."

They finished the rest of the oat biscuits.

"Mia's been telling me about this hobby people used to have on Terra One," Cole began.

Arden tried to remember who Mia was as Cole rambled about something called a garden. Eventually, he had to ask, "Mia...She's...?"

A wrinkle of hurt flashed over Cole's face. "They're one of my partners."

Partners! Arden really hadn't been paying attention. He didn't know Cole had paired up with one person, let alone more than one. "I'm an awful friend, Cole, you know that. How..." It felt like a tactless question, but Arden asked, "How many people are you seeing?"

"Well, Mia and Wei live together, but I stay over a lot."

"Wei Han?"

Cole nodded.

"And Alexander and I, we've been thinking about moving in together. He stays over most nights I'm home and, uh, well. Things aren't going great with him and Zira."

"You're with Zira's...Zira's Alexander? Aren't they married?" He recalled Zira getting married for sure. It had been a while ago, maybe eight or nine years.

Cole looked at his hands and picked at a non-existent hangnail. "Yes."

"And you and Alexander, that started before or after they got married?"

"After, but it's not about us, their issues. I don't think so anyway. It's about, uh, you know, other stuff. They don't like the same things, I don't think. They fight about Lex a lot. How to raise her and all that."

Arden always forgot Zira had a daughter. He'd never considered Zira the parenting type and it had shocked everyone that she'd had a baby, let alone had one intentionally and as young as she had.

"So, Alexander might move in. If things don't turn around with them."

"And you've told me all of this before?" Arden asked because none of it sounded familiar.

"Not all of it."

"Good, I was wondering if I had memory problems. Although, honestly, I don't listen to anything anyone says anyway."

"We know."

"It is one of the perks of being Autarch. You can be as rude as you like, and no one says anything."

"You've been rude all your life, Ardi. We're just used to it by now."

Arden chuckled. He paid for breakfast, made his farewells, and promised to see Cole tomorrow for lunch at their usual place.

The next day, as he walked in a few minutes late, the table hushed. He found the way they all looked at him while trying not to stare unsettling.

Once he'd settled into his seat, Zira immediately asked, "So is it true?"

He wanted to ignore her for being so vague.

"You put a thrall in charge of one of the hydroponics bays?" Mace clarified before Arden could be impolite.

"I...What? He's not in charge. He's just...advising," Arden said.

"You're having a thrall advise Raleigh, though," Zira said.

"Yes."

"That's sort of a bit much, even for you," Cathie said.

"I don't follow," he said with the hope that his tone made it clear he better like what they were implying.

"That's so..." Cathie began.

"Disrespectful," Cole supplied cautiously. Not necessarily cautious for himself, but he glanced around the rest of the table as though he wondered what turn this could take.

"It's rude?" Arden demanded.

"I mean. Letting a thrall tell someone what to do." Cathie shrugged and looked at her food.

"Raleigh won't like it," Cole said.

Arden had not considered for a single moment what Raleigh would like. "Raleigh's an idiot. He needs all the advice he can get."

"But from a thrall?" Zira asked.

The table quieted again.

Mace took a large bite of food, then said, "Uh, big match tomorrow."

"I take advice from a thrall," Arden pointed out.

They all looked at their lunches.

Arden huffily stabbed a bit of fried tofu in his salad. It split and he had to chase it around his plate. For once, he finished his entire meal since he was so intent on not talking to anyone. He didn't know who had told them he'd sent a thrall to advise in Hydroponics Three. He'd only told Raleigh just that morning.

He thought he'd worded it nicely, too.

He hadn't even told Rhys.

Fuck. He should do that, shouldn't he? Especially if word was already going around.

He left the lunch early and sent for Rhys.

They arrived back at his chambers at about the same time.

Rhys followed him inside and Arden caught him eyeing the couch. They hadn't seen each other since Rhys's injury.

"Your Eminence, how can I serve?"

"You're recovered, I take it?" He eyed the scab and fading bruise on Rhys's head.

Rhys nodded. "Three days' rest, doctor's orders."

"Mmm, well, I hope you enjoyed it. You won't be getting much for a while."

Rhys's face remained smooth. "Your Eminence?"

"I'm sending you back to Hydroponics Three."

He nodded. "Of course, they have much need there."

"Not to lug around crops or...whatever else it is they do. You're going to advise Raleigh."

Those void-dark eyes widened slightly. "I...I'm sorry?"

"What? You've been whispering little pieces of advice to me without me even asking for years. Don't act like this is something unusual."

"Your Eminence, it *is* unusual."

"What's the difference?"

Rhys glanced out the window and then at the floor. He looked everywhere but at Arden.

"Honestly, tell me your reservations."

"Raleigh isn't you."

"No, he's doing a much worse job than I am with a fraction of the number of things to oversee. He can't even get two hydroponics bays in order. He needs the help."

Rhys closed his eyes and gave a small bow. "As you command, Your Eminence."

He hated that. "Rhys!"

The thrall flinched.

Arden's stomach twisted. "Just tell me the fucking truth."

"You...you wanted help. You knew you needed it. That's the only reason you let me get away with any of the things I've said to you. It took months for you to even take my first suggestion and that was just to turn up the heat in the Quarters so people could get enough sleep to do their jobs."

Arden crossed his arms. "I didn't *know* it was cold there."

"You *wanted* to do better, and it still took time. Raleigh...he won't listen to me. He doesn't think..." Rhys risked a glance at Arden's face. "He thinks it's everyone's fault but his own. All I'm going to do is piss him off and that's going to come down on me."

"I'll make sure he leaves you alone."

"Then he'll take it out on the other workers."

Arden scoffed.

"Which won't fix anything," Rhys reminded.

"No. It won't." He sighed. "Fuck." His throat tightened. "It's too late to take it back. I already told him."

Rhys nodded.

"What do I do?" Arden asked. He'd never openly asked Rhys for help before. He'd always just pointed him in a direction and waited for the suggestions to come.

"I don't know."

Arden reached for his tablet with an unsteady hand. He didn't know what to do but look through a few reports. He moved back and forth between different pieces of useless information.

He threw the tablet and it clattered against the viewing window.

Rhys recoiled. "I'm sorry, Your Eminence, I...I'll have better advice for you once I think about things a little more."

"I'm so fucking *stupid.*"

"No, Your Eminence, it was—"

"It was fucking stupid, Rhys. I can't see two feet in front of my own face." He kicked the nearest piece of furniture. Pain lanced through his toes. "Fuck!"

"Please," Rhys whispered.

"We'll all fucking die because of how *fucking stupid* I am!" He swiped the knick-knacks off his coffee table and the ones that didn't break clattered across the floor.

It had never come to this before.

Arden had never let his insecurities show so openly, not among friends or family, certainly not in front of a thrall. He'd lashed out at people, and lost his temper, but never with tears in his eyes, never insulting himself. He hadn't had a tantrum like this since he was a child and Mother had tried to make him do something he hated. Except Mama couldn't scoop him up and tell him he wasn't bad, just shy.

"He's not shy, he's spoiled," Mother would always scold but she would never make Arden go out if she thought he'd have a tantrum. It would have embarrassed her too badly.

Spoiled, careless, selfish. Mother had always known exactly how he would turn out. He'd seen it in her face every time she'd told him he would become Autarch. He'd seen it when she'd told him his time as Autarch would come sooner than they'd thought.

Rhys watched him warily.

Arden threw something else, the closest thing to him. A pillow from the couch that barely made it five feet and plopped harmlessly to the floor.

Rhys covered his mouth.

Arden bit his tongue.

They glanced at each other. Eye contact unraveled their composure and sent them both into giggle fits, nervous and uncomfortable.

"I'm so sorry," Rhys panted through his fingers.

"So fucking *stupid,*" Arden breathed. He threw himself on the couch and squeezed his temples to see if it would make his headache go away.

"Am I still speaking honestly?" Rhys asked.

"Might as well." Vomit almost came up instead of words.

"You aren't stupid."

Arden snorted.

Rhys approached the couch. He gingerly sat beside Arden. Not close at all, but too close given their relative positions on *Eden*. "You're not stupid. You don't have to worry about people not wanting to listen to you. They do what you say because they have to do it. There's no want involved. But as soon as you leave me alone with him it will become my word against Raleigh's. I already know how that will play out."

Arden looked at him. "How will it play out?"

"The same way it always does when a thrall speaks out against a peer."

"You mean I'll take Raleigh's word over yours."

"Without a doubt."

Arden didn't like that. "Rhys, I trust you."

Rhys shook his head.

"Don't!" A whine had crept into his voice. "I said I trust you. I've staked the lives of everyone on *Eden* on that."

Rhys furrowed his brow.

"What if you were wrong? All those little things you've whispered and insinuated because you know I'll eventually listen. What if I listened and you were wrong? Or have you never considered that?"

"I'm not wrong often enough that I think about it much," Rhys admitted softly.

"Well. Think about it."

Rhys retrieved the pillow and tablet Arden had thrown, his face drawn as he moved about the room. He replaced the pillow and set the tablet on the coffee table. He started to pick up the knick-knacks, broken and whole, from around the room.

"Oh, don't...I'll call for someone."

"I'm already here," Rhys answered and continued to tidy. Finally, he stood to the side of the couch, hands folded, eyes lowered.

Arden drew his legs up to his chest and rested his chin on his knees. Just as he'd watched Rhys clean, he watched Rhys stand there for a while. He didn't know what to say. He *wanted* to say something, too, which he found unusual. And irritating.

After a while, he settled on, "I have no reason to do anything of the things you suggest other than that you're the one who suggests them."

Rhys shifted subtly.

"Half the shit you ask me to do doesn't make any sense. Like...upping the heat. What does heat have to do with productivity? Or, uh, what was it last year?"

"Increasing the work age."

"Right. But it helped. Everything you suggest helps and I need all the help I can get to stop *Eden* from turning into another failed Terra outpost."

"*Eden* won't fail."

"Unless we should look into hyperspace and try to ship everyone to Terra Four."

"*Eden* won't fail."

Arden sighed. "Then tell me how to fix it."

Rhys glanced up. Something strange moved over his face, something Arden couldn't untangle. "As you wish, Your Eminence. Is...it would be helpful to know your intentions with H-Three."

"To make it better. Six dead in one quarter? We can't lose thralls like that. And we can't have two of the hydroponics bays struggling. Figure out what Raleigh is doing wrong, tell me how to fix it."

"Yes, Your Eminence."

"I...Rhys, I mean it. I'll take your word. Don't let Raleigh push you around."

"Yes, Your Eminence."

Arden pointed to the tablet. "Hand me that."

Rhys handed it over.

Arden created a new user profile for Rhys and spent some time debating what user privileges to give him. Eventually, he logged out of his own profile and logged into the new one.

He handed it back to Rhys and said, "Daily reports. Honest ones. And message me directly if something's wrong."

Rhys raised an eyebrow. He stared down at the tablet and ran a nail over a crack in the screen.

"I mean it. If this goes right..." Arden stopped himself. "It has to go right."

"I'll do whatever I can, Your Eminence."

Arden unfurled himself from the couch. He approached Rhys and then realized he didn't know why he'd stood. He settled on saying, "The passcode is my birthday backward."

"Thank you, Your Eminence."

"Go. Get ready for tomorrow."

Rhys left with a small bow.

Arden went to check his messages then realized he'd given his only tablet to Rhys. He sent for a thrall to bring him a new one and spent an hour setting up the tablet and adjusting the settings to be exactly the way he liked.

He lost another hour flicking through old pictures. He'd had to download his old albums onto this one and had gotten distracted perusing the memories.

Once he became Autarch all the images of him were ones taken at formal functions by hired photographers.

He tried not to dwell on that, or on how terrible he looked in a lot of them. A corpse, lightly warmed, although the past five years or so had seen improvements.

There was even one of him and his uncle Winslow laughing together at Founder's Day a few years ago.

He checked his messages, found nothing interesting, and invited himself to dinner with Burton Riley's family.

He hated every moment of it, but he learned what he needed.

Reports rolled in from Rhys every evening for a week. He offered detailed explanations of what was wrong and proposed careful solutions. Each report ended with the proviso 'Supervisor Raleigh has declined to take these suggestions into consideration.'

One day, a little after breakfast, Arden received a message from Rhys that read, 'Please come to h3 assoonehff.'

He frowned at the message. He dressed in a hurry, once again grateful for a wardrobe that he could mix indiscriminately. He grabbed a pair of shoes, plain athletic shoes that he hadn't seen in ages.

Four.

He owned four pairs of shoes, he realized distantly as he hurried out of his chambers. The silver ones, the gray boots, a pair of black oxfords, and these. They must have been left over from the last time he'd thought to get back into handball.

In Hydroponics Three, he found the thralls lined up against a wall, facing it. That unnerved Arden. A tank of water and crops had tipped onto the floor and the tablet he'd given Rhys lie face down in the puddle.

All the thralls had their eyes trained on the floor and their hands at their sides, as motionless as toy soldiers. A few of them were wet. He picked out Rhys from the lineup, a little taller than most, and not quite as still. He had his hands clenched, balled in the soggy, beige fabric of his trousers; they quivered ever so slightly.

"What happened?" Arden asked him as he stepped around the puddle.

Rhys lifted his head and turned around marginally.

"I said don't move!" Raleigh roared.

Arden's head whipped towards Raleigh's office.

The man stomped out and over to Rhys. "What part of that didn't you understand?"

"I asked him a question," Arden said, keeping his voice low.

Raleigh looked over. "Your Eminence! Oh, I'm...these thralls, they're out of hand today. I apologize for the mess."

Arden glanced at the thralls again.

Something about them motionless and facing the wall really unsettled him. It reminded him of a Hollow Night ghost story. "Turn around, face forward."

The thralls obeyed almost in unison.

"What happened?" Arden asked.

"Not to point fingers, Your Eminence, but this one," Raleigh said and pointed at Rhys, "Got it in his head that he can do whatever he likes. He started giving orders to the other thralls, telling them *not* to listen to me."

"Hm. And how did the tank get on the floor?"

"I may have...I made my point with him. How I needed to."

Arden scanned the thralls.

Rhys had returned his eyes to the floor.

"So, what? You pushed him or something?"

"Your Eminence, with all due respect, you don't know thralls as I do."

Arden couldn't argue that. He barely interacted with most thralls. "So...this sort of discipline is common here?" A mild disquiet made its home in his stomach.

Raleigh lifted his chin. "I do what I have to."

Arden nodded. He eyed the puddle, the half-grown crops with their broken stems and tangled roots. He gestured towards it and said, "Save what you can."

A handful of thralls moved forward like slinking cartoon rats.

"Rhys?"

A rustling whisper went through the thralls as they glanced at each other, but especially at Rhys.

"Is Raleigh's telling of things correct?"

"Yes, Your Eminence."

Arden nodded again. He paced towards Rhys, then back towards the puddle. He knew already what he needed to do, but he'd never done it before. He circled back towards Rhys and when he put a hand on the thrall's shoulder, every thrall in the room flinched for him. He tightened his grip. "What did you do?"

"Mr. Raleigh wanted two of them to move the tank. I told them not to move it without four. Sherah has a bad heart already. Mr. Raleigh said one person could move it and...and threw me into it to prove it, I suppose."

Arden pressed his lips together, gave another useless nod, then said, "Okay." He couldn't stop nodding. He sucked in a breath, let it out, and released Rhys. He turned to Raleigh, who seemed just as disturbed as the thralls that Arden had spoken to Rhys. "Charles, you're fired."

Raleigh stared. "Your Eminence?"

The thralls whispered.

The ones scooping the salvageable crops froze.

"For years you've run not just the least productive hydroponics bays, but the least productive ones by a pretty wide margin. I sent someone to help you and you not only ignored him, but you also destroyed crops and broke one of my tanks. This isn't your bay, Raleigh. Everything in this bay you've rented from me. The thralls, the tanks, the space itself. And now we're done. I'm terminating our contract effective immediately."

The system was a bit of a scam, but Bex hadn't been exactly upright when it came to business deals. Aside from personal property, no one on *Eden* truly owned anything except the Autarch. Every living space and business, every piece of equipment was rented.

"My family has run this—"

"Get out."

Raleigh stared, frozen, his eyes bugged out of his face.

"Now," Arden insisted firmly.

Raleigh stormed out, seething with all the rage of impotence.

The thralls eyed each other.

Arden said, "Well. Get to work. Clean this up. Someone get a new tablet...Get Raleigh's tablet."

They scurried around the bay, most of them doing something that looked fairly meaningless.

They had to be shocked.

Arden didn't think a supervisor had ever been fired before. Suggested for early retirement, sure, but never fired in front of the thralls. Never dressed down with an audience like that.

"I'll, uh...I'll get a new supervisor in a few days. You'll be able to manage until then."

Rhys nodded.

"Are you hurt?"

Rhys shook his head.

"You sure? This is definitely covered under worker's compensation."

A small smile appeared on Rhys's face. It didn't last. He eyed the other thralls, the puddle of water, and the tablet one of the thralls offered to Arden.

Arden used it to revoke Raleigh's privileges and make his termination official. It took a while to go through and cancel all the contracts. He handed the tablet to Rhys when he finished. "Are you sure you're alright?"

"Shaken, I suppose, Your Eminence."

Arden smiled even though he felt like screaming. He put his hand back on Rhys's shoulder. "Come by tonight. We should talk."

Rhys nodded.

Arden didn't want to let go of Rhys's shoulder. He didn't want to leave the bay, but he imagined he'd be more of a distraction than a help if he hung around while the thralls tried to get things in order. "Wasteful," he said. "We couldn't tolerate that, not with things being how they are."

"Of course, Your Eminence."

Arden took his hand back. He hesitated a little longer, then left.

Before lunch, fourteen separate people messaged him about Raleigh. Some of them friends with gossip in mind, some supervisors with concerns.

He took the time to draft a single message to send to them all. Without vitriol, he explained the need for a change in those bays and Raleigh's unwillingness to meet that need.

By the time Rhys arrived that night, Arden had stopped replying to messages. He hid his tablet under a pillow so he couldn't hear it vibrate and sat in front of the viewing window. He watched Terra One.

People still lived there, at least, that's what the most recent scan said.

"Your Eminence?" Rhys murmured as he approached.

Arden turned to look at him. "Come sit with me."

Rhys sat beside him on the floor in front of the vast window.

"How did the rest of the day go?"

"Fine."

"I'm going to send you Mason Baker as a new supervisor."

"Oh."

"We went to school together. He's fairly eager to do something other than handball and modeling. He, uh, he won't have the same ego as Raleigh. His parents, sister, and cousins supervise most of the engineering crews."

"A wise choice, surely."

"He'll do whatever you tell him," Arden shared candidly.

Rhys raised an eyebrow.

"He will. He's good at taking directions. It's why he's so good at handball."

"Was his coach a thrall?"

"Oh, shut up, Rhys," Arden huffed.

"Apologies, Your Eminence."

Arden stretched out and lay on his stomach. He pressed his ear to the floor. "Come here."

Rhys followed Arden's example.

"Listen."

The sound of music came up through the floor.

"Every night their mother makes them practice for two hours. Lisette Gavroche, she's a singer. She thinks they'll all be singers too."

"I've heard them sing on Giving Day."

"The older girl has a pretty voice." Arden kept his eyes on Rhys.

The thrall noticed and met his gaze.

Arden waited for Rhys to say something submissive and avert his gaze.

He didn't do either.

They lay on the floor and looked at each other.

It wasn't like anything Arden had ever done before. No subservience or defiance, not even the type of false, bubbly flirtation he might get from an interested peer. His friends bustled too much to do something like this unless they'd drank too much to move.

It meant nothing, lying on the floor like this. Rhys did it because he had to do what Arden told him.

Rhys started to hum along to the song that came up faintly through the floor. "Are they practicing for Giving Day already?"

"No, it's, uh...it gets sung at pretty much every official function."

"Oh. I wouldn't know."

"You'd get just as sick of it as the rest of us." Arden turned onto his side and used his arm as a cushion.

Rhys folded his arms beneath his chin. He opened his mouth, then closed it.

"No, say it."

Rhys hesitated, but asked, "Do you do this a lot?"

"More than I probably should."

In the quiet between them, the buzz of Arden's tablet resounded.

"Your tablet keeps going off."

"I'm ignoring it. It's just people asking about Raleigh."

"They must have a lot to ask."

"No, just the same thing a million times." Arden drew in a breath.

Rhys shared, "The other workers had dozens of questions."

"Really?"

"Like how you knew my name."

Arden let out an embarrassed giggle. He'd spent years not knowing the thralls had names. They went by numbers in the programs used to track their work and debts and Arden hadn't ever had occasion to address one personally. Rhys had gently corrected that misconception a few months after they'd met. "Is it that unusual?"

"For someone of your status."

"I see you all the time though."

"I know that," Rhys reminded.

"You probably want to go home."

"It was a long day."

Arden said, "You know, if this goes well..."

"Your Eminence?"

"I just...I really need you to make this work."

"Of course, Your Eminence. I'll do whatever I can."

"Goodnight, Rhys."

"Goodnight, Your Eminence."

Arden stayed on the floor listening to the Gavroche children sing.

Arden gave the two of them a week to settle in before he visited Hydroponics Three again. They'd rearranged the general lay out of things for some reason or another. Arden trusted that it made sense.

All the tanks had been sown this time.

He spied a few sprouts with little splints to hold their broken stems together. He peered at them. "Does that work?" he asked the nearest thrall.

The girl seemed shocked that Arden had spoken to her. She whispered, "Uh," then cleared her throat and added, "We hope so, Your Eminence."

He smiled at the mending sprout. "Where's Rhys?"

She kept her eyes on the ground. "I think he's in the office."

He nodded and moved toward the office. He hesitated and looked over the girl again. She had to be about eleven, which dipped far below the standardized work age. Only orphans and children with disabled parents got permission to work before they turned fourteen. He wondered which one had landed this girl here.

Her eyes darted towards him, but never reached above his knees.

"What's your name?"

"Linley, Your Eminence."

"You're a little young to be here, aren't you?"

"No, Your Eminence, I'm fourteen," she insisted quietly. "Just short, I suppose."

Short and thin and underdeveloped, too. He put a hand on his hip then tapped his password into his tablet. He glanced around and saw what must have been a few other exceptionally small fourteen-year-olds. "What's your number?"

"Oh, Your Eminence," Rhys greeted him.

He looked over.

"We're honored to have you in Hydroponics Three. We've made a lot of changes since you visited last, Your Eminence."

"Do you have to call me that every time you say anything to me?" Arden demanded.

Linley glanced between him and Rhys.

"You've got children working here, Rhys."

The little girl let out a pathetic sort of squeak.

"Go ahead, Linley, back to what you were doing," Rhys said. When she didn't go fast enough, he shooed her away. "Let's address your concern in private, Your Eminence."

"Mmm." Arden followed Rhys to the office.

Mace looked up from his tablet and said, "You know I almost flunked mathematics every year. This was a stupid idea, Ardi."

Rhys raised an eyebrow, maybe at the nickname.

Arden squeezed Mace's shoulder. "You're not here to do math, Mace."

"Why am I here?"

"To listen to Rhys."

Rhys opened his mouth, then snapped it shut, his eyes wide.

Mace snorted. "What are you here for?"

"Checking in my two favorite boys," Arden said. "Although, maybe not my favorites anymore. You have little kids out there."

Mace shot a look at Rhys.

"Your Eminence..." Rhys sighed.

"I thought better of you."

"Those children...we do the best we can for them," Mace offered. "Light duty, you know, things like that. They're in rough positions at home."

"That girl lied to me about her age."

Mace widened his eyes and looked at Rhys again.

"Your Eminence, if I may explain?" Rhys asked.

"I hope you can."

Rhys glanced out towards the floor, his eyes following the small form. "Linley works because her mother can't."

"Then she shouldn't lie about her age."

"She has to. Her mother's disability isn't...officially recognized, so Linley couldn't get permission to work without...modifying a few things in her paperwork. Technically, her mother is considered in dereliction of duty and Linley can't apply for special work circumstances."

Arden crossed his arms. "And the other children?"

"Their parents died or were disabled working here. I thought...We thought it might be best if we could do for them what we could," Rhys said.

Arden didn't like it. "Her mother's sick?"

"Something like that."

"Bad luck."

Rhys made a face but didn't say anything.

Arden almost wished he would. He didn't stop to dwell on that feeling, not sure where it could possibly take him. Instead, he told Mace, "Well, if you think it's the right thing to do, then I trust your judgment."

"I don't know if it's right, but it's, uh...it's the best we can do," Mace said.

Arden clicked his tongue. His mother had stuck to the rules like glue, not an ounce of leniency, not in business, politics, or at home. "Well. I guess it is what it is," he finally pronounced.

He looked around the office a while longer.

"Did Your Eminence require anything else?" Rhys asked.

Arden poked him in the ribs. He didn't know why Rhys's formality bothered him so much. It shouldn't have. It should have bothered him when he showed those subtle bits of insolence. Maybe he just didn't like him being so formal in front of Mace. The juxtaposition did feel uncomfortable. "Call me Arden for once."

"I don't think I can," Rhys answered softly with his eyes on the ground.

"Oh, Ardi, don't be weird," Mace scolded. To Rhys, he said, "He gets a little funny sometimes, don't take it personally."

"Very rude, Mr. Baker," Arden scolded.

Mace rolled his eyes. "You didn't come down here to hang around all day."

"I have lunch with Cathie later." Cathie and, for some awful reason, Bull. Arden didn't plan on staying long.

Mace nodded.

Arden glanced at the time. He was, actually, already running late. To Rhys, he said, "Have someone get me a shot of Twelve before I go. I'm going to need it."

Rhys hesitated but went anyway. He must have assumed Arden had taken one with breakfast, too, which Arden had.

He needed something to get him through this lunch. He'd agreed to it before he'd known Bull would be there.

Rhys took a while to bring him the Twelve and when he did, it was only half full.

Arden eyed it, and Rhys, with suspicion.

Mace cleared his throat. He'd personally witnessed Arden have a full-blown shitfit over not being brought exactly what he'd asked for, especially when it came to formulas.

Arden reflected on those moments with embarrassment as he took the shot Rhys offered him. "What happened?"

"I spilled it, Your Eminence, I'm sorry. I can get you another if you like," Rhys said with all the deference and sorrow in the world.

Not a drop on the glass or tray to indicate a spill. And, not to mention, even if Rhys had actually spilled it, he knew better to bring a peer anything less than what they'd requested.

"Ardi," Mace began shakily. "I'm sure he'll—"

Arden held up a hand and threw back the shot. "I'm not the same sort of mess I was then, Mace, don't worry."

Mace showed his teeth, but it was guilt and nerves and second-hand embarrassment, not a smile.

"I'll check in later," Arden assured them. He hugged Mace goodbye and poked Rhys again on his way out.

Rhys's face barely changed, but it changed all the same.

Arden grinned at him. His legs felt weak and not just because he thought Rhys was handsome. He couldn't ask Mace to come with him, not in a thousand years, so he said, "Rhys, walk with me."

"Of course, Your Eminence."

They made it out of the bay before Arden had to reach out for Rhys to steady himself. Feebly, he said, "Good thing you spilled half of it."

"I'm sorry, Your Eminence."

"Just help me walk."

He'd made thralls help him walk before, sometimes even made them carry him, so nothing should have felt strange about leaning against Rhys like this.

"Where are we going?"

"This place called Mint, it's off Curie's Esplanade," Arden said. "I just need help getting there. It will wear off by the time lunch is over."

"Whatever you need, Your Eminence."

Warmth and calm filled him up. He nestled his face against Rhys's shirt. "Let's skip the stairs today."

"Wise choice, Your Eminence."

"Arden."

"No, I'm Rhys."

Arden giggled. "You're really funny sometimes, Rhys."

"I do my best to amuse when it seems appropriate." He shifted his grip on Arden.

Half-way through their walk, the Twelve settled and Arden could move on his own again. He leaned on Rhys a little longer than strictly necessary.

By the time they reached Mint, Arden could mostly control his limbs and his emotions. He straightened his clothes and asked, "How do I look?"

"Very well, Your Eminence."

"Be honest."

"You look high."

"Well, I am, so that's probably good." Arden flashed him a smile. "Good luck in Hydroponics Three. Did I ever say that?"

"No."

Arden patted his arm, then turned away to walk inside the restaurant.

He saw Cathie and Bull immediately but stopped to talk to a few people that he wanted to see marginally more than he wanted to see Bull. When he did make his way to the table, Cathie threw her arms around him.

"Oh, we thought you weren't coming!"

"No, no, I just, I got caught up in one of the bays," he lied as he sunk into her embrace. He badly wanted to stay there. He tightened his arms, which made him feel better until he remembered why he felt so awful about being here.

He spied Bull over her shoulder.

He stepped out of her arms. "You shouldn't have waited for me."

"Don't be silly, Ardi, of course we waited for you."

"I told you to order," Bull said.

A thrall appeared to take their orders as soon as Arden's ass hit the chair.

"Nice what kind of service being Autarch gets you," Bull mentioned.

Arden bared his teeth in the semblance of a smile. "The position has one or two perks," he agreed as amiably as he could.

He snagged a piece of bread and shoved a piece in his mouth, then shredded the rest of it over a plate as he waited for someone to say something.

Cathie started to talk about her ladies' club project, which had something to do with getting presents for disadvantaged children on Giving Day.

Arden ate another piece of bread. "Uh. What children?" he asked.

"Some of the poor little dears whose parents have had a hard year. So many businesses are...temporarily closed."

Arden snorted and slid down in his chair. "Those children."

"What else did you think I meant?"

He had thought she meant awful little urchins like Linley. "I thought you meant getting the ugly ones surgery."

"Arden, that's so bad!" she scolded.

"You're right, sometimes the ugly ones grow up okay-looking. Better to wait." He looked at Bull. "Maybe start one for disadvantaged adults. Some of them really could use work."

Bull huffed and crossed his arms. He was good-looking, in a meaty sort of way that appealed to certain people.

Arden's eyes found the pale, circular scar on Bull's arm. His heart sped up and he ate more bread as if that would help.

"Will you come visit my ladies' club?" Cathie asked. "I know you'll be a good influence on them."

"Will I?"

"You've been so charitable lately. It will impress the importance of it on them," Cathie said.

"What charity?"

"Oh, well, just...how you've been with that thrall. Going above and beyond, really. And now Raleigh's family will be so put upon," Cathie said. "It's only right..."

Arden tried to interpret what she'd said and figure out how what he'd done in Hydroponics Three could count as charity. It took more than a few minutes, so he gave up. "I don't know, send me a message. I might be busy."

"You should make time. You might find someone, too."

Arden wrinkled his nose. He liked Cathie, but he'd met her friends and didn't think they held anything for him romantically.

Or sexually. His taste in women got finicky.

"Like I said, message me, I'll try to make time."

She put her hand over his. "I hope so. They'll be thrilled."

"I'm sure they will be," Bull said.

"What about you, Bull? Any fancy clubs that need special guests?" Arden asked.

"I don't think you'd be interested," Bull said.

Cathie said, "Bull's taken up this new sport, uh, cross...crossby?"

"It's a combination of two old Terran sports," Bull explained. Everything he said to Arden seemed to come out through clenched teeth.

"Fascinating. Tell me more," Arden encouraged flatly.

He fantasized about assorted other things while Bull talked about a sport that sounded irrationally dangerous. Eventually, that coupled with the Twelve he'd taken started to make him, well, not exactly drowsy, but languid and cozy. He felt that way until Bull cleared his throat, then grunted.

Then it got hard to ignore what had happened.

He made himself swallow a few more bites of food. This much Twelve on an empty stomach wouldn't do him any good.

"How's your soup?" Cathie asked.

"Good," he said with the realization that this was soup and not just a dish of pasta unusually light on pasta and heavy on sauce.

"You're looking at it kind of funny," Cathie pointed out gently.

"Uh. I'm." He sat up straighter in his chair. "I'm a little warm."

"Are you alright?"

He nodded. "Yes. Yeah. I'm fine." He took a few more bites and dredged a piece of bread through the soup. "Are you still in that book club?"

Cathie laughed, assured him she was, and told an amusing story about the last book club meeting.

After lunch, Arden went to visit his uncle, Mama's brother Winslow. He was old, older than Mama by about twenty years. It made him a little doddering, but he was a sweet, jolly little man. He always gave Arden sweets, which made him feel like a little boy.

He let himself into Winslow's apartment and called, "Winnie?"

He got no answer and a horrible, cold fear sliced through him.

"Winnie!" he demanded.

A round face framed by white curls peeked out from the bedroom. "Oh, Arden, I thought I heard someone hollering. Let yourself in, why don't you?"

Arden scowled. "I'm Autarch. I don't have to knock."

Winslow secured a housecoat around himself. "What can I do for you this afternoon?"

Arden shrugged. "Aren't I allowed to visit?"

"Of course you are, of course you are." Winslow shuffled over to a side table, picked up a lacquered wooden bowl, and shuffled over to Arden with it proffered.

Arden took a candy.

"Come have a seat." Winslow replaced the bowl and went to a stuffed chair.

Arden seated himself on a similarly plump couch. "How've you been?"

"Oh, you know," Winslow began and meandered into a vague but lengthy description of his last two weeks, which was that last time that Arden had visited him.

After that he told a few stories from Arden's childhood, asking him if he remembered things and filling in the details Arden couldn't. From there, he moved into his own youth and told Arden about the girl he'd somehow almost married.

Arden had heard all these stories before, but he liked their familiarity and the warmth with which Winslow told them.

Finally, Winslow started to yawn and start talking about a nap. He stretched.

"Alright, Winnie, I won't keep you anymore."

Winslow offered him another candy and hugged him long and tight. He patted his back and said, "Come back anytime."

"Have a nice nap, Winnie." Arden kissed the top of the old man's fluffy curls. "Love you."

"Oh, you too, you too."

Arden retreated to his chambers for a nap of his own. He really shouldn't have had that much Twelve, because he napped until the middle of the night. He did have some lovely dreams, soft, pillowy ones that made him want to stay in bed for another day.

It took Rhys and Mace, but mostly Rhys, Arden assumed, three weeks to sort out the production issues in Hydroponics Three and Four. Some of it had to do with the new workers Arden had transferred to their bay, a lot more of it seemed to do with the fact that the thralls weren't too afraid to sneeze anymore.

Those bays still lagged behind their counterparts to some degree, but Arden deemed that acceptable given what Mace had inherited and the short time they'd had to implement changes.

He invited the two of them to his chamber to celebrate.

Separately of course.

He had different things to tell both of them.

He lavished Mace with praise and served him bubbly drinks that tickled their noses and made them giggle like they were teenagers again. He asked him to keep doing exactly what he was doing and told him that Rhys would leave at the end of the week.

"And I really like your haircut!" Arden insisted for the third time.

He might have had too much to drink.

Mace touched his hair, now much shortened and parted to the side. "I thought it looked a little more professional. Maybe if I look like I know what I'm doing..." He chuckled.

"You pull it off." He almost reached out to touch Mace's hair. He could have gotten away with it. They were friends and Arden was Autarch. He could have gotten away with anything he wanted, though they might not have been friends afterward. Instead, he grabbed Mace's hand. "I'm proud of you."

Mace grinned. "I know, Ardi, you told me four times already." He set down a half-full drink. "I, uh." He glanced at the time.

"You have somewhere to be?"

"I..." He blushed. "I sort of have a date."

Arden squealed then covered his mouth. "With who!"

"Lourdes Guzman."

"No, oh, she's so pretty!"

Mace nodded his agreement.

"Didn't she *just* get divorced?"

"A few months ago."

"Mason!" he scolded.

Mace shrugged. "We've always been, uh, fond of each other."

Arden gave him a push. "Then go, fuck, what are you doing here with me?"

Mace hugged him before he left.

Arden waited about five minutes, slugged back the rest of Mace's drink, then buzzed for Rhys. He'd expected Mace to stay a little longer.

He poured himself another drink while he waited and poured one for Rhys as well.

He stared at the drink and reconsidered.

He'd taken a little bit of flack recently for this whole business with Rhys. All the struggling supervisors had gotten touchy, Raleigh's friends and family had been cool, and the Council had outright hated what they'd done.

They hadn't even cared when he'd shown them the increase in productivity. They didn't care about eggplants unless theirs came out cooked wrong.

In fairness, badly cooked eggplant tasted disgusting.

Rhys came in and gave a small bow.

Arden snorted. "So fucking formal all the time."

"I apologize, Your Eminence."

Rhys had acted strangely the past few weeks, too. Skittish, almost, or worried about something. He'd declined to tell Arden about it and Arden had only asked once. If Rhys didn't want to tell him and could promise it wasn't about work, then Arden wouldn't press the issue.

"Come sit."

Rhys sat and awkwardly took the drink Arden handed to him.

"You did a nice job this month."

"H-Three and H-Four have good projections for the quarter."

Arden tapped Rhys's drink. "It's good."

Rhys took a sip.

Arden stretched out on the couch and nestled into the pillows. "Don't you feel excited?"

"Of course."

"You don't seem like you feel excited."

"Your Eminence?"

Arden pushed himself up and sighed. "Mace is excited about it," he pouted.

"Supervisor Baker will get credit for revitalizing a years-long failure. He has every reason to be excited."

Arden felt a smile grow on his face. He sipped his drink, then set it down. He scooted a little close to Rhys. "Are you jealous?"

Rhys took an enormous swallow of his drink and winced, either at the bubbles or the taste.

"Rhys, are you mad at me?"

"Of course not, Your Eminence."

A lie, plain as the nose on his face. Arden grinned and pushed a little harder. "Then why are you so grumpy?"

"Why the fuck do you care!"

Arden's stomach dropped and his heart tightened. He stared at Rhys, then grinned. He forgot about the conversation he'd meant to have.

Rhys looked horrified.

Arden moved in to wrap himself around Rhys. A thrall couldn't have given a stronger come-on, not even if he'd stripped naked and crawled into bed with Arden.

Rhys put his hands on Arden's shoulders. "No." Not defiant, not pleading. Just firm. Sincere.

"No?" Arden asked. He settled back a little.

"No."

Arden sat back all the way. "Okay." There wasn't anything else to say.

Rhys swallowed. "You own me."

"I own everything," Arden pointed out. Rhys didn't look in the mood to hear about the technical differences between indenture and slavery.

"I can't do this if you own me."

"Oh." Arden rubbed his nose. He'd drank too much to figure out what Rhys was angling at. "So..."

Rhys glanced at the drink he'd swallowed as though he suspected it of something.

"They're strong but not strong enough to make you say that after one drink," Arden told him. "Three or four is when we get into unexpected outbursts."

Rhys rubbed his mouth.

"So...what exactly are you asking me for, Rhys?" Arden asked. He honestly had no idea, but he did want to know where this would go. He could give Rhys anything he wanted as long as it existed on *Eden*.

Rhys studied him. Cautiously, he proposed, "Clear my debt."

Arden took a few seconds to consider it. He slugged back the rest of his drink, shrugged, and said, "Okay."

He had thousands of thralls and four generations of their slow, steady trickle of attempts to pay back his family. Peers rented the thralls from Arden and what they earned went towards their debt, minus their rent and provisions. Rhys's debt made no difference to him.

Rhys shook his head. "You...Arden, you don't...You don't mean it."

"Sure, I do!" He stretched and rolled so he could reach his tablet. It took him a few attempts, his fingers a little clumsy, to do it, and asked, "Eight one three five seven two?"

Rhys barely nodded.

Arden squinted at the tablet, then went in to manually clear the debt from Rhys's account. He could technically control anyone's account, even the peers. Bex had written a lot of fine print into the tickets to *Eden*. Financial supremacy for the Torre family must have seemed like a small price to pay compared to staying on Terra One.

He handed over the tablet to Rhys to show a single, perfect digit in his account.

Rhys covered his mouth with one hand. He shook his head.

Arden sidled closer. "So...can I kiss you now?"

Rhys choked back a sob. He pressed both hands over his mouth.

"Oh, hey, now," Arden soothed. He put a hand on Rhys's arm. "What?"

"You couldn't understand," he insisted raggedly.

"Do I have to?"

Rhys shook his head.

Arden tried to offer something cheerful. "You're the first thrall to ever clear his debt, you know."

"I know," Rhys whispered shakily.

"You didn't think I'd do it."

"No. I thought...I thought you'd get mad at me for even asking."

Arden brushed his fingers through Rhys's hair. He wanted to see it out of that messy little bun. "Do you mind?"

"I don't know."

"Mmmm, well." Arden worked the tie out of Rhys's hair and finger-combed it. "Pretty color."

"It's brown."

"Still pretty." It felt nice between Arden's fingers, thick and a little wavy with a little bit of texture so it didn't slip right through his fingers. "Do you want another drink?"

"That might help."

Arden giggled and smiled. He nuzzled against Rhys for a second, then poured them both drinks.

Rhys stared into his drink.

"What?"

"I just. I can't believe it."

"Well. I really like you, Rhys. If that's what it takes to make this comfortable for you, then it's no skin off my nose." Arden pushed the drink gently up towards Rhys's mouth. "You need to catch up with me."

Rhys drank it in two big sips.

"Maybe not that fast."

Rhys looked more distraught that Arden anticipated.

Maybe that outburst had been just an outburst, not a come-on. Maybe he'd been trying to backpedal.

He could just be overwhelmed. Arden had given him an exceptional sum and they hadn't arranged any sort of *quid pro quo* ahead of time.

Arden proposed, "I have an idea."

"Okay."

Arden stood, grabbed his tablet, and grabbed Rhys by the wrist. "Come on."

Rhys followed him to his bedroom.

"Shoes."

Rhys removed his shoes.

Arden shimmied out of his robe and draped it on the back of a chair. He rolled into bed and gestured for Rhys to join him.

Rhys sat on top of the covers.

Arden didn't push it.

Rhys probably hadn't done this before. He seemed too upright and noble for this kind of thing. Too self-assured to barter sexual favors for new shoes or a warmer coat.

And he really did need new shoes, Arden noticed. His were patched, and lumpy with glue at the seams.

Arden hadn't done this before, either. He'd never slept with a thrall.

Except Rhys wasn't a thrall anymore.

He certainly wasn't a peer, though.

Not that it mattered.

Arden pulled up the movies on his tablet. "Whenever I was in a particularly grumpy mood, Mama and I would have snacks in bed and watch a movie."

"Oh."

"It's, uh, it's not quite the same without the snacks. And it's not the same without someone to watch with me. But..." Arden shrugged. "She might be gone, but she left me a really good movie collection. Do you want some snacks?"

"Uh."

Arden handed over the tablet. "Here, pick something out." He rolled over to dig through his bedside drawer. He kept an emergency stash of chocolates there. He'd outgrown the habit of eating his feelings, but he kept them for nostalgia's sake. "They're a little old but I don't think chocolate goes bad." He handed a bar to Rhys. "What'd you pick?"

"I don't know."

Arden peered at the title. "That's a sequel."

"Oh."

"We'll watch the first one though, that's fine."

He found *Searching for Haven* and started it. He rested his head on Rhys's arm. He hadn't had someone to do this with in years.

Mother hadn't liked movies. Or, if she had, she had never made time to watch them.

He explained, "There's three or four more of these, they're like...low budget sci-fi movies, but there was this actress in them, Abercrombie Winston, and she had a huge cult following. People who went to see whatever she was in no matter how bad it was."

"Oh."

"This one's pretty good, though." Arden burrowed a little closer to Rhys, who still hadn't joined him under the covers. He peeled back the wrapper of the chocolate.

Rhys didn't talk much. He didn't eat the chocolate or come under the covers or put his arm around Arden. He remained stiff and uncomfortable beside him.

Finally, Arden had to ask, "Have you done this before?"

"Which part?"

"I don't know. Any of it. Had an affair with a peer?"

"No."

"Been with a guy?"

Rhys scowled and his cheeks darkened.

Arden didn't know what that reaction meant, so he teased, "Had sex?"

Rhys chuckled. "Yeah. I've done that."

Arden nestled up to him. "I really do like you, Rhys. I'm...You know. These things between classes, they're usually just...quick bits of nothing, no names, no anything. I'd be okay if we took it a little slower than that."

"We do already know each other's names."

"Is that wild?"

"Slow is fine."

Arden squeezed Rhys. He fell asleep before the movie finished.

In the morning, he woke up to a quiet voice saying, "Your Eminence."

He burrowed his face harder against...against someone's back. He tightened his grip. Rhys. He smiled.

"Please, Your Eminence, I have to go to work."

Arden released him and pushed himself up. "How about that kiss, though?"

Rhys kissed him. A slow and somewhat hesitant kiss that warmed when

Arden gripped the front of Rhys's shirt.

Arden didn't want to let go but when Rhys stepped back, he let him. "Have a nice first day at work."

"It's not..." Rhys paused. "Uh. I guess it sort of is."

"I'll see you later?"

"I should go home."

Home. What a concept. It dawned on Arden that Rhys might have people to tell. Parents or siblings, or just friends. "Mmm. Okay. Different night. Bye."

"Goodbye, Your Eminence."

Arden watched him go and snuggled back into the covers. He should get up.

People would be buzzing once they found out that a thrall had cleared his debts. All of *Eden* would want to know how he'd managed it.

Arden figured he could officially call it a commendation for good work done in the hydroponics bays. Or for a decade of good advice.

Really, for the opening of a new era on *Eden*.

From bed, he drafted an announcement of what he'd meant to tell Rhys last night. He bathed, then reconsidered what he'd written. He took a shot of Twelve and had a bit of breakfast, then sent his final copy, first directly to the Council members, then to all of *Eden*.

Effective in eight weeks, all the current Council members were dismissed from their positions and ineligible to run again for another five years.

Arden made the first nomination of the new campaign.

Cole Baker, the poet, who called him in hysterics about five minutes later.

Arden had underestimated how much people would panic in response to his announcement. Almost nothing got done on *Eden* for two days such was their distress, so he called everyone to the Amphitheater. In the mezzanine, hordes of thralls crowded together, too far away to see Arden as anything more than a speck.

The peers, though, he could make out some of their faces.

It seemed faintly ridiculous that with so few citizens the mezzanine saw any use at all.

He stepped up to the microphone and said, "We have been your Autarch for more than ten years now. This Council has served since our mother's time. Although we've often wished that her reign over *Eden* had not ended so soon, it is time for us to step out of her shadow. It is time for *Eden* to step out of the shadow of what it was meant to be and become what it truly is. We cannot do this with a Council elected in a different mindset."

The crowd rustled, tense, impatient.

"We cannot have incapable supervisors who balk at good advice. We cannot waste and expect that we will never want. *Eden* will survive because it cannot fail. A new Council is not a desperate act. It is a hopeful one. Make your nominations for new members and make those nominations with hope."

None of this applied to the thralls. They got no vote.

Something Rhys had said rolled around in Arden's mind. Something that had never occurred to him and which he had written off as foolishness. Even Rhys hadn't taken it seriously.

He made a split-second decision.

"For years, the keenest mind we know has not belonged to the peerage. This person lacked the education and advantages of our upbringing but has shown endless resourcefulness. Because of this, we welcome another change to the Council. The indentured will have their voice, too. Their votes now decide a single seat."

A rush of noise went through the crowd.

Gasps, yes, but something from the mezzanine. At first, he thought it must be screaming, but they were cheers.

What difference did one seat out of eleven make? Probably hardly any, but if there were other thralls out there as smart as Rhys, maybe having them vote would lend something to Arden's vision.

"We welcome a new era, all of us, together. Thank you."

He retreated to his chambers before the Amphitheater could empty, ducking through servant passages.

He didn't want to face the crowds up close.

He locked the doors to his room and requested he not be disturbed.

He also sent messages to safety officers to tread carefully.

Half an hour later, someone knocked on his door.

He expected Cole or Mace, or maybe Cathie, and he would turn them away, but when he saw Rhys, he opened the door.

"You've gone absolutely mad," Rhys accused as he entered.

Arden smiled. Warmth fluttered from his stomach up to his face. He'd been so busy managing the minor political crisis he'd caused that they hadn't seen each other. "It is a little rambunctious of me, isn't it?"

"They're going to tear *Eden* apart."

Arden shrugged. "Let them try. She was built to withstand an asteroid."

Rhys seized Arden by the shoulders. "Why are you doing this?"

"Because I can."

"It's a game," he accused.

Arden stepped back. "No. It's...You see the same quarterly reports I do, Rhys. You know we can't keep doing this. You made it work with Mace. Together, us, a new Council, we'll make it work on the whole station. It's this or slowly die over the next century."

"I fixed an obvious and glaring problem. I can't conjure more workers out of nowhere!"

"It's not about how many thralls we have. It's about how hard they're working."

"They're already working as hard as they can!" Rhys's face twisted, a flash of real emotion that Arden had never seen from him before.

Arden rubbed the fabric of Rhys's shirt between his fingers. "No. They're working as hard as they *want* to, given their current circumstances. Improve circumstances. Improve morale. Improve productivity. Hopefully."

Rhys stared at him like he'd changed languages.

Arden sidled closer and put his arms around his shoulders. "Let's pretend you haven't been yelling at me. Let's try this again."

"I..." Rhys glanced at the arms around him but didn't pull back.

"I'll go first. Rhys, I've been busy, I missed you."

"I. Things...things have been busy," Rhys agreed. He put one hand on Arden's side.

"I didn't get to hear anything about what it's like to be...uh. Emancipated? Let's call it that. How is it to be emancipated?"

"It's...unreal."

"Hmm, that's it?"

"It's fucking amazing."

Arden grinned. "Yeah?"

"Yeah."

He kissed him and drew him in closer. Something didn't feel right about this, but Arden couldn't put his finger on what. He worked his fingers into Rhys's hair. He wanted to do more. He wanted to drag him in and kiss him hard. He wanted to tear him out of his clothes.

He wanted, honestly, to do anything. Even if it was watching another movie or laying on the floor. He just wanted to feel something, something that wouldn't be latched onto a person he couldn't have, who didn't want him.

Cathie had never wanted him, neither had Mace, though in different ways. None of the people he'd slept with had done it because they liked him, not really.

He stepped back. "Do you like me?"

Rhys tilted his head.

"I mean. Honestly. Not between Autarch and the man he owned. Because I meant it when I said I like you, Rhys. It'd be great if you liked me, too."

Rhys smiled gently. "I, yeah. I like you."

"Really?"

"Yes."

"So why does kissing you feel like kissing a pillow?"

"You kiss a lot of pillows?" Rhys asked.

"Rhys," Arden whined. He nearly stomped his foot.

"I like you, Arden," Rhys assured. "But...My whole life got turned upside down because apparently you like me a lot more than I thought. Things feel...unreal. Like it's a joke or a lie or...or a test."

"Upside down in a good way, right?"

Rhys smiled at him. "Yes." He took Arden's hand. "And then you sent the whole station topsy-turvy. We're all reeling."

Arden twisted his fingers with Rhys's and kissed his knuckles. "I planned to tell you about it first but, uh, you started yelling at me and asking me for things."

"I...!"

Arden turned their hands and kissed his inner wrist. "Yeah. You."

A dark flush came across Rhys's cheeks.

"Come lay down with me. We can finish our conversation from last time."

"You fell asleep last time."

"Drinking does that to me," Arden admitted easily. He gave Rhys a tug and when he came along, Arden slung an arm around him to pull him close. He slipped off his shoes and rolled into bed.

Rhys watched him with a funny expression on his face.

"What?"

"You've been acting different."

"I've been feeling different. Take your shoes off."

Rhys took longer than necessary to remove his shoes. He sat on the edge of his bed when he had.

Arden rested his head on one of Rhys's thighs. "You've gone all the way with girls?"

"I'm twenty-nine," Rhys pointed out as though it meant something.

Arden pursed his lips, then offered, "I didn't until I was thirty-two, so let's not take things for granted."

"Oh."

"But you haven't with a guy?"

"I've done plenty of things with different kinds of people. You don't have to worry about me being inexperienced."

"Really?"

Rhys gave a bit of a rascally smile. "It's the cheapest way to have fun."

Arden giggled. "Do you get around, then? Lots of friends in lots of places?"

"I used to."

"Mmm, coping mechanisms of a desperate youth. I understand that."

Rhys ran his fingers over the soft fabric of Arden's sleeve. "Who says my youth was desperate?"

Instead of pointing out the look in his eye, his careful poise, and the thin scars Arden had glimpsed on his arms, he said, "Mama treated food like tangible love. She was so round and chubby. And so pretty. She had the warmest hugs. I was a chubby little boy, too, until Mama passed and..." Arden rubbed his nose. "And Mother pointed out chubby cheeks and a jiggly belly wasn't as becoming on me as it was on other people."

"Oh."

"Lost it like that." Arden snapped his fingers. "Formulas helped." He gazed up at Rhys. "Now it's your turn to share."

Rhys shook his head. "No one wants to hear that." He slid his fingers through Arden's hair, combing it out so it draped down his back.

Arden came close to saying, "I do," but the chance escaped him because Rhys brushed his fingers over Arden's ass and it sent a quiver of longing through him.

Rhys jerked his hand back. "Your, uh. Your hair is so long. I didn't..."

Arden pushed himself up, then climbed over to the center of the bed. "Come lay next to me."

Rhys stretched out next to him. "I'm supposed to be at work."

"Then you should have gone to work instead of coming here," Arden pointed out. "Besides, do you think anyone's working right now? I mean...They're in their crews, but I'm sure they're not working."

"Can I come back tonight?"

"You can come back every night."

"I meant can I leave?"

"Oh." He felt awkward and sort of stupid. "I'm not the sort to keep a body where it doesn't want to be."

Rhys tucked a piece of Arden's hair behind his ear. "I'll come back tonight."

Arden had lost the plot of their relationship completely at this point. His suspicions that Rhys had not meant to start this firmed up, hard and cold in his belly. "Don't come back if you don't want to do this."

Rhys blinked a few times. He pressed his lips together, then licked them. "I don't like to miss work."

"I did notice that."

Rhys kissed him, another slow, careful press of his lips.

Arden kissed back a little more fiercely than Rhys had given in the hopes the other man might respond.

It worked for about a minute.

"I have to go to work," Rhys breathed into his mouth.

Arden kissed him once more. "Fine, then go."

Rhys gave him another quick kiss.

Arden watched him go.

He spent the rest of the day waiting for Rhys to come back. Here and there he tamped out fires the rumor mill had started, but mostly he waited.

Sometimes he paced.

He washed, even though he'd washed that morning. He changed into more casual clothes, then into something nicer, and then back into the clothes he'd put on the first time.

He combed and braided his hair, then stared in the mirror, reconsidering his choice.

"What the fuck?" he asked his reflection.

He stared at the thralls who came to tidy up his room and they slunk around beneath his gaze.

Finally, he went over to the window to watch Terra One. That always distracted him, although not always for the betterment of his mood.

No one alive on *Eden* had set foot on the planet. They still had shuttles that could go down, but no one ever did. Just like no one from Terra One ever came up to *Eden* anymore. Their civilization might have degraded so much that they didn't know what *Eden* was or how to contact it.

He checked the time and checked the Council nominations. So far, seventeen members of the peerage had received nominations.

He sat and looked down at the planet, then lost some time staring at his reflection, muted, in the clear glass between him and the void.

Fuck, what a reflection. A pinched face with wide eyes and a thin mouth.

Well.

Not that thin. Not unattractively thin, but it must have belonged to his father, whoever he was. Mother's mouth had been full and handsome.

He had been handsomer years ago, before he'd gotten so thin. Not that his mouth had changed.

He should have eaten more and relied on formulas less, but it was better to be scrawny than pudgy. Not that he had anything against pudgy people, or fat ones. He liked them a lot, for the most part.

But he didn't want to be one of them because all he could think of was Mother frowning when he outgrew clothing in width faster than he did in length.

In retrospect, he probably would have thinned out when he'd hit his growth spurt naturally since that was when he'd gone from average to skinny.

Rhys knocked before he let himself in.

At least he let himself in.

Arden liked that. He turned, leaned against the window, and gave a small wave. "Hi."

"Hi."

"You came back."

"I said I would," Rhys reminded.

"I thought you might reconsider things."

Rhys came over to sit next to him. "A few weeks ago, I might have."

"Oh. What changed?"

"A lot," Rhys admitted.

"Did you want to be more specific than that?'

"Mason Baker had a lot of good things to say about you," Rhys said.

Arden didn't know if it was an explanation or a change in subject.

"Would you take it back if I said I didn't want to do this?" Rhys asked.

"You mean put your debt back?" Arden asked.

The thought had never crossed his mind. It seemed poor form to ask for a lover to return gifts when things came to an end. He'd never done it before, not even when he'd given Faust Reins his favorite robe and Faust had turned out to be a rotten lover. And a cheat. Arden didn't mind sharing but he liked to know he was doing it.

"That feels rude," Arden settled on saying.

Rhys sighed.

"Fuck, if you don't like me, get out, Rhys."

Gently, the other man assured, "I like you."

Feeling slightly sick, but mostly small and stupid, Arden drew his legs up to his chest. "I'm trying to do something, Rhys, but I can't do it without you."

"No, probably not."

Arden chuckled.

Rhys put an arm around Arden's shoulders and tugged him in closer. "I'd be lying if I said I didn't feel funny about all of this, but I like you."

Arden nestled under his arm. "But it's okay to kiss you."

Rhys nodded.

"Will you come lay down with me? I know I keep saying that but maybe third time's the charm."

Rhys stood and held out a hand to help Arden up.

Quiet but hand-in-hand, they walked to Arden's bedroom.

Rhys took off his shoes without Arden saying anything.

"What do you want to do?" Arden asked.

"Whatever happens, I suppose, is alright with me."

Arden rubbed his nose. "That's a lot of options."

"I may not have done every kind of thing with every kind of person but...you know, I do like to try new things."

"Do you? I hate new things. They terrify me." Arden shucked off his shirt and tossed it on a chair. He did the same with his pants but missed the chair and had to retrieve them. When he straightened up, he saw Rhys placing his own shirt, folded neatly, on the bedside table.

He twisted his hair into a loose knot and secured it to keep it out of the way.

Undressed, they slid under the covers.

Rhys flinched when Arden touched his side. "Your hands are cold."

"Oh! Sorry, they're always like that. Mother had cold hands too..." He trailed off, realizing that bringing up his mother in bed might not be the sexiest thing to do. "I guess it's genetic," he finished, like an idiot.

Rhys smiled, though, and brought Arden's hand to his lips.

Arden inched a little closer and kissed his shoulder. He tried not to say anything else unbecoming. He warmed all over when Rhys wrapped an arm around his waist and pulled him into an embrace.

He wanted to impress Rhys but ended up melting altogether when Rhys kissed him. The last person he'd kissed had thrown up on him and that had been almost a year ago.

No, two years ago! Where the fuck had the time gone?

Distantly, he wondered what Kenji was up to.

Rhys's hand between his legs brought him back to the moment.

Oh, this would be fast. Wretchedly, embarrassingly fast.

He should have done something beforehand so he would last.

Except he hadn't even been sure Rhys would show.

"I, uh," he whispered.

"Hmm?"

"I might go too fast."

"Alright." Rhys took his hand back and kissed Arden's throat. "I can work with that."

A bit of Twelve would take the edge off, slow things down. And Seven had been made for people with exactly this need without any of the other effects.

What would be better? Cumming too early or stopping things to take a shot?

Rhys kept his hands away from Arden's cock for a while, paying attention to other spots on his body that evoked fuzzy, warm feelings, but didn't tip him towards the edge.

He slid his hands over Rhys, delighted to have someone to touch, someone that leaned into his touches once his hands warmed up.

They pressed hard against each other, no room for hands any more, and slid their way to a climax.

Arden didn't cum half as fast as he'd expected he would.

He giggled a lot afterward.

Rhys frowned. "Are you alright?"

Curled up in near hysterics, Arden nodded and insisted, "I'm fine!"

Rhys didn't ask again, just laid down.

Once he calmed down, he reached over to call for someone to bring washcloths, because they'd smeared all over each other's bellies, and snacks. He found himself in the worst mood for a snack.

He stopped himself and studied Rhys, who had his eyes closed. He hadn't fallen asleep, he had them intentionally closed.

Maybe he'd found Arden's fit of laughter unbecoming. Or he knew he wouldn't like what he saw when he opened them.

He probably wouldn't like a thrall coming in to see him like this. Arden barely knew one from the other, but Rhys might have known whoever came in personally.

Arden kissed his nose.

Rhys opened his eyes.

"Do you want a snack?"

"I'm okay."

He pointed. "Bathroom's through there." Rhys already knew that, but Arden felt the need to point it out. "If you want to clean up."

Rhys nodded.

When he left the bathroom, Arden took his turn to wash up. He came back out to find Rhys with some of his clothes pulled back on. "Oh."

Rhys shifted. "I didn't know if..."

"Well. You could stay."

Rhys hesitated.

Arden felt awful standing there naked. "I'd like it if you did. If you want to."

"I could."

"Please," he mumbled.

Rhys raised his eyebrows. "If Your Eminence commands it."

"Are you going to pick on me this much all the time!"

Rhys grinned. "I would have picked on you a lot more if you hadn't owned me before."

Arden scowled and pouted his way back to bed, then curled up in the sheets.

Rhys sat on the bed, legs crisscross.

"No, I don't care if you stay, go do whatever it is that's more important or interesting or..." Arden huffed.

"I didn't know if you were going to kick me out," Rhys offered softly.

Arden uncurled.

"Peers do that, you know."

"As a matter of technicality, we are not a peer, we are the Autarch. We should not be compared."

"Well, I've heard he's worse."

Arden scooted over to place his head on Rhys's thigh. "I was a beast for a while."

"I remember."

Arden scowled.

Rhys played with a loose strand of Arden's hair. "I remember you throwing that tray across the Public Chamber."

"Mm."

"And calling Lazlo Frakes an 'irredeemable fucking cretin'," Rhys continued. "Or the time you poured a pitcher of water over the laps of everyone at your dinner table."

Arden remembered that but didn't remember Rhys being there for it. It had been right before his inauguration and people had kept telling him he had big shoes to fill, that his mother had such grand expectations for him, things like that. He'd dumped the water, smashed his dinner plate, and stormed out. "I didn't even know you then."

"I was working."

"Oh." A little slither of shame wormed through Arden. "I was an awful beast."

Rhys's fingers moved through his hair, slow, steady strokes. He didn't argue.

Arden stretched out.

Rhys's touch wandered away from Arden's hair. His shoulder, his chest, over one nipple.

Arden flinched. "Huh! Oh, don't do that."

Rhys withdrew his hand entirely. "I'm sorry."

"No, it's, they're just weirdly sensitive, uh, after I had surgery. I was supposed to get all this rest and not use my arms but," Arden snorted, "It was handball season and I didn't want to miss practice too much. I thought the other kids wouldn't like me as much if I didn't show up for practice and keep my spot on the team."

"What kind of surgery?" Rhys scanned his chest.

"Oh!" Arden rolled onto his back and tugged down the sheets. He traced over a few short, thin lines, barely there after so many years, on his stomach. "The whole thing, all of it. Uh. Gene therapy, removing things, attaching other things." He pointed to one scar, most obscured by reddish curls, at the base of his cock.

With vague concern, Rhys asked, "What happened?"

"Well, nothing *happened*, Rhys. I was just...you know, born with a body that needed a few adjustments before I felt cozy in it."

Rhys's brow knit.

"It happens with plenty of people," Arden reminded defensively.

"No, no, I know, I just..."

"What?"

"The people I know who need those procedures never get them."

"Why not?"

"Cost too much."

Arden pressed his lips together. He'd been young when he'd realized what he needed, and it had taken a few years to convince his parents of what was right for him. Mother had planned her heir carefully and a son hadn't factored into that.

In the end, she'd gotten him everything he needed, every available procedure to make his body his own. He'd never thought about cost.

He'd never thought about a lot of things.

He played with his dick a little bit, flipping it from side to side, and told Rhys, "Grew this in one of the labs upstairs. Works like I grew it myself. Miracle of modern science, right?"

"A miracle," Rhys agreed.

Arden stretched. "Are you sure you don't want a snack? I'm dying for one."

"Did you eat dinner?"

"Uh. No."

"You should do that."

"Mmm. Are you hungry? Come on. Where do you want to eat?"

Rhys shook his head. "I don't think that's a good idea."

"What?"

"Bringing me out to eat with you."

Arden blew a raspberry.

"I think you're underestimating how much people are freaking out."

Arden blew another raspberry, this time into Rhys's side. "Fine, they're freaking out. I'm ordering something, though, so what do you want?"

"I'm not picky."

He grabbed his tablet, ordered a handful of favorites, then laid back to wait. When he heard the thrall enter, he called, "In here!"

Rhys shot him a look.

"What?"

Rhys pressed his lips into a thin line, then slunk down in bed when the thrall entered.

"Over there." Arden pointed to a table beside the armchair where he'd tossed his clothes.

The thrall set it down. "Anything else, Your Eminence?"

"That's all."

Rhys scooted even lower in the bed until the thrall had left.

Arden grabbed the tray and brought it over to the bed. He didn't point out that Rhys had hidden from the thrall. Instead, he pulled the cover off the tray and said, "Here, try this, it's amazing." He speared a forkful and held it out to Rhys.

Rhys took the bite. His eyes fluttered close.

"Right?" Arden asked.

Rhys nodded.

They ate, then nestled back together under the covers. Arden fell asleep almost as soon as Rhys put an arm around him.

In the morning, Rhys woke him as he tried to untangle them.

Arden said, "You keep trying to leave."

"I have to go to work."

"You keep saying that."

"It keeps being true."

"Take that tray with you?"

"Of course, Your Eminence."

Arden snorted. He grabbed Rhys's hand and kissed his palm. "See you soon?"

"There's a Council meeting tomorrow."

"Oh, fuck, there is. I'll see you tomorrow."

Rhys tried to walk away, but Arden didn't let go of his hand, not until Rhys came in and kissed him.

"Bye," Arden said.

"Bye."

Arden snuggled into the pillow Rhys had used until the absolute last minute. He washed and dressed in a hurry, then headed to his first appointment of the day. Some young peer wanted to talk Arden into renting her a storefront.

Arden had little intention of opening a new store anytime soon. Not until they had engineering, farming, and maintenance sorted out. He told the peer as much, but also said he'd keep her idea in mind when things looked up.

Arden arrived at the Public Chamber significantly earlier than the rest of the Council. Rhys had come and woken him rather early, which Arden had attempted to protest, but Rhys had convinced him with a kiss.

Arden put his feet up on the table while they waited and looked at Rhys in his usual place. "I don't know why you wanted me here so early."

"It looks better."

"Does it?"

"You want to impress your new Council, when you have it, don't you?"

"Yes."

"No one's impressed when you show up in your bedclothes."

"I only did that a few times." Arden tipped back his chair so he could see Rhys better. "Have you been thinking all these mean things about me for the last ten years?"

"Since before that."

Arden frowned at him.

His hand folded over his stomach but his eyes on Arden's face, Rhys gamely shared, "At first I didn't think I could like you less than I already did, and then I really didn't like you at all."

"And then...?"

"And then you started to take my advice."

"Oh."

Rhys softened what he'd said with a smile. "You're nearly a real person now."

"You really are very bold!" Arden scolded.

Rhys's smile widened.

The other members of the Council filed in and interrupted anything either of them might have said.

The Council members fixed Rhys with hideous stares, eleven pairs of eyes, livid and ugly.

Arden returned all four legs of his chair to the floor and sat up straighter.

"He should not be here," said Don Wiess.

"He's here by my invitation," Arden reminded.

"No one but Council members are allowed in the Public Chamber," Madge Yarrow said. "We've tolerated his intrusion—"

"You've got two months left to keep tolerating it. You all received my agenda for today's meeting?"

Now those pairs of eyes fixed themselves on Arden with icy distaste.

"You're going to ruin *Eden*," Burton Riley accused.

"All the shuttles in the docking bay are still functional if you'd like to take your chances somewhere else," Arden said. "You do go to the evacuation drills, don't you? You should know how to work one."

Riley scowled. Most peers blew off the drills. Children went because their teachers brought them, but the vast majority of adults had better plans. Arden went every time, though. He would have been a poor example otherwise.

"The purpose of today's meeting is to prepare a, uh, a conspectus of sorts for the incoming Council members. It's been a while since we've had an election and there's a lot of information to pass on. I'd like to make it as smooth as possible."

"It might be easier if you hadn't barred us from running again," Riley huffed.

"I don't *want* any of you running again. You're...obstinate, narrow-minded, and uncooperative. You're trying to make things how they were, but that's not what we're doing anymore," Arden said.

Weiss tried to insist, "You're making a mistake, Arden—"

"Excuse me!" he said.

Weiss bowed his head. "Your Eminence."

"We're here to work on this conspectus and anyone who says anything unrelated to the Council's business this day will...will be put on rations for a week."

"Rations?" Riley asked.

Arden nodded. "Mmm. You'll get what the thralls get to eat. And you can fucking join the vent cleaners, too, if you don't get your shit together."

"You can't do that."

"I can do whatever the fuck I want. I've been sitting here for twelve years trying to dance around you idiots to get things done when I've been able to just do things the whole time. You all understand that, don't you? This Council is a farce. Just a...a way for me to delegate things and keep the peerage happy."

The Council stared at him.

"My mother knew that. But I was young and unprepared and…and I was easily led. Not anymore."

They kept staring.

Arden smacked his hand on the table. "Not anymore! Bigley, you first, go. What's your summary of engineering?"

Bigley sputtered, nearly dropped his tablet, then started to give a shaky recount of the past decade or so.

Arden made himself sit up straight. He wanted badly to slouch back into his chair and cross his arms, but he didn't. He stayed upright and listened keenly as they gave their reports. Most of them had come ill-prepared.

They broke around lunchtime and Arden reminded them they'd reconvene tomorrow morning, and every morning thereafter, to finish this.

Rhys moved for the first time when all the Council members had left.

Arden had forgotten about him. He gestured to a chair.

Rhys sat.

"How long have you known?"

"Your Eminence?"

"That I'm an idiot."

Rhys smiled. "You're not an idiot."

"Then why do I act like one?"

"Because you've been spoiled all your life."

Arden sighed. He folded his arms on the table and rested his chin on his arms. "Is that all it is?"

"The last Autarch never believed she would die, not even while she was dying."

"Did you whisper into her ear too?"

"No, but I've listened to you talk about her for a decade."

Arden groaned. "Should we have lunch in here? I need to organize my notes."

"If you'd like me to join you."

"Of course, I do." Arden tapped out a lunch order on his tablet, then paused to ask, "What do you want?"

"I'm not picky."

Arden stuck out his tongue. "I never realized it, you know, until today. Until I was yelling at them, that they've been leading me along like I can't think on my own. Like I don't own everything."

Rhys remained quiet.

Arden lifted his head. "You must have figured it out pretty quick."

"Your Eminence?"

"Barely two years into my reign and you're sneaking up behind me making these little comments," Arden accused limply.

Rhys lowered his eyes.

Arden's stomach hurt. "Well?"

"Do you really want me to answer that?"

"I do now."

"You, uh. Do you remember that flu outbreak ten years ago?"

Arden nodded.

"We had to scrub everything, the whole station, top to bottom. As soon as we stopped puking, they had us out cleaning. I was wiping down one of the stairwells. It was late, but it was round-the-clock work."

Arden straightened up.

"So I was, you know, wiping down the railings and this fancy-looking boy was sitting on the stairs, head in his hands. I didn't realize you were crying until I was a few stairs away. You'd been at it for a while 'cause it was just a few sniffles every now and again."

Arden cleared his throat. He didn't like this story.

"Anyway, you noticed me and you yelled at me for bothering you. I asked if you needed anything. You said you needed help and I said, 'What usually helps me is washing my face and a drink of water' and you just...you stared at me. You asked me for a glass of water, and I walked you back to your room and got you a glass of water and wet a washcloth so you could wash your face and told you to go to bed. And you went to bed."

"I don't remember that."

"You were shitfaced. But you...you so badly wanted someone to tell you what to do. You were like a lost kid. So...I kind of. I thought I should give you what you wanted."

"Mmm. Out of the goodness of your heart?" Arden asked.

"Better me than one of them," Rhys said and slung his eyes towards the other empty Council seats.

"Then this is some long con?" Arden asked. The stone in his gut grew heavier and colder by the second.

"I don't want *Eden* to fail either. It's my home."

"And sleeping with me?"

"Not remotely part of the plan."

"No?" Arden asked.

"Like I said, I didn't even like you at first."

Arden took his hand and squeezed it. "I didn't like you either."

Rhys smiled at him.

A thrall brought in their lunch.

They ate before they started to review the reports. They spent three or four hours doing what they could with what they'd been given. An awful pain started behind Arden's eyes, so he called it quits. He retreated to his chambers, skipping dinner and taking shots of Three and Nine.

They spent a week like that, listening to the Council in the morning, having lunch together, then trying to put things together for the incoming members. They separated in the evenings for some reason or another.

This evening it was because Arden had agreed to visit Cathie's ladies' club. He approached the event with absolute dread, but a thrall served him a saucer of fizzy wine as soon as he walked in the door, so he felt better about it immediately.

They'd completed the conspectus, pending a few minor revisions, so he felt he deserved to indulge.

He expected a group of bored, gossipy women of the peerage, which he got. Fifteen women between twenty-six and forty, dressed up for no one but themselves and each other.

He settled himself into an available armchair and raised an eyebrow. "Ollie?" he asked.

The young man looked over at him. "That's me, Your Eminence."

Ollie Brown had been years behind Arden in school, but Arden had played ball with Ollie's older brother.

"Are you part of Cathie's club?"

"When there's nothing else to do," Ollie said. "What about you?"

"Oh, Cathie wants me to impress the importance of charity on you all."

Ollie smiled. "Between the two of us, I'm here because I'm desperate to get Tiz to notice me and she thinks it's so funny of me to show up to a ladies' club."

"That humor's a little antiquated."

"Isn't it though!" Ollie agreed. "But she has wonderful tits. I saw them once and I've been chasing that dragon for three years now."

Arden smiled.

"Ardi!" Cathie cried when she saw him.

He rose to meet her.

She wrapped him up in a hug and started showing him off to all her friends, making introductions.

She glowed with the attention.

He found himself talking to Tiz Rivera and catching sour looks from Ollie. He motioned for a thrall to bring him another drink. When he had it, he watched the thrall walk away, then eyed Tiz's breasts. He didn't care that they were wonderful, he was sure they were, but he did wonder how much she'd paid for them.

She noticed him looking and gave him a funny kind of smile. Somewhere between irritated and flattered. Something else, too.

Calculating, he realized. He immediately wanted to dispel any notions she'd gotten. "Did you know thralls can't get the right procedures?"

"What?" she asked.

"Oh, you know, the ones with gender things to take care of." He made a vague gesture.

"And?"

"I didn't know. Did you?"

"No. Why would I, Your Eminence?" she asked cagily.

"No reason. Just. I thought everyone could get them."

"I never had those sorts of issues."

"No, but how much did you pay for those?" he asked and nodded towards her breasts.

She gaped at him, then mumbled a number under her breath.

It did seem outside of most thralls' budgets.

Tiz made an excuse to get away from Arden.

He finished his drink, picked over the snacks, and made some light chitchat with the other ladies.

When he felt he'd spent enough time with them, he left without saying goodbye to anyone.

He planned to curl up in bed and watch a few shows, or maybe a movie. He'd changed into his pajamas and retrieved his tablet from its charging dock when someone knocked on his door.

He checked it and let Rhys in. He smiled at him. "Miss me?"

"I actually needed to talk to you about something."

"Oh."

"Can I?" Rhys held out his hand for Arden's tablet.

Arden handed it over, then took it back to look at the page Rhys had pulled up. His account. "And?"

"I can't live on that."

"Um." Arden stared at the number. It seemed meager, edging back toward the nothing he'd started with a little while ago. He flicked through a few more pages.

People rented thralls from Arden and what they paid went either towards a thrall's rent and provisions or towards their debt. It worked much the same way for Rhys. People paid Arden for his time and the money got funneled automatically towards rent or his personal funds. The system smelled funny, even to Arden, but people had signed up for that when they'd come to *Eden*.

Arden noted, "No rations."

"Only people with debt get rations," Rhys reminded. "I don't qualify anymore."

"Mmm."

"And the only food for sale is meant for peers."

Arden nodded his head. "That is a problem, isn't it?"

"I tried to buy tomatoes today and I would have gone back into debt for it."

"Hmm. Well. Do you want me to put you back on rations? Or..." He studied Rhys's face. "Or pay you more?"

"How about both?" Rhys proposed.

"I did think you'd say that." Arden took the tablet over to the couch and did a little digging through the files. "Did you know you've never gotten a raise?"

"I did know that."

Arden studied the files a little longer and weighed the options and consequences, near and far. "What I do for you is going to set a precedent for everyone who pays back their debt."

"And how likely is that?" Rhys asked archly.

"I'm just saying, down the road, history will look to you as an example."

"So?"

Arden shrugged. "So, I really hope whoever's Autarch in four or five generations can afford what I'm about to give you." He doubled Rhys's pay, put in a note to figure out a raise schedule later, and gave him access to ration credits again. If Rhys paid back his debt and word got around that he'd lived better beforehand, then no one would ever have the motivation to work off their debt. "The thing with the food, we'll sort that once we have a new Council settled. Figure out some kind of middle ground on pricing. Is that all you wanted?"

"A man has got to eat," Rhys pointed out.

"I've fed you lunch every day this week," Arden returned.

"Some of us eat more than once a day."

Arden ignored that. "I was going to watch a movie. You could stay."

"You seemed pretty sick of me earlier."

"That's just work, though!" Arden assured, a little chagrined that he'd snapped at Rhys earlier. "Outside of work, I'm desperate to see you."

"You didn't call for me."

"It felt like you might think it was obligatory."

"Isn't it obligatory for everyone to answer when the Autarch calls?" Rhys asked.

"Well, *yes*, but I'm not, you know. I'm trying to make you sleep with me. I just, I had fun. I thought you did, too."

"I had fun."

"Besides, it's just a movie."

"I'll stay for a movie," Rhys agreed.

Arden grinned and pecked him on the cheek.

He snuggled up to Rhys as they watched.

Rhys ended up staying for more than a movie. He agreed to stay for a late dinner, which didn't surprise Arden given the state of his funds.

They ate sitting on the floor on opposite sides of the coffee table in Arden's viewing room.

Arden, as he ripped apart edamame shells, offered, "If you haven't got anywhere really pressing to be, I could suck your dick, too, if you're interested."

Rhys pressed the back of his hand to his mouth. He'd just taken a large bite of pasta and had to struggle to chew it.

"If you're interested," Arden repeated.

"I...Are you sure?"

Arden nodded.

"I'm interested."

Arden popped a few edamame beans in his mouth. He pulled up his leg and rested his knee on his chin. "You don't look interested. You look uncomfortable."

"I usually am around you."

The confession didn't surprise Arden, but it did hurt. "I super fucking hate that."

Rhys chuckled. "Is that the kind of language you learned in your superior education?"

"Sure fucking is. It's also where I learned how to give head and I'd like to share the benefit of that superior education with you. Poor unfortunate wretch that you are, we must give alms." Arden gave Rhys a smile he hoped came off as soft and inviting.

Rhys pushed a little bit of pasta around his plate. He gestured to it with his fork. "I, uh. Can I heat this up later if I don't finish it now?"

Arden tittered. "You can have a whole second plate of pasta if you want. You can have three. We can make you a little to-go box if you're going to try to feed me that excuse about having to work."

"I do have to work!"

Arden scooted around to the other side of the table. He gave Rhys a nudge towards the couch. "Go ahead."

Rhys hesitated.

Arden gave him another push. "Go on."

Rhys pulled himself onto the couch.

"Stop thinking about your pasta."

The other man murmured, "Sorry."

"Think about me for once."

"I think about you all the time."

"No, you think about *Eden*, and the Autarch, and the man who owned you, and the Council, and the thralls. Think about *me*." Arden slid between Rhys's legs, ran his hands up his thighs, and skimmed a finger under the waistband of his trousers. The rough fabric tickled his finger, a delicious contrast to the softness of Rhys's skin.

Rhys drew in a breath. He stared down at Arden, his dark eyes bright.

Arden kissed him, slow, but not slow how Rhys kissed slow. Not careful but savoring. He kissed his throat and untied the front of his shirt. He pressed his mouth to Rhys's chest, his fingers moving down to work at the buttons of his pants.

Rhys sunk lower into the couch, all sighs and soft, sweet gasps.

He stayed like that, running his fingers through Arden's hair when Arden lowered his head.

He found Rhys ready, straining, and made the eager work of him. Not hurried, no, just attentive and enthusiastic.

He liked this, Rhys's fingers in his hair, the taste of him in his mouth, and hopefully, the thought of Arden in Rhys's mind.

He pulled back after Rhys had cum. He licked his lips and wiped his mouth.

Rhys pulled him in for a kiss. Slow, but not careful.

Arden settled into his arms. "Do you want to stay?"

"I'll stay," Rhys consented. He sounded a little sad, but he kissed the side of Arden's face and pulled him closer into a hug.

Arden almost said thank you, but he stopped himself.

He warmed Rhys's pasta up and lent him pajamas.

He felt hazily content, even when Rhys woke him up in the morning to kiss him goodbye.

"Do you want me to call someone for you?" Rhys asked.

"No. Didn't I give you today off?"

"Day off means I'm not getting paid."

Arden stretched. "Okay. I'll see you soon?"

"Mmhmm." Rhys kissed his forehead.

Arden snuggled into the pillow Rhys had used for about half an hour. When he felt good and ready, he got up and drew himself a bath.

Once upon a time, he'd done this regularly for himself. He'd sit around in a bubble bath with his hair piled on his head.

Today he sunk all the way in and scrubbed his scalp. He washed it and then smoothed conditioner through the length of it. He twisted it and sat it on top of his head to let it soak in.

There'd been a time when he'd taken care of himself a little better. Gotten exercise and the closest thing to fresh air *Eden* could offer. He hadn't used so many formulas and he'd eaten more than one full meal a day.

What had changed?

Mama had died, and then Mother had gone and died, too, and he'd become Autarch...Really, he'd been worse off then than he was now.

Maybe he'd ruined his sense of self and overall health. Maybe this was as good as it got.

Shit, if it was, he should probably find someone to have his kids, because he couldn't be long for this world if this was as good as it got.

What would happen to *Eden* if he died without an heir? He had cousins. That would have to do.

He curled his lip thinking of his cousins. Some of them were too much like their father and the others were too afraid of their father to be worthwhile.

He rinsed his hair, dressed, and went to surprise Uncle Winslow for breakfast.

Winslow hugged him and told the same stories he always told. He both complimented and complained about their breakfast in the same cheerful tone so that Arden didn't know which was which. He had no idea if 'very cooked' or 'just as dry as the desert' were good or bad.

He honestly didn't care, either.

"You look happy today, Arden," Winslow noted as he spread jam over his biscuit.

Arden stirred his oatmeal. "Do I? What's that look like?"

"Those sweet little dimples on your cheeks, for one." Winslow reached over and gently pinched Arden's cheek.

"Winnie." He pushed his hand away. "I'm not five."

"You were such a cute little thing then. Chubby little cheeks."

Arden reached over and patted Winslow's cheek. "Wonder where I got them from."

"Ah, what's the harm in spoiling a child a little? You're only young once."

Arden had to make himself smile.

"You're still so young..." Winslow sighed.

"Winnie?"

"Hmm?"

"Mama, she, um. She and Mother were happy together."

"Very happy."

"How did they fall in love?" he asked.

"Oh. Hmm." Winslow wiped his mouth. He leaned back in his chair. "It started with you, Ardi."

A pleasant warmth bubbled through Arden.

"Your mother decided it was time to have an heir. She interviewed potential fathers, potential surrogates, settled on the two she did. The whole time Rani carried you, the Autarch watched over her like a hawk. Do this, do that, blah blah." Winslow waved a hand.

That didn't surprise Arden.

"Rani liked that. She liked being taken care of. She was always such a child like that. And the Autarch liked that Rani listened. They, just...they made sense together. Isn't that nice?"

"It's lovely," Arden agreed.

It sounded awful, honestly, but his mothers had been much different people than he was. But it was nice that they'd loved each other, even if they'd only gotten thirteen years together. Maybe closer to fourteen, if he counted Mama's pregnancy and the fact that she hadn't dropped dead on exactly his thirteenth birthday.

"Why?" Winslow asked.

Arden shrugged. "Thinking about how awful it would be if Uncle Morris inherited the position."

Winslow grimaced. He and the other Stones had never cared much for the Torre family. The feeling had been more or less mutual, with the exception of Mama and Mother themselves.

Arden had to side with the Stones. They might have been silly and indulgent, but at least they were fun. He didn't even share genes with the Stones and he liked them better.

Sounding mildly concerned, Winslow told him, "You're still young, Ardi, you've got time. Children are work, best not to rush in before you're ready."

"Oh, idle fantasy only, Winnie," he assured seriously.

He had about another quarter of a century before he started to worry about being past his prime for child-rearing. Mother hadn't decided to have an heir until her eighties and she'd still been spry.

Before she'd gotten sick.

What an awful sickness, it had shriveled up her mind and her body. All the resources on *Eden* had meant nothing.

If Morris Torre hadn't been such a shit, he might have sat as regent for a decade. Who wanted a twenty-three-year-old as Autarch? Most of his schoolmates had still been tooling around in elective lessons, playing sports, and refining their taste in hobbies.

Even in his darkest moments, Arden could at least rest assured he'd done better than Uncle Morris would have. Based on the reports that came out of the med centers he supervised, everyone on decks six and seven would take to the halls to celebrate if Morris dropped dead.

"You never had kids, Winnie," Arden pointed out.

"I suppose I didn't. I guess I wasn't inclined towards it. Some men are better as uncles."

"You're an amazing uncle."

"Flatterer."

"An absolutely fabulous marvel of an uncle."

Winslow blushed and smiled. "Oh, go on, Ardi, don't tease an old man."

"You're not old, Winnie! I need you around for *at least* a hundred more years."

Winslow chuckled. He put some jam on a biscuit and passed it to Arden. "Try this, it's much too sweet!"

Arden ate it and agreed, "Pretty sweet."

"Your hair looks nice. Did you do something with it?"

"Brushed it."

Winslow clucked his tongue.

Arden reached over to ruffle his curls. "What about these! Do you brush them?"

"Arden!" Winslow scolded. He even managed to appear convincingly cross before he smiled. "You're a very fresh boy."

Arden grinned at him. He reached over to hold Winslow's hand. "Eventually someone's going to find it becoming."

Winslow laughed and tightened his pudgy fingers around Arden's thin ones.

Arden put Rhys in charge of organizing the thrall side of the elections. Or, at least, he had in his head. He had yet to tell Rhys.

He would tell Rhys as soon as he stopped looking so happy with himself. He thought he'd talked Arden into making a concession on something, some edit in the conspectus that they'd bickered about before.

Arden had taken the correction Rhys wanted personally at first and he'd argued about it out of spite until he'd stopped to listen to what Rhys had to say.

It had made sense, too much sense to ignore.

He reached his hand across the table in the Public Chamber, palm up and open.

Rhys regarded it warily.

Arden wiggled his fingers.

Rhys took his hand.

"I want you to organize the elections for the thralls."

Rhys tried to take his hand back, but Arden didn't let go. He sighed. "In a month?"

"Just, uh, you know, do it the same way we do the peers."

"There are a lot more workers!"

Arden smiled at him. "You can have help. Do you want help?"

"Do you...Arden—"

Arden grinned. "I like it when you say my name."

"Have I done something to give you the impression that I can do the work of half a dozen people?" Rhys demanded.

"You sort of have."

"Disabuse yourself of the notion immediately," Rhys requested.

"How many people do you want?"

"Thirty."

Arden returned, "Twenty, paid, full-time. As many volunteers as you want, as long as they're not missing work."

"And tablets for them?"

"Mmmm, ten refurbished ones."

Rhys frowned.

"I'm not made of money!"

Rhys's face shifted through about a dozen emotions, none of them favorable.

Arden tittered. He squeezed Rhys's hand and leaned over to kiss him. "I had you there, didn't I!"

"It isn't funny."

"It was a little funny."

Arden settled back in his chair. "Are we done with this?"

"Almost."

"Can we finish it tomorrow?"

"You just dropped an enormous burden in my lap—"

Arden blew a raspberry. "Fine. We'll finish it now." He dragged his tablet over. Not much work remained.

Distracted, he checked the list of nominees. Nineteen people running. Two had targeted thralls as their demographic. The rest hadn't paid their new voters any attention.

"Do you know Cole Baker?" Arden asked.

"Not personally, no, but everyone knows who he is."

"You read a lot of poetry?"

"I like to read," Rhys answered. He attempted to sound casual.

Arden narrowed his eyes. "You like Cole's poetry?"

"Um. Yes."

"You like love poems."

"Sure. Aren't we working on something?"

"You like love poems, or you like subversive anti-capitalist poetry disguised as love poems?" Arden asked.

Rhys cleared his throat. "Hmm? No, I just. You know. I guess I'm a romantic."

"So you do think I'm an idiot."

"Arden," Rhys sighed.

Arden gave a little shimmy. "I really like when you say my name."

Rhys took his hair out from his bun, ruffled his fingers through it, and retied it. He fidgeted with his clothes. He didn't look at Arden.

"It's okay, you know. That you don't like how things are," Arden said.

Rhys eyed him.

"It's not working and all of the weight is bearing down on, on you.

People like you. The thralls. We're making changes, I promise, but I'm not looking to start a revolution. It will take time, but we'll fix things."

"How?"

"I don't know yet. But we can figure it out."

"Okay."

Arden came over to perch on the table near Rhys. "I promise."

Rhys nodded.

He put a hand on Rhys's shoulder. "I don't like it either. Or this. It's all new. New things—"

"Terrify you," Rhys finished for him. His voice came out strangely, wet and thick.

"Hey."

He shook his head.

Arden tightened his grip on his shoulder. "Rhys."

He shook his head again but put his hand over Arden's. He pressed his cheek against their hands.

Arden touched his hair.

Rhys sniffled.

"Do you want a drink of water?"

He licked his lips, then nodded. "Please."

Arden handed him one of the glasses left over from their lunch.

Rhys sipped the water and wiped his nose. "Sorry."

"It's okay. We'll, uh. I know we can do this." He gave Rhys a small smile.

Rhys returned it, tight-lipped.

"Do you want to come over tonight?"

"I think...I think I should get started on the election."

"Oh. Sure."

"A different night," Rhys promised.

"Okay." He checked the time. "Do you want to get started now?"

"Please."

Arden slid off the table.

Rhys stood abruptly. He pulled Arden into a tight hug.

Arden patted his back, not sure what else to do. They'd never hugged, not in a purely platonic way. Physical affection between them usually didn't come from Rhys and that which did come never amounted to anything more than carnal. Arden had written it off as part of his personality or maybe part of his upbringing. "Are you alright?"

Rhys nodded. He cradled the back of Arden's head and kissed his temple. "Yeah."

"Okay."

After a minute or so, Rhys's grip loosened. He stepped back, looking embarrassed.

Arden smiled. He kissed his cheek. "Maybe you're tired. Why don't you get some rest tonight? Worry about the election tomorrow."

"No, I—"

"I won't pay you until tomorrow!" Arden half-teased, half-threatened. "Get a really good night's sleep. That's a direct order from your Autarch."

Rhys chuckled. "Fine."

"Send me a list of who you want to work with, I'll change their work orders over in the morning."

Rhys nodded.

Arden gave him a push towards the door. "Go, before I change my mind."

"About what?"

"About whatever I want!" He pushed Rhys more firmly this time.

Rhys went, glanced back once, then walked out of the Public Chamber.

Arden stayed a while longer to finish the conspectus. He stared at the nominees for Council. He knew all of them. He didn't feel strongly one way or another about most of them. Bull had thrown his name in, or someone had nominated him, and Arden knew he wouldn't confirm him if he won a seat.

Cathie would be pissed, but Arden couldn't sit through Council meetings with him.

He also wouldn't confirm Ulrich Narrows, not based on personal dislike, but because Ulrich embezzled. Oh, he'd avoided a conviction, but Arden wouldn't let him anywhere near the Public Chamber and the funds the Council managed.

To Arden's excitement, Shayla Mbye had a nomination. She'd always impressed him with a level-headedness that seemed to be the product of sheer will alone. He hoped she won a seat.

He headed back to his room for an early night.

He'd had a lot of those lately, but he preferred them to sleepless ones.

Halfway back, he bumped into a few of his mother's friends, wrinkled old women with their feet firmly in their second century. With bright eyes and pinched mouths, they looked him over and invited him to come along with them to dinner.

He accepted. He had no choice.

He listened to everything they said with rapt attention. Mother had brought him to many social events with these women and had chastised him frequently and harshly when he'd ignored them or seemed like he'd ignored them.

He wondered if his mothers had ever considered another child, either as a companion for him or as a failsafe if Arden turned out a disappointment. If they had, they'd never spoken of it to him.

Maybe he would have liked that, a sibling or two.

Much more likely, he would have hated it. Having to share Mama? He would have terrorized whoever had come after him.

Maybe he was meant to be the youngest child. He should have had an older sibling, someone for Mother to focus on, while he could stay safe and cozy in Mama's arms.

Another child could have happened if Mama hadn't died.

Her death had happened abruptly, not illness, but an accident.

Hopefully, an accident and not a murder. Her lift had crashed, taking her life and the life of two of her friends.

"You're just on another planet, aren't you!" scolded one of the ladies.

"I'm sorry, Eula. I was thinking about Mama and Mother."

The women exchanged pitying looks.

One placed a knotty hand on his. "We all think about your mothers. They were such lovely friends to us."

He forced himself to smile.

"Good women," another agreed.

"And you so young, too, to have lost both of them..." a third sighed.

Arden lost his grip on the smile. He sipped his drink and pushed some food around his plate.

Home, he needed to go home. He made an excuse to leave as early as he could. It took forever, but he did escape eventually.

He curled up in his bed.

He resisted the urge to ask Rhys to come over.

Instead, he messaged Cathie and asked if she was busy. She had plans with friends already but invited him out to join her.

He declined.

He tried Cole and Mace, and even Zira, and got similar answers.

Finally, the inevitable took its course. That spiral of uncomfortable emotions. He'd coped with them in other ways before, but this time he called for a shot of Nine.

The time it took the thrall to bring the shot dragged, slow, nearly agonizing.

When the thrall did arrive, Arden called for them to bring it to his bedroom.

They came, eyes down.

"Took you long enough," he said.

"I beg your forgiveness, Your Eminence," the thrall murmured.

He reached for the shot, then hesitated. He pulled his hand back and placed it on his hip.

The thrall remained still.

Arden sighed. "How often do you answer my calls?"

"Your Eminence?"

"I mean, how often do you come to my room, bring me stuff?"

"Uh. Frequently, Your Eminence."

Arden looked the woman up and down. A little older than he was and unfamiliar to him. "What, like, once a month, twice a month...?"

"Almost every day, Your Eminence."

"Are you bullshitting me?"

"Um. No, Your Eminence."

"Alright. Well. What's your name?"

Shakily, she began, "Seven four three—"

"No, your name."

"Fari, Your Eminence."

Arden took the glass. "Thanks, Fari."

She remained stock still.

"You can go."

She scurried out faster than thralls he'd thrown things at.

Fuck, he'd really been a beast. Throwing things at people. No wonder Rhys hadn't liked him.

Instead of thinking about that any further, he threw back the shot and flopped onto his bed. He fell asleep before he made it all the way under the covers.

He woke up fully clothed, excepting his shoes, and twisted up in his blanket. He squinted up at the face of the man who'd woken him. "Mace?"

"Oh, Ardi, that hurts!" Cole scolded. "You know we aren't even twins."

"Could have fooled me."

"My eyes are much greener than Mace's!"

"Still both hazel," Arden reminded.

"And now he's got that stupid haircut. Professional. He looks like a careerist." Cole jumped on to the bed beside Arden. "You didn't message me back and I got sort of worried you might be doing that *thing* you do."

"Which one?"

"Oh, you know." Cole stretched out on the bed beside him and propped his chin up on one hand. "With the formulas and the regrettable choice of bedmates."

"Regrettable?"

"The one who threw up on you, the one who stole your robe—"

"I gave him the robe!" Arden protested.

Cole snorted. "Besides, I'm not worried about your lovers, that's your own business. I just wanted to make sure you hadn't put yourself into a coma."

"I've never been in a coma."

"There's a first time for everything. Come on, get up."

"Why?"

"I don't know, aren't you important? Don't you have something important to do? You should have come out last night; we had a lot of fun."

Arden rolled over and buried his face in the nearest pillow. He yawned into it. "Can you get my tablet?"

Cole handed it over. "Lots of missed messages. That's what happens when you make us worry."

"Not enough to come over," Arden pointed out. He rolled onto his back and held his tablet up so he could see it, hoping he wouldn't drop it directly on to his face.

Cole raised an eyebrow. He gestured to his outfit, which was not an 'off to morning handball practice' outfit so much as it was a 'night at the club' outfit, all shiny, stretchy fabric with large expanses of olive skin exposed.

A funny bloom of warmth spread through his chest. He put aside his tablet and latched onto Cole, dragging him into a hug.

Cole giggled and hugged him back.

Arden let out a little laugh, too, but after a moment, he didn't feel silly or warm. He felt strangely empty. He tightened his embrace.

"You alright, Ardi?"

"I think so."

Cole pulled away, stood up, and stretched. "That couch did something to my neck..." he grumbled.

"A hot shower usually fixes it for me," Arden suggested. "You could have come in the bed."

"Oh. I...well. I'll keep it in mind."

Arden checked his messages and found the one he'd wanted to read. He skimmed over Rhys's message and started assigning the requested workers to Rhys's crew. He glanced over at Cole. "Go ahead, you first."

"Breakfast after?"

"Mm."

"Let everyone know you're still alive."

"Ugh. Fine. Go shower," Arden mumbled. He reread Rhys's message, just to make sure he hadn't agreed to anything awful.

Not that he thought Rhys had awful plans.

After his shower, Cole padded around the room undressed. He pawed through Arden's closet and glanced back to ask, "Shouldn't you be in the shower?"

"Nothing will fit you in there." He continued to watch Cole move aside the various garments. A lazy sort of appreciation for the other man hovered at the forefront of his mind. Despite their similar appearances, he'd never felt the same attraction towards Cole as he had towards Mace.

Maybe he only wanted people he couldn't have. Mace, Cathie...Nothing he'd had with anyone had ever lasted long. A few months, maybe close to a year, and then things changed. People changed. The fun of fucking the Autarch wore off.

"You appreciating the view, Your Eminence?" Cole asked.

"After six years of handball, you look more normal to me naked than otherwise."

Cole giggled. He held up a loose pair of pants. "If I try these on and they rip, are we still friends?"

"Go ahead."

Arden rolled out of bed and puttered his way through a shower, keeping his hair out of the water. He left it braided and coiled on top of his head as he dressed. He grabbed the first pants he could but when he looked for the shirt he wanted, he found it on Cole.

The flowy tunic probably was the only shirt that would fit the other man.

He wondered if Rhys could fit into his clothes, what he would look like dressed up instead of those rough thrall garments.

Some of his clothes might fit Rhys. He stood a little taller than Arden and weighed more, though they wouldn't have been much different in body type of Arden had weighed the proper amount for his height.

Arden usually liked being skinny. He didn't think anyone else liked it for him, but he did. He enjoyed the press of his bones against his skin, the narrowness of his waist and wrists, and the hollows of his cheeks. It made him feel...

He examined his fingers.

It made him feel delicate. Like something worth protecting, worth taking care of. He had all this money, all these things, all these people, he had to be worth something.

He didn't think about it too much because he knew it was wrong to feel that way.

He picked a different shirt and slid his feet into his favorite silver shoes.

Cole draped an arm around his shoulder and leaned on him. "Breakfast?"

Arden sagged slightly under Cole's weight. "Breakfast," he agreed without any real conviction.

He ate, though, and carried on a conversation with his friends, or whatever these people had become to him.

Maybe this was what friendship became in adulthood. Everything seemed so much duller than it had when he'd been young.

Zira asked, "So you're really letting the thralls vote?"

"Zira, if you ask me again, I will jettison you into the void," he reminded.

She scowled at him.

"Then stop asking!" he scolded. "I told you a thousand times, *yes*."

"I don't see why."

"Because you can't see past the end of your nose," Cathie pointed out. "They're so miserable, might as well let them think they're making a choice.

Right, Ardi? What does one seat do out of eleven?"

"One voice is more than they've ever been given," Cole said. "One voice can do a lot."

"Especially when it's sleeping with half the station," Zira huffed.

Cole's face crumpled and he turned red from the neck up.

"Don't be a bitch, Zira!" Arden snapped.

At the same time, Mace added, "That's rude!"

Cathie, quietly, added, "Completely uncalled for."

"What!" Zira growled. "He *is*."

"There's no fucking reason to say it like that," Arden said. "Very rude."

Cole shifted around in his chair and pushed some food around his plate. His brother put a hand on his arm.

Arden nudged his foot under the table and gave him the kindest look he could manage when Cole looked over.

Breakfast turned into an uncomfortable silence and people made excuses to leave, first Zira, then Cathie.

Arden said, "People will listen to you because your voice matters. Because it's beautiful."

Cole blinked at him.

"I really like your poems," Arden reminded softly.

Mace rested his head on Cole's shoulder. "Zira's just mad that she can't work things out with Alexander."

"That doesn't make me feel better."

"It's between the two of them."

"I know but..."

Mace squeezed his brother's hand. "Their issues are theirs and have been theirs since Zira decided to treat Alexander like a sperm donor instead of the kid's father."

Cole sighed. He snuggled against Mace and heaved a long, dramatic sigh.

Mace patted his back.

Arden tried to keep his face from doing anything weird.

Mace and Cole made their way to practice, which Arden declined to join, though the idea did tempt him terribly, albeit briefly. He did promise to go to their match next week.

He made a brief tour of some of the farming bays, hydroponic and otherwise. He genuinely enjoyed visiting the orchards. The strict, pruned shapes of the fruit trees appealed to him.

He touched the pinkish skin of an immature apple.

Had their ancestors ever dreamed of such a thing? Not just the ones on the planet below them, or on Terra Prime, but on their homeworld. Earth, if it existed. When humanity had first emerged, had a single creature ever dreamed of their children living among the stars?

He hoped so. He hoped they'd dreamed of it with wonder, instead of terror, which was how Arden felt about it sometimes.

So far above the world, fixed in an infinite void. Arden had never felt ground beneath his feet, or seen a beach, or a sunset. He'd read about them, viewed their ghosts in various forms of media, but he'd never felt the wind or heard a river babble.

Did it matter? Would it change him if he did?

The supervisors in the bays asked him simpering, careful questions, the thralls averted their eyes, and Arden hated all of them.

Not personally, of course, but the whole ridiculous farce of it.

He visited Winslow for lunch but found the old man napping in his armchair. He wanted to wake him but refrained. He picked up a book and settled into Winslow's couch to wait. He read for a while, but Winslow never woke up, letting out wheezy little snores. Arden finally called it quits, left his uncle a note, and moved on to his next appointment.

Later in the day, Winslow sent him a message apologizing for being asleep, scolding Arden for not waking him, and asking him to dinner.

Arden smiled down at his tablet and Winslow's formal, stuffy way of messaging. He accepted the invitation, of course.

Staunchly apolitical, Winslow chattered about everything except the upcoming elections. Food, books, movies, clothes, Arden's love life, or lack thereof, old friends and old memories.

"What about you, Winnie?"

"Hmm?"

"Are you seeing anyone?"

The old man's cheeks turned pink. "Me? I'm a little too old…"

"Nonsense, Winnie."

"Oh, well. I've had a few very good friends in my time, Arden."

"Like Marcus?"

Winslow had never introduced Marcus as anything more than a friend, but they'd been nigh inseparable for years until the other man had passed.

"Marcus was a good friend to me," Winslow agreed.

"Never anything more?"

The old man looked a little embarrassed…No, not embarrassed, uncomfortable. "I never wanted anything more," he said with a particular and gently informative tone.

"Ah."

Winslow pushed his food around his plate.

"It must be lovely to have that kind of friend," Arden offered.

His uncle nodded. "Lovely indeed."

Arden smiled. "So have you made any new friends, then, Winnie? You can't be too old to make new friends."

Winslow smiled. "I have friends. Just none like Marcus. Not at the moment."

"I expect you'd introduce us if you did."

Winslow placed his hand over Arden's wrist. "Of course, I would, dear." He gave a reassuring squeeze.

Arden took a few more bites of food. "Well. I have to go check in with a few things. Election stuff."

"Oh, I don't need to hear about that."

"Winnie, you know, you could take an interest."

Winslow dabbed his mouth with a lacy napkin. "I support you, Arden, but I don't need to hear about it."

He wondered if Mama had been like that. He hugged his uncle goodbye and walked to the storefront he'd assigned to Rhys for the election preparations. He'd needed an office of some kind and Goshawk had empty shops in the dozens.

Through the window, he watched the thralls within bustle around under Rhys's direction. He'd given Rhys permission to raid a few old storage bays for supplies and they'd helped themselves to a lot. More than desks and chairs, they'd taken sofas, rugs, and countertop appliances.

He stepped inside and everyone stilled.

"Your Eminence," Rhys greeted him.

"Was this everything they had in storage or did you leave something for the mice?"

Rhys frowned. "Mice?"

"It's...I think it's an old expression. I've heard in movies."

"Hmm."

"Just, you know, you seemed to have helped yourself?"

Rhys shrugged, a little bashful. "We were enthusiastic to get started."

"Everything going well?"

"As well as it can this soon in."

The thralls looked between Rhys and Arden, expectant.

"Your Eminence," Rhys added for good measure.

"You have everything you need?" Arden asked. His hands smoothed over his clothes of their own accord.

Rhys glanced around. His eyes lingered on a few of the thralls.

He'd chosen an odd bunch, pregnant women, people with chronic injuries or illnesses, elderly people.

"Friends of yours?" Arden asked.

Rhys shrugged. "Friends, or friends of friends. People I trust."

"Hmm."

Arden paced around the office then lingered near the office. "You sure you don't need anything else?"

"I'll keep you apprised."

"Thanks, Rhys. Uh. Cole might be by."

"Cole Baker?"

Arden nodded. "He likes you lot." He gestured vaguely around the store-turned-office. "Bleeding heart, if you ask me."

Rhys smiled.

Arden hesitated, then left without another word. He'd wanted to say more but hadn't been sure how much he should say in front of the thralls, or how much Rhys would want him to say. Some thralls, he knew, judged the ones who slept with peers for favors and he didn't think any thrall had gotten more than Rhys had.

He decided to leave Rhys alone for a few days. He had a lot to do.

Of course, he made sure Rhys knew that Arden would offer him whatever he needed to accomplish the task at hand. He might have told him too many times, but this mattered to Arden. It mattered to everyone on *Eden* whether they knew it or not.

The lead up to the elections kept Arden busy, despite not having to run to keep the position of Autarch. He had to keep track of the candidates and decide which ones he would confirm, should they win a seat. That meant attending fundraisers, campaign events, and very boring luncheons. He actively enjoyed Cole's event tonight because soft-eyed artists and well-muscled athletes circled warily around each other, trying to pull Cole in two different directions.

Cole's partners represented the divide in his life almost too perfectly. Wei and Mia ranked among the top athletes on the station, in gymnastics and squash respectively. They stood upright and proud, moving through the room like the world owed them something. Alexander lingered off to the side, standing in a small circle with a few other people. He had a drink clasped in both hands and shook his head a lot.

Arden hung back and watched as Wei and Mia approached Alexander. He didn't know the state of things between sides.

Alexander gave a small wave to the other two and seemed uncomfortable when they came closer.

The three of them shook hands and exchanged greetings.

Cole noticed that they'd started to interact and politely pushed his way over to the other three. He seemed nervous, but that could be because the election was tomorrow.

Arden finished his drink and continued to watch.

Things seemed to grow comfortable between the four of them before Cole had to go speak with potential voters.

He had confidence that Cole would win a seat. Good family, well-liked, popular writer. Even if the thralls didn't throw their weight behind him, a decent number of peers would.

He got another drink, grew bored of watching, and pushed his way over to Cole. "Excited?"

"Terrified."

"Try drinking."

"Oh, I'll throw up for sure."

Arden gave him a nudge. "You'll win."

"That's what scares me."

"Well, I promise I won't let you fuck up too badly."

Cole gave a thin, nervous smile. He forced a chuckle.

"You mingle. I'm going to, uh...probably just find another drink," Arden declared, suddenly uncomfortable.

He found several more drinks, then found his way home.

He stared out the window for a while, then messaged Rhys to come over.

Rhys came over. He didn't have a choice, which Arden knew. Arden lay on his back on the floor and waited for the sound of his door sliding open.

"I'm over here!" he called when he heard it.

Rhys approached. "You summoned me?"

Arden grinned. "I did, didn't I?"

"Any particular reason?"

"I wanted to see you. I haven't seen you much."

"We've been busy," Rhys reminded.

Arden held out his hand.

Rhys didn't take it, but he sat beside him.

Arden wiggled over and rested his head on Rhys's lap. "Do you think everything will change tomorrow?"

"Depends who wins. You have some pretty staunch centrists running. If Baker takes a seat, he'll support your agenda, and—"

"Do you ever relax?"

"You asked me a question."

"But I wanted you to say, 'yes, Arden, it will all be different.' I wanted you to say..." He twisted and stared up at Rhys. "I wanted you to say, 'it will be different thanks to you' and I wanted you to smile when you said it."

"Is that why you're doing this?" Rhys asked.

Arden tittered. "You want me to say it's all for you?"

"I'd be worried if it was."

"I just don't want *Eden* to fall apart. I want...I want this place to be what it should have been in the first place," Arden confided. "I mean, Bex never..." He sighed. "When Bex called it *Eden* she meant it. Paradise. For people like her. Like me. And it was until, until, you know, the cracks started to show. Until the cost of paradise needed to be paid."

Rhys twisted a bit of Arden's hair around his finger.

"Do you want to stay tonight?"

"I have—"

"Work in the morning. I know. But we have the same work tomorrow, don't we?"

Rhys tilted his head.

"I did think I should be there. It's a historic occasion. An historic...a historic..." Arden nuzzled his face into Rhys's lap. "We can go together. I mean...as, as Autarch and, uh...election official? Freedman? Advisor...as whatever you are. You know. A government thing, not a...a personal thing."

"Oh."

"It makes sense. First election for them. I should be there. Don't you think?"

"It makes sense," Rhys agreed.

"So stay tonight."

"Alright."

Arden wrapped himself around the other man, squeezing him tight. He buried his face in Rhys's shirt, against his shoulder. "I really want to get drunk."

"You're already drunk."

"Like absolutely blackout wasted."

"Tomorrow."

Arden snorted. "Promise?"

"Sure."

Arden tightened his grip, then stood. He took Rhys by the hand and pulled him to bed. He threw his clothes on the nearest piece of furniture, then curled himself around Rhys, who'd undressed as well.

He wrapped them in blankets and twined his legs with Rhys's. He knew a few ways they could get closer to each other, but those all seemed unnecessary. He skimmed his fingers over various parts of the other man, careful to avoid anything too intimate.

And to avoid the barely-there scars on his arms.

Maybe it was too obvious to avoid them.

Maybe it would make Rhys uncomfortable, maybe it would make him think Arden found the marks disturbing.

Rhys took Arden's hand and stopped his fingers from wandering. "You should get some sleep. Early morning."

Arden kissed his cheek and loosened his grip so they could both get comfortable. He fell asleep quickly but woke throughout the night. Most times he found Rhys nearby or still in his arms, but the third or fourth time, he found him not at all.

He glanced around the room. No Rhys, but his clothes hadn't left. He pulled on a robe and headed out to search for him.

He found him in front of the window, also wearing a robe.

Arden's nicest robe, one made of warm, black velvet.

Arden cleared his throat.

Rhys looked over. He grimaced. "Sorry."

Arden shrugged.

"I couldn't sleep." He pulled the robe a little closer. "I didn't think you'd mind..."

"I don't. Do you want something to help you sleep?"

Rhys shook his head.

Arden came to sit beside him. "Are you sure? I know a couple good ways to tire you out."

Rhys sighed. "No."

Arden placed his head on Rhys's shoulder. He didn't say anything else for a while. Rhys didn't seem to have appreciated his offers or his jokes. He wondered if he'd wanted to get away from Arden.

Quietly, after a while, he said, "It's a beautiful view, isn't it?"

"Mmm."

"Sometimes I can't look away. I sit here for hours and hours and I think about how big everything and how small we are and how...how nothing matters but somehow everything matters."

Rhys shifted a little.

"When I was really little, uh..." he trailed off. He felt stupid all of a sudden. Rhys didn't care about Arden's stories.

"Go ahead," Rhys urged gently.

Arden sighed. "I, uh, I just...I used to get so scared of things. Of the whole world. Everything is so cold and hard and *big* and I would just...I would cry sometimes just so I wouldn't have to leave my room. It's...it's so *awful* that we're up here, floating in this...this *awful* thing my family built. It frightens me and I feel so stupid for being afraid."

Rhys started to say something, then swallowed. He twisted himself to rest his chin on the top of Arden's head. "I was never frightened of anything, not my parents or teachers, or the peers, or the big kids...I was always angry. And, then, uh...then I found something out and I got this hideous cold feeling all over me. Like my guts had gotten stirred up and yanked up to the back of my throat."

"Twelve smooths things out," Arden murmured. "What are you afraid of?"

Rhys shook his head. "Don't worry about it."

Arden didn't press. He took Rhys's hand. He kissed his knuckles, then he nestled his cheek against Rhys's palm. "I hated being afraid."

"I liked being angry. I lived for it. I showed it off, how angry I was. I wanted everyone to know that..."

"That something hurt?" Arden guessed.

A sad smile played on Rhys's face. "Yeah."

Arden smiled back, just as sad. He wanted to cry.

He really wanted to cry. He let go of Rhys's hand and it dropped away from his face. Arden rubbed his eyes. He sniffled.

"Are you okay?"

"I don't know. I..." He pressed his lips together. "I'm fine. I am. I'll...Come back to bed."

"Okay."

Arden went to the bathroom first. He blew his nose and splashed his face with cold water. Once he settled down, he crawled back into bed with Rhys. "Sorry," he mumbled.

Rhys put an arm around him and nestled close to him.

Arden didn't sleep at all for the rest of the night. He didn't think Rhys did either. Neither of them spoke or moved, they just lay together, eyes closed, waiting for the morning.

Arden couldn't eat breakfast.

Rhys could. He tucked away a healthy portion and bounced between excited and nervous, but always collected.

Arden stayed calm, but he had help. He called for a half-shot of Twelve, better for an empty stomach, and dressed in his nicest plain outfit. He had to look put together but more approachable than he usually did at public appearances.

Rhys started to pull on the same clothes he'd worn yesterday.

Arden shook his head. "Don't wear that."

Rhys raised an eyebrow.

Arden pulled him towards the closet. "I, uh. I thought you might need something." He ran his hand over a set of clothes he'd ordered a few weeks ago. Tidy and plain, not vastly different from what Rhys usually wore, but finer fabrics and deeper, richer colors. Rust and sage, instead of washed-out browns.

The colors would complement the pale brown of his skin and warm his dark eyes. They'd glow just like they did in the light. He'd look put together and approachable. He'd stand out from peers and thralls.

And he would look handsome.

He always looked handsome, really, but the clothes would help.

Rhys rubbed the fabric of the shirt between his fingers. "I..."

Arden shrugged. "Don't say anything, just wear them."

Rhys smirked. "Yes, Your Eminence."

Arden snorted and left him in the closet. He sat on the bed and waited for him to emerge. When he did, he let out a sharp whistle.

Rhys scowled.

"You look good."

"Thank you." Rhys smoothed his clothes.

Arden grinned at him. "Ready?"

He nodded. "You?"

"No. I'm terrified."

Rhys chuckled. "You know, if the rest of *Eden* knew you were such a baby, no one would be afraid of you anymore."

"They'll be afraid of me as long as I have direct control over the entire economy," Arden reminded.

Rhys made a face, an odd, reticent sort of grimace.

"It's fucked up, isn't it? I didn't even get good grades," Arden agreed gamely.

He strode out the door, trying to prepare himself for the day.

He spent hours at the polling station, circling through the crowds, but finding his way back towards Rhys every hour or so. He didn't do it intentionally and normally he wouldn't have come back to the same person so many times, but Rhys was the only person he knew. At parties, he liked to bounce between different friends, or better yet, find a comfortable chair in a slightly secluded corner.

This wasn't a party, he reminded himself.

The day almost had the air of a party, but it was too anxious and almost solemn. Somewhere between a funeral and the nerves before a particularly tough handball match. It felt, he realized, like walking into surgery, desperate for the results but afraid of the process.

He reflexively touched his chest.

He pulled his hands down and turned his mind away from memories of hours of his childhood spent in front of the mirror trying to figure out what it was that felt so *strange* about the way he looked. Not wrong or bad, just...not his own.

Arden had been eight when things had clicked. He'd put on a program just for noise while he played, all his toys spread over the living room carpet. An interview with a dancer, who'd mentioned she'd missed a few performances recovering from surgery.

He didn't remember her name or her troupe, but he recalled the confident, sweet cadence of her voice when she'd said, "It was part of my transition to make my body more comfortable for me to live in."

Comfortable. Arden had clung to that idea, that he could be comfortable.

Gene therapy, a few surgeries spanning a few years of his life, and he didn't know how much money, but here he stood on the other side, comfortable.

He looked out over the lines of people waiting to vote, the crowds milling around, their voices sometimes spiking in frustration or excitement.

How many of these people couldn't have what he did? Not just because of their gender, but on any level.

Had a thrall ever been comfortable on *Eden*?

And there were so many of them.

Thousands of the awful, squirming worms, pushing towards him, wanting to vote, their grubby hands grabbing at the small scrap of hope he'd dangled before them.

He saw it in his head, so many hands reaching towards the filthy tatter he held out. Reaching, touching, closing around him.

Pulling him down.

Shit.

Fuck.

He sucked in an unsteady breath.

He found Rhys and hovered beside him without saying anything.

Eventually, Rhys must have sensed his presence or caught a glimpse out of the corner of his eye. He turned away from his conversation. "Did, um...Do you need something, Your Eminence?"

He swallowed. "I think I'm about to freak out. Do you have a quiet room somewhere?"

Rhys frowned.

"Please," Arden rasped, his throat dry, his lips sticky.

"This way."

Arden followed Rhys to a small room that he eventually recognized as a bathroom. He voiced the concern.

Rhys answered, "You seem like you might be used to crying in bathrooms at parties."

Arden normally would have scolded him or pinched him, or at the very least called him rude. Instead, he pressed his lips together and blinked back a few tears.

"This is where I come to cry at work," Rhys offered with helpful cheer.

Arden could not imagine Rhys crying.

"Why cry at home when you can get paid to cry at work?"

Arden let out a horrible gurgling chuckle. He ground his knuckles into his eyes.

Rhys remained in the doorway of the bathroom for a few seconds, then said, "I'll...I'll leave you to it."

"Twelve," he demanded, then slammed the door in Rhys's face. He crouched in the cleanest corner of the bathroom and allowed himself a few piteous sobs into his hands before he tried to pull himself together in earnest.

He didn't know what had bothered him so much, the throng of people or how he'd routinely failed them for years.

Both, probably. He hated people, crowds, strangers, and he hated the thought of *Eden* falling to ruin under his rule.

And it would, fuck it really would. He was smearing liquid bandage over gaping wounds and dabbing rubbing alcohol over festering sores.

He didn't have much luck gathering himself.

He wished he'd stayed home.

He wiped away his tears as soon as they came and tried to hold back the worst of the crying. It didn't work.

Rhys let himself in a while later with a half-shot held carefully in one hand. "Sorry it took a while, no one's, uh, no one's working today. Anywhere." He crouched in the doorway and held it out to Arden.

He took the shot from Rhys and nearly dropped it, a little bit of slippery liquid sliding down his fingers and wrist.

If he'd dropped it, he would have lapped it off the floor.

He threw it back and waited, eyes closed.

It rolled through him, smoothed the world for him. Numbed the sandpaper sorrow grinding at his throat and eyes. He had to sit for a while before he had control of his limbs again.

Rhys still crouched in the doorway. He watched Arden.

If he didn't stop, Arden might start crying again.

"You okay?"

"I guess."

"What happened?"

"I don't know. Too many people."

Rhys took Arden's hand. "You really meant it when you said you were scared."

He nodded.

Rhys pressed his lips together. "Are you ready to come back out?"

Arden nodded, even though he wasn't ready. He washed his face with cold water and patted it dry.

He asked, "Presentable?"

"You look like you've been crying."

"Well, I have been crying."

Rhys stepped into the bathroom. He put his arms around Arden and held him wordlessly for much longer than Arden expected. He held him until he felt better. He stepped back, didn't say anything, and gave a nod back towards the polling area. "Twenty minutes, then you can leave for lunch. Check in a few other places. Come back in a few hours."

Arden tried to smile, but it came out thin and ungrateful. He did what Rhys had advised. He kept himself together for the rest of the night.

When the polls closed and every thrall of eligible age had voted, Arden presented the poll workers with a bottle of fizzy wine, which most of them regarded warily.

"Open it. Someone get glasses!" Arden insisted.

They scurried to obey.

No one sipped it even once they had a mug or cup in hand. Not proper drinkware, but whatever they'd scrounged from their office.

Someone had found a gaudy chalice that Arden assumed had been part of some play or costume party.

They'd given it to him.

He frowned at it.

Rhys grinned at him. At the glass in his hand.

A lot of people seemed to find the chalice amusing, a joke Arden didn't get.

Arden handed it over to him and took the plain mug meant for Rhys.

The thrall passing out glasses exchanged looks with another one.

When everyone had liquid in their cup, be it wine or something soft, Arden said, "Someone should say something." He looked at Rhys.

The thralls shifted uncomfortably. A few sniggered.

Rhys looked into the chalice and didn't meet Arden's eyes.

"Good work, all of you. It's...things are changing. And that can only be good." He raised his cup.

Everyone sipped. A few people mumbled in agreement.

Arden excused himself from the office building but didn't go far enough that he couldn't see what happened as soon as he left. Through the display window of the former storefront, he watched as someone elbowed Rhys, goaded him.

Rhys shook his head. He handed the cup to someone else.

The thrall who took it changed their posture, exaggeratedly snooty and sort of mincing. She said something Arden couldn't catch. She raised her cup.

Arden heard the room erupt with laughter.

He recognized what had happened. It didn't hurt. He understood that the thralls did not love the peerage.

Rhys had a smile on his face.

That did hurt.

Their eyes met through the display glass.

Arden hurried away.

Other people walked the streets, bottles and glasses in hand, waiting to celebrate the election results. They'd be calculated and posted on the big screens around *Eden* before midnight. Further celebration would come when Arden confirmed members a little while later.

Rhys caught up with him. "Arden."

Arden stopped and turned towards him. He raised an eyebrow minimally.

"Did you still want to get drunk?"

His insides hurt.

"You don't have to do this."

"No, I—"

"So don't if you don't want to," Arden insisted, trying to sound firm, but feeling desperate.

"Eulie was just making a joke. It wasn't...it wasn't even mean, not really."

"I'm sure it was a good impression."

Rhys started to smile. "It was, uh, it was what she said, really, that made me laugh."

"And that was...?"

Rhys rubbed his nose, reined in his smile, and said, "She, uh, she said, 'well, as uncomfortable as this has made *you*, I promise it's been much worse for me. Now, I've got bigger and better bathrooms to cry in at much nicer parties.'"

"And that's funny because...?"

"Because it's exactly something you'd say."

"I guess my subjects know me better than I give them credit for," Arden said, "Or they've been getting really good material directly from the source."

Rhys turned red.

Arden could see it even in the dim light of the artificial night. "*Don't do this if you don't want to.*"

"Listen, people...you know, they figured out pretty quick how I ended up the first worker to pay off their debt. And how I got this job. And how I got them all their jobs. It was really funny to them, that *I* was the one who finally bent over for the right peer after years, and Arden, I really mean *years* of being much less subtle about how I felt than I've ever been with you."

"Ah."

"And you weren't there and I was and I don't like it when people laugh at me. So, yeah, I found something else for them to laugh at."

Arden wanted to be angry, but he'd be a liar if he said he hadn't hurt other people to make himself feel better. It still stung. He sighed. "Nothing a few drinks won't fix, I guess. Come on."

They walked together.

"Where are we going?"

"The Big Room," Arden said.

Rhys eyed him.

"It's, uh, I think it's actually called the Bex Torre Recreation and Dance Hall, but it's just...a big empty room."

"I know what it is. Is this a party?"

"Of course. It's an election. And I have confirmations to give out."

"Am I allowed to be there?"

"You followed me into the Public Chamber without asking. You're worried about a party?"

"I followed you into the Public Chamber without you noticing," Rhys pointed out.

Arden couldn't help but smile. "Well, people will notice you tonight. If anyone's rude, tell them to fuck off. Or get me, and I'll tell them to fuck off."

Rhys kept a companionable closeness as they walked, more than he'd ever shown before. Arden wondered if he meant it as an apology. It didn't feel like one and he didn't know if Rhys had anything to apologize for. It just felt friendly.

It felt like a good time for Arden to say, "I, uh. I wanted to propose something to you."

Warily, the other man said, "What's that?"

"You don't actually have a job. I mean, especially now that the election is over. I know you've been acting in this advisory capacity for years now, but you've always just been listed as a floating worker."

Rhys shrugged. "Keeps me on my toes."

"Well. If you want it, there is an official job that you could have. My Chamberlain. Uh, my mother had a few on and off throughout her life. Especially when she got older."

"That's not..."

"It's a position meant for a peer," Arden confirmed. "But that doesn't mean anything. It's not in the rules and even if it was, I can fucking change the rules, can't I?"

"And if I say no?"

"I mean, you'll hurt my feelings, first of all, and you won't get a considerable pay raise, which is probably more important to you."

Rhys's mouth twisted.

"I didn't mean it like that. I just. I know...I know money matters to you in a way that it doesn't matter to me. Water matters more to the fish on the floor than the one in the sea."

"Is that another saying from an old movie?"

Arden shrugged. He didn't know.

"Can I think about it?"

"Of course." Arden had hoped for an enthusiastic acceptance, but Rhys tended to think about things before he agreed to them. Sensible of him.

Arden didn't know what that was like, being sensible.

"Take as long as you need," Arden added. Generously, he thought.

Rhys hesitated when they neared the Big Room. They could hear it before they saw it.

Arden paused when he paused. "What?"

"I really fucking hate these people."

Arden smiled. He took Rhys's hands in his and kissed his knuckles. "Well, I hate them too, and most of them aren't very pleased with me, and they definitely *all* hate you, so you're not alone in disliking your company tonight."

"Arden, what are you doing?" asked a voice from behind him. "Who is that?"

Rhys yanked his hands back.

Arden turned around. "Hi, Zira. Alexander. You two headed inside?" Between the couple, he spotted a small girl of maybe six. Or possibly younger or older. Arden had no idea. She had to be less than eight or nine because they'd only been married that long. He should have known her age. "You three."

"Lexira?" Zira prompted her daughter.

"Pleased to see you, Your Eminence." The child gave a perfect little bow. She was a picture-perfect child: big eyes, a button nose, with her father's full mouth and dark coloring, although rather diluted by Zira's paleness. She had a cloud of curls decorated with tiny jewels that hung in her hair like stars.

Zira had dressed her up, too, like a perfect little doll.

Every time he saw the girl, she was the model of politeness and prettiness.

Arden remembered being dressed up like that. He gave the little girl his very best bow. "Extremely pleased to see you, Lexira."

She smiled, pleased and nervous. She looked at her mother. Her eyes also darted to Rhys.

Alexander put a hand on his daughter's shoulder. "Any early reports?"

Arden smiled. "Ohh, now, even the candidates don't get previews. Come inside." He nodded over his shoulder. "Do you know Rhys?"

"I don't think we've met," Alexander said.

Zira eyed Rhys suspiciously.

Arden thought about saying, "Yes, *that* Rhys," but decided it was Rhys's place to decide how much he wanted people to know. In his nice new clothes, a stranger would never know he wasn't an underdressed peer without him saying something.

He placed a hand on Rhys's back and guided him along inside. "Let's find somewhere to sit before all the good seats fill up."

"Have you ever let anyone take a seat you wanted?" Zira asked.

Arden held his tongue for the sake of her daughter's ears. He winced at the sight of the Big Room packed with so many people. Dimly lit with pools of color here and there and glittering decorations on the ceilings and walls, the room had several distinct sections tonight, all of them similar in aesthetic but different in purpose. The bar crowded with people standing and holding their drinks, a dance floor already frantic with bodies, a distant, screened-in corner full of cushions and pillows and low couches filled with bodies doing other things, and then a sitting area with tables and chairs and a buffet.

Rhys's eyes swept over the whole room, drinking it in and looking simultaneously fascinated and disgusted.

Arden brought him over towards the sitting area. He settled Rhys into a seat, then raised a hand to call over a thrall. He thought better of it and made an awkward, aborted motion that turned into smoothing his clothes. "I, uh. I'll get you a drink. I'll get us drink. Drinks." He checked to see if Zira and Alexander had peeled away, which they had. "What do you want?"

"I'm not picky." Rhys sat upright and still in his chair.

They had a secluded corner table with room for more friends, but far enough from the fray people would need to seek them out to find them. A thin string of lights illuminated the space, but only modestly.

"I'll be right back."

Rhys nodded.

The crowds parted for Arden as he moved through them. He got his drinks as fast as they could physically be made. Still, it wasn't fast enough because, by the time he returned to Rhys, people had found him.

Cathie had seated herself in the chair Arden had claimed and Bull lounged in the one next to her.

Arden placed a drink in front of Rhys. "Cath."

She grinned at him. "I saw you two come in together. I was just talking to, uh..."

"Rhys," Rhys provided.

"Mmm, Rhys. You know, I've seen you two together before but I never, uh, I never knew that *this* was *that* thrall," she said.

"Well, he's not a thrall anymore."

Cathie grinned louchely at him. "No, I guess not."

Arden wished she hadn't said anything. He sat next to Rhys, between him and Cathie. He took a sip of his drink. "Snacks?" he asked.

"I'm not...Uh. Yeah. Yes. Your Eminence, I'll be right back." Rhys left the table and beelined for the buffet.

Arden hoped he'd hadn't taken Arden's question as a demand.

"Funny, bringing him here," Bull noted.

Arden ignored him and asked Cathie about her sister, which he knew would eat up a lot of time. She loved her little sister to bits and had been a second mother to the girl.

Rhys returned with laden plates.

He sat quietly while Cathie chattered.

He stiffened when more people came to join them.

Mace, at least, had the decency to say, "Oh, Rhys, hi!" with a genuine smile on his face.

Cole eyed Rhys, but with curiosity, not cruelty.

"Do you know my brother?" Mace asked.

"I'm afraid not, Supervisor—"

"Rhys, shit, don't do that, I'm not at work!" Mace insisted cheerily. "Just Mace. Anyway, this is Cole."

Rhys nodded. "I've, uh, I've read your poems."

Cole smiled shyly. "I hope you like them."

Arden touched Rhys's knee under the table. Just a bit of reassurance. He carried on talking to Cathie for a while, then the conversation spiraled out to include the rest of the table. Other people visited, Cole's partners, a few of the ladies from Cathie's club, pals of Bull's.

Arden picked at the snacks Rhys had fetched and ferried empty glasses and drinks back and forth between the bar.

The third time he came back he found that Cathie had taken his seat, again. She had her elbow on the table and her eyes on Rhys.

The sight made Arden's stomach bubble.

Cole tried to talk to him, but he couldn't stop listening in on the entirely friendly and banal conversation Cathie had pulled Rhys into.

The big screens mounted around the room turned on and showed a loading screen.

Cole grabbed onto Arden's arm. "Oh! It's time."

Arden squeezed his shoulder. "You'll win."

Cathie smiled at Bull. "And you too, hon!"

Arden had forgotten that Bull had a nomination. He'd entirely forgotten. If there was any bit of luck in the entire universe, the votes would get rid of Bull so Arden wouldn't have to deny his confirmation.

He slung back the rest of his drink, just in case.

The room quieted and everyone's faces turned towards the screens, hundreds of faces illuminated in green and blue.

Arden held tight to Cole's hand and Cole gripped back just as hard.

Numbers counted down from then, then the names appeared, alphabetical by last name.

"Cole Baker," a synthetic voice read over the hushed music of the dance floor.

Cole squeaked, then buried his face in his hands, somewhere between laughing and crying.

Mace hugged him.

Across the room, Arden heard Wei Han let out a whoop.

"...Istis Frakes, Riley Hmong, Jon Keats..."

Arden's stomach dropped.

He didn't hear the rest of the names.

Cathie let out a whoop of delight and threw her arms around Bull.

Arden tuned back in to hear the last name.

"Shayla Mbye."

Thank fuck Shayla had gotten elected.

He fumbled for his tablet and his hands shook as he pulled up the right page to confirm the candidates. The synthetic voice read them off a few seconds after he'd checked the boxes and saved the page.

"Cole Baker, confirmed."

People whooped.

Cole hugged Arden, his face still wet. "I'm gonna try really hard," he promised weepily.

"I know." Arden squeezed him back like hugging Cole could make things better.

Alexander had hurried over to embrace and congratulate his partner.

The artificial voice continued to list confirmations. It said, "Jon Keats, denied."

The room quieted.

People started to boo. Some people cheered.

Cathie stared at Arden. "What?" she demanded stonily.

Arden shook his head.

"What do you mean denied!" she demanded.

Bull stood up.

The voice went on confirming the rest of the candidates.

Arden shook his head. "He can't...he *can't* be on the Council."

Rhys had his eyes fixed on Arden, a strange kind of wonder on his face. "He's not a good fit."

Mace had curled up on himself, shoulders hunched. His hands clasped his arms but not hard enough to quell his shaking.

"What do you mean he's not a good fit? You're just being petty, Arden!" Cathie shouted.

"No," Cole said. "Ardi's right."

"Easy for you to say. You're fucking ridiculous," Bull growled at Arden.

"I'm...!" Arden paused. He sucked in a breath. His teeth felt funny, which meant he'd absolutely drunk too much. "Does she know what you did?"

Bull turned red. "Don't you dare—"

"Does she know!"

Cole had a protective arm around his brother and spoke softly into his ear.

"Rhys, take them for a walk," Arden demanded.

Rhys stood. He put a hand on Mace's arm. "Come on."

The three of them left.

"It was a million fucking years ago, you can't still be pissed," Bull said.

"What was?" Cathie asked.

"If it was a million years ago, we'd all be dead, but we aren't and I'll be pissed, I'll be fucking livid as long as I'm alive," Arden told Bull.

"Livid! He's not the one with a permanent *bite mark* on his arm."

"Bull," Cathie said. "What's going on?"

"He fucking wanted it!" Bull shouted.

Arden didn't think about it. He hucked his glass at Bull's face and, to his seething delight, made contact. All those years of practice hadn't amounted to nothing.

Bull clapped a hand to his nose but couldn't stop the blood from seeping between his fingers.

"Arden!" Cathie shrieked.

Arden shoved the table out of the way so hard it toppled. "Say that again."

Bull grabbed Arden by the face, his heavy palm wet. He squeezed so hard Arden's jaw ached. "He. Wanted. It. You little fucking pricks flaunting everything and then crying as soon as you get what you deserve."

Arden shoved a finger into Bull's eye.

The bigger man bellowed.

"Stop it!" Cathie screamed. "Stop! Both of you, stop it!" She grabbed onto Arden's arm and pulled him away, shoving herself between him and Bull. "What are you fighting about!"

"Bull can tell you," Arden said. He snatched a napkin off the ground and wiped his face.

She had tears on her face, but Arden didn't care.

"He can tell you and then you can ask me again why he can't be on the Council." He threw the napkin at her feet.

Safety officers had shown up finally, though they looked like they'd been celebrating too, judging by the lean of their stance and the crookedness of their uniforms.

"Bring him to lockup."

Arden scanned the room for Rhys and the Baker brothers. He had to ask around for them, which turned out the be a feat because more people were interested in telling him he had blood on his face and asking what had happened with Bull than they were with answering Arden's questions.

He found them eventually in a mostly empty room meant, Arden assumed, for thralls to hide the work that went into hosting events such as this.

The three of them were standing around, drinks in hand, and seemed to be uneasily and pointedly making conversation about something other than what had happened.

"Is that your blood!" Mace cried.

"Oh. No. I drink my glass...I threw my glass at his face."

Rhys choked back a laugh.

"Fucking...Arden." Mace sighed. He rubbed his face.

"What?"

"You shouldn't have done that."

"I can do whatever the fuck I want."

Mace sighed again.

Arden hugged Mace. He murmured, "I should have done more than bite him."

"Ardi, don't, I don't even want to think about it," Mace whispered.

He tightened his hug. "Come back to my room. All of you, we can...we'll finish this party off right, huh? A few more drinks. I think I still have knuckles, too. Or we can play jumble."

Weakly, Mace protested, "You always win at jumble."

"I know, that's why I like to play."

All of them somewhat uncomfortable, they made their way back to Arden's rooms. When they arrived and exchanged awkward glances, Arden gave Cole a nudge towards the bar in the corner and said, "Drinks!"

He washed his face, then gathered up all the pillows and blankets he could find. He found enough to exceed his grip, blankets tangling around his legs and pillows dropping as he walked.

Rhys gathered up what Arden lost and trailed behind him to the empty floor before the viewing window.

Arden spread out the pillows and blankets and added the couch cushions to create a comfortable nest.

Cole and Mace made themselves at home quickly, stripping shoes and jackets, and bits of confining clothing that might inhibit their lounging. They had done this before.

Rhys didn't acclimate as quickly.

Arden started to worry he wouldn't at all. He wanted to hug him but didn't know how Rhys would respond. He never knew where he stood with Rhys or what boundaries they had, or what ones they lacked but should have had.

He settled for giving him one of the drinks Cole had made and placing a guiding hand on his elbow. "Come get comfortable."

Rhys sat stiffly on a pillow, all his clothes on.

Arden pressed his lips together and didn't say anything. He shucked off his jacket, kicked his shoes into the corner, then stripped off the high-collared shirt he wore, too. The pants could stay, for now, loose and soft as they were. He sat next to Rhys, but not too close.

He stretched over and poked Mace's leg with his foot. He raised a quizzical eyebrow.

"I'm fine," Mace said.

Arden made a face. "You always say that."

Mace shrugged. He sipped his drink.

Arden left it alone. He placed his hand halfway between him and Rhys, just in case.

Cole said, "I don't think I made them too strong—"

"You always make them too strong!" Mace said.

"That's why we have him make the drinks," Arden reminded with a smile.

Rhys shifted and adjusted his jacket.

No matter how much he wanted to slide his hands inside that jacket and ease it off his shoulders, Arden refrained. He draped a blanket over his lap and one shoulder so he'd have something to do with his hands. He traced the pattern stitched into the blanket.

"How'd Cathie take it?" Mace asked quietly.

"I didn't tell her. It's not my business to tell...I mean..." Arden shrugged. "She should hear it from you or Bull."

A pinched look flitted over Mace's face. He replaced it with a forced smile. "She's going to be so mad at me!" he joked tremulously.

"No, she won't," Cole insisted.

Mace shook his head. "I'd..." He rubbed his nose. "I'd be mad at me."

"Mason," Cole scolded softly. He put an arm around his brother. "This is why Dad thinks we're stupid. Because I actually am, and you say stuff like that."

Mace snorted.

Rhys made a sound, some aborted word that he choked off.

They all looked at him.

"Sorry," he muttered.

The Baker brothers giggled into each other's shoulders.

Arden covered his mouth but still smiled.

Rhys flushed. He started to stand up.

Arden grabbed his arm. He scooted closer. "Don't be grumpy."

"I'm not grumpy."

"Then what's wrong?" Arden asked softly.

Rhys glanced towards Cole and Mace. He half-whispered, half-hissed, "I don't belong here."

"No, of course not," Arden agreed gamely, "We're all idiots and you've got more than three coherent thoughts in your head."

Rhys tilted his head warily, eyes narrowed.

"Thank you for gracing us with your company."

"Now I know you're making fun of me."

"You make fun of me all the time."

"It's...It's not the same."

Arden smiled. "No. You can go if you really want to, Rhys, you can always leave whenever you want. But don't go just because you feel like, uh, like you're not here as an equal."

"Arden, you don't *have* equals."

"Out there, maybe. In here..." Arden shrugged one shoulder. He glanced at the Baker brothers. "Don't go."

"In here, he's just Arden," Cole said. "It's always been like that."

"Even to the workers?" Rhys challenged.

"You're not a thrall," Arden reminded.

"That's not the *point*."

"What's the point?" Arden asked.

Rhys scowled.

"It's a real question!" Arden said. "Tell me the point."

Rhys clenched his jaw.

Arden took Rhys's hand. Gently, he pointed out, "Look, you've got a Council member and a supervisor and, well, little old me, waiting to hear what you have to say."

"And I really do want to hear," Cole asked. "You know, it's...It's kind of hard to get opinions out of most thralls."

"It's hard to give an honest opinion when disrespect is seen as a come-on," Rhys pointed out.

Arden's face got hot. He adjusted his blanket.

"Then speak for them, Rhys, so that I can take that to the Council," Cole asked.

He looked sweet and earnest, which must have worked on Rhys, because Rhys said, "The point is that I'm not a peer. I never will be and that makes me...that makes me less. An inferior being in the eyes of everyone who lives above deck six."

Arden squirmed. He wanted to say it wasn't true out of instinct, but he knew it was. He knew he was part of it and had been and maybe still was the worst of it.

"Thank you," Cole said sincerely. "Can we talk about this more another time? I didn't mean to put you on the spot."

Rhys nodded.

Arden finished his drink. He absolutely was the worst of it, the worst of all of them. He made himself another drink, straight liquor, and slugged it back. He nearly choked for the tightness of his throat. He thought about taking another drink straight away but settled for bringing the bottle back to the blanket nest with him.

He set it off to the side, centrally enough that whoever wanted it could grab it.

Rhys hadn't worked his way through his first drink yet. He always drank slowly, ate slowly.

"Do you like it?" Arden asked, nodding towards the glass in his hand.

"It's good."

"Too strong?"

Rhys shook his head. "No. Or, if it is, it's smooth. Not what I'm used to, at any rate."

Arden watched him fiddle with the glass swizzle stick. He searched for a word and when it came to him, he declared, "Scuff."

"What about it?" Rhys asked.

"That's what you drink in the Quarters."

"That's what we drink if we're not worried about losing our eyesight or slipping into a coma. Scuff is...it's nasty stuff. You never really know what's in it. People who hope to wake up in the morning usually stick to rakka."

"And that's safer?"

"It's just fruit wine, made from whatever's no good to eat. Some people have a better hand at it. My auntie made good rakka. But it's not as nice as this." Rhys nodded towards his glass.

"You should bring me some."

"Sorry?"

"Next time you come visit. We can trade." He jabbed a thumb towards his well-stocked bar.

"I don't know where I'd get enough to be worth a trade."

Arden shook his head. "A bottle for a bottle." Not a fair trade, but also somehow the fairest deal that had ever been made on *Eden*. Before Rhys could say anything else, Arden got up, rummaged through his desk, and came back with a game. He emptied the little sack of pieces. They clattered and pinged against the floor daintily. "You know how to play jumble?"

Rhys started flipping over letter tiles. "More or less. At least, I've watched enough supervisors play."

"Not Mr. Baker, I hope."

Mace leaned over to smack Arden. "Don't be mean."

Cole took the pack of cards and started to shuffle. He set down the stack facedown, glanced around to see if the others were ready with their first ten tiles, then flipped the first card to show a picture. All the cards bore an image and the first person to make a word related to the image would win the card.

Tiles could be swapped, but only one at a time.

Arden's fingers itched already. He wasn't as good at making words as other people, but he always remembered where people had put back letters.

The first card showed a bathtub.

Mace won the first card by spelling soap and they flipped the next to show a picture of a woman. Cole spelled a word, tight, which Arden readily called bullshit on. They debated the merit of the association and ruled that tight couldn't be played based on the argument that women wore tight clothes sometimes.

Jumble could become a game of alliances just as easily as it became one of wits or memory. With an even number of players, the odds weren't so bad, unless three decided to gang up on one.

That didn't happen tonight.

They played a few dozen rounds and interspersed drinks, gossip, and some mild philosophizing. Nothing serious, just the sort of thoughts people indulged when they drank.

After the last round, they counted the cards, declared Arden the winner yet again, and settled in among the cushions.

No one voiced their tiredness or made mention of getting home, but slowly, they trickled to the bathroom and came back in more comfortable clothing, or no clothing at all, in Cole's case.

Cole glanced towards Rhys, who'd taken Arden's velvet robe and cocooned himself in blankets an hour before the rest of them. He caught Arden watching Rhys sleep. "You really do like him."

Arden tightened the blanket around his shoulders. "I wasn't trying to hide it."

Cole settled on the cushion nearest to Arden and started making himself cozy. "No, no, of course not, I...you know. There's rumors and I've never, uh. It's been a while since you've spent time with anyone, Ardi. Longer since you spent time with someone new."

"Most of the people I wanted to spend time with ended up not wanting to spend time with me."

"You were an awful shit for a while there."

Drunk enough to be openly self-pitying, Arden said, "Come back to me when both your parents are dead."

Cole rubbed Arden's arm. "Ardi, I'm sorry."

He shook his head. "I just. I never know...I mean. I *do* know, I guess that's the problem. I know I disappointed Mother. I wonder if Mama would have been disappointed, too, eventually."

"The last Autarch was hard to please," Cole offered.

Arden glanced at Rhys to make sure he was asleep. He could hear Mace's soft, even breathing. "I think I stopped pleasing her as soon as she realized..."

"Don't," Cole warned gently.

"Just, you know, she picked me out. Everything about me, I think, she designed. That I would be this height, with this skin, and hair and...and I think she would have sculpted my very face if she could have. Picked out the exact shade of brown for my eyes. But she didn't design a son."

"She designed *you*. She designed a son."

"You know what I meant."

"I know that we're more than our parents' expectations. My parents don't even read my poems. Not a single one since I was ten."

Arden sigh as dramatically as he could and swooned back onto the cushions. "I hope I'm not like that. If I have kids."

"No, me neither."

Arden snuggled deeper into his nest. "Goodnight, Cole."

"Goodnight, Ardi."

Arden woke up with a sticky mouth and his forehead butted up against someone's chest. He didn't care who, anyone who'd been here last night would be a fine person to cuddle. It was Rhys, though, he realized with a pleased flutter in his stomach.

He'd have felt more pleased if he didn't feel so thirsty and greasy and generally unpleasant.

Rhys didn't wake when Arden got up.

He called for enough breakfast for everyone and showered. By the time he emerged, the thralls had delivered the food and the other three had started picking at it.

He took a piece of toast out of Cole's hand.

Cole smacked him on the leg.

Arden grinned and flopped down next to him. "Be kind to us, Councilmember Baker, if you're wise."

Cole took the toast back and took a bite. "Cut it out."

Mace reached over his brother and took a carafe of water. "Fuck," he groaned.

"Shower," Arden offered.

"No, I've got to go, I'm supposed to see Lourdes for lunch."

Arden sniffed him. "You still might want to shower first."

Mace punched him lightly in the back. "You're such a shit, Arden."

Arden smiled at him.

He gave the brothers both long, warm hugs when they left and congratulated Cole again. "I'll see you tomorrow."

Cole groaned and tightened his arms around Arden. "See you tomorrow."

When they'd gone, he cautiously approached Rhys. "Are you doing anything today?"

"I have a few things to do at home."

"Mmm."

"You'll come to Council tomorrow?" Arden asked.

Rhys nodded, his mouth too full of pear to speak.

"And, I mean, don't think I'm rushing you, but consider that Chamberlain job!"

"I will."

Arden kissed his cheek, then settled his chin on Rhys's shoulder. "You have to go right now?"

"I wouldn't mind a shower."

"Mm. Anything else?"

Rhys kissed Arden's forehead. "You could come in the shower with me."

Arden wrapped his arms around Rhys's waist and squeezed. "That sounds nice." A second shower did sound nice, even nicer with Rhys.

It was nice, though relatively tame, mostly kisses and soapy hands. Arden didn't mind. He liked just touching Rhys, any kind of closeness the other man afforded him. He stepped out of the shower and Rhys followed right on his heels.

Arden glanced back. "Hm. Oh!" Rhys had pushed him up against the counter from behind. The abruptness of it sent a ping of warmth through him.

Rhys drew back a little. "Sorry, was that...?"

Arden assured, "No, it wasn't! It's...that's fine." He reached back and took one of Rhys's hands. "Really good."

Rhys knotted his fingers in the loose bun of Arden's hair. "And that?"

"You could probably do anything to me and I'd like it," Arden admitted breathlessly.

Rhys gently butted his forehead against the back of Arden's skull and let out a little laugh, more disbelieving than amused. He kissed Arden's shoulder. "Tell me if you don't, in any case."

Arden arched back against him. He pulled open a drawer. "Check in here. Or the one underneath."

Rhys rummaged around and came back with a bottle.

Arden understood, in a way, Rhys's impulse to treat him roughly and his desire to give in to it. It didn't really matter, the whys of it, because it felt wonderful. He eagerly let Rhys fuck him against the counter, his cheek against the cool stone of the countertop. He played into the roughness of it, which had them both moaning during it, then panting afterward.

Rhys kissed his shoulder again.

Arden giggled.

"Do you always laugh after?" Rhys asked.

Arden turned around and leaned against the counter. "Only when it's funny." A look he couldn't interpret crossed Rhys's face. "Which it usually is! The whole thing is...I mean, don't you think it's kind of funny? Unless it's really bad, I suppose that isn't so funny..." Arden pulled his hair out of its bun and finger-combed it over his shoulder. It needed redoing now. "You don't think it's funny?"

"I never thought of it."

"The whole thing is ridiculous. In the best way."

"Hmm."

"I really like being ridiculous with you." He tossed his braided hair over his shoulder, then hugged Rhys.

Rhys sighed wistfully.

"What's wrong?"

"I wish things were different."

Arden smiled. "Well. We're making things different, aren't we?"

Rhys smiled without it reaching his eyes.

Deep, dark eyes, beautiful as the vast emptiness outside *Eden*. Maybe more beautiful. Arden could lose himself in those eyes. He pecked Rhys on the lips. "Get dressed. You have better places to be."

Rhys dressed without saying anything.

"I'll see you tomorrow."

"Mmm. See you."

Arden walked him to the door, gave him another kiss, then called, "Oh, and start thinking about what you want for Giving Day!"

Rhys glanced back, his mouth pulled into a frown.

Arden grinned at him and closed the door.

The holiday was a few months off, but Arden always had a hard time thinking of what he wanted. As a child, he'd wanted a lot of things, toys and games and trinkets. Now, peers all sent him gifts in hopes of currying favor, but he never wanted any of them and did a lot of strategic regifting. He had piles of things he hadn't gotten rid of yet in his guest bedroom.

He hoped to spend the rest of his day recovering from last night, but in the afternoon, Cathie came by looking absolutely awful. Her normally bronze skin had gone sallow, she had bags under her eyes, and she still wore what she'd worn last night.

"Cath, what..." He stopped himself from asking the obvious. "Come in."

She hugged him and he sank into her arms. "Why didn't you tell me!"

"It wasn't my business to tell."

She squeezed him harder. "You didn't have to tell me *who*, Arden, but you didn't have to let me date a rapist!"

He hadn't thought of it that way. "I'm sorry, Cath. I...I never thought of it."

"All these years thinking you two were just...bickering over something stupid. Something petty."

He rubbed her back. "I'm sorry."

"Mace wouldn't even talk to me."

"He doesn't like to talk about it." He brought her over to the couch. "Just tell him you love him and he'll tell you he loves you too and leave it at that."

"I feel so *disgusting*."

Arden held her hand and talked her through what he could while she vented. Mostly, he told her it wasn't her fault and that no one was mad at her, which was what he always said when someone felt bad about something.

She stayed long enough that they ordered dinner.

Arden met the thrall at the door to talk the tray and made sure to say, "Thank you..." He squinted at the youth.

The thrall squirmed as Arden struggled to remember his name.

"Thank you, Peter?"

"Of course, Your Eminence, whatever you need." Peter hurried away.

Arden thought the thralls disliked his attempts at manners as much as Arden disliked making the attempts. He didn't know how much it mattered, either, but all those little things Rhys had whispered to him hadn't seemed to matter when he'd started either.

Small things mattered.

They had to.

After they ate, he walked Cathie back to her room. He visited Winslow because they sort of lived near each other. He regretted it within ten minutes.

Winslow gave him an earful about starting fights and acting uncivilized.

Arden tuned him out and elected to lay on Winslow's couch and study the carpet pattern.

"You aren't listening!" Winslow accused.

"I'm not a little boy."

"You acted like one last night."

"Winnie, are you really mad at me?" Arden asked, pushing himself up on one elbow to study his uncle.

"I thought you'd outgrown this sort of behavior."

"Bull isn't a nice person, you know. It's not like I attacked a stranger."

"That doesn't mean you have to roughhouse like some thrall."

"Winnie."

"No, no, Arden, I'm quite disappointed in you. I don't condone violence."

"I'm sorry, Winnie."

"It's so hideous." Winslow came to sit beside him.

Arden moved his legs and sat up all the way. Winslow always had been sensitive to these kinds of things, but Arden hadn't understood how sensitive until now. He'd tuned out most of the scolding he'd gotten as a youth. He didn't like the way Winslow looked at him.

His uncle took his hand. "It's just ugly."

"I'm sorry." He hated seeing his uncle so distraught.

"You ruined that man's eye, you know."

"I..." Arden hadn't known. He didn't even feel bad. He wished he could put out both of Bull's eyes. "Well. He was being awful."

"Don't go saying people deserve things like that."

Arden sighed. He wrapped his arms around his uncle. "I'm *sorry*, Winnie, don't be mad at me."

"Don't try to soften me up."

"Don't be mad," Arden insisted, "You're my only family in the whole world. You know I couldn't bear if you were mad at me."

Winslow didn't hug him back. "You'd do better laying this on Morris if you want sympathy for what you did."

Arden's stomach turned at the thought of being compared to Morris Torre. His arms loosened. "Don't say that."

"It was an ugly thing you did, Arden, something he would do."

Arden shook his head. Morris hurt people because he liked it, for his own gain or pleasure. He'd hurt lots of people and Arden had only gotten into a scrap with someone who'd hurt his friend. "It wasn't like that, Win. It wasn't. He hurt my friend."

Winslow pursed his lips.

"Don't say I'm like Morris."

His uncle's face softened a little. "No, I don't suppose I ever saw Morris look upset at being reprimanded."

Arden swallowed.

Winslow touched his cheek. "Be a good boy, Arden."

He nodded. "I'm sorry."

"Would you like something to eat?"

Arden wanted to go home, but he said yes anyway because he apparently hated having his uncle upset with him. He hadn't anticipated it.

In the morning, before the first meeting of the new Council, he went to lockup to have a look at Bull.

He had purple bruises around his nose and eyes, and a bandage over the one Arden had poked.

Gauged, really, if the damage was that bad.

He jammed the buzzer on the intercom so he could talk to Bull. "Wake up."

Without moving from the cot or opening his good eye, Bull answered, "I'm awake. What do you want?"

"My uncle says I shouldn't have hurt you. I say you shouldn't have raped my friend or told people that he wanted it."

"He didn't fight me. *You* did. You were just jealous I fucked him before you did."

"I..." Arden sighed. He wished he had another glass to throw at him; the only thing that stopped him from finding one was thinking of Winslow. "Anyway. Mace isn't having you charged with anything. So, you can go home." He tapped in the code to unlock the door. "How's your eye?"

Bull bared his teeth and walked away.

"Bull."

The man stopped and turned around.

"You did put hands on your Autarch. We've decided on our own justice."

"You're such a petty little bitch."

"You're going to volunteer at a med center. I messaged you the details."

Bull took a step towards Arden.

Arden flinched.

The other man laughed at him but didn't touch him. "Exactly."

Arden made his way to the Public Chamber, where Rhys looked visibly relieved at the sight of him.

"We didn't know where you were."

"Oh. Sorry. Are you ready?"

Rhys nodded.

Arden entered the Public Chamber and engaged in the obligatory formalities involved in changing over a Council: a short speech thanking the former members, accompanied by a small commemorative gift for their service, and another speech welcoming the new members. Everyone shook hands and when the former members left, Arden messaged the conspectus to the new Council and went over a few rules and regulations related to being on the Council.

Shayla Mbye watched Rhys for most of the time Arden spoke.

When he asked, "Any questions?" with the hope that everyone would have the sense to say no, Shayla raised her hand.

"I have a question."

"Of course."

"*Eden*'s statutes prohibit any other than the Council or the Autarch from entering the Public Chamber. Why has that been ignored?"

Arden glanced at Rhys. "Because the last subsection of the statutes says that the Autarch, as the owner of the station, can, without Council or prior declaration, change any aforementioned statute at any time for any reason."

Shayla folded her hands on the table. "Begging your pardon, Your Eminence, that's *how* you've ignored the rules. Not why."

"Oh." He looked at Rhys again and could tell Rhys wished he'd stop looking at him. "Uh." Pulled between a flippant answer and a meaningful one, he finally said, "Rhys has given us good counsel for some years now. It's easiest for him to do so if he's well informed."

Shayla didn't exactly look satisfied. "Thank you, Your Eminence."

"Any other questions?"

No one had any.

"We'll adjourn for the day. Reconvene the same time tomorrow. You'll have time to review the conspectus and we can figure out supervisory areas from there."

Arden stood first and meant to invite Cole to lunch but didn't have the chance. Shayla, Istis Frakes, and Xio Benevides approached him as Cole headed out with the rest of the Council.

"How can I help you?" Arden asked.

"We thought you might like to join us for lunch," Xio offered.

Arden eyed the three women and thought this Council might end up giving him a harder time than he thought. All three of them outclassed Arden by a mile when it came to intellect and ambition. "Of course," he agreed because he saw no other course. He made himself look at them and not at Rhys. "I'll be out in a moment."

The trio exited the room.

Arden allowed himself to turn around. "I, uh. That didn't go so bad?"

"No."

"Do you want to come to lunch?"

"I don't think I was invited."

"Mmm. Well. I'll see you?"

"Arden...uh. About what you said."

Arden eagerly waited for Rhys to accept the position of Chamberlain. He smiled. "Yeah?"

"About Giving Day," he added, shoulders hunched and eyes on Arden's feet.

"Oh."

"I don't have anything that I could give you. And, uh, knowing that, if you want to give me something, the only thing I can think to ask for is to clear someone else's debt."

Arden sat on the table. He hadn't expected that. And it wouldn't do, not at all. The request entirely missed the point of Giving Day. Maybe it was different for workers. They had less to give and more people to give to. "Someone specific?"

"I...I have friends, you know. And family."

"Okay. I'll think about it. It's not for a few months."

Rhys nodded.

Arden didn't need to think about it, he'd already decided exactly what he wanted to do. He hopped off the table, put a hand on Rhys's shoulder, and said, "You could come to lunch anyway."

"That's alright. I don't want to ruffle any feathers."

"See you later?"

"I'll stop by."

Arden patted his shoulder, then went out to catch up with Shayla and the other two. They led him to a restaurant he didn't care for, but he kept that to himself. He tried his hardest to find something he wanted on the menu but ended up ordering a hodgepodge of items from different dishes.

He chased his peas around his plate, spearing them one at a time. He said, "Uh, I was really glad to see you got a nomination, Shayla."

"Oh, Your Eminence, just Shay, please."

"Oh. Shay. Well. I think you'll be a wonderful member of our Council."

She smiled. "Thank you, Your Eminence. I'm excited, too."

Xio chimed in, "You inspired a lot of us with that speech of yours. A new era."

"Hopefully," he said.

Istis laughed, a pretty charming little sound that made him smile too.

As they lunched, Arden started to think he'd been wrong to worry about them. How could having three bright, capable young women on the Council hurt? From what he could tell, they supported his vision for *Eden,* and he would need that support. The peers had elected several centrists to the Council and though none of them seemed unreasonable, they would need convincing. It would be good to have help.

After about four Council meetings, a thirteenth chair appeared. Arden didn't know who'd put it there. No one took credit, or blame, for it, but no one protested when Arden told Rhys, "Well, no use in you standing all the time."

Rhys stayed quiet during meetings and didn't pull his chair up to the table, but he sat readily enough.

He gave his advice less surreptitiously than he ever had before, although almost never in front of anyone but Cole. He had a soft spot for Cole. Maybe because Cole had won the thrall vote or maybe just because Rhys liked him, but he talked more easily in front of Cole.

He brought Arden the bottle of rakka he'd agreed to trade and went home with a bottle of expensive cherry wine Arden had received on his twentieth birthday. He stayed over some nights and sometimes even showed up without Arden asking him over.

Those nights always warmed Arden from head to toe. Such a small thing meant so much.

Giving Day inched closer and Arden liked to think about all the nice things he could give Rhys. Sometimes while Rhys slept Arden would look at him, idly planning gifts for years to come.

He wondered if thralls celebrated their birthdays. He'd have to find out, and look up Rhys's, and get him something nice for his birthday. Rhys had asked for cleared debts, and he would get them, even if he lived to be two hundred, Arden wouldn't run out of thralls to liberate in Rhys's name. But he wanted to give him things.

He kissed Rhys's shoulder and the other man stirred in his sleep. He rolled over. "Hmm?"

"Nothing."

Rhys nestled back into the pillow.

Arden stretched and cuddled up next to him. Normally, on a sleepless night like this, he'd have called for a shot, but he liked the quiet peace that existed in these late hours.

"Are you watching me sleep?" Rhys asked after a few minutes.

"No."

"Mmm."

"I am listening to you breathe, though."

Rhys rolled over and pulled Arden into his arms. "Go to sleep. We have to be up in the morning."

Arden pulled in a slow, deep breath. He pretended to sleep and drifted off eventually.

In the morning, Rhys accompanied him to visit a few of the engineering offices. They visited the different work crews so often that they'd started to feel like social calls instead of productivity and safety check-ins.

All the Council members visited different areas on the station so that at least once a week every supervisor had received a visit.

The thralls had become much less squirrely during these visits. A handful of times, a worker had even spoken directly to Arden without staring at the floor.

As much as Arden came to like the visits on a social level, they did make him worry. Everyone had the same problem: not enough bodies.

Productivity did go up, overall, as safety regulations and morale issues came to light and were resolved. It wasn't enough, though.

Not yet, Arden reminded himself. It had been a few months since the election. They needed time.

As they walked toward Engineering Two, Rhys said, "I've been thinking."

"About what?"

"The position you offered me."

Arden glanced over. They hadn't spoken about that in a while and Rhys's answers had grown evasive, so he'd stopped bringing it up. "And?"

"You didn't offer it to me because we're involved."

"No."

"Arden, promise."

"I mean, I might not have thought of it if we weren't, but I don't just want your advice because I find you both fun and enjoyable."

"That's not a promise."

"Promises always come with fine print on *Eden*, though, don't they? You really want me to promise this job isn't a *quid pro quo*?"

"Yes," Rhys answered.

Arden shrugged and said, "Fine. I promise. The offer stands, regardless of our involvement. Are you accepting?"

"I think I have to."

Arden made a face. "I super hate when you say things like that."

"No, it's not...It's not like that. Not like you're making me. I just have to do it for a lot of reasons."

"Okay. Well. Congratulations, Mr. Malek." He offered his hand for Rhys to shake. "Welcome to the company."

Rhys shook it with a funny kind of smile on his face.

"I'll send over a contract and everything tomorrow at some point. I think I need to make some changes to the old one." Arden kept a hold of his hand, though he shifted the way he held it, and continued walking towards Engineering Two.

"Aren't we going to negotiate terms?"

Arden chuckled. "If that's what you want to do."

"I do."

"It will be very boring."

"I'll survive."

"Maybe *you* could trust *me* for once," Arden suggested.

Rhys made a sweeping gesture with both hands to indicate the entirety of the space station around them.

"Alright, but that was like a super long time ago."

Rhys raised his eyebrows and tilted his head.

"And I'm not...I'm not like Bex, you know. She actively swindled people."

"And you just, what, inherited them?"

"Well. Yes, but it's..." Arden huffed. He crossed his arms.

"Tell me again how many people you own."

"Technically, I don't *own* people. Just things."

"Is there a difference to you?"

Arden opened his mouth to protest, to explain the difference between indenture and slavery, but he couldn't. Rhys had been teasing, but the question stung. He closed his mouth.

Rhys reminded, "You never got picky about the details before. Whether you own our bodies or everything that surrounds them, your family positioned themselves as gods."

"Shouldn't you be a little nicer to me then?" Arden sulked.

"Why don't you threaten to jettison me into space?"

This had started to feel like a fight even though Rhys spoke in a pleasant, almost jovial tone. "No one's ever actually done that."

"Mmm."

"I don't know what you want me to say."

Rhys shrugged.

"Be nice to me," Arden wanted to demand. He could demand it and if he did, he'd get it. Rhys would have to be nice to him.

Somehow, that didn't make him feel better.

He stayed quiet.

He inspected a few things in Engineering Two, tried not to glower at anyone, and left without saying anything while Rhys chatted with the work crew.

He deliberately went to find Cathie, who had been sort of a wreck since she'd ended things with Bull. She'd really liked him and couldn't reconcile the man she'd loved and the one who'd hurt her friend.

Arden felt bad about letting her get in so deep with Bull.

Once he'd made the mistake of reminding her that he had told her several times that Bull was awful. She'd laid into him, making it clear that his warning had not been serious or sufficient.

He'd mostly offered platitudes since then.

Today he found her in better spirits as she bustled around her room, tidying up. She had a large pile of things on her couch, shoes and clothes, trinkets, jewelry, a few books, and a shimmery silver faux-fur coat.

He ran his fingers over the coat, marveling at the silkiness and shine.

"Oh, just let yourself in, Ardi," she scolded when she saw him.

"I rang. You didn't answer."

She turned down the music. "Sorry. I'm just trying to clean up a few things."

"Mmm."

"I'm getting rid of everything that doesn't make me happy."

He lifted the coat out of the pile. "This doesn't make you happy?"

"Oh, I hate that thing. My brother got it for me. He has awful taste."

Arden slung the jacket around his shoulders like a cape. "I don't know, I think it's great."

"Then take it."

He shimmed his shoulders.

She shook her head. "It's hideous on you too, Your Eminence."

"I'm still taking it. Tell Mathis I said thank you."

"Only if you want him sniffing around you asking for favors."

Arden put his arms through the sleeves. "I don't think Mathis has even spoken to me since school."

"Well, you did call him a disgusting worm in front of our parents."

"Fuck. Well. Then I guess really say thank you."

"Alright," she said in a tone that made him think she wouldn't. "You know, if this is another one of your pity visits, you don't have to stay."

"Uh."

She put her hands on her hips. "I figured it was pity instead of you trying to get laid like every other guy who's started talking to me again."

"Oh. Well. Neither? Is that an option?"

"You know I was teasing."

He nodded. He sat on the couch next to her pile of discards. "How are your parents?"

"Fine."

"And your sister?"

"Lane is good!" she answered and launched into a thirty-minute update on her little sister's life.

He helped her pack all her unwanted items into boxes and bags, even when she insisted that she would just call for a thrall.

When he started shoving items into bags, she said, "You know, you've gone a little soft on them."

Arden shrugged.

"It's not a good look, Ardi, letting Rhys talk you into all these changes," she advised. "People are starting to talk."

He paused, then stuffed a few more things into a bag. He hated that. Did he really seem so easily led? Had he acted so awfully towards people that he was considered incapable of concern for others?

Was he even concerned for others, or did he just dislike feeling guilty over treating people badly now that he thought of them as people?

Did it make a difference? Did it matter if he cracked down on safety in the workplace because it boosted productivity or because he cared if people got hurt? The result was the same, wasn't it?

"I. I'll see you later. Lunch tomorrow, right?"

"Of course."

He left.

He found Rhys waiting outside his door. He held out his tablet. "You left this in E-Two."

"You could have put it inside."

"What are you wearing?"

"Cathie didn't want it anymore."

"It's...interesting."

Arden opened his door. "Did you want to come in?"

"I wanted to talk."

Arden wrinkled his nose. He laid down on the couch and draped an arm over his face. "Go for it."

Rhys sat on the floor in front of the couch. "I hurt your feelings."

"Not really."

"I didn't mean to."

Arden let out a puff of air in the hopes it would get the faux fur away from his mouth but had no luck. He brought his arm up to pillow his head. He had things he wanted to say but they all got stuck in his throat. He rolled over to face Rhys. "Just. Sometimes I feel like you don't like me very much."

"I like you."

"But you don't trust me."

Rhys shifted. He sighed, then reached up to take Arden's hand. He kissed his knuckles. "I...As a person, as Arden, I trust you in personal matters. I don't think you'd ever do anything to hurt me, at least not on purpose. But as an employer, well...I'm sorry. I want to make sure I get what I need."

"I'll give you whatever you need."

Rhys shook his head. "Not like that. Not between people. Between employer and employee. It's different."

"I guess," Arden admitted unhappily.

Rhys kissed his hand again. "I know that's hard to understand."

He sighed.

Rhys ran his fingers through the shimmery fur of the jacket. "Cathie just gave this up? You didn't have to fight her for it?"

"Shut up. I like it."

"You would." Rhys wrapped a lock of Arden's hair around his finger. "I bet if you cut all this off you could make a jacket out of it."

"Ew!"

"Yeah, but you'd wear it, though."

"Rhys, don't make fun of me."

Rhys kissed him. "You can't sulk. You have three appointments coming up."

Arden groaned. "Fine, but I'm wearing the coat."

"They'll think you've gone mad."

"They already think I've gone mad, thanks to your influence."

"You're very trendy with workers, and there's more of us," Rhys pointed out.

"Jettison the peers into space, then I'll finally be popular."

Rhys kissed him. "Now you're talking. Say it again."

Arden snorted.

"Oh, come on, Arden, say it for me. Eat the rich. You know I like it when you get subversive." Rhys pressed his lips to Arden's throat.

Arden laughed and pushed him away. "I thought I had appointments."

"Just say it just once," Rhys wheedled.

"Eat the rich?"

Rhys kissed him with a grin, not exactly romantic, but definitely playful. "Alright, now say—"

"No, stop it, we're not doing this!"

"Not into roleplay?"

"Not when it involves killing my friends and family."

Rhys blew a raspberry.

Arden pushed himself up. "Who are my appointments with?"

"Lazlo Frakes—"

"Fuuuuuck," Arden groaned. "Ugh. I take it back. Let's roleplay a violent revolution. I think I have a really fuck-off big dildo in the guestroom somewhere. You can take out all your latent anger on me."

Rhys squinted. "Should I ask?"

Arden stood, rummaged through the various unused gifts in the guestroom closet, then came back with an overlarge glass dildo. He turned it so Rhys could read the inscription.

"The biggest dick I could find for the biggest dick I know." Rhys frowned at it.

"What? You never just irresponsibly bought awful presents for your friends with your parents' money?" Arden guessed.

"No."

"One year I got Cathie this ancient taxidermy, uh, like a big ugly fish with this horrible sharp beak."

Arden turned the dildo over. "I don't think this is even functional. I think it's for drugs…" He couldn't think of any other reason it would be hollow and have holes in it. Someone on his handball team had gotten it delivered to his hospital room after one of his surgeries. He tossed it on the couch. "It was really funny when we were fifteen." Maybe being looped on painkillers had made it funnier.

"Can you please put that away so the people who clean your room don't think you're using it on me?"

Arden raised his eyebrow.

A little embarrassed, Rhys said, "Everyone in the Quarters already thinks I'm your pet, I'd rather not have rumors getting around that you use a cock the size of an arm on me."

Arden could imagine how those rumors might upset someone like Rhys and returned it to the guestroom closet. Instead of getting ready to see Frakes, he sat beside Rhys. "You really don't like people knowing we're together."

Rhys's eyes crinkled ever so slightly. He licked his lips. Then that look was gone, replaced with sadness instead of discomfort. "I don't like people thinking that I'm being used."

"Oh."

"And I don't…" He gave a small smile. "I don't like people thinking that I'm doing this to get things from you."

"Aren't you?" Arden almost asked, but he didn't. He smiled and a funny kind of hope filled him up. He took Rhys's hand and kissed it, then said, "I guess let's go see Frakes."

Frakes hadn't improved much since the last time Arden had seen him. As soon as Rhys walked in beside Arden, Frakes frowned.

"I'd hoped we could speak in private, Your Eminence."

Arden made a small gesture with his hand to indicate that Rhys should go, which the other man did, though not without a quick flash of displeasure showing on his face. Arden seated himself without waiting for an invitation. "I hope you're not wasting my time."

"Oh, Your Eminence, I don't want you to feel obligated to meet with me—"

"Just get to it," Arden growled.

Frakes took out his tablet and cast a few documents to a large screen on the wall. "This is my proposition for the new programs for the next quarter." He pointed to one image of a large, happy thrall family. "This one is for a drama about—"

Arden sighed loudly. "Come back to that one."

He disliked Frakes as a person, but he also disliked having to put thought into what bits of entertainment the government would use to influence people. His mother had made it seem so necessary, a polite way of informing people of what they needed instead of what they thought they wanted.

Frakes made it feel so slimy.

Once, Arden had gotten bored and said, "Do whatever you want," which had been the wrong thing to tell the Entertainment Minister. The resulting songs, movies, and shows that Frakes's crew had created that quarter had bordered on directly accusing thralls of being lazy.

Since then, Arden had kept an eye on Frakes and looked for someone to replace him. No one Arden had approached had wanted the job and those who had approached him had lacked the talent and resources to do the job.

So Frakes had stayed.

Arden eyed the image of the family again.

"Birthrates are lagging for thralls," Frakes reminded gently. "If we want more thralls, we have to convince them that they want children."

"What if they don't want children for a reason?"

"What?"

"I wouldn't want children if I lived in the Quarters. Especially not if I was the one carrying them."

"Oh, well...That's why we need to convince them—"

Arden shook his head. "Things are a little different now."

"Meaning what, Your Eminence?"

"Scrap it. I want...uh. I want you to put on something fun. Something light and sweet, something that will make people, anyone who sees it, just smile for a little while."

"Sorry?"

"Make it seem like things are okay. I don't want people to worry. We've been making them worry, I think."

Frakes frowned.

"We've been making me worry anyway. Let's lighten things up, hmm?"

"So, you want me to redo everything?"

Arden shrugged. "Is that a problem?"

"Of course not, Your Eminence."

"I want to do something about, uh, getting more screens down in the Quarters, too. If we want people to watch things, we've got to give them somewhere to watch them. No one likes to be crowded into a room like that."

"That's very smart, Your Eminence."

Arden forced a smile. "So you'll see to it? Set up a new meeting when you have some new ideas."

"Of course."

"And try to make, uh, make conserving resources seem cool. Think of something for the peers."

Frakes frowned. "Are things going poorly with the changes to work crews?"

"No. But it doesn't help to be more mindful of what we waste." Arden let himself out.

Rhys had waited for him right by the door. He had his hands folded over his abdomen and dropped into step behind Arden when they started walking.

Arden fell back and linked arms with him. "Don't take it personally. Frakes thinks if thralls find out that movies are propaganda then *Eden* will fall apart."

Rhys widened his eyes. "You mean the four movies they showed about settling down and having kids last quarter were trying to trick us into having kids?"

Arden chuckled.

"And those dirty movies they show afterhours about how sexy it is to get a lot of women pregnant, are those propaganda too?"

Arden blushed. "Sounds like it."

"And the little cute cartoons they play for kids, the ones about being a hard worker and doing your share—"

"Alright, fine." Arden tightened his grip on Rhys's arm. "I didn't say he was smart or good at it, but I haven't been able to replace him either."

"Try harder."

Arden rolled his eyes.

"I know some really good cartoons that can teach you how to do your share to help out," Rhys teased.

He walked away from Rhys.

At least, he pretended to. He only went a few feet before he glanced back to check on him. "So who's next?"

"Supervisor Corbin."

"Maintenance?"

Rhys nodded.

"Corbin's pretty with it. Did she say what she wanted?"

Rhys shook his head.

It turned out that Corbin wanted to take leave to stay home with her child who needed surgery, which Arden granted.

She seemed surprised and he tried not to take offense.

After another quick and painless appointment, he and Rhys sat down to hammer out the details of Rhys's work contract over dinner. Arden had dug up the last few contracts between his mother and her Chamberlains.

Rhys poured over them for most of their meal.

Arden shredded his food into little bits while he waited. Every so often, he said, "So, what do you think?"

Rhys said, "I'm still reading," the first few times.

The fourth time Arden asked, Rhys set down the tablet. "Do you need something?"

"No, just, they're not that long."

"Checking for fine print."

Arden stuck out his tongue.

Rhys said, "I assume there's changes you want to make."

"Sure. The salary's got to change, for one."

Rhys nodded.

"I mean, the most recent one is over a decade out of date, so we've got to adjust for that. And the expected duties need to change."

"Say that again."

"The duties need to change. Those are more secretarial than advisory."

"About the money."

"Oh. Well. I figured we'd have to change it. So you're fairly compensated."

Rhys stood up from the small table Arden had acquired a few months ago. They ate together often enough that he'd thought it warranted having a table with chairs, instead of always sitting on the ground around the coffee table or eating in bed.

He paced over to the viewing window.

Arden watched. When he stayed there for a few minutes, he called over, "What?"

Rhys didn't answer.

Arden gave him a few more minutes, then went over to him. He leaned against the window. "What?"

"Money doesn't really mean anything at all to you."

Arden shrugged. "I understand what it does for me and my position. I understand what it lets me do."

"But that much, Arden."

"It's not that much at all. It's not more than what a starting supervisor would make."

"It's at least ten times what anyone I know has ever made."

"Do you want me to not pay you more?"

"You're missing the fucking point."

"Explain it to me."

"I can't...I don't even know where to start. And I don't want to. I don't always want to explain things to you, you know!"

"Then don't explain it. Just sign whatever contract we come up with and stop asking me why I don't care about a bucketful of sand when I've got a whole beach." Arden smiled at him and tried to take his hand.

"I think I need to go."

Arden straightened up. "Why?"

"Because this is too much."

"Oh. Well. Can I walk you home?" He didn't want Rhys to leave but knew he couldn't order him to stay.

"Is that a fucking joke?"

Arden shrugged. "I've never seen where you live."

"You've never been to the Quarters."

"No reason to."

Rhys studied him, then shook his head. "Maybe some other time."

"Oh. Okay."

"I'll come by in the morning."

Arden nodded.

Rhys looked like he wanted to say something else. He touched Arden's arm, then left without saying anything.

Arden tried to find something else to do, but nothing he tried got rid of the tight feeling in his chest or the ugly thoughts swirling in his head. He called for a shot of Nine and slept like a rock, dreamless and cold, until someone tried to wake him.

His eyes couldn't quite open and he tried to rub them.

"Ardi, hey."

He rolled over. "Nother minute."

"Arden," a voice insisted.

Not Rhys.

Whose voice was that?

A harder shake, then a disgusted scoff.

He fell back asleep.

How much later he didn't know, but someone opened his mouth and poured something down his throat.

Uncomfortable alertness made his heart patter and his fingers twitch within minutes. His eyes popped open when he realized what had happened.

Six would do that.

Cole and Cathie hovered over his bed.

He pushed himself up and dragged his covers around him, disoriented and displeased. "What?"

Cole began, "We were out at Crystal and, uh, there was this group of kids, like right out of school, and they were shit-wasted, and they started picking on the thralls who were serving drinks."

Arden groaned. "And?"

"The safety officers broke things up but—"

"They actually fought?"

"One of the bartenders threw a punch."

"They're all in lock up. But people are freaking out. I don't think a thrall's ever hit a peer before," Cathie said.

Arden hadn't heard of it happening in years, not since before Mama had died. He didn't remember it, but he'd read the reports and knew the justice the last Autarch had doled out for the offending thrall.

He dragged himself out of bed and pulled a robe on over his pajamas. He shoved his feet into shoes. "Go down to the Safety Office, tell them to double patrols, send out a message for everyone to be cautious. Tell all the thralls who aren't working essential positions to go home."

"All that just for this?" Cathie asked.

"I don't need anyone doing anything stupid."

"Where are you going?"

"Lockup."

He didn't want to go, but a glance at a clock made it apparent that he should deal with it now so the morning could be productive and mostly normal.

A safety officer followed him to lockup, which he appreciated because the people he passed seemed nervous, angry, or both. Mostly younger people out enjoying the night, so probably drunk or on formulas, or some combination of that and likely a few pills throw in for good measure.

In lockup, he found a crowd of young peers and three thralls.

The thralls looked much worse for wear, but one particularly puffed up and irate looking peer girl had a bloody lip.

Arden addressed the safety officer watching the lot and asked, "What happened?"

"Fighting over a boy or something."

"She was bothering my friend, Your Eminence," the bloodied peer informed him. She shot a vicious look towards the youngest thrall, a blonde girl with beige skin. Arden guessed her to be in her early twenties.

Arden looked at the peer who'd addressed him. "And then?"

"I told her to get away from her and she didn't listen."

Arden didn't exactly follow. He couldn't focus well at the moment, too busy taking in the minute details of everything in lockup.

Six did that.

"Who was the worker bothering?"

"She wasn't bothering me," a peer piped up from the back. Short-haired and tomboyish, but a girl from what Arden could tell. "We were just talking."

"Talking about stupid shit, Ridea," the bloodied peer snapped.

"Is anyone pressing charges?" Arden asked the officer.

"I am!"

"What's your name?"

"Paget, Your Eminence."

To one of the safety officers, Arden requested, "Will you take Paget and get her report?"

The officer nodded, took the girl, and walked her to another room.

Arden approached the thralls, who looked like shit. They'd been outnumbered, clearly. "What about you lot?"

"I want to press charges," the blonde said.

Arden smiled. "Great." He glanced at the other two, who shook their heads.

He had officers take statements and arranged bail. Once the peers' parents and guardians had come to bail them out and apologized for their children causing problems, Arden typed his code into the padlock.

He gestured towards the door.

"No one paid our bail," the blonde thrall said.

"Yeah, and no one ever fucking would, I bet," Arden said.

"Mara, let's go before you start something else," one of the thralls hissed at the blonde. To Arden, he said, "Thank you, Your Eminence. We appreciate very much everything you've done for us."

Arden wrinkled his nose. "Head home."

The other two scurried away.

Mara didn't go as fast.

Arden caught up with her. "What were you talking about with that girl? Ridea?"

"She asked if I had kids."

"Oh."

"I think she was trying to be friendly. Everyone assumes that workers start having kids as soon as they can but..."

"Propaganda, am I right?" Arden joked.

Mara didn't seem to know what to make of that. "We started talking about why I didn't and why I didn't plan on it."

"Mmm. Have you been to a med center?"

"One of the officers checked us out. Said I was fine."

"Are you fine?"

She didn't look okay, not just in the sense that she'd been in a fight. She looked angry and exhausted, a bone-deep expression of both emotions on her face. Bags under her eyes and a scowl that hadn't gone away. She spoke to him like she hoped he'd pick a fight, too.

She answered, "Fine as I'll ever get."

He grimaced. "Do you know Rhys?"

"Your Rhys? Yeah, everyone knows about him. We don't all know each other though."

He didn't like the way she'd said Rhys's name. He walked quietly alongside her until they reached the lift that would bring her to the lower decks of *Eden*. He pushed the button for her.

She glanced at him. "Uh. Thanks. Your Eminence."

He shrugged. "Keep your head down. People are going to be mad you're pressing charges."

"I don't care."

"I don't want to have to assign a safety officer to keep you alive. We had to do that when that woman pressed charges against a peer a few years ago."

It had been Rhys's idea to give the woman protection.

The lift arrived.

"I'll keep an eye on your court case. Try not to punch the judge when he rules in her favor."

"She started it," Mara insisted.

Arden gave her a smile and waved when she stepped onto the lift. He wandered back to his room and couldn't get back to sleep.

By the time the Six wore off and he felt tired, he'd already showered, washed his hair, and gotten dressed.

He deflated halfway through breakfast and wanted a nap. He picked the berries out of his oatmeal.

Rhys found him staring vacantly into his oatmeal. "Busy night?"

"Mm."

"I heard what happened."

"I bet everyone has." Arden yawned. He rubbed his eyes. "How are you?"

"I didn't get much thinking done. People were up all night talking."

Arden gestured towards the mostly untouched breakfast. "Help yourself."

Rhys yawned and poured himself a cup of tea.

Neither of them said much.

Finally, Rhys stretched and said, "I'm sorry I walked out like that yesterday."

"I don't know, I want to walk away from things all the time."

"It's overwhelming."

"I can tell." He rubbed his eyes and poured himself more tea. He wondered if he needed something stronger. Maybe more Six if he wanted to make it through the day. "Do you want to write up your contract today?"

"Can you stay awake for it? Maybe you should go back to bed."

"No, no, I can...We should get this done." He looked around for his tablet and collapsed onto the couch with it. He curled up on his side, opened a new document, and set it to take dictation. "Let this contract show the arrangement between the employer, one Arden Torre, Autarch of *Eden*, and the employee, Rhys Malek, for the position of First Chamberlain to the Autarch. This contract ensures the following terms outlined below for a period of one year from the date of its signing by both parties."

He closed his eyes, took a breath, and carried on outlining a standard work contract. Once they had the barebones, they hashed out the details, free of tricks or loopholes.

Arden fell asleep at one point.

He woke up to an edited version of the contract waiting for him.

Rhys snored quietly at the other end of the couch.

He read through the contract one last time. He signed it then poked Rhys in the side with the corner of the tablet.

Rhys woke with a gasp.

"Sign."

"No more changes?"

He shook his head.

Rhys signed the contract.

"Do you want to take a nap?"

"You have appointments—"

"Cancel them. Do you want to take a nap with me?"

Rhys nodded.

Arden took the tablet, set it on the table, and dragged a throw over them. He nestled up against Rhys and fell asleep almost as soon as he got comfortable.

Arden woke to dozens of gifts piled outside his door, delivered discretely by thralls in the night. He called for help bringing them into his rooms, then hopped into the shower with a bouncy, nervous energy. He washed his hair and took care picking out his clothes.

When Rhys arrived, which Arden had made him promise to do, his heart had shimmied up into this throat.

He hadn't been excited for Giving Day since he was a kid, really, but something felt different. He'd always had people to give things to and plenty of things to give, but it had never felt important before. His friends and family had never needed anything.

He hurried over to Rhys and grabbed his hand. "Hi!"

Rhys's eyes slid over Arden to all the shiny packages and parcels piled on his coffee table.

Arden flapped his hand toward them. "You can help me open those later. Sometimes I get really nice chocolates. Come in here." He gave Rhys's hand a tug.

Rhys went, but Arden had to give a pretty hard tug to get him to move. "I said not to get me anything."

"Uh, no, you actually asked me to give a vast sum of money to a person I don't know. Eight two six whoever," Arden said, still holding his hand and pulling him towards the bed. "Here, here, sit."

Rhys didn't sit. "Arden, I—"

"I did it, shit. Same deal I gave you. First thing this morning, but you can't open that."

His eyes, dark and beautiful as the speckled sky outside, widened. His lips parted.

For years and years, Arden had not thought of Rhys's lips. He'd never felt warm when Rhys had murmured in his ear. Had he been too miserable? Too numb? Or just a fool?

He didn't know why Rhys looked so miserable. "I wanted you to have something to open," he offered meekly. "Is that awful of me?"

"No."

"Will you open it?"

"Of course."

"And will you get that look off your face?" Arden teased.

Rhys forced a smile.

Arden kissed him then took a few boxes out of his closet. He placed them in Rhys's lap then sat on the bed beside him, knees pulled him to his chest. He watched and tried to wait, but soon enough, he urged, "Go on!"

"I didn't get you anything."

"Yeah, but everyone else did, so I won't miss it."

Carefully, Rhys tugged one end of a ribbon. It took him a million years to open the first box. Three shirts of various styles, neatly folded, of finer fabric and richer colors. The same for pants. A nice jacket, some good socks. A new, well-made pair of shoes. A tidy little update to his wardrobe for his new job.

Rhys examined each object awkwardly but with reverence. The shoes seemed to impress him the most.

Arden understood why. The shoes he wore now had lumpy seams where they'd been glued back together.

"I thought about getting you new undies, but I didn't know if you'd like that."

Rhys chuckled.

"Besides, you can afford that now."

"Thank you."

Arden pointed to the last box, smaller than the rest, and less neatly packaged. He had purchased it last minute and hadn't had the heart to make a worker wrap it in the middle of the night.

"It's heavy."

"Open it."

He peeled back the wrapping paper and opened the box to reveal a metal tin that could fit in the palm of his hand. Within rested a dense cake of soap, richly scented and laden with moisturizers.

"I know how much you like that scent. Now you have one for home, too."

Rhys smelled it and grinned. He gave Arden's leg a quick, friendly rub. "Thank you."

Arden pecked his cheek. He heard the door. "Oh, that's lunch. I figured you wouldn't want to go out."

"It's a little wild out there."

"Mmm, well, everyone's got to see if the Public Chamber is any different from any other year. I think we're giving out oranges this year."

Arden went out and directed the worker to put their lunch on the table. He then realized he'd covered it in gifts and rushed over to make space for the tray. "Thanks, Fari!"

"You're welcome, Your Eminence. Is there anything else I can do for you?"

Arden nodded towards the gifts. "Yeah, grab one of those on your way out."

"Which one?"

"I don't care, pick one."

"Where...Where should I bring it, Your Eminence?"

"Home."

She openly frowned at him. She looked to Rhys for reassurance.

"Take two," Rhys advised from where he leaned against the frame of Arden's bedroom door. "He won't notice."

"You're so bad!" Arden scolded, giving Rhys a playful smack on the arm.

Fari took only one package, the one closest to her, and looked uncomfortable the whole time.

After they ate, Arden and Rhys opened his gifts.

He only wanted about six of them, the ones from people who knew him.

What a problem to have. He'd have to make room in the closet.

"Come help me make space."

"Why keep them?" Rhys asked. He selected another chocolate from an array and took a bite.

Cherry-filled.

Arden would have spit it out.

Rhys ate the whole thing.

"Uh. It would be sort of awful to throw them away. And very rude to send them back."

"I'm sure you could think of something else." Rhys took another candy and waited, chewing the caramel slowly.

Arden put a hand on his hip, trying to think of something else.

"Doesn't your friend have a charity for poor unfortunates?" Rhys suggested mildly.

"What? Cathie's ladies' club?"

Rhys nodded.

"Well, I don't..." Half an idea rattled across his brain. He tried to grab it.

"It is *Giving* Day," Rhys suggested more strongly.

"Oh!" He looked at the pile. "You want me to give them to people?"

"I didn't say that."

"To thralls," Arden clarified more for himself than Rhys.

"I didn't say that."

Arden snorted.

"You gave one to Fari."

"I don't have enough for everyone!"

"You'll figure it out."

Arden sighed.

"I'll be impressed."

As much as Arden didn't want to admit it, he wanted to impress Rhys.

Rhys snagged his tablet and settled onto the couch. He burrowed under a blanket with his knees pulled close to his chest. Every so often the tablet let out a beep or a chirp.

He was playing a game.

Arden smiled at him, though Rhys didn't notice. He returned his attention to the pile of gifts. He tried to puzzle it out for a while. "I don't know, do you just want to invite your friends?"

Rhys looked up from his tablet. "Hmm?"

"Invite your friends."

"Um."

"Alright, maybe not."

Eventually, he had laundry carts delivered directly to his room. He piled the gifts, old and new, into the carts.

Rhys watched.

"Impressed?"

"Are you planning on bringing those to the Public Chamber?'

"No, let's go to the Quarters, see who's home. Help me push the other one."

Rhys put on his shoes and picked a cart.

Arden wheeled the cart out into the hall, fighting with a finicky wheel, and realized halfway down the hall he'd have to take a lift. He tried not to think about it and steered the cart into the nearest lift.

Except it wouldn't fit.

"You have to use a service lift."

"Ugh."

"They're at the end of the hall."

Arden whined, backed up, and pushed towards the service lift.

Three workers stood beside the two of them on the large lift. They huddled into a corner, far from their Autarch as they could get.

"You want one?" Rhys asked.

The trio exchanged looks.

"It's Giving Day," Rhys encouraged.

One older woman stepped forward, peered into the cart, and selected a glittery black vase. She examined it, then stepped back with it cradled in her arms.

Arden smiled at the other two, which didn't help the situation.

They didn't take anything.

He left the lift on a random level and glanced at the signs.

Quarter Three.

People milled around doing various chores. A few children chased each other around, giggling and wrestling. They climbed over the hodgepodge furniture in the common areas. Patched screens showed cartoons and a few adults sat off to the side, either mending clothes or preparing meals.

On either side of the halls, people had their doors open. Cords stretched between apartments, over the common areas, draped with laundry.

The whole place smacked of oranges.

"Careful!" one adult scolded.

The child they'd warned didn't listen. A ball bounced towards Arden and he plucked it out of the air, appraised its many scuffs and patches, and tested its heft. The ball didn't quite hold air. His fingers sunk into the sides.

The child who'd thrown it, a girl of maybe six, eyed him.

Three more children crowded around.

"Can I have it back?" the girl asked.

Arden tossed it up and bounced it back to her using his elbow.

She smiled but barely caught it.

"That one's in rough shape," he pointed out. "Hard to play with."

"It's my best one."

"Not anymore." He dug deep, all the way to the bottom of the cart. He knew he had a handball in there somewhere. When he found it, he gave it a bounce, first on the floor then on his knee.

He saw Rhys watching him and had to show off. He bounced it up on his knee again, did a spin, caught it on one shoulder, rolled it down his arm, and elbowed it towards the children.

"That's not a regulation pass," Rhys pointed out.

"Knees *aren't* feet. It's regulation."

"You must have been a pleasure to play with."

The child who'd caught the ball stared at it. "We can really have it?"

Arden nodded. "Sure."

The kids scampered off with it, back to their chasing and climbing without a second thought for Arden.

None of the adults had noticed them yet, too absorbed in their chores.

Arden wheeled a little closer to the common area. He caught smells of long-simmering stews and snippets of conversations, little snatches of songs, as he passed by the rooms.

One man caught him looking inside.

Arden lifted his chin, then checked himself. He settled his posture to be friendlier. "You want something?" He jabbed his thumb towards the cart.

The man limped over, steadying himself on a cane. "Can I help you, Your Eminence?"

"If you pick something out. Our rooms needed tidying."

The man kept his gaze lowered, or, he did when he thought Arden was looking. He peered into the cart and cast a lot of suspicious glances towards Arden when he thought he wasn't.

Rhys pointed out a set of sheets and said, "They'll be soft as petals."

The man took the sheets and shrunk away from them. "Thank you, Your Eminence."

"Thank you."

They handed out a few things to interested parties in Quarter Three, which Arden came to understand was colloquially known as Giant Step because the lift sometimes stopped too early or too late on their floor, leaving a drop between the lift floor and the exit.

He advised them to put in a work order.

Rhys covered his mouth.

One woman shook with the effort to keep her response contained.

They stopped in on other floors, not in any order.

Children picked things out the most eagerly. Most of them didn't seem to recognize Arden and just understood that he had a cartful of things they could take. One little boy picked out a furry scarf, wrapped it all the way around his face, and ran away, bumping several corners as he went.

They didn't visit every deck in the Quarters, but they did get rid of all the sundry items Arden had brought.

He recruited someone else to return the carts to the laundry.

Back in his room, he made Rhys try on some of his new clothes. "To make sure they fit!" he'd insisted.

Rhys had played along for a few outfits, while Arden had watched, laying on the bed on his stomach with his feet in the air. Rhys hadn't gotten dressed after. He'd folded up his new clothes and put them back in the boxes.

Arden didn't complain.

He liked to watch Rhys, especially because he'd spent a lot of years barely noticing him. He wanted to make up for lost time, maybe. Appreciate what he'd overlooked for years. Not the whole ten years they'd known each other, but longer than he should have.

Rhys rolled on to the bed beside him so they lay shoulder to shoulder. He nudged Arden. "I kind of had fun today."

"And normally you have...more or less fun than this?"

Rhys put an arm around him and pulled him over. He kissed his temple. "I really do like you, Arden."

"But just sometimes," Arden guessed.

"A little bit more than that."

"You, uh. You wanna...?"

Rhys kissed him. "Might as well."

"Such enthusiasm!"

Rhys kissed his neck. "Get undressed."

Arden kissed him hard, then shed his clothes and slid up against Rhys. He pressed as close to Rhys as he could, until they couldn't get any closer, one flushed creature moving together, breathing together. A few times it felt like they even thought together, anticipating what the other would want without a sound.

He held onto Rhys long after they'd finished, his cheek against Rhys's warmed chest. He could hear his heart, a beautiful rhythm beneath a beautiful shell of bone and flesh and skin. He kissed his ribs.

Rhys played with Arden's hair.

He'd have to redo it.

"You didn't laugh," Rhys pointed out.

"It wasn't funny."

"Does that mean it was bad?"

"No," Arden murmured.

"You okay?"

"Think so."

Rhys shifted to get a better look at Arden. "You sure?"

"Uh. Just." He swallowed. "I don't know."

"Alright." Rhys adjusted them so he spooned Arden. He kissed the back of his head.

It helped.

He dozed off, then woke with a start in the late evening. He pushed Rhys. "Hey!"

"Uh!" Rhys woke with a start.

"I'm supposed to be at the thing, the...the big...!"

Wide-eyed, Rhys said, "Oh, the...! Shit, the party."

Arden clawed his way out from under the sheets and hurried towards his clothes. Nearly an hour ago, all the peers had gathered in the Big Room, the same as they did for any formal occasion, for the Giving Day festivities. A lush, themed party where people came together to celebrate, but really to show off their most luxe gifts.

He seized the clothes he'd worn earlier but realized they wouldn't do.

Rhys got out of bed, pulled Arden into his arms, and kissed his shoulder. "Go wash up. I'll find you something to wear."

"Come with me."

"I don't belong there."

Arden squeezed him. One night that he'd attended without a partner for nearly every year he'd been alive, but the idea of going alone tonight made him want to cry.

Rhys squeezed him back. "Wash up."

Arden washed up, but it didn't make him feel any better. He climbed into the fancy clothes Rhys handed to him. He wanted to beg Rhys to come with him.

"I'll see you when you get back," Rhys assured, which was not the same as offering to come along, but it was the next best thing.

Arden kissed him, shoved his shoes on, and practically ran to the Big Room. People milled around, drinks in hand, and turned towards the door when he entered. He must have been the only peer not in the room, save for the homebound and antisocial ones. He hesitated, then made his way to the podium set up for him.

He'd given a dozen of these speeches, silly things written by Frakes months ahead of time.

He stepped up to the mic. "Hi! Sorry for the wait, everybody. I got a little caught up."

The crowd rustled.

A nervous chuckled escaped him. He glanced at the speech Frakes had written for him. Unity, peace, blah, blah. He rubbed his nose. "We are..." He took a breath and closed the document with the speech. "We are glad to be here and see you. We all have a new agenda, we're sure you've noticed. And we've wasted your time enough tonight so we...I. I just want to say, please, bear with me for a while more. I'm doing my best and I need you to do your best, too. Be kind, not just to the people in this room, but to the ones who don't have the same lovely things as you and I. Thank you."

The crowd didn't make a sound.

A thrall stood frozen near the podium.

Arden stepped down, took a drink from their tray, and raised it. "Cheers!"

A few people near him raised their drinks and returned his salute.

He took a big swig of his drink and delved into the crowd to find a friend. He found, unfortunately, one of his cousins. He engaged in the necessary niceties, then took off as soon as he could.

After that, he found Zira and Alexander, who seemed sort of warm toward each other that night. Lexira carried a stuffed toy in her arms and gazed at it lovingly while the adults around her talked. Arden insisted on getting them drinks, as well as a sweet, non-alcoholic one for Lexira.

Cole wandered their way, which brought Wei and Mia by, too. Arden got them all drinks, too, and more for himself.

By the time he encountered Cathie, he was drunk.

He ran into Winslow sitting with a group of his friends and invited himself to sit at their table. He thanked Winslow at least three times for the gift he'd sent over.

Quietly, Winslow suggested that Arden might want to drink some water.

Arden agreed but never managed to make his way towards any drink not containing alcohol.

He ended up, some hours later, on the dancefloor with Wei Han, not sure entirely how he'd gotten from Winslow's table to Wei's arms.

Cole and Mia danced together a few feet away and both seemed deeply amused by Arden and Wei dancing together.

Arden asked, "Did I ever give you a handy in the stairwell?"

Wei frowned.

Cole's mouth popped open. "Arden!"

"What! They're *identical*."

Cole scowled. "Still, it's pretty rude!"

Arden blew a raspberry, peeled away from Wei, and slung an arm around Cole. "You know I love you, right?"

"I love you, too. Have you had any water?"

Arden shrugged. He honestly didn't know.

Cole navigated him to a table and brought him water.

"Did I hurt his feelings?"

"I mean, I don't think so, but honestly, would you want someone asking you that?"

"Fucking, I don't care, I'm...Who cares? It was like, one handjob a million years ago. Listen, Mia, are they...Uh. I don't think Mia likes me very much. They keep giving me this look."

"Before or after you asked Wei if you jerked him off in the stairway?"

Arden rolled his eyes. He drank his water, even though he didn't think it would do much. He rubbed his eyes, desperately longing for bed now that he'd sat down for a few minutes.

He stood and, without goodbyes, walked out.

He found his way home on his own.

He heard a movie playing and followed the sounds to find Rhys soaking in the bath watching the screen above the tub.

Rhys looked up. "I thought you'd be out longer."

"Would it ruin your bath if I threw up?"

Rhys sat up. "Do you need to throw up?"

"No, I can wait, I just...if I make myself barf now, I'll feel better in the morning. Actually...you know what? There's a bathroom off the guestroom. I'll be right back."

Rhys started to stand.

"Nononono, stay, I'll right...be right back." He wandered off and returned when he had emptied his stomach.

He sat on the bathmat beside the tub. "How was your night?"

"Fine. Are you okay?"

"Mmm." Arden couldn't feel his teeth. He put his chin on the edge of the tub. "What'd you do?"

"Not much."

"Hm. You like baths?"

Rhys sloshed a bit of water around. "Apparently I do."

"D'ya mean?"

"There's no baths in the Quarters."

"Oh." That made sense, as best as Arden's fuzzy mind could figure. "Where do you live?"

"Quarter Two, you knew that."

"Uh. No, I mean, what's it like? Your apartment?"

"Oh. Small. Sometimes...uh, somewhere between crowded and cozy. But it's home."

"Who's making it crowded?"

"Well, no one lives alone in the Quarters. We can't afford it."

"Oh. Well. You could—"

Abruptly, Rhys continued, "But it's nice to have company all the time. You know. I never have to be alone if I don't want to be. And if I need to breathe, I can always go for a walk. Have you ever been down below deck fourteen?"

Deck fourteen marked the end of the inhabited part of the space station.

"You aren't supposed to go down there."

Rhys smiled. "Are you going to send me to lock up?"

"It's not safe. What if you got hurt? No one would know where you were."

"Oh, one of the maintenance crews would find me eventually."

"Or find your body," Arden warned severely.

Rhys put his hand over Arden's. "It's fine. You want to come in here?"

"Mhm."

Arden struggled out of his clothes and splashed gracelessly into the bath. It was big enough for two, or even three, depending on how close people got. He put his head on Rhys's chest, the water lapping at the side of his mouth and nose.

The water stayed hot for ages thanks to the heated tub. They could have stayed in all night, though Mother had always teased Arden that he'd boil if he stayed in too long. He'd believed her until the age of eight.

"Both my parents are dead." A bit of soap foam splashed into his mouth as he spoke.

"Um. I know."

"Yours?"

"Oh. No. Not dead. Very much alive in Quarter Five."

"You don't sound happy about it."

He ran his fingers over Arden's side. "I think my parents were a little different than yours."

"Different how?"

"Like I have fourteen siblings different. Like one of my aunties named me when my parents didn't. After seven they were tired, after ten exhausted...A few days of maternity leave, and we went off to the care of those too old to work."

Arden had known, in a vague way, how childcare worked in the Quarters. He knew three days was standard leave, up to seven for a difficult birth. He knew thralls reproduced like rabbits to get their debt split as many ways as they could. He knew it in terms of numbers, not in terms of people. "I'm sorry."

"You were probably what, seven, when I was born?"

"Six."

"Things weren't your fault. Yet."

Arden whined.

Rhys gave his flank a sharp pat. "Don't. It's my turn to be sad."

"Are you sad?"

"No."

"Don't be sad."

"Are you ready for bed?" Rhys asked.

Arden closed his eyes and considered the proposition. "I might throw up."

"You already threw up."

"Mmm. That was on purpose. This time won't be." Arden didn't move. He hoped this wave of nausea would pass if he stayed still.

It worked.

He climbed out of the tub, made sure to brush his teeth, then climbed under the sheets.

Rhys joined him not much later. He smelled like Arden's soap and shampoo. He put an arm around Arden and said, "There's a bowl next to you if you change your mind about throwing up."

"I'm sorry you had a shitty childhood."

"Go to sleep."

Arden tried to sleep, alternating between mildly queasy and deeply tired.

He drifted off at some point and woke late in the morning.

A shot of Three waited for him on his bedside table.

He took the shot, checked around for Rhys, and found a message teasing him for sleeping in and reminding him that some people had work to do. He smiled at the note and gave himself the day to recover.

Rhys stopped by later to see how he was, which Arden really liked.

Arden settled himself into a chair in the back of the room. It had taken a long time for Mara's case against Paget to come to court. Half a dozen times the courts had dismissed and she had needed to refile, which was normally how thrall cases against peers went.

Each time Mara had refiled her case against Paget, she'd needed to get a certain number of signatures, with at least one from a member of the Council.

Multiple members had signed her petition each time she'd brought it before them.

Arden had signed it, too, for what it was worth.

Today a court had finally allowed her to bring her case before them. It was her last chance, honestly, because she'd filed with all the other courts on *Eden* and couldn't file in the same court twice.

The courts had immediately accepted Paget's charges against Mara, of course. They'd postponed their judgment on that case, though, so they could have one case to settle both sets of charges.

Arden waved to Mara when she came in.

She looked just as tired and pissed off as always, which he liked about her. She waved back begrudgingly.

Paget entered the courtroom looking every ounce the pampered darling of her family. She had bought her outfit within the last week or so because Arden had noticed it on display in one of the remaining Goshawk storefronts recently.

Arden scanned the gathered thralls for Rhys. He wouldn't miss the case for anything but had declined Arden's invitation to sit together.

Specifically, he'd said, "I don't want to be around a bunch of peers for this."

Arden didn't blame him.

Shay, Xio, and Istis approached him. "Are these seats taken?" Shay asked quietly.

A sign at the end of the row marked these seats as reserved, so Arden had five or six empty seats on either side. He couldn't bear the idea of being packed with other people like that. A peer would never dare to ask for permission to sit in a reserved area unless they knew Arden counted them as a friend.

Shay looked a little uncertain that Arden would let her in.

He pushed aside the stand for the cordage barrier with his foot. "Come on in."

The trio settled into their seats as the last handful of spectators trickled into the courtroom.

Arden had watched a lot of cases. His mother had always kept up with the courts and she'd brought him along. The rooms never got this full unless something really juicy had happened.

The Hmong divorce case a few years ago had lasted four sessions and had played out like an old teledrama.

This one felt a little grittier.

He hadn't yet decided if he would intervene on the results. He could, of course, but since his Giving Day speech, he'd been on delicate ground socially. Some people had liked it, and Rhys reported that the thralls had thought it very funny. A certain demographic had hated it, though. A few people, mostly older ones who'd known his mother, had deemed it necessary to tell him how much they'd hated it, either through a message or to his face.

"Have you followed the case closely, Your Eminence?" Shay asked.

"Oh, I don't follow anything closely, but I'm interested to see how it plays out. Have you met Mara?"

"Only to sign her petitions to file," Shay confided.

"You'd probably like her." He spotted Rhys among the workers and waved.

Rhys met his eye but didn't wave back.

Probably too crowded. They'd packed in shoulder to shoulder over there.

Arden listened with half an ear to the court proceedings. He knew this story already, having gotten both versions first-hand from both parties.

Ridea, the peer who'd spoken to Mara in the first place, and the thralls who'd worked with Mara that night came to speak on Mara's behalf. Even her supervisor went on record to say she had a temper but always kept it in check during business hours.

The friends of Paget who'd been there spoke endlessly of Paget's good character and distaste for low-class activities. They spoke as if brawls represented a common thrall activity, which played into stereotypes but didn't line up with crime reports.

Either the Quarters had a generally peaceful atmosphere or thralls didn't report crimes. Both seemed equally likely.

The whole case quickly became little more than one woman's word against the other's.

"Get to the bar recordings!" Arden called eventually, bored of listening to various testimonies on personal character and eye-witness accounts from people who'd readily admitted to drinking on the night in question.

As a rule, any place thralls worked unattended had cameras.

People murmured.

Quite a few turned to shoot him a dirty look until they realized who had called out.

The court took a recess to find the footage.

Arden slipped through the peers and found Rhys in the throng of workers. He tapped him on the shoulder.

Rhys turned to face him.

The people around him shrunk back when they saw Arden.

"I think we have time for a quick lunch if you want," Arden offered.

Rhys looked at the people near him, his unease plain.

"Uh. No, I, you already had plans?" Arden asked.

"Not plans as such, but..." Rhys glanced again at the people with him.

Arden looked at them, too. "You, uh. You all could come, too. If you wanted." He looked at Rhys. "If you want."

Rhys's friends looked deeply uncomfortable, even with their eyes lowered and their hands folded.

"That's, uh. Thank you, Your Eminence, that's kind of you, but..." Rhys said.

"We ate at home, Your Eminence," one of the workers supplied, clearly lying.

"I, alright, well. See you later," Arden said.

He left before the mix of emotions inside him could get the better of him. Discomfort, embarrassment, anger all rising from his guts to his throat.

Shay called to him as he stalked down a hall, no longer interested in the case. "Your Eminence! Lunch?"

He lunched with her, Xio, and Istis out of something between obligation and guilt. He couldn't hold up his end of the conversation for shit.

The trio, to their credit, took his mood in stride.

Xio acted a little too kindly towards Arden, which he tried to write off as empathy and politeness, as well as his status as Autarch. She did put her hand on his leg once, but then immediately pulled it back and looked mortified, so he thought of it as an accident.

He wanted to go home. Instead, he followed the Council members back to the courtroom to see how things played out.

They played the footage of the incident. It showed somewhere between both accounts. Mara had gotten much closer to Paget than she admitted, but she hadn't struck the first blow, as Paget had claimed.

A quick brawl ended by safety officers dragging the women apart.

The court, in the end, charged both women. Mara with inciting violence, and Paget for assault.

Arden confided to Shay, "That's kind of bullshit, isn't it?"

"Seems fair to me," Shay said. "They both acted out of turn."

Arden rolled his eyes. "I suppose." He pushed past the crowd to get to Mara. He offered her his hand. "Congratulations."

She didn't shake. "I didn't win."

"You didn't lose, either."

"Community service. When am I supposed to find time for that?" she asked.

He shrugged.

"Typical."

"You *really* don't like me."

"I'd spit on you if it wouldn't get me more community service."

Arden grinned. He couldn't help it. A strange kind of feeling fluttered in his stomach, only to have it replaced with discomfort. He had to ask, "How old are you?"

"Twenty."

He wrinkled his nose. "Ugh, never mind."

"Never mind what?'

"I don't know, but whatever it was, forget about it."

"Are you as crazy as they say, or just stupid?"

He shrugged. "Probably a little of both. Let me know if you need help working something out with that community service."

She scowled at him.

He patted her shoulder and walked away. He could practically feel her eyes burning his back as he went.

In the evening, he dropped by Mace's handball practice. He caught Mace before it started.

Mace placed his hands on Arden's shoulder and his chin on his hands. "Ardi, you should come play with us."

"In this?"

"We can find you a spare set."

Arden looked towards the players already stretching. He hadn't played in years.

"Come on," Mace pleaded.

Arden sighed. "Alright."

Mace straightened up. "Really!"

"I guess."

Mace bounced on his toes and practically dragged Arden into the changing room.

Self-consciously, Arden stretched. He felt ridiculous and wanted to leave, but he'd look even stupider if he ran off half-way through warm-ups in someone else's clothes. Most of the people on the court he'd played with before, so they knew he'd been a barely competent player.

Mace patted him on the cheek. "Don't think I've ever seen you play with your eyes all the way open."

"Haha, so funny, Arden was a teenage addict."

Mace looked reticent for a second, then pushed him. "Don't be a baby."

Arden stuck out his tongue.

Mace pelted him with the ball.

He caught it and threw it back, just as hard.

Mace cackled.

Everyone took it easy on Arden, for the most part, at least until he started showing off. Then they went for him just as hard as they went for everyone else.

He winded easily, but that came from not exercising for years.

He complained once to Mace that his legs felt like dead weight, which Mace responded to by poking him in the ribs and telling him to take better care of himself.

Before the end of practice, Arden had to take a seat, breathless and sweaty. He sipped water and watched the other players go at it now that the delicate Autarch had stepped off the court.

Mace came over and kicked him in the foot. "Come on, showers."

"How dare you kick us."

Mace kicked him again, a little harder. Then he extended his hand to lift Arden.

Arden took it.

Mace pulled him so hard he felt like he was flying for half a second.

"Oh, Mason, you're so *strong*," he purred.

Mace snorted, looped his arm around Arden, and pulled him towards the locker room.

Arden remembered exactly why he'd wanted to date Mace all those years ago.

Mace poked him in the ribs again. "What would Rhys think if he caught you staring at me like that?"

"Oh, shut up. You don't even like boys!"

"But you do," Mace said. "And you really like Rhys."

Arden shrugged. He stripped off his borrowed practice clothes and stepped into the spray of the shower.

Mace took the next showerhead and continued, "It's so obvious that it's kind of cute."

Arden flushed, which he knew would be highly visible with his complexion. He turned up the heat of the water and hoped that would disguise it. "Shut up."

"No, it's a good thing! Much better than the last person you dated."

Arden winced, thinking about Faust. "Maybe I only like people who don't like me." He grabbed the soap and turned away to wash so he wouldn't have to see the pitying look Mace gave him.

"He likes you," Mace assured.

Arden got soap in his eyes and focused on rinsing it out instead of wondering if Rhys liked him.

"Arden."

"What?"

"You don't think he likes you?"

"I have soap in my eyes."

"Well, you have to open them to rinse it out," Mace advised.

Cleaned and redressed, Mace and Arden wandered in the vague direction of Mace's rooms.

They didn't talk about much. Arden had brushed off any further attempts to talk about Rhys. It made him feel sick and hopeful all at once.

He put away twice what he normally ate at dinner, which made his stomach hurt.

Mace teased him a little about that too but sent him home with a hug and a serious sounding, "Be good."

Arden lay awake contemplating the meaning of goodness and whether he could ever achieve it. He had, by anyone's standards, never been good, except as maybe a baby. Mama had always said he'd been a happy baby.

He woke up stiff and sore.

Punishment for not stretching enough.

Mace had sent him a message asking him to pretty please consider coming to practice more often.

Arden wrote back that he'd consider it when he could move without hurting again.

When he and Rhys met up outside the Public Chamber, they both shifted and couldn't look at each other. During the meeting, Arden could feel the discomfort rolling off Rhys. He wanted to adjourn the meeting to talk to him but knew it would be poor form and do nothing for his standing.

Somehow, despite his vast power, it remained important to keep people from hating him. If people started to hate him, he'd have to keep them in line with fear, which he didn't enjoy thinking about.

"Arden," Cole called.

He pulled himself out of his thoughts.

"There's rumors about your uncle."

"What could Winnie possibly be up to?"

"Your other uncle," Shay clarified.

Arden wrinkled his nose. "What are they saying about Morris now? We've already got rape and assault. I hope he's not moving towards anything worse than that."

"There's been a little talk of him, uh. Well. A few people overheard him saying he'd be a better leader than you," Xio said.

"He's been saying that since before Mother even died."

"People might agree with him," Riley Hmong suggested.

He scanned the faces in the room.

"Not us!" Istis quickly assured.

"No, not us. We think you're a wonderful Autarch," Xio added.

He blushed. No one had ever said anything that kind about his reign and the compliments he had received never sounded sincere. Hers had, though.

"We wouldn't have brought it up if we didn't think Morris was...a poor candidate," Tule Marrow pointed out. "We might disagree from time to time, Your Eminence, but your uncle...I much more than disagree with him."

People around the table murmured their agreement, even the centrists.

Thank fuck for that.

"But there are some people who see Morris as a better option," Riley added.

"Such as?"

Cole cleared his throat. "You might have really pissed off Bull and his friends."

Arden groaned. "Can you name names?"

"Not presently. I mean, they're just rumors, and you know how rumors get," Istis said.

"Alright. Well. Keep an ear out."

Morris was vicious, but he wasn't stupid. He wouldn't stage an outright rebellion. He would wait until Arden showed public weakness.

"This business with the thralls, maybe we could make our changes more gently," Tule suggested.

"The changes *have* been gentle," Shay pointed out.

"I'd be afraid of Morris in an enclosed space, but I'm not afraid of him politically," Arden said. "And when push comes to shove, there's more workers than peers."

Cole covered his mouth to hold in a giggle.

Half the table looked openly scandalized. At least three sent vicious looks towards Rhys.

"Don't!" Arden warned. "It's not him, it's history. You know what happens to people like us when there's too many people and not enough food?"

The table exchanged uneasy glances.

"Work with me here."

"We are, Your Eminence," Salim Bowles assured. "No one wants to see *Eden* fail."

Arden nodded, somewhat satisfied. His weak and newly discovered morals had their place and he tried to rely on those to motivate the Council, rather than the threat of violent political revolution. He didn't even like to think of it, but it felt like a distinct possibility. If not within in his lifetime, then soon.

If he'd paid better attention in school, he might have figured out *Eden's* trajectory a lot sooner.

Quietly, after everyone else had left, Rhys suggested, "When it comes to your uncle, you might want to take advantage of the workers he uses regularly."

"Advantage how?"

"They hear a lot. They'd hear a lot more if they knew someone would pay for it."

"Fine. You can arrange that?"

Rhys nodded.

"Good. Keep me updated."

"Yes, Your Eminence."

They looked at each other, then looked away.

Arden cleared his throat.

Rhys smoothed his clothes.

"You really don't like people knowing we're together," Arden said.

Rhys glanced up. "Uh. No...not. Some of my friends aren't..." He sighed. He took out his hair and retied it. "Some of my friends don't exactly believe in taking things one step at a time."

"Eat the rich?" Arden guessed.

"It would have been a mess."

"You don't hate me, then?"

Rhys met his eyes. "Of course, I don't hate you, Arden."

Arden looked at his nails.

"Even when I did hate you, I wouldn't have ever wanted you to eat lunch with that lot," he teased with an easy smile.

Absolutely without warning, Arden's eyes started to burn. He clenched his jaw and blinked, but tears spilled anyway.

Rhys looked actively afraid. He took a step forward, then stopped.

"What...?"

"I super fucking hate when you say things like that. I just...I just want you to like me and I...!" He scrubbed his face with his sleeve, angry at himself for crying and angry at Rhys for upsetting him.

"I do like you," Rhys rushed to assure him.

Arden shook his head.

Rhys hugged him. "Come on, Arden, I like you. You're alright." He rubbed his back. "You're alright."

Arden didn't feel alright.

Rhys hugged him harder, like he thought he could crush the sadness out of Arden.

It worked, in a way, because Arden couldn't really breathe.

Rhys wiped his face for him. "Come on, let's get you some water."

He nodded.

Once he'd washed his face and didn't look like such a mess, they went to the Solar Deck together to walk around.

Arden stripped off his jacket due to the heat and so he would have something to hold. He wanted to hold Rhys's hand but also knew Rhys didn't want him to. Dozens of people milled around or lounged to take in the light from the star.

After two loops around the deck, in a stretch without anyone to overhear, Arden asked, "Are you embarrassed by me?"

"No."

Arden didn't look at him. He kept walking.

Rhys stayed beside him. "I'm actually...Arden, are you listening?"

Arden shrugged.

Rhys put a hand on Arden's arm and moved in close to him. "Arden."

"Hmm?"

"I'm proud of you."

"Shut up."

"No, I mean it. You have every reason to let us all rot and starve, to live a decadent life and let *Eden* drift towards death. To do what every Autarch before you did."

Arden didn't think Rhys could understand how much it hurt to hear that. People had such low expectations for him that they considered a basic concern for the human race something for him to take pride in. "That's my mother you're talking about."

Rhys sucked his lower lip in and dug in his teeth. He rubbed his nose. "I..."

"You think she didn't care about this station? Or that she didn't love me enough to keep *Eden* alive long enough for me to grow old?"

"I think..." Rhys sighed and dropped his gaze. "I'm sorry. I didn't mean to offend you."

"No, don't pull that thrall bullshit. Look at me. Tell me what you think."

Rhys lifted his eyes to meet Arden's, the entire world in that dark gaze, as he said, "I think she saw what she wanted to see. Your family could do anything for so long they forgot they weren't the gods they pretended to be. You can't swindle or bully your way out of food shortages or failing infrastructure." He took Arden by the hands. "I think you might be the only Autarch who doesn't feel entitled to their position. And I don't know why. I don't know if it's because you're an insecure brat or because you're so deeply sensitive that you avoid everything that makes you feel anything."

He said it so gently that Arden almost forgot to take offense at being called an over-sensitive brat. He wiggled his hands deeper into Rhys's grip. "I feel very seen right now." A wisp of a smile turned up one corner of his mouth.

"Then take the compliment."

"You want me to say thank you for being called a big baby?" Arden asked, his smile growing.

Rhys tugged him in for a one-armed hug. "Are you done being mad at me?"

Arden sighed into his chest. "Can we do one more loop?"

"Of course."

Rhys held on to his hand as they walked. He even swung his arm a little and had a bit of a jaunt to his step. "It really is nice up here!" he declared a few times.

He seemed particularly impressed with the plants that grew in the heat of the Solar Deck. He would touch their glossy leaves and ask questions about them.

For once, Arden knew something he didn't. He supplied the names of the plants easily.

Mother had liked plants.

Rhys asked, "Do you think these grew on Terra?"

"They grew on Terra One, so they grew on Terra Prime, too."

"How do you know?"

"Because Terra One was empty when the scouts from Terra Prime found it. Just dirt and water and sunshine. They seeded the planet and made it habitable. Didn't you learn that in school?"

"I never liked history," Rhys admitted, but it sounded like a lie. Not that he secretly liked history, but that he had another reason for his gap in knowledge.

"Rumor has it that some of the plants they grew on Terra Prime had come from Earth if it existed at all. I mean...it probably had to. We know Terra Prime wasn't empty and humans had to come from *somewhere*. Sometimes people even say there were, well, other people there when humans came. Although...other people think the other 'tribes' our ancestors fought were only different sects of humans. That Earth was just a section of Terra Prime, not a planet." Arden shrugged. "No one really knows."

"Do you think it's real?"

"Earth? We had to come from somewhere, right? But I don't know. Does it matter?"

"I don't know. What do you think?"

Arden wanted to shrug again, but he stopped to think about the question. "Uh. It...Where we came from is important, but not as important as where we're going. And someday, maybe, if we get far enough, we'll understand where we've been." He glanced at Rhys. "Right?"

"I don't know."

They finished their loop around the deck and attended to meetings and inspections that Rhys had discreetly rescheduled while Arden had washed his face and sipped a glass of water.

Nothing interesting happened.

Nothing interested happened for most of the next week, except for one time in the middle of dinner, a worker had come and whispered something into Rhys's ear.

He'd gone wide-eyed and pale, then he'd practically begged Arden to excuse him from dinner, which Arden had.

He didn't see Rhys for a few days after that, having received a message saying he had a few things at home to take care of.

When Arden did see him next, he declined to talk about what had happened. "Everything's fine."

"You took off in a super big hurry."

"I know. I'm sorry."

Arden hadn't wanted an apology, but he accepted it. Instead, he asked, "You want to stay over?"

"Oh. I don't know. I should get back."

"I thought everything was fine."

"It is. It is."

"You missed work, though."

"Hmm?"

"It's not like you."

Rhys wrapped an arm around his neck and pulled him into a headlock, gentle but still playful. "Maybe now that I get paid like a peer, I can afford to stay home once in a while."

Arden squirmed out of his grip and pushed him.

Rhys pushed him back.

They roughhoused for a few minutes, dissolving into to giggles when Rhys scooped up Arden and threw him over his shoulder.

He hurried to put Arden down when someone rang at the door.

Arden straightened his clothes. "What!"

A safety officer, followed by Mara, stepped just inside his rooms. "Your Eminence, uh, this thrall has been looking for you. Normally, we'd send her away, but..." The officer glanced at Mara. "She said—"

"I said you be pissed if they did that," Mara answered.

The officer said, "Ah, I know Your Eminence was involved in her trial."

"Barely!" Arden protested.

"I can take her away."

"No, don't be stupid, she's all the way here already and you've ruined the mood," Arden said. He waved away the safety officer.

"What mood?" Rhys asked.

Arden rolled his eyes and smacked Rhys's arm. He gestured to the couch. "What can I do for you, Mara?"

She sat. "This community service bullshit."

Arden grinned and settled beside her, casual and relaxed. Cool-looking, he thought.

Rhys choked on some half-formed word.

"What about it?" Arden asked.

"I don't have time."

"And you'd like me to...?"

"Get rid of it!" she demanded.

"Give an inch," Arden murmured.

"You can," she insisted.

"Well, yeah, I *can*. Why should I? You did pick a fight with that other girl."

Mara shook her head, blond wisps flying about her face. "She picked a fight with me."

"Arden, maybe..." Rhys began, then clamped his mouth shut.

Mara gave Rhys a horrible look, the kind of vicious hate for which only young people had the energy. "I don't need you sticking up for me, either!"

Rhys pursed his lips, then paced over to the bar. He didn't do anything over there except look put off.

"Is that what it takes to get something out of you?" Mara asked Arden. She still had those cold, pale eyes fixed on Rhys.

He had an uncomfortable idea of where this would go. He straightened up. He didn't think he looked cool anymore.

"I'll fuck you if I have to," she growled as though he'd propositioned her.

"Ew!"

From the bar, Rhys echoed, "Ew," though more quietly.

Arden told her, "I *don't* want to have sex with you."

"You did it for him." She slung her glare towards Rhys again.

"That's different."

"You don't like girls?"

"Listen, that's…that's personal. And also, I already said no, so…just. No." Her age had firmly removed her as a person of interest for him, and it had only been a passing interest in the first place. "We'll figure something out."

"How? You can't add more hours to the day."

Arden considered that option. "I actually think I could. But, how about…How about!" Arden grinned at his idea. "I'll commute your community service on the terms that you supply me with information gathered in the course of your usual work."

"What kind?"

"Like the kind that drunk, unhappy peers might let slip at a bar. You do work at that bar regularly, don't you?"

"Yes."

"So?" he asked.

She rolled her eyes. "Fine."

"Good! Uh, weekly reports. Go down and get a refurbished tablet."

"How long am I on the hook for?"

He shrugged. "Until I'm satisfied that I don't need you gathering information for me anymore."

She looked livid.

"Or you can go scrub the blood off the floor in a med center!" Arden threatened.

"I said fine."

"Alright, then go away."

She stalked out.

Rhys came back over to the couch and took her spot. "Well, fuck."

"I know. Were you that angry?"

"I was better at hiding it, that's for sure." Rhys scooted closer to Arden and poked him in the side. "You really are a big softy."

Arden blew a raspberry.

"Or do you just like people who are mean to you?"

"That's the one."

Rhys rested his head on Arden's shoulder.

"You could be mean to me right now, if you wanted," Arden suggested.

"Arden, I'm so tired…"

"You do look like shit. I wasn't going to say anything."

"Ugh, I get the *worst* bags under my eyes. You should have seen me when I was fifteen; I looked like one of those old horror characters they show around Hollow Night."

Arden pictured him as one of the spooky wraiths that parents used to threaten children. The tradition of Hollow Night came purely from *Eden,* started by a small group of peers with an affinity for all things dark and gloomy. They'd had movie nights which had grown and grown until now every year on Hollow Night, teens and adults stayed up scaring themselves silly while their children tried to sneak glimpses of the screens.

Arden hated it.

He offered, "Do you want to take a nap?"

"I should get home."

"What's so great about home all of a sudden?"

Rhys smiled hazily, eyes closed. "No place like home." He nestled his cheek against Arden's shoulder. He yawned.

"You're not getting sick, are you?"

"No."

"You should go to a med center."

"I'm not sick. Just sleepy."

Arden kissed the top of his head. "Go home and get some sleep."

"You don't mind?"

"No."

Rhys didn't move for some time, but he did eventually stretch and yawn and rise from the couch. He gave Arden a peck then ambled out.

Arden didn't know what had gotten into him. This tired, playful contentedness lasted for a few weeks and lingered, generally, as part of Rhys's personality.

Arden liked it. He liked that Rhys seemed happy. He felt happy, too, and hoped that they were happy together.

Each week, Mara had sent in her reports, short and begrudging.

A big blonde lady said you suck. Her husband thought so too.

Four teenagers bet each other they could fight you but they were pretty drunk.

A man named Praetor said you're ruining everything.

Fallon Thomas said you're a piece of shit.

Arden didn't know what he'd expected, asking her to tattle on drunken peers. Today, though, her report came early, long before her shift ended.

A couple of old guys said they were going to 'get rid of that thrall bitch' you're fucking and I think they meant it.

Apparently, her dislike for Rhys didn't extend to wanting him dead.

He made his way to the bar she worked at and sat for a drink.

She came over to him right away, not unusual for his station, but she did elbow someone out of her way to get to him. "You got my message?"

"Mhm."

She glanced towards a pair of older, but certainly not old, men.

Arden's stomach hurt upon seeing the younger of the two, about thirty years his senior, but still spry and shrewd.

Morris Torre had been born years after Arden's mother had become Autarch, the last son of an ancient father. Unattended by anyone but thrall nannies who hadn't known how to discipline him, Morris had grown from brat to terror to active threat to those around him.

His elder sister had never cared much for him, his father had died, and his mother didn't exist as far as Morris was concerned. Popular rumor said she lived below deck six.

Arden wondered if she knew what a horror her son had become.

"You didn't want to mention which old guys it was? And, a pink ivy, too."

As she made his drink, she said, "I don't know who the fuck they are."

"Alright, well, here's a bit of advice, if you're ever alone with the tall one, run."

She placed his drink in front of him.

He winced. "Little heavy on the syrup."

"Do you want to know what they said or not?"

Now that he knew it had been Morris, he worried in a different, but less immediate, way. Morris made threats and often followed through with them but in an unexpected manner. "What did they say?"

"That you're thinking with your dick."

"Oh, probably."

"They mentioned getting rid of your current pet and replacing it with one who'd influence you in a different direction," she confided.

"Don't call him my pet."

She raised an eyebrow. She topped his drink with an aggressive splash of bubbly water. "That's what you're worried about?"

"Morris is scum but he's not stupid. And he won't get his hands dirty with murder. Those charges stick better than the skeezy, backhanded shit he does."

"Hm."

"Keep me posted."

"Sure."

"Don't you mean 'of course, Your Eminence'?" he asked.

She narrowed her eyes.

He took his drink and headed out into the crowd. He didn't want to bump into his uncle and knew he had to have friendly acquaintances out here somewhere. He'd gotten dressed for this, after all. He'd expected a dangerous plot on Rhys's life, not some petty plan to infiltrate Arden's bedroom.

He found Zira looking abjectly alone with a drink and no friends at her table. He sat across from her.

She glanced up.

"Don't look happy to see me or anything."

"Hi, Arden."

"What's that look?"

"It's the look that says my husband moved out and filed for divorce last week."

He grimaced. He had heard about that from Cole. Cole had seemed pleased with the change, even mentioning that he had finally gotten to spend time with Alexander and his daughter as a provisional sort of family unit.

Alexander and Zira still had to work out a custody agreement, but the girl had spent a few nights with each parent over the past week.

"I guess there is that," he admitted. "How...How are you?"

She heaved a sigh and rolled her eyes at him.

"That's why no one ever asks how you're doing, you know!" he accused. "It's got to be hard, Zira. Go ahead and say it's hard."

"It's fucking awful."

"It's got to be."

"Cathie said I should find someone new, get back on my feet."

"Or off your feet," Arden suggested with a silly, sort of louche smile.

She glared. "That's not funny."

"I thought it was. Do you want to talk about it?"

"No."

He sipped his drink.

After an awkward silence, she declared, "I just don't understand! I did everything. I did!"

"What's everything, exactly?"

She sipped her drink and stewed.

"Zira."

She huffed.

Arden stretched across the table and held his hands out. He pouted at her. "Zeenie-beenie, come on, if you can't tell me, who can you tell?"

She glared, then put her hands in his. "I don't know what went wrong."

"Does Alexander have any insight?"

"He says we started fighting one day and never figured out how to stop."

Given what he knew of their relationship, the assessment sounded accurate. "You guys were really young when you got married. Maybe too young," he said. "Maybe you didn't know what you wanted yet. I mean...who even gets married in their twenties!"

"My parents did."

"We are not our parents," he reminded. He could see how Zira would want to be like her parents, though, deeply infatuated with each other after fifty-plus years.

Married young, children young...The pieces settled into place.

"The good news is you have lots of time to find someone new. Or take time for you. You and Alexander...Shit, I mean, did you two even date other people beforehand?"

"Not seriously."

"Mmm."

"My parents didn't."

"Oh, I thought your name was Zira, not Sharie," he said.

She yanked her hands back. "You know, you always were my least favorite cousin."

"But am I your favorite *second* cousin?" he asked.

Growing up, he and Zira had seen a lot of each other. Mama and her cousin, Sharie, had grown up close and shared the same predilections for shimmer and shine, for dressing up their little doll-faced children, and watching silly old shows. Zira and Arden had called each other's mothers auntie, snuggled in on the couch for movies, and secretly helped each other out of the itchiest parts of their outfits.

It had been Zira that had spread the nickname 'Ardi' to the rest of their friends.

As they'd gotten older, they'd drifted in and out of each other's lives. Sometimes friends, sometimes less.

Right now, he thought they might be less than friends. He had a hand in that, but Zira did, too.

"You know none of us are picking sides, right?" he reminded.

"It kind of feels like people are."

"We're still friends," he told her.

"That's what Cathie said."

"And Cathie's usually right. Do you want another drink?"

"No, Lexira's at home. I should go soon."

"You don't like me, do you?" he pouted.

"Not really." She smiled, though.

"Zira?"

"What, Ardi?"

Very seriously, he said, "Promise me something."

"What?"

"Promise me that Lex's dresses aren't as itchy as ours were."

She snorted. "Do you remember Founder's Day, that poufy green skirt?"

He giggled. "Yes! Oh, you *tore the shit* out of it climbing up onto the railing."

"No, sliding down it."

"Oh, yes, right, right. Auntie Sharie was *livid*."

"Not as angry as the Autarch was when you chipped your tooth the day before your birthday party."

"I spent the whole day in a chair getting it fixed."

"Your face swelled up so bad," she tittered.

They reminisced for a little while longer about clothes they'd ruined, times they'd cut their own hair, things they'd gotten stuck in their hair, and the other mischief they'd caused. She teased him about his temper tantrums; he teased back about her being such a brownnoser. Finally, she said she really had to go.

He walked her home and hugged her goodbye. He told her, "If you ever need a night out and want someone to watch Lex, let me know. I hear trauma is formative for children."

That made her laugh.

She didn't take him up on his offer to keep an eye on Lexira, which he hadn't expected her to.

He thought about it, though, for the following week. Maybe it would do him some good to spend time around children, start considering if he wanted some of his own one day. It seemed like a venture one should go into with a general knowledge of children. He likely wouldn't do it by accident, he rarely slept with people who had a womb, and even if he had, he didn't know for sure that he could get anyone pregnant.

Other options existed and the whole thing was so far off that he didn't think about it too much.

He did think about it now, lazily content as he cuddled up to Rhys. They'd really gone at it and Arden thought he might fall asleep. He snuggled a little closer. "Hey."

"Hmm?"

Arden gazed at him for a little while. He looked so calm. Eyes closed, his arm around Arden, skin against skin. He even smelled good. It made Arden warm, not the overwhelming heat of lust, but a different, smoother warmth. This feeling, this warmth, was not entirely foreign to him, but he hadn't encountered it for a long time. "Do you want to meet my Uncle Winnie?"

"What?" Rhys's voice came soft, not quite fully awake.

"We could drop by sometime tomorrow. Take him out for lunch. He'd like that."

"Oh. Does he not get a lot of visitors?" Rhys asked. He opened his eyes.

"No, not...I meant you should come meet him." Arden sat up a little. He adjusted a lock of Rhys's rumpled hair. "I'd like that."

Rhys sat up all the way. "Arden."

"No, just, Rhys. I really like you." He kissed his shoulder. "Maybe, you know. Definitely more than—"

Abruptly, Rhys pulled him into a hug. He looked miserable as he crushed Arden against him. "Don't."

"What?"

"Arden, I'm so sorry. I am. I can't."

"Winnie's really nice! He'll like you, too," Arden insisted. He understood where Rhys's concerns lay.

"You don't understand."

Arden hugged him back. It would terrify him to meet Rhys's family if Rhys had ever been inclined to make those introductions. "No, I do, it's scary meeting someone's family but I promise—"

"I can't do this anymore."

Arden squirmed out of his arms. "What!"

"It's not right. I'm sorry, I thought..." Rhys licked his lips and swallowed.

Arden stared. His whole body flipped between hot and cold. He couldn't think. "I'm confused," he whispered.

"This...this relationship means something to you. Something more than what it means to me," Rhys said. He spoke in exactly the same way Mother's doctor had when she'd told them she couldn't help anymore. "I can't do it anymore."

"Don't say that."

"I'm sorry."

Arden pushed him, not hard, nothing more than palm to shoulder. "Why would you say that!"

Rhys pressed his lips together.

"You said you like me!"

"I do."

"I said *don't do this*, I said *don't* if you don't like me!" Arden insisted.

"Not like that." He placed a hand on Arden's arm, likely meant to soothe him.

It pissed Arden off, that sad look on his face, like Rhys wasn't the one hurting him. "Tell me this is a shitty joke."

"I'm sorry. I can't do this."

Arden pushed him again, much harder. "Why did you do it if you don't like me!"

Rhys put up his arms. "It's not like that. I thought. I thought this wouldn't go anywhere. I thought it wouldn't matter if I didn't love you because I never thought you would love me. I didn't even think you could."

Arden shoved him out of the bed. "Get out."

He stumbled as he went. "Arden—"

"No, get the fuck out! Get the fuck out of my room!" His voice pitched up, nearly a shriek by the time he finished.

Rhys glanced around for his clothes.

Arden scrambled after him. He threw the first thing he could find, not at Rhys, but definitely toward him. He practically chased him out of the room, throwing things and shouting, "I don't ever want to fucking see you again."

He threw Rhys's clothes after him, so he had to scramble around the hall to gather them. "Ever fucking again."

He wanted to chase him down the hall, he wanted to shove him and scream at him. More than that, he wanted for this to not have happened.

He threw his shoes last.

Rhys flinched as they whizzed by him.

He stormed away, leaving Rhys naked in the hall.

He flipped his coffee table and threw a chair into the bar. He threw the other against the viewing window, where it broke. He threw the pieces around his room, too.

Finally, he couldn't keep himself from crying any longer. He sat down, curled in on himself, and sobbed. He screamed, too, meaningless things and wordless shouts.

His eyes hurt. His throat hurt, and his chest, and everything else.

Fuck.

He still had cum inside him, sliding down his thighs.

He wanted to fucking die.

He lay on the floor and stared out the window. Dying planet, dying *Eden*, and something dying inside Arden, too. Hope, or love, or whatever that warmth inside him had been.

Nothing made sense.

He stayed on the floor for hours, until he had to use the bathroom or piss himself. He curled up in bed after that, except he couldn't stay there. Not when the pillows smelled like Rhys.

He slept on the couch.

Or, he lay on his couch, awake and tired for hours.

Eventually, he got his tablet and watched *This Endless Life* until he fell asleep.

He woke with drool crusted onto his face.

He used the bathroom, then went back to the couch.

His stomach hurt with hunger, but he ignored it until his guts numbed.

Sometimes he cried, sometimes he stared at his tablet watching episodes he'd seen at least three times already.

He ignored messages. He locked his door, changed the code, and wouldn't open it for friend or thrall.

He didn't know how many days it had been before someone forced their way inside. He heard the repeated attempts to guess his code.

Finally, the door opened.

He should have picked a better passcode.

"Go away," he croaked.

Mace and Cole came in, stepping around the mess he'd made throwing things. "Ardi, you in here?" Mace asked.

Cole flicked on the lights. "Oh, Ardi," he sighed.

Arden curled up and pulled the blanket over his head. "Go away."

Mace sat beside him. "What happened?"

Arden didn't move.

Mace tugged down the blanket. He rubbed Arden's back. "Are you alright, at least?"

He meant to growl, "Yes," but instead a weak, "No," eked past his lips.

"What happened?"

"Rhys ended it."

"Oh," Mace sighed. "Oh, Ardi, I'm sorry."

Cole started to pick things up.

Arden turned and buried himself in Mace's arms. He thought he'd cried himself out, but he cried as Mace held him.

He went when Cole told him it was time for a bath.

He soaked for a while wishing he couldn't hear his friends discussing him and the mess he'd made.

He sank under the water so he couldn't.

Cole helped him wash his hair, which it badly needed, while Mace changed the sheets. The brothers wrapped him up in a robe and made him eat some oatmeal. He went along with it since he'd skipped enough meals to make him weak and lightheaded.

He felt like a child.

He'd acted like a child.

An awful, spoiled brat.

He must have scared Rhys.

That made him cry again.

Mace and Cole stayed for the night.

He'd asked them to stay with him, next to him, which they did without hesitation. He nestled between the two of them, safe between his friends.

He felt like shit. Worse than that, he had to live with the inalienable knowledge that he had acted horribly toward Rhys.

"I fucking threw stuff at him," he whispered into Cole's back.

"Did you hit him?" Cole asked.

"That's not funny!" Mace warned.

Arden started to cry.

"Look what you did!" Mace scolded.

"No, it's okay," Arden sniffled. "I'm a piece of shit."

"No, shh, Arden," Cole soothed.

He fell asleep again eventually.

The brothers got him up, got him breakfast, and got him dressed. When they left, Cathie stopped by not much later.

She made him take a loop around the Solar Deck with her. They walked arm in arm. She validated all his feelings and reminded him she'd gone through a breakup not too long ago when he said she didn't know how he felt.

That shut him up pretty well.

After all, she'd been unwittingly sleeping with someone who'd hurt one of her closest friends.

He'd just gotten dumped by someone who didn't love him and considered Arden incapable of love.

They ended up walking for hours.

He felt better. A little empty, still tired, but better after hours of talking with Cathie.

A few days later, he took slightly too much Twelve in preparation for a Council meeting. Cole had to half-carry him there. He didn't know what he would do if he saw Rhys, but vomiting seemed a good option.

Except Rhys didn't come.

They waited for him, but he never arrived.

They held the meeting without him.

And kept holding meetings without him.

Arden fumbled his way through the meetings, not any more confused than usual, but certainly less confident without Rhys by his side.

Arden hung around the bar.

He'd hung around this bar a lot lately, but Mara's scathing reports cheered him up and getting them from her in person cheered him twice as much.

The drinks helped his mood, too.

"People aren't going to say anything about you if you're sitting right there," Mara pointed out as she placed a drink in front of him.

"What's this?" He didn't recognize the pale blue concoction.

"Oggie's freak of the week. He calls this one High Water."

He sipped it. "That's nice."

Oggie came up behind Mara and put his elbows on her shoulders. "It's the mulberry syrup. Glad you like it, Eminence."

Mara glared at Oggie more kindly than she glared at anyone else. She elbowed him in the stomach and walked away.

Oggie rubbed his stomach. He leaned on the bar across from Arden. He confided happily, "If she wasn't my sister, I'd probably kill her."

Arden smiled. He sipped the drink. He liked the siblings quite a lot. The pair looked alike in some ways, though they'd never be mistaken for twins. Mara had a lighter complexion and narrower features, as well as tighter body language. Oggie had a languidness about him, a luxurious sort of boredom complimented by his tawny skin and golden hair.

Arden liked that they talked to him instead of to the floor. He drummed his fingers. "Can I ask you a personal question?"

"Open book."

"The two of you, you're not..." He tried to choose his words carefully. "You're not scared of peers like everyone else."

Oggie smiled. "Do you want to know a secret?"

"Always."

Oggie leaned close. "Our mother is a peer."

Arden raised his eyebrows.

"Her and Pop had quite the affair, long enough to have both of us. Mam kept us in her rooms, away from the other kids, and never let Pop come around during the day. I guess he got sick of it, and she got sick of him being sick of it. Booted us all out."

"Oh."

"That! That was a wake-up call. Going from a nice peer apartment to the Quarters. I guess we're poorly socialized."

"You seem pretty well socialized."

Oggie smiled, a brilliant, handsome smile. "That's all outside. Inside I'm spare parts. Ask Mara. Oh! Sorry, Eminence, there's orders waiting."

Arden waved his hand to indicate Oggie could leave.

Not that he ever waited for Arden's permission.

Arden sat with his drink, watching the people around him. People stopped to say hello and chat, but most didn't stay long.

He glanced at the time. He had a breakfast date with Winslow tomorrow, so he couldn't stay out too late.

Except he would.

He always did. He hated going home these days.

It felt empty.

He hadn't seen Rhys in months. He'd stopped coming to work. He hadn't sent Arden a single message, not even to tell him off for acting like a beast or to apologize for breaking his heart.

The thought of sending him a message made Arden sick to his stomach. He'd learned to function without a Chamberlain.

Eden had elected a functional Council this time. Arden had become uneasily thankful for each member, fond of even the ones who argued with him.

Productivity had even climbed a hair in the past few months.

People were happier at work and happy people simply did better work than stressed, exhausted ones.

He had bought *Eden* a few more years, he hoped.

If he could get peers to stop being so ridiculously wasteful and bellyaching about the shortage of luxe items, he could die happy.

Or he could die right now, still raw and feeling like his insides had gotten scooped out.

"Nother one?" Mara asked.

His teeth had started to feel funny. "Water?"

She served him a glass. "Don't you have friends?"

"I have a few positions open, actually, if you want to apply."

"I'd rather spit on you."

"You can spit on me when I'm dead," he offered.

She scoffed and walked away.

Several hours and drinks later, he wandered home.

By some stroke of luck, he made it to breakfast with Winslow on time. His uncle told his usual stories as Arden picked apart his food.

"You look tired," Winslow told him.

"I am tired."

"You should get some rest."

Arden rubbed his nose.

He couldn't sleep.

One night, on an empty stomach he'd taken enough Nine to knock out a person twice his size, which he was told could have killed him. He doubted that, but the doctor had insisted he needed to lay off the formulas for a while.

He'd agreed to when his friends had threatened to start keeping an eye on him.

He'd also agreed to go to practice with Mace and Cole when they'd pulled him into a group hug and refused to let go until he agreed.

All of it was fine. Food, drinks, practice, his friends. Sometimes, things dipped firmly into 'not fine' when he couldn't sleep, or he drank too much, or he spent all night staring at Terra One. But for the most part, he was fine.

He needed to be.

He kept busy.

He had to.

During his third night at the bar in four days, Oggie came up to him. "So."

"So?"

"Mara slides you little tasty bits of gossip, right? In exchange for something."

"Something like that."

"What could a boy like me do to get a deal like that?" Oggie asked.

"You have information?"

"I might. I might have other things, too." Oggie winked, but it was strangely dead-eyed. Most of the emotions on his face never affected the look of his eyes.

"What kind of information?"

"What's in it for me?" With each word, he walked his fingers across the bar towards Arden's arm.

"What do you want?"

"Money."

"Ah. Well. I have that. What do you have?"

Oggie slid up onto the bar to whisper into Arden's ear. "Your uncle asked me to do something."

Arden met his eyes.

There were too many people around to talk right now.

"Come to my room later," Arden murmured back.

Oggie slid back and tapped Arden's nose. "See you soon."

Arden watched him discretely as he whispered something to another man, someone Arden knew as a friend of Morris's. If Morris even had friends. Maybe accomplice would better describe him.

He waited up late for Oggie to stop by.

As soon as he stepped inside, the thrall surveyed the apartment. "Oh, how *nice*, Eminence. A little austere..." His eyes flicked over Arden.

Arden hadn't replaced most of the things he'd broken when he'd had that hissy fit. "What's the information?"

"Aren't you even going to invite me to sit?" Oggie asked. "A fellow might think you didn't like him very much!"

Arden gestured to the couch. "Drink?"

"Never touch the stuff. I see too many people on the wrong end of a bottle." Oggie settled into the couch as if he belonged there. He crossed his legs.

Arden sat next to him. "So?"

"Your uncle—"

"Just call him Morris."

"Morris has noticed that you, uh, are currently pet-free."

Arden grunted.

"And he may have noticed you being super extra nice to me and my sister. Big tips, always talking to us, knows our names..."

"The point, Oggie?"

"You don't go for foreplay, do you?" Oggie asked.

Arden, to his surprise, blushed. "Get on with it."

With a serious eye roll, Oggie said, "Morris asked me to seduce you so he could use me to feed you his ideas."

"I wouldn't get involved with him."

"Mmm, but I'm going to because he offered me money."

"You're not doing a very good job of seducing me."

"Morris is a bastard and I don't think I'd like whatever his vison for *Eden* is. But if *you* give *me* information to give *him*..." Oggie made a hopping gesture with one finger, then shrugged. "I think it's smart."

"It is."

"So?"

"So fine."

Oggie shimmied his shoulders and flashed a smile. "Good. You're going to have to start giving me nice things, then, if you want people to think you're keeping me."

Arden rolled his eyes.

"And I could give you nice things, too," the younger man purred. It really didn't reach his eyes that time.

"I don't think we need to do that."

"No?"

Arden sighed. "We can pretend we do. But I'm..."

"If you say you're heartbroken, I'll throw up."

"You're sort of rotten."

Oggie grinned. His green eyes sparkled. "Spare parts."

"Do you want to stay tonight?"

"That's sort of soon! No, I'll just tell people you had your way with me."

"I suppose."

"Would you like to provide some details?"

Arden didn't. "Tell them whatever you want."

"Well, did we go all the way?"

"Not on a first date!" Arden scolded. "I'm a nice boy, you know, from a good family!"

They laughed.

"Blew you behind the bar, got it," Oggie said. "See you soon, sugar." He let himself out with a delicate wave that was mostly wiggling his fingers.

Arden stayed on the couch watching his tablet.

He worked up a good sweat at practice the next day.

Xio waved to him from the sidelines.

He waved back.

Cole waggled his eyebrows at him when she looked away.

"Shut up," Arden grumbled.

Mace hip-checked him. "You two playing or scouting the sidelines?"

Arden gave him a push.

In the showers, the brothers teased Arden a little more, but in a kind way. Arden thought they might be happy for him.

After all, he'd felt ecstatic when Mace and Lourdes had started going out officially and he bubbled with delight whenever he saw them in public together. He adored them together. Sometimes, Lourdes came to their group lunches and Arden couldn't help teasing Mace extra then. Mace would blush and tell him to cut it out, but he would also grin.

He strolled through the shops after practice to get an idea of what kind of gifts he should get Oggie. Rhys had never wanted things like that, but Arden had wanted to give him things. Maybe this would be fun. He held off on buying anything until he knew Oggie better. Nothing worse than giving someone something they didn't want, that awkward sinking feeling when they opened it and their face changed.

He stayed in that night, trying to think of which lies would be most beneficial to send his uncle's way.

He couldn't think of much, mostly because he didn't know Morris's plan. He'd have to wait and see.

He wished his mother had coded more patience into his genes.

Then again, he didn't know if that was possible. He'd never investigated the process used to make designer children. He didn't like hearing about it, any more than most people liked hearing about their parents making them.

He stayed up late reading the most recent reports about Terra One. Bio scans and satellite images. People still lived down there, scavenging, huddled together in a few small groups. Barely clinging on to life.

That or some big primates had evolved and started tribes, which didn't evolutionarily make sense.

Had to be humans.

Fucking humans, grasping on to whatever scraps they could get.

He wondered if they would outlast the ruination of the planet. *Eden* had to survive several more centuries until Terra One could sustain large scale human life again. He tried to do some math in his head, wondering if *Eden* would make it. It could go either way: not enough people or too many.

Fewer people than anticipated had come aboard, even including the indentured. Bex had thought they would need methods of population control, but even five generations later, they had plenty of room to grow.

Two generations in a horrible sickness had seriously damaged the population. Many people who got it had died and some survivors had ended up sterile.

Maybe if that hadn't happened, *Eden* would be in better shape.

Or maybe it would be worse, overcrowded and famished.

No use in worrying about that now.

Sometimes Arden marveled at the sheer size of the station. Keeping the unused parts in working order ate up more time and resources than they could spare, but he worried what would happen if part of the station fell into disrepair.

"You look deep in thought."

Arden flinched and spun around.

"Sorry, sugar, didn't mean to scare you," Oggie said. "You didn't come by to say hi tonight, so I thought I'd come see you."

"Is it that kind of affair?"

"You're obsessed with me."

"Come sit."

"On the floor."

"You're a fucking thrall, Oggie."

"You're a terrible beast to me!" Oggie declared. He came to sit next to Arden anyway. "Do you want to spit in my mouth?"

"Do…do you want me to?"

"Mmmm, maybe when we get to know each other a little better. Dear Morris wishes me to gain your trust before he gives me any brainwashing to do."

"Huh."

"What should I tell him?"

"Tell him I'm too empty to trust anyone right now."

Oggie placed his hand on Arden's thigh. "The kind of empty that hurts?"

"Emptier."

Oggie nodded. "Do you want to talk about it? I can make you a drink."

The idea tempted him. "Maybe not."

"Hope for you yet, sugar."

"Did you plan on staying?"

"Just as long as it would take for you to pretend to fuck me."

Arden thought about it. "A few games of knuckles."

Oggie smirked. "You really don't go for foreplay!"

Arden clucked his tongue. "Shut up. Do you want to play or not?"

"By all means."

Oggie stayed for three games of knuckles, just so they could break the tie. As he left, he asked, "Should I come back tomorrow night?"

"I'm not insatiable."

"Night after?"

Arden nodded, then corrected, "No! I, uh. I have plans. After that."

"Alright, sugar, see you soon. You could drop by the bar and say hi."

Arden already knew he would.

Mara scowled at him when he stopped by and told him, "He won't shut up about fucking you."

"Only good things, I hope."

She rolled her eyes. "Oh, you're a *stud*, Your Eminence," she spat.

He felt kind of bad for lying to her, but a secret didn't stay kept when too many people knew it. "I'll take good care of him."

"Like you did the last one?"

"He left me."

She snorted. "Yeah, and you threw him out naked in the hallway."

He couldn't meet her eyes.

"Don't fuck him up any worse, he's already spare parts." Her eyes burned, pale and terrifying.

"I'm starting to think both of you are," he murmured. He took his drink and went to sit with Zira and Cathie.

"Holding up okay?" Cathie asked when she hugged him hello.

He let himself melt into her embrace momentarily. "All's well."

"And how's *Eden*?" Zira asked when he sat.

"Hmm?"

"You're making all these changes..."

"Oh. Things are going well."

"Any chance you'll let some of the shops open up?"

Arden tried not to grimace.

"I don't know, I think it's been sort of fun," Cathie said. "Makes me more creative with how I put outfits together."

Zira sighed. "I don't have an eye for that stuff like you do, Cath."

"I'll come over!" Cathie enthused.

Zira brightened a little. "I'll need to look good to find someone new."

"On the prowl already?" Cathie asked.

"I guess. It's lonely without Alexander..." Her usual sourness and boredom faded from her face, replaced with an open sadness.

Cathie took her hand. "I understand."

Arden understood, too, but took a drink instead of chiming in. He couldn't whine about being lonely if he wanted this affair with Oggie to seem real.

He steered the conversation toward their respective favorite family members. The two of them fell into a conversation about the stupid shit children got up to, fed from Zira's current experience and Cathie's recollections of her sister's childhood.

Arden couldn't think of anything to add.

He called it an early night and went home to read reports.

A few nights later, Oggie stopped by to tell Arden his uncle had suggested a few ways for Oggie to earn the Autarch's trust.

"He says you overuse formulas."

"I certainly used to," Arden agreed. "The tendency still shows its face from time to time."

"He thinks I can get you using Twelve again. That it will make you more suggestible."

"It likely would."

"What do you say, do you want a shot?"

"No. But you can tell him I took one." Arden stretched across the couch, close to Oggie but not touching. He looked up at him. "Do you think you'd stay the night?"

Oggie watched him, a glimmer of mistrust in his eyes. "Maybe if you really wore me out."

"What if we stayed up late playing board games and I made up the couch for you?"

Oggie raised an eyebrow. "Not exactly torrid."

"Tell people whatever you want. I'm asking if you want to—"

"Hang out? Are we friends, now, sugar?"

"I hope so."

Oggie smiled. He smoothed a piece of hair away from Arden's brow. He had thin fingers; he was thin all over, not scrawny and forced like Arden's body, but a natural, willowy elegance. He was a beautiful young man. Not handsome like the Baker brothers or Rhys, but artistically ideal. Arden's mother would have called it 'good breeding' if she hadn't known his father was a thrall.

"I'll stay. Do you have a deck of cards?"

"At least six. Check behind the bar."

They stayed up late playing cards, laughing and flirting harmlessly. Arden made up the couch for him and tried not to think about the time he'd done it for Rhys.

He fluffed the last pillow. "Your sister will be pissed."

"Mara's always pissed."

"Does she hate me?"

"Not more than she hates most people." Oggie started sliding out of his clothes. He glanced at Arden as if checking his level of interest.

Arden wanted to touch him. He wanted to know if he felt as soft as he looked. He didn't think he wanted anything more than that.

"What about you?" Arden asked.

"She might hate me, too."

"No, I meant, do you hate me?"

"No." Oggie smiled. "No, I think I might actually like you." He pronounced it softly and with a degree of reverence like he'd discovered something unexpectedly nice.

That made Arden smile, too. He said, "Sleep tight."

"Good night, sugar."

The next time Oggie stayed over, Arden had cleaned up the guest bedroom, gotten sheets for the bed and added a few homey touches like decorations and toiletries for the bathroom. He showed it to Oggie.

Oggie looked around, ran his hands over the soft bedspread, sniffed the soap, and glanced at the pajamas in the drawers. He held up one pair against himself to check the size. He looked at Arden.

"I figured you were about my size..." Arden shrugged. He nodded towards the bed. "It's more comfortable than the couch, at any rate."

"Couch is more comfortable than my bed."

"I bet."

Oggie sprawled on the bed. He watched Arden for a reaction. He'd stretched himself out deliciously.

"Are you *trying* to get me to fuck you?" Arden asked.

Oggie sat up. "It's what people end up wanting."

Arden sat beside him on the bed. He ran his fingers over the embroidery on the covers. "People like me," he murmured.

"All kinds of people. Not just peers. You get used to it. People chasing you whether you want them to or not. Cheapest way to have fun in the Quarters and I look like a lot of fun, don't I?"

"Have people hurt you, Oggie?" He had no business asking, but he felt like he could say anything to Oggie. They talked all the time and about everything.

"Not yet. A few close calls."

Arden licked his lips.

"I'm just waiting for you to make your move. Or, I don't know. Trying to get you to make one so I finally know where I stand with you."

"You could ask."

"Most people lie."

Arden nodded. "You're good-looking, Oggie, but you knew that already. And you're fun and sort of awful, and I like you."

"Weird come-on."

Arden scoffed at him. "Shut up, Oggie. I'm trying to tell you that I'd be blind if I didn't think you were attractive—"

"A couple of blind people have told me I smell incredibly nice."

"But I don't want to have sex with you."

"Not even a little?"

"Well. I mean. *Yes*, in a physical sense but not, uh. I just. Last time I had an affair, it kind of went different than I thought it would," Arden admitted. "I don't want that again."

"What did happen with you two? People have come up with about a thousand reasons you'd kick him out like that."

"He ended things."

"That's all? I heard he was sleeping with someone else."

"No, he just ended things."

Oggie lay back down. He placed his head on Arden's leg. "The balls that must have taken. Why?"

"I..." Arden swallowed. "Cause I asked him to come meet my uncle."

"Morris?"

"No, ew, no. My Uncle Winnie. He was, uh, my mama's brother. He's the only family I have."

Oggie made a sympathetic coo. "Poor thing. And he, what? Really didn't want to meet your family?"

"I don't know. I guess he just didn't love me."

Sounding surprised, Oggie asked, "Did you love him?"

Arden nodded. "I never got to tell him. He didn't want me to."

Oggie smiled up at him. He seemed to like that it hurt Arden. "The one thing you can't make people give you. Everything on all of *Eden* and you couldn't make him love you."

Arden's throat tightened.

Oggie sat up. He put his arms around Arden, his chin on Arden's shoulder. "What's it feel like?"

"It hurts."

"Where?"

"Inside. Like I can't breathe, like there's something in my throat. Like soap in my eyes. Like I'm going to throw up."

Oggie pulled in a slow breath. "Like you'll never go home again," he murmured so quietly Arden didn't think he'd meant to say it aloud. He pulled back and kissed Arden's cheek.

They gazed at each other.

"Do you want to play jumble?" Arden asked.

"I always win."

Arden grinned. "We'll see about that."

Oggie's eyes twinkled.

Oggie gave him a run for his money, the toughest dozen rounds of jumble he'd played since Mother had lost the capacity to play.

She hadn't held him on her lap or smothered him in kisses, but she'd taught him how to play jumble, and read to him every night, and taken him for long walks on the Solar Deck. She'd kept an eye on his handball career, weak as it had been, even though she'd have preferred that he played lacrosse.

He wondered if Oggie's mother had taught him to play jumble. It was popular in peer ladies' clubs.

He knew better than to ask.

They eventually called it quits, since they both had places to be in the morning. Oggie made himself at home in the guestroom.

It took a few weeks for things to become routine, but just like that, Oggie became part of his life. A few nights a week, he came over for board games and stayed the night. He relayed everything Morris wanted him to do and Arden sent back pieces of information.

Arden would peruse the shops at least once a week and pick out some trinket, a bit of jewelry or luxe beauty product. Nothing too expensive, their affair wasn't *that* serious yet, they'd decided.

He liked the way Oggie cooed over things. He'd always say something like, "You really do spoil me, sugar," and kiss Arden's cheek.

Arden made sure not to let it go any further than that. Kisses on the cheek, or hugs, or sometimes a bit of cuddling, but he knew if it went any further, it would hurt Oggie somehow. Someone had treated him badly, or maybe a lot of people had. He didn't want to be one of them.

When his friends asked him about it, he'd shrug and say, "It's something to do, isn't it? Better than moping."

They would murmur insincere agreements, which he thought was kind of judgmental of them.

A tour of Maintenance Six put Arden in a mood. Not angry or upset but puzzled. He wanted someone to talk with, someone who'd have a keener idea of what to do about the unused parts of *Eden*.

If they could do less work there, then they could take better care of the inhabited parts of the ship, dedicate more workers to farming, engineering, and maybe even reopen a few shops, just to placate the peers.

He knew Rhys would have an idea.

He'd overacted.

He always did. Spoiled.

It was a stupid idea, but he did it anyway.

He took the stairs to Quarter Two.

As he walked, he started to get indignant, thinking that Rhys still happily collected his Chamberlain's salary without putting in a day of work.

It was petty, not showing up for work just because *he'd* chosen to break things off with Arden.

People shot him funny looks as he walked through the Quarter, weaving around people in the common areas and dodging rambunctious children.

Everyone seemed to be outside their rooms, gathered together in groups, chatting or doing chores.

He checked the numbers on the apartments, growing closer to Rhys's registered address. As he moved deeper into the Quarter, he spied fewer children, almost none, and more people started to give him openly hostile stares.

Turning back might prove a wiser course.

He walked a little further, his stomach starting to prickle with fear.

No one would do anything to him.

A baby gurgled.

The sound instinctively drew his attention. His head swiveled towards it.

An umber-skinned woman about thirty years of age held the baby. Not newborn, but less than a year old.

What a tiny creature.

Arden couldn't remember the last time he'd seen a baby. Most peers left theirs with nannies until they were large enough to effectively dress up and show off. He lost his train of thought when the woman passed the baby to the man who came out of the apartment.

She ducked inside.

He saw the number on the door. The same as Rhys's.

And, of course, there was Rhys holding the baby.

Arden just stood there, watching. Staring at Rhys, holding that baby with a stupid smile on his face.

Fuck.

Did people smile like that at babies that weren't theirs?

Arden turned and pushed through the people behind him. He walked as fast as he could out of the Quarters and back to his room, nearly breaking into a run once or twice. He worried that if he didn't get home fast enough, he'd collapse. His legs felt heavy and floppy all at once.

He shoved into someone in a crowded part of the hall.

"Oh, Arden!" she said. "You okay?"

He had to focus to remember her name. One of the players on his handball team.

"Sick," he mumbled.

"Not coming to practice?"

How did these idiots have practice so often! "No."

"We'll miss you."

He grunted and kept walking.

Slower now. The initial panic had oozed out of him, leaving him numb and feeling sort of slimy.

He curled up on the couch with his tablet. He found Rhys's page. It detailed things like his birthday, blood type, medical conditions, and so on. He dug a little deeper to find his relatives; that page contained direct connections only, parents and children, a way to trace where his debt had come from and would go.

There were his parents, and here was a new entry, not there the last time Arden had looked through Rhys's information to find his birthday.

A baby girl.

Born before Rhys had broken up with him and, a bit of math revealed, conceived before they had started their affair.

He checked the child's other parent.

The other person whose debt he'd cleared, at Rhys's request.

The few pieces that existed settled into place.

The only child in the Quarters born without debt in the history of *Eden*.

The whole time, Rhys had been with someone else, a relationship serious enough to produce a child. Hardly anyone did that by accident anymore.

Arden felt sick at just how thoroughly Rhys had used him. The whole thing had been a way to clear his family's debt and get a cushy job.

He looked at the number in Rhys's bank account. He nearly wiped it.

But that baby.

Fuck.

He should at least fire Rhys from being Chamberlain, give the job to someone who would turn up to work.

In the end, he did nothing.

He tried but couldn't bring himself to type anything. He tossed his tablet on the coffee table with a groan.

He made himself a drink, then another.

Oggie came over for the night, listened sympathetically, and took over the drink-making. His creations turned out more palatable and less intoxicating.

Cole let himself in and found them sprawled on the couch. "Uh."

Arden pointed to the bar. "Oggie made a whole pitcher."

Cole stared at Oggie. "You, uh. You missed practice. Larista said you weren't feeling well. I thought I'd stop by."

"I'm fine."

Cole kept looking at Oggie.

Arden asked, "You know each other?"

"I've seen you at Crystal," Cole said.

"Raspberry vodka fizz," Oggie recited, "Twist of lemon, extra ice."

Cole barely smiled. "Ardi, are you—"

"Ardi!" Oggie giggled, then smothered his laugh with his hand.

"Are you okay?" Cole asked.

"I'm fine. Do you want to stay?"

"No, uh. You seem busy."

Arden didn't look busy at all. He had a drink in his hand and his legs tangled with Oggie's...Oh. That kind of busy. He blushed. "Stop by some other time."

"Maybe knock first," Oggie suggested mildly.

Cole ducked out of the room.

"Your friend doesn't like me."

"Well, we have sort of positioned you as a lascivious pet getting me re-hooked on formulas," Arden pointed out.

Oggie sighed and stretched. "Lascivious."

"Mmm."

He folded himself into Arden's arms. "Sugar, tell me I'm a little more than that."

Arden drained his drink, set the glass down, and pulled Oggie close. Having him close felt comfortable. "When we figure out what Morris is up to, you should meet my other friends properly."

Oggie hummed.

"I can't believe he's a dad."

"I'm sorry, sugar."

"No, it's just..." Arden sighed. "I thought, I don't know. I don't know what I thought anymore."

"You thought he liked you."

"I would have given him anything on *Eden*."

"Give it to me instead."

Arden ruffled Oggie's hair, wavy and blond, but not as pale as his sister's. Like gold, it had a richness Mara's lacked. Thick and slippery. "What do you want?"

"I want what I should have had. Can you bend time?"

"Sorry."

"I forgive you."

They stayed quiet.

Oggie refilled their drinks.

"I thought you didn't drink," Arden noted.

Oggie looked at the glass in his hand. "I don't."

Arden raised an eyebrow.

Oggie smiled but offered no further explanation.

They quieted, existing on the couch. Minutes ticked past in a peaceable companionship. No need to impress each other since they'd already declared their intentions without worrying about feelings.

Arden said again, "I don't know why I went down there."

"Because you loved him and you missed him," Oggie offered simply.

"I was mad he stopped coming to work."

"Maybe send him a message?"

"Do you think I should?"

"Do you hate him?"

"I didn't. Now I...I." Arden frowned. He snuggled back up to Oggie. "I hate that he tricked me. I hate that he pretended to like me. I told him, I really did, I told him not to do it if he didn't like me. I thought that mattered. I thought any of it meant something to him, that he thought I was a person, not just a means to an end."

Oggie hummed. He played with the hem of Arden's sleeve. "Nice shirt, what is this?”

“Uh. Silk blend.”

“Do you think it would fit me?”

Arden slipped it off and handed it over.

Oggie took the shirt but stared at Arden. He ran his fingers over Arden’s ribs, exploratory and firm.

Arden almost said something, but instead, he watched Oggie, lips slightly parted. Words rested on the tip of his tongue, and thoughts bumped off each other in his head, but he was confused more than anything else.

Oggie dug his fingers in.

Arden flinched. “Ow!”

“Sorry,” Oggie breathed. He reached out but stopped himself. He stood up. “You’re so skinny, but I bet a lot of your clothes would fit me.” He grabbed Arden’s hand and pulled him into the bedroom. He nudged Arden to sit on the bed. “Mara and I used to do fashion shows with Mam’s clothes. Mam got so mad!”

He started going through Arden’s closet, his hands trembling.

“Oggie.”

“No, I...Spare parts, remember? Let’s do something fun.” He grabbed a pair of pants.

Arden recognized that nervous energy and didn’t press matters.

They spent a few more hours drinking and playing dress-up.

Before they fell asleep, wrapped in Arden’s two nicest robes, Oggie whispered, “Sugar?”

“Hmm?”

“Are you mad at me?”

“No.”

Oggie nestled closer. “Buy me something nice so I know for sure.”

Arden giggled. “I’ll take you shopping tomorrow.”

“You spoil me, sugar.”

In the morning, Arden attended a Council meeting and spent most of it trying not to look at Rhys’s empty chair.

After that, he met up with Oggie on Goshawk. He offered his arm to him.

For a moment, Oggie looked nervous, but he took Arden’s arm. “So. What do I get?”

“What do you want?”

“I’ll know when I see it.”

Arm in arm, they walked through the shops.

They didn’t look like a couple, not with Oggie in the shabby, bland clothes of a thrall. Arden took him to a clothing shop first.

People watched Oggie as he moved around the store, their eyes narrowed.

Arden stayed close and made a show of doting on him.

If they were going to sell this, they'd have to really sell it.

The more sway Morris thought Oggie had over Arden, the easier it would be to find out Morris's plan, catch him conspiring, and make him politically irrelevant.

Oggie played the role well.

Arden bought him several new outfits in that shop alone.

A bad look for an Autarch that preached restraint.

But, to be fair, Oggie didn't have any nice clothes.

New shoes, new outfits, and even new underwear, during the selection of which he made a show of blushing coyly.

He looked so happy, grinning and cooing over the materials. He touched just about everything in every shop they entered.

Arden liked making him smile. "You should go back and change."

"Back where?"

"Home?" Arden suggested.

"Then what?"

"I'll take you to dinner."

"Oh, sugar," Oggie sighed and looked miserable.

"What's wrong?"

"I..." He licked his lips. "Oh, I'd hate that, I really would." His green eyes shone.

Arden, without thinking, touched his cheek. "Then never mind."

"Really?"

"Of course."

They carried Oggie's bags back, heading towards the Quarters.

Oggie hesitated at the lift. "Maybe..."

"Hmm?"

"I don't know. Maybe I should keep them with you." He turned a ring around and around his finger, a twisted silver band on his forefinger. "People do notice the things you get me." He'd never looked so unsure.

"Isn't that the point?"

He blinked quickly. "I know."

"Oggie..." Arden trailed off. He'd meant to tell Oggie he was being silly, but this wasn't silly. He looked genuinely distressed at something.

Oggie looked at him.

"Let's put everything in your room, you're right." Arden put a hand on Oggie's arm and led him back toward Arden's rooms.

They hung things in the closet or folded them neatly into drawers.

"Do people bother you about things? About us?" Arden asked.

"Some people are so ugly..."

Mara had given Rhys absolutely scathing looks. She made no secret of how much she disliked Arden sleeping with her brother. He wondered what she said when she wasn't holding back. She must have been awful behind closed doors.

Arden held out a hand. "Come sit with me."

Oggie sat beside him on the guest bed. He burrowed up against Arden's side, his head on his shoulder. "Sugar, I'm in such a mood. I'm not any fun like this. I'm sorry."

"Do you want to stay here?"

"It wouldn't be any fun for you."

"I mean stay here permanently."

Oggie straightened up. He stared at Arden. "You don't mean that."

"I do. I like when you're here."

"You wouldn't like me after a while. I get to be too much. Best in small doses, and better yet, bent over or on my back or something like that..."

"Move in, Oggie. Morris will think you've got your hooks in. And I *like* having you around. I like you."

"I shouldn't."

Arden hugged him. "Are you going to make your Autarch beg?"

"I keep terrible hours and I'm a beast in the mornings—"

"I know that already."

He pulled out of Arden's embrace. "And I'm spare parts, Arden. I'm no good to have around like that."

This side of Oggie had never shown its face before. He always acted so carefree, sultry and haughty, like the spoiled peer he'd almost been. Now, he sounded sad and sort of ashamed.

Arden took his hands. "What's the worst that could happen?"

"We wouldn't be friends anymore."

That made Arden's chest tighten. He didn't know how Oggie had become so important so fast, but here they were. "How long do you think it would take for me to get sick of you?"

"A month."

"Then let's try it for a month. Revisit things then. Hmm? And don't cry, you look like you're going to cry."

"I'm not!" he protested but rubbed his eyes anyway.

"You're too—"

"Don't tell me I'm too pretty to cry," Oggie warned tremulously.

"I wasn't going to. I was going to say you're too worked up. We should have a drink."

"I don't drink." Oggie dabbed the corners of his eyes with a sleeve. He walked out of the room and Arden could hear him mixing something at the bar.

They drank enough to get tipsy, but not drunk. They built a blanket and pillow nest on the floor in front of the window and Oggie demanded, "Why do you like looking down there so much?"

"Don't you wonder where we came from?"

"No."

"You don't think about what Terra One was like at all?"

"I didn't even know it was *called* Terra One until I was twenty-three."

"Oh, so, like...right now?"

"Shut up, you wretch. I'm *almost twenty-six.*"

"You're a baby."

"I'm so old, sugar! I'm going to get wrinkled and saggy and lose my hair and then I won't be any good to anyone."

Arden rolled over next to him. "You'll always be beautiful."

Oggie snorted.

"No, not...I mean. I can't imagine you ever acting like you're anything less than gorgeous, which means you always will be."

"Are you trying to tell me confidence is key?" Oggie scoffed. "It's not. It's all bone structure."

Arden rolled his eyes. "Someday when we're old, you're going to realize how stupid that is."

"Not if we both live to be two hundred."

"Come meet my Uncle Winnie. He's old and the cutest little thing I've ever seen." As soon as he said the words, he realized his mistake.

"Will he hate me as much as your friends do?"

"Cole doesn't hate you."

"You don't see the looks they give me when they're at Crystal! Like I'm serving them poison."

"Winnie's never mean to anyone."

Oggie sighed. He twisted and snuggled into the blankets. "I hope you're not lying to me, sugar. I might have to go run away and get someone pregnant."

"Oggie!"

Oggie grinned.

"You are, you're *awful.*"

He didn't have the good grace to look reticent. He looked pleased.

Arden let out a long, heavy sigh. "Do you think he's happy?"

"No."

"You're just saying that."

"No, I think he's miserable. I think he's a wretch. I think that's the only way you let someone with no one else fall in love with you when you have a woman and a baby at home," Oggie declared.

It didn't make Arden feel better.

He didn't like to think of himself as *that* alone.

He had friends. He had Uncle Winslow.

But having Rhys, that had felt special. It had felt warm and complete, fulfilled, in a way that no friend or lover had done before.

He had been content.

Comfortable.

"Oggie?"

"Hmm?" The other man had nodded off. He pushed himself up.

"We're really friends, right?"

"Of course we are sugar," he mumbled, then settled back into the pillows.

Arden watched him sleep. His thoughts churned too much for him to get much rest.

In the morning, Oggie kindly pointed out, "You've got the worst bags under your eyes."

Arden frowned.

Oggie smoothed one thumb under Arden's eye. He did it slowly, deliberately.

He was going to shove his thumb into his eye, Arden knew. He imagined it clearly, that perfectly filed and smoothed nail jammed straight into Arden's eyeball.

But it never came.

Oggie tucked a piece of hair behind Arden's ear. "I'm going to take a bath, shug. After that, I need to go get the rest of my things. I'm sorry I got like that. I have these awful moods...Spare parts. You know."

Arden patted his leg. "I'm going back to sleep."

Through his doze, he vaguely heard Oggie leave. By the time Arden had roused himself and washed, he hadn't come back.

When Arden came back from what he needed to do that day, Oggie wasn't there, but more of his things were in the guestroom.

He glanced over the small collection of items. A bag, a small jewelry box, a suitcase. Nothing much.

He didn't go through the bags, but he did peek inside the jewelry box. Some of the pieces he recognized, either because he'd bought them or seen them on Oggie. Others needed polishing and some looked too large or too small for Oggie. A heavy watch, a bracelet made for a child, a gaudy brooch an old woman would have worn.

He closed the box.

He spent the night in bed.

In the middle of the night or the very early morning, the door opened.

It frightened Arden awake, had his heart thudding and his eyes open wide, staring into the blackness of his room.

"Og?" he called.

A light came on. "Sugar, are you awake in there?"

"Just making sure."

Silhouetted in his bedroom door appeared Oggie. "Did I wake you?"

"Uh. Just..."

"I'm sorry, sugar. I told you I keep bad hours."

"No, I'll get used to it. Goodnight, Oggie."

"Good morning, shug."

Arden drifted back to sleep and woke at a more reasonable time on his own. He could hear Oggie quietly snoring from the guestroom.

No.

Not the guestroom. *His* room.

Oggie came home at a more reasonable hour that night and they played a few board games.

"You should come to practice tomorrow."

"If you try to make me play, I'll absolutely screech."

"No, just to watch."

Oggie raised an eyebrow.

"Don't boyfriends usually do things like that? Come cheer people on at practice."

"I'm not your boyfriend, I'm your pet. It's different."

Arden tossed the dice and counted his total, then rerolled. After a few more rounds, he asked, "Does it have to be different, though? I mean, what's it matter?"

"Boyfriends you can marry. Pets you trade in for a new model every few years."

"Is there something in between that?"

"Yes, but there isn't a word for it, and you get sick of those too, it's just harder to get rid of them. It's whatever my father was to my mother."

Arden made a sympathetic face. He didn't know what to say to that. "Do you think...?" He swallowed the rest of the question when Oggie looked up at him. "Never mind."

Oggie rolled the dice. He sipped his drink. He didn't reroll despite having a shitty hand. He passed the dice back to Arden.

"Will you come, though?"

"I don't belong—"

"I don't care where you belong," Arden snapped. He hadn't meant to, but he was so sick of being told things like that. "I'm the fucking Autarch and I invited you, which means you belong there."

Oggie stared at him, eyes the size of saucers. "I'm sorry. I'll go."

Arden's stomach twisted. He scooted around to the other side of the coffee table and drew Oggie into his arms.

The younger man didn't resist, but he stayed stiff in Arden's embrace.

"I didn't mean to yell at you."

"You didn't," Oggie whispered. He cleared his throat. "You should hear what people say to me if I mess up their order. That's really being shouted at."

Arden hugged him closer. "I'm sorry."

Oggie leaned further into Arden's arms, but it was entirely forced. A practiced relaxation.

How much did Oggie do for show? Carefully practiced, meant to give the right impression, but not an honest one.

"I'm sorry," Arden said again. He meant it, for what he'd done, for what everyone else had done. He was sorry for all the bad, cruel, and ugly things in the world.

"It's alright, sugar."

"I just...I want you to be there. I want you to be my friend. Really my friend."

"I know."

They never finished their game. They went to bed. The next morning, they sat down to breakfast like nothing happened.

Oggie came to watch practice, even though Arden tried to walk back his insistence that he come. He did a good job pretending to be fascinated with Arden. Cheering him vapidly from the sidelines, waving and smiling. He looked the part, dressed up nice, sitting with Cathie, Zira, and a few of their friends.

Arden had asked them to keep an eye on him, which they did, but it wasn't with particularly kind expressions.

They would smile at him when he spoke to them, then glare and whisper when he had his back turned.

Arden saw it all.

Oggie couldn't make lunch afterward, he had work.

As Arden, Zira, and Cathie walked together, he said, "Oggie's nice, isn't he?"

"He's very good-looking," Zira said.

"Mmm. But he's nice, too."

Neither of them responded.

"How've you been, Arden?" Cathie asked after a while.

"Good."

The women exchanged glances.

"What?"

"Nothing," Cathie assured.

After a few long, uncomfortable moments, Zira said, "I think he used to see Richter Paulsen."

"Who?"

"Your pet."

Cathie said, "And Emmie Ulster."

"Quite a few others," Zira added.

"Never moved in with any of them, though," Cathie noted.

Arden tried to smile at her. "He's good company."

"Hmmm. Really? Did, he, uh...Did you pay off his debt, too?" she asked carefully.

"He. I."

Arden didn't know how to answer. He didn't know what was worse. Sleeping with someone he owned or trading freedom for sexual favors.

He never came up with an answer, just waited a while and changed the topic.

When they parted ways, Cathie firmly, kindly insisted, "Take care of yourself."

Not too many days later, Oggie came home red-eyed and scrunch-faced, went into his room, and cried into a pillow.

Arden could still hear it through the door, but Oggie wouldn't answer or unlock the door when he asked what was wrong.

Oggie had come home crying again. He'd always say something like, "Just some rough customers!" and go into his room.

He'd be back to his usual self in the morning, teasing Arden, spoiled and luxurious.

Arden knocked on the door and said, "Og, let me in."

"No, sugar, just...! I'm *fine*."

Arden sat outside the door and listened to him sniffle. It made him sick.

He didn't know what, exactly, was wrong, but he knew it had to do with him. He didn't know how he knew, but he felt it in his gut that pretending to be Arden's pet took a toll on him. Maybe the thralls picked on him, or maybe the peers did, or maybe having to spend time with Arden took too much out of him.

He toyed around on his tablet, then put on his shoes and headed out.

Down to Quarter Two.

This time he didn't care about the awful looks sent his way as he went deeper in.

He rapped on Rhys's door. Half a dozen people listed this place as home, common enough in the Quarters.

A man he didn't know answered it. His smile faded when he saw Arden. He'd been expecting someone else.

"Get Rhys."

The man stared, then disappeared back inside.

Half-dressed and sleep-rumbled, Rhys emerged. His face changed from confused to fearful when he saw Arden.

"Can we talk somewhere?"

Rhys licked his lips. He nodded. "Uh, it's..." He glanced behind him. "It'll be a little more private this way."

Arden followed him to a seemingly abandoned part of the Quarter, a common room with the barest furnishings. He took a seat on the rickety chair Rhys indicated.

"How can I serve, Your Eminence?"

"Oh, shut the fuck up," Arden snapped.

Rhys physically flinched. Subtly, but Arden saw it.

He sighed. Huffed, really. "Sit down."

Rhys sat. He kept his eyes down.

"We..." Arden struggled to think of the right way to say this. "We have unfinished business."

Rhys nodded without looking up.

"I, uh. We'd talked about you setting up a few contacts, people who'd keep an eye on my uncle."

"Yes, Your Eminence."

"But you know lots of people, right? Like. You could get me information about anything, anyone, I wanted."

"Yes, Your—"

"Call me that again and I swear I'll fucking screech," Arden said.

Rhys looked up briefly, his brow knit. "I..."

Arden had meant only to find out what he needed to know. He didn't want to talk about anything else. He really didn't want to see Rhys.

Except that he did.

He had really, genuinely liked him, enjoyed his company. He missed him, didn't want to miss him, resented him, and felt guilty all at once.

Enough to make a person sick.

Or, at least enough to make him drink.

He sighed.

Rhys had taken a seat far away from him, significantly out of arm's reach, how he would have before they'd started their affair.

Arden pulled his feet up onto the chair and rested his chin on his knees. "How are you?"

"I."

"I know already. You don't have to keep pretending."

"Know?"

"Did you have some kind of accident? Hit your head again? I know about her."

"Her...Oh!" Rhys let out a breath, half-chuckled, then shook his head.

"What's her name?"

"Gertrude."

Arden couldn't help himself when he said, "What a hideous fucking name for a baby."

Rhys opened and closed his mouth. "The baby's name is Darcy."

"That's better. Gertrude is your...partner?"

Rhys shrugged. "Gertie's...It's sort of complicated with Gertie."

"Right."

"We were sort of seeing each other. She was sort of seeing other people, too. We broke it off a while ago. Better as friends, you know. But..." Rhys shrugged. "She found out she was pregnant. So, we're, uh. Co-parenting. As friends."

"Not partners?"

Rhys shrugged. "She's seeing a few people. I'm...not."

Arden's throat tightened. "And you just, you never wanted to mention any of it? Months and months together and you never wanted to say a fucking thing?"

"I didn't know how you'd take it."

"Well, I would have gotten you a fucking present, for one." Arden crossed his arms.

Rhys undid and redid his hair.

"I didn't come here to talk about any of this. I just." He pulled in a breath, then sighed.

"Arden, I'm—"

"If you say you're sorry—"

"I am!" Rhys insisted. "I didn't ever mean for it to get that far."

"No, you just wanted to get rid of your debt and that woman...Gertie. Her debt. And be done."

"No."

"Well, it's what you did!"

"I didn't think it would get that far. I didn't think you'd do those things. I thought I'd ask for too much, or you'd get bored, and you'd call it off. But you kept giving me things. You kept wanting me around."

Arden shouldn't have come. There had to be someone else who could help.

"And I..."

Arden started berating himself for having hope. It struggled inside him and he kept crushing it. He dreaded what Rhys would say next because no matter what, it would hurt. It would feel awful, twisting and shredding him up inside. He shouldn't have come here.

"I really did...I really *do* like you. I really am sorry I hurt you. Please don't...Please don't cry."

Arden blinked but couldn't keep the tears back. "I just needed help with Oggie."

"Oggie," Rhys repeated.

"He's my—"

"I know who he is."

Arden tried to say something, but he couldn't. His throat hurt too much, his mouth slimy and swollen. He sniffled, sucking snot back in with the most hideous sound. He scrubbed his face with his shirt. "Stop looking at me."

"I'm worried about you."

"Fuck off," Arden gurgled.

Rhys came over closer to him. He hovered.

Arden wiped his face again, like wiping his face would make him stop crying. "Just stop standing there!"

Rhys stepped back.

Arden had never wanted to hit someone so badly and not done it. He curled tighter around himself.

Fuck.

Rhys sat down beside Arden's chair. He put his hand on Arden's shin. "I didn't want to hurt you."

Arden took his hand. "You stopped coming to work."

"You said you never wanted to see me again."

"I."

"And you threw a lot of things at me."

"I didn't hit you," he reminded childishly.

"Oh, thanks."

"I could have."

"You're something else, you know that."

"I have good aim."

Rhys squeezed his hand.

"Come back to work. I need help."

"Okay."

Arden oozed out of his chair. He wrapped his arms around Rhys and squeezed, more because he needed it than he thought the gesture would be welcome.

Rhys patted his back.

Arden gave himself a few moments, pulled back, and wiped his face one last time. "I need help with Oggie."

Rhys nodded. "The formulas will be hard to kick, but—"

"What? No. He's upset about something. I think people are giving him a hard time, but he won't talk to me about it."

"You came down here to ask me for relationship advice?"

"I...Yes. Well. I want to know what people are saying to him."

"He's...Listen. He's involved in shady stuff if what people say is true," Rhys said.

Arden waved a hand. Oggie hadn't shied away from sharing his less than savory exploits with Arden.

"And you know he's, uh...he sort of does this professionally, right?

Sleeping with peers."

"We're not even sleeping together. It's, uh. It's this whole thing, I'll fill you in some other time. Just talk to whoever it is you know in this seedy underbelly and find out what I need to know."

Rhys nodded.

Arden sucked in a breath. "What a fucking mess."

"How have you been, though?"

"I. Uh. I've been okay. You?"

Rhys smiled. "I've been spending all day with Darcy. I've been great. She can roll over and she's babbling."

"Adorable."

They sat in stilted silence.

Arden said, "I, uh. I'll see you tomorrow, right?"

"Yes."

"Okay."

They stood, looked at each other, and fidgeted. With a few starts and stops, they headed back towards Rhys's apartment.

They parted ways without saying anything else.

Oggie had stopped crying by the time Arden got home. "That you, sugar?" he called and appeared in the doorway of his bedroom looking a hair less exquisite than usual.

"You feeling better?"

"Oh, I...Don't you worry about me, shug, I just." He waved a hand. "You want a drink?"

"I was going to head to bed."

Oggie nodded.

"Do you..."

"No, no, I was getting ready for bed, too. Goodnight."

"Night, Oggie."

In the morning, Rhys came by while Oggie still slept. He lingered in the door when Arden answered, his eyes taking in the changes to the rooms.

Since Oggie had moved in, Arden had gotten a few new things—most to replace the things he'd broken.

Oggie's had picked most of them out and his taste ran differently than Arden's. The rooms didn't exactly look mismatched, but the furniture and decorations Oggie had selected stood out as accent pieces.

Arden liked it.

"Quick turnaround," Arden said, just so he had something to say.

"No, I uh...I thought you wanted me to come back to work."

"Oh. That."

"I thought you'd be asleep."

"I've had to wake myself up and get to meetings on my own for a while now."

Rhys looked at the floor.

Arden smiled. "Come in. There's stuff to go over anyway. New reports and everything. Unless you've been keeping current?"

"A little bit."

Arden raised an eyebrow.

"I've been home with Darcy."

"One baby and suddenly our revolutionary is complacent."

"I..." Rhys's face flushed, more than what gentle teasing should have provoked.

"What?"

Rhys sighed.

Arden gestured to the table.

They sat.

"Go on," Arden insisted.

"So. The thing is..." Rhys looked at the curio on the table, a plant leaf in a piece of amber. "I never told you a lot of things. About me. About how, uh, I swore I'd never have kids, never feed into this capitalist machine that eats us alive."

Arden kept quiet but couldn't help but widen his eyes.

"This group of us, we've known each other for years, we all decided we'd put our foot down, take direct action. It ended up being mostly, uh, complaining and stealing things like medical supplies, extra rations, or things from rooms we cleaned. Stupid shit. But it felt, well, it felt better than nothing."

Arden nodded. "Sure."

"Then I got in with you, started feeding you ideas, started making actual changes, which was great. People really thought I was getting stuff done. People got a little funny about me sleeping with you. I felt funny about it, too, especially when I basically did it to get out of debt. But I knew...you know, I couldn't bring a kid into the world and saddle her with debt she'd never repay. Watch her work herself to death."

"I already figured out that you had ulterior motives, Rhys, but thanks for the details."

"I'm just, I just want you to know that...that however it started, however I used to feel about you, it's honestly different now. I just, I would look at Darcy and think about how we all get born without asking to and do the best with what we've got. With what we're given. So I." Rhys sighed. "I meant it when I said I was proud of you. And I ended things because it was wrong for me to use you like that. You should have someone who...who cares for you the same way you care for them. We don't have to talk about it ever again, but I wanted you to know."

Arden shrugged. "Alright."

"That's it?"

"What else should I do? Tell you I loved you, that I might still love you, that you made me feel happy? Beg you for another chance?"

Rhys shifted. "No."

"I am sorry I threw you out like that. It was shitty of me."

"It was," Rhys agreed without venom.

Arden licked his lips. "Maybe one of the shittier things I've done."

Rhys almost smiled.

"So can we move on? I can't pretend it never happened, but I still need you. *Eden* still needs work. Alright?"

"Alright."

Arden got up and searched for his tablet, to have something else to do, to give himself time to settle.

He wanted to throw up.

He nearly called for a shot.

He hadn't done that in a while. He hadn't need to do that in a while. His body had made its own numbness, but this might be too much. The jagged edges of the world had started poking at him again.

Maybe they'd go away.

He returned to the table with his tablet, pulled up the most relevant reports, and started showing them to Rhys.

It kept him focused.

After an hour, Oggie came out of his room and called, "Sugar, I...Oh!" He spied Rhys and pulled his robe closed.

He liked to walk around half-dressed, watching Arden for a reaction.

Sometimes Arden thought about giving it to him, but he didn't know what kind of test this was. Years in a locker room made him good at ignoring the nudity of others.

He thought it kind of frustrated Oggie.

"Didn't know we had a guest, sugar," Oggie scolded.

Arden watched the two of them watch each other. He wouldn't have wanted to walk between them with the way they were trying to kill each other with their eyes. "Just work."

Oggie came over and leaned in.

Arden prepared himself for a kiss on the cheek. He got one on the mouth, warm and possessive. He nearly pulled back. He placed a hand on Oggie's chest and murmured into his neck, "He knows we aren't sleeping together."

"Not very good at keeping secrets," Oggie whispered back.

"Sorry."

Oggie tweaked his nose. "Could have warned me a little sooner. You want a drink?"

"Maybe breakfast," Arden suggested.

Oggie ordered breakfast and put a splash of vodka into his juice. He offered it to Arden.

"No, thanks."

He didn't offer any to Rhys. All the while he ate, he kept a judgmental eye on Rhys.

When he went to take a shower, Rhys mentioned, "So he really doesn't like me."

"You weren't exactly making nice either."

Rhys took a bite of fruit salad instead of saying anything.

"Don't!" Arden warned. "Say it."

"I still have permission to speak freely?"

Arden rolled his eyes. "I guess."

"He's a bad influence. All the formulas..."

"Just as fake as us sleeping together."

"That kiss didn't look fake. You got carried into the Public Chamber the other day, was that fake, too?"

"Yes."

"Arden."

"It was! My uncle's up to something, we're trying to figure out what it is. Morris has to believe he's got, uh, influence over me through Oggie. Otherwise, he'll try something else."

"I don't like it," Rhys sulked.

Arden blew a raspberry.

"Be careful."

Arden pushed the tablet back toward him. "Are you going to be ready for Council tomorrow?"

"Mhm."

"You plan on coming to check on Engineering Three with me?"

"Unless you're telling me not to."

"Might as well jump right back into it." Arden poked his head into Oggie's room. "I'm heading out."

"What for?" Oggie called from the bathroom.

"Work, Og."

"Come in here for a second."

Arden went into the bathroom. "What?"

Oggie pulled back the shower curtain half-way. "I'm sorry I made a fool of myself like that. I just...you know, coming out of the guestroom felt a little suspicious if we're sleeping together."

"Oh, I'd make you sleep in your own room anyway if we were, I've heard you snoring."

"You awful beast!"

Arden smiled at him.

Oggie reached out a hand.

Arden took it and gave a reassuring squeeze. "See you for dinner."

"Bye, sugar."

"And hey."

"Hmm?"

"Play nice with Rhys."

"Absolutely no promises on that." Oggie closed the shower curtain.

Arden smiled about that all the way to Engineering.

It took a few days to readjust to having Rhys by his side. The Council seemed actively relieved to see him at meetings again, with a few exceptions.

Cole smiled at him and asked him how he'd been, which Arden resented a little. Rhys had, after all, broken his heart.

It was nice, though, to have someone to talk to again, someone who understood *Eden* as well, or better, than he did.

By the end of the week, Rhys reported that a few of Oggie's coworkers had taken to harassing him. Over what, Rhys didn't say, but Arden had them reassigned and went down to Crystal to personally chew out the supervisor for letting it go unaddressed.

Mara watched him chew out the supervisor, her face cold and unreadable. When it was over, she said, "Must be nice."

"What?"

"Og has it made these days. New clothes, fancy apartment, someone to watch his back, and all he needs to do is blow you. Must be nice to have friends in high places." She said it like an accusation.

Arden had to remind himself not to bristle. "Maybe you'd know if you weren't so fucking mean all the time, Mara."

She glared.

"Is someone giving you trouble?"

"No one has the balls."

He believed that.

As if she resented having to ask, she inquired, "How is Oggie?"

"You see him at work, don't you?" He knew they didn't always work the same shifts, but Oggie mentioned having seen his sister pretty frequently. Once or twice a week, he had a story about something the two of them had gotten up to at work.

She shrugged. "Yeah, but he's a liar. He says he's fine."

Arden debated what he should share. "Come over and see him."

"Has he been drinking?"

"Uh. Yes."

"Good."

"Sorry?"

"If he's not drinking, he'll get up to something worse," she said.

"Come over for dinner."

"I'm working."

"We're up late."

She scowled. "Whatever. I'll think about it."

Oggie came home that night, stood in front of the couch, and demanded, "What did you do?"

"Hmm?" Arden glanced up.

"Tylia is *pissed* at me."

He set down his tablet. "Is she giving you a hard time?"

"No, she was super extra nice, which is absolutely terrifying. What did you do?" Oggie asked.

"I. Did I overstep? You wouldn't tell me what was wrong."

Oggie crossed his arms.

Arden took his hand. "And you were coming home so upset!"

"Can't believe you got involved," he mumbled.

"I..." Fuck, he wanted to cry or throw up. He'd go back to a shot of Twelve every morning if *these* were the feelings he'd been staving off.

"I'm not mad, sugar!" Oggie added quickly. He sat and put his arms around Arden. "Just surprised."

"Why?"

"I'm not the sort that gets looked out for."

Arden squeezed him. "Well, that's what friends do."

"Careful, sugar, I might fall in love," he teased.

Arden giggled.

"What do you want to drink?" He pulled out of Arden's arms and headed towards the bar.

"You're making me fat, you know."

Oggie laughed. "What!"

"A lot of extra calories in those drinks."

"Sugar, you look *perfect*. I can still count all your ribs and everything."

Arden snorted. He approached the bar. "Sure, ribs. The sexiest thing since lacey undies."

"Oh, no lacey stuff for me."

"No?"

"Straps," Oggie declared with a shimmy of his shoulders. "Buckles." He bit his lower lip.

"Oggie," Arden half-scolded.

He grinned. "All tied up so I can give those ribs a good count. Or how about the notches in your spine..."

Arden didn't know if he was serious or not. Pointing out how unbecomingly thin he'd made himself didn't seem like flirting but Oggie looked strangely hungry when he'd said it. He didn't know if he wanted Oggie to mean it.

Oggie didn't look like he knew either. He stared at Arden for a moment, then started making a pitcher of drinks in a hurry. "Mara said she'd be gracing us with her bright and cheery company tonight. Your idea?"

"She's your sister."

"Hmm. I'm really going to have to fake it. She knows what it looks like when I'm sleeping with someone."

"Pointers?" Arden asked.

"Yeah, treat me like shit and talk to me like I'm an idiot."

"Yikes."

"Yikes," Oggie agreed. He took a sip of his drink. He handed Arden a glass. "A little strong, but you'll need it."

"Mara isn't that bad."

"No, but I'm going to tell you my sexual history, so you won't act surprised when she brings things up to embarrass me."

"You don't have to do that."

"I'd rather have you hear it from me in any case."

Arden tried his drink and made a face.

"I knew you wouldn't like it..." Oggie sighed.

"No, just, it's sour! I wasn't expecting it. It's nice." He took another sip to prove his point.

They made themselves comfortable on the couch and for two hours, told stories back and forth about what they'd done, where they'd done it, and occasionally with whom. Oggie had started listing things off clinically and Arden had felt the need to chime in, to tell the funniest sex story he had.

He'd wanted to make him laugh, not hear him rattle off exes and exploits.

His retelling of Kenji Saito throwing up on his dick had lightened the mood and in exchange, Oggie had offered the story of how he'd literally run away the first time he'd seen someone else naked.

"It was just...*there*, ugh, just all red and angry-looking. Throbbing." Oggie shuddered. "I didn't even try with anyone for a whole *year* after that."

By the time Mara arrived, they were drunk, and anything she said to get a rise out of either of them provoked a giggle fit.

Eventually, they got her drunk, too, and she lightened up. She wasn't nice, but she wasn't so aggressive.

Oggie stayed glued to Arden's side the whole time. Complimenting him, playing with his hair, kissing his fingers and throat and wrist. He'd squeeze Arden's thigh and make insinuations about what they'd do later.

Mara let it be known that she found the display disgusting.

When she left, Oggie stayed glued to Arden but got less handsy.

Arden got him a glass of water and put him to bed.

"Sugar?" Oggie held on to his hand but spoke into his pillow.

"Hmm."

"You want to stay?"

"I don't know, tell me again about the time you shit all over your boyfriend's bed. That was attractive."

"I was fifteen! How good were you at fucking when you were fifteen?" Oggie demanded petulantly. "*He* was old enough to know better, I don't even feel bad. He couldn't have given a fellow a heads up?"

Arden sniggered. "Get some sleep, Og."

"Maybe I'll come puke on your dick later."

Arden gave him a playful smack. "Good night."

He couldn't go to bed. He lingered in Oggie's doorway, watching him twist and burrow until he got comfortable. When Oggie hadn't moved for a few minutes, when Arden could hear his quiet, steady breaths turn into gentle snores, he left and curled up in his own bed.

He dreamed of stupid things, petty worries leftover from his childhood and dredged up by too much drinking. He stood alone on Terra's dust, surrounded by hungry cannibals. He didn't know if Terra had cannibals, but people had made movies about it and he'd always been overly influenced by movies. He fought and ran, clawed his way out of people's grasps, twisted in their arms, and ran some more.

This dream had worried Mama. She'd brought him to talk to a therapist about it, who'd simply called Arden an 'anxious, sensitive child' and prescribed a series of mindfulness exercises.

The next night, when he couldn't shake the dreams, he got up and woke Oggie, and made him watch a light-hearted movie with him.

Oggie fell asleep during the movie, bunched up on the couch with his head on Arden's thigh, but the weight reassured Arden as surely as the fluffy, serene images on his tablet.

"Sugar, you've got to breathe," Oggie scolded.

"I am breathing," Arden lied through gritted teeth.

Oggie said, "I can *feel* you not breathing."

"It hurts."

Oggie eased up. "Hurts like we should stop or hurts like it's mild discomfort and you're a big baby?"

"Like I'm a baby," Arden admitted.

"Last one. Roll over."

Arden rolled onto his stomach and Oggie twisted him into another stretch he promised would help with Arden's back.

"I worked for three years doing PT in the med center on deck seven," he'd told Arden. Then he'd taken it upon himself to torture Arden with a series of stretches.

When Oggie finally released Arden, he had to admit his back did feel better. Much better. He'd slept funny, or done something during practice, he didn't know, but the stretches had worked. He'd heard it got easier to do these sorts of things as he got older and thirty-six wasn't as far off as it had been.

He lay on the floor, his arms folded beneath his chin. "Why don't you work in PT anymore?"

"Mmm. I might have gotten fired."

"For what?"

Oggie declined to answer.

"For what, Og? I can just look it up."

"I might have been stealing things, but you know, they never proved it." Arden snorted.

Oggie kissed the back of his head. "You're tense all over, sugar. I can fix that, too." He smoothed his hands down Arden's back, his fingertips warm through the thin fabric of Arden's undershirt.

Arden nearly said yes.

Oggie dug a knuckle into Arden's back so hard that Arden whimpered, high and breathy.

It felt terrible and blissful all at once.

Oggie did it again.

Arden rolled away. His skin felt empty where Oggie had touched him, cold where it should have been warm, and raw and yearning all at once. He wanted that pressure back. He shouldn't have.

Oggie watched him, green eyes trained on Arden, lips slightly parted.

"Ow," Arden said pointedly past the lump in his throat.

"Didn't you like it just a little bit?" Oggie asked.

"It hurt."

The bright, hungry look in his eyes faded. He dropped his gaze. "Sorry, sugar," he whispered, sounding more disappointed than apologetic.

Arden pushed himself up and scooted closer to Oggie. He nudged his leg with his knee. "My back feels better."

He cheered a little and smiled at Arden. "I told you to trust me."

"It'd be a lot easier if I didn't think you liked hurting me," Arden accused gently. He'd meant to keep that thought in.

Oggie blinked a few times. "I...It's. Not like that. I don't want to *hurt* you, not...Never mind." He started to stand up.

Arden put a hand on his arm. "Not never mind. Go ahead."

"I'd never do anything that...that *really* hurt you. You know. Not the kind that lasts. It's just, I don't know, sometimes I just, I just *want* to do something. Just to see what would happen, or just to...to feel it."

Arden didn't understand that at all.

"I don't know, Arden, I don't. I'm nothing put spare parts zipped up in a nice exterior."

"Well, maybe ask next time."

Oggie pressed his lips together, then chuckled. "Sure. I'll ask," he agreed without sounding sincere at all. He sounded sad and doubtful, and something else Arden couldn't name. "Your back really feels better?"

"Mhm."

He smiled.

Arden smiled back.

They sat there smiling at each other.

They'd gotten good at pretending uncomfortable moments like these never happened. Sometimes Arden wondered if those moments were even that uncomfortable. Sure, he didn't exactly know how to navigate them, but he didn't feel *bad* about them.

He usually didn't feel bad around Oggie. Confused or mildly concerned, but that seemed to be a given for anyone who knew him.

Arden proposed, "Let's go out."

"What do you mean?"

"Well, uh, I know the Bakers and Zira and Cathie are probably going out tonight. They're always on my case about going with them."

"I don't want to go to work on my night off," Oggie protested weakly.

"So pick a different club. I know you're going somewhere when you're out late."

"You wouldn't want to go to that kind of place."

"Try me."

"And you'd attract a lot of attention..."

"So?"

"So, they're, uh..."

"Are you doing something illegal?"

"Usually."

Arden gave him a little push. "You know what I meant."

"I don't want to get anyone in trouble, shug. Please, don't make me tell you."

He looked desperate, so Arden agreed, "Alright. Then will you come out tonight with me?"

Oggie whined, "Shug!"

"What! Come *on*, we'll have fun, and if we don't, we can leave."

"Promise?"

"I promise."

"Fine," he sulked.

Arden poked him in the ribs and went off to look through his closet. He brought his tablet along so he could get details of where they'd be from Cole, who must have jumped up and down with excitement judging by how many exclamation points he put in his messages.

He dressed up, not fancy, but extra nice. Silver shoes, tight black pants, a metallic black top, and the shaggy, silver coat he'd taken from Cathie. Well-made and well-fitting clothes, except for the jacket, but that worked, an outfit put together with care. He did his hair, twisting it up into a bun and shoving in a lot of shiny little pins to keep it in place.

He skipped the makeup. He hadn't touched the stuff in years and didn't trust himself not to mess it up.

Plus, he thought as he surveyed himself in the mirror, he looked pretty good anyway. Not so pinched and gaunt these days.

He smiled at his reflection. His mouth wasn't *too* thin. It balanced out the wideness of his eyes. He had a nice smile when he meant it. A fuller mouth would have looked out of place on his face.

He looked good, he decided again.

He smiled at Oggie when they met up in the living room. "You look great!" he declared.

"Look at you dressed up, shug." Oggie looked perfect. He would have looked great in an old sack but dressed up in luxe clothes and his hair carefully disheveled he looked radiant.

For once, though, Arden didn't feel shabby in comparison. He was glad to have someone so special on his arm, even if it was fake.

Cole grinned when he saw Arden, but his face fell when he saw Oggie. He kissed Arden's cheek and said, "Glad you came out tonight!"

Arden let go of Oggie to give Cole a squeeze.

He hugged everyone, the whole group that had turned out tonight. He even hugged Zira. When he finished greeting everyone, he turned back to Oggie.

He looked sort of scared.

Arden took his hand and brought him in closer to the group.

Everyone looked them over.

Evaluating them.

Checking for weaknesses, in their own ways. He knew the look on each of them.

"Drinks?" he offered.

They held up their glasses.

"What do you want, shug?" Oggie asked.

"I'll get—"

"Don't be silly," Oggie said. He kissed Arden on the cheek and whispered, "Don't you fucking leave me alone with these people."

Arden nodded and let him go. He turned back to find his friends all watching him. "What?"

"We didn't know you were bringing anyone," Mace mentioned.

"Well, we're...uh. Well, he's my...Why shouldn't I have brought him?" Arden demanded.

"No one said you shouldn't have," Cole soothed. "We're a little surprised."

"Why, though?" Arden asked.

"Didn't know you wanted to have that kind of night," Cathie said. "I mean, we haven't partied like that since our twenties."

"Oh, no, no," Arden insisted immediately. The others had come under the impression that Arden meant to get wild, downing shots of formula and snorting crushed pills meant for other purposes. "No. Not like that."

"Is there another reason you brought your pet then?" Zira asked.

"Cause I fucking like him," Arden snapped.

She scowled. "Heard he supplies a lot of people with certain things is all."

"Be nice to him."

"Ardi, of course we'll be nice to him," Cathie promised. "We're…"

"You look good," Cole interrupted. "I like this jacket."

"No, you don't."

"It works on you," Cole assured. "You know I'd tell you if it didn't."

Arden did know. He ran his fingers through the faux fur. "It's atrocious."

"Deeply," Mace agreed.

They all gave Oggie fake smiles when he came back.

He handed Arden a drink. "I had to tell off Garen for copying my drink. Trying to make High Water with *blueberry* syrup, the idiot. If he's going to do it wrong, he ought to at least call it something else. Anyway, I got you a vodka soda…" He trailed off. "That okay, shug?"

"Perfect."

"Good to start with, nothing to throw off your palate. They are making pitchers of pink ivies tonight, and Garen's decent at making those—"

"I thought it was your night off."

"You're the one who brought me to work."

Arden nudged him. "You going to come dance with me later?"

"Can you dance without being shitfaced?"

"I actually can. But will I? Nope."

Oggie grinned.

They stood around and chatted with the others, sipping their drinks and waiting to get drunk.

At least, Arden was waiting to get drunk. The others seemed happy enough to talk.

Oggie snuggled up under Arden's arm. He put on a good act, the perfect pet, flattering and flirty.

Arden didn't know how much was fake. He got very drunk. Not too drunk, not drunk enough to be a mess, but enough to have fun. Enough to pull a protesting Oggie out onto the dancefloor.

"Shug, really, I'm not that coordinated—"

"Doesn't matter. Everyone's just…jumping around."

"Sugar—"

Arden grabbed both his hands and dropped to his knees. "Ogden Theodore Nielsen, will you please dance with me?"

"Oh, fucking, Arden, get up, get up, people are looking."

"Will you dance with me?"

"Yes. Get up!"

Arden popped up to his feet and dragged him to the center of the floor. He twirled them together.

After a few songs, he told Oggie, "You're not a bad dancer!"

"I know. I didn't want to dance."

Arden giggled. "Why not?"

"People are looking at us," he pointed out as a non-answer.

"They're supposed to be." He threw his arms around Oggie and hung off him for a few songs.

They came back to a cluster of Arden's friends whispering together. Oggie had mentioned getting more drinks and now that they had them, he said, "Sugar, can we sit for a little bit?"

"I, uh. You sit, I'll be right back. Bathroom."

Oggie nodded.

Arden headed towards the bathroom.

Mace followed right on his heels.

"I thought you didn't like boys," Arden teased.

"Ardi, I wanted to talk for a second."

"Okay..." He lingered outside of the bathroom. "What about?"

"We're worried about you."

"We?"

"Your fucking friends, Arden. Don't be an asshole for once in your life," Mace snapped.

Arden raised his eyebrows. As a rule, people didn't talk to him like that.

"Whatever's going on between you and Nielsen, keep it in the bedroom."

"Excuse me?"

"You were in such a good place, Ardi, and we, you know, we all hear about the formulas, all the things you buy him. Cole says you fell asleep in Council the other day."

"It was boring," Arden sulked.

He'd stayed up later than he should have a few nights in a row, yes, but it had been a tedious meeting.

"We're worried about you."

Arden fidgeted. He turned and went into the bathroom because he really did have to pee.

He hated this.

He headed back to find everyone sitting around the table. He hung back and watched them staring at Oggie while he fidgeted with the swizzle stick in his drink. His lips moved every so often. He looked at his drink more than he looked at them. He had a flat smile plastered on his face.

They were asking him questions.

He went over and nuzzled against Oggie's throat. "Let's go home."

Oggie kissed his shoulder. "Anything you like, sugar."

Arden held tight to his hand while they walked away without much of a farewell. He got the feeling that if he said anything, Oggie would cry, or maybe scream.

In their rooms, while Oggie undressed, Arden went into his bathroom and drew a bath.

"What are you doing?" Oggie called from the closet.

"You'll feel better."

Oggie came to stand in the doorway of his bathroom, undressed. "Who says I need to feel better?"

"That look on your face."

"You don't ever stop to think I fake feeling bad just the same as I fake being your pet?"

"No." Arden sat beside the tub. He tested the water. "Should I?"

"You don't ever worry that I'm not your friend?"

"I worry everyone isn't my friend. I joined the handball team so people would have to spend time with me. Before that, I spent most of my childhood pitching a fit anytime my mothers tried to make me do something social."

Oggie came over to stand next to Arden.

Close.

Really close.

Arden avoided looking up to get too much of an eyeful.

Oggie crouched. He tested the water. He sighed.

"What's wrong?"

"Sometimes I feel like someone peeled off my skin and the world is made out of sandpaper."

Arden kind of understood that.

They stayed on the floor like that, the water churning and steaming, waiting for the bath to fill.

When it did, Arden turned off the faucet. "I'll go if you want to be alone."

"I don't know what I want." He sounded exhausted. He climbed into the tub. His skin went ruddy with the heat.

Arden had made it too hot. He reached for the cold tap.

"Don't." Oggie sunk up to his shoulders in too hot water.

"Are you okay, Oggie?"

Oggie looked at him.

"I mean, my friends—"

"Your friends are worried about you. People believe what we've told them to believe. Isn't that a good thing?"

"It can't be easy, people thinking you're the bad guy."

Oggie sighed. "Go get some sleep, sugar."

In the morning, he couldn't find Oggie. He hadn't taken his things, so Arden didn't worry. Sometimes Oggie went out. Part of Arden doubted he'd even gone to bed last night.

Rhys came to get him for work, and he spent all day away from his rooms.

Oggie hadn't come back by dinner time.

Maybe he'd come home and then gone back out. He did that sometimes. A few times he hadn't come home for a couple days in a row. Once or twice, he'd brought someone back, late at night.

He'd tried to keep it secret, whispering at the other person to be quiet, but Arden could always hear them.

These clandestine visitors never stayed long. Arden never asked about them, either.

He went down to Crystal to check if Oggie had gone to work.

Mara said, "He traded shifts last minute."

"Oh. Well. If he comes by, tell him I was looking for him."

"You lose him?" she asked disdainfully.

"I didn't lose him, he's an adult."

"Mm."

He rolled his eyes at her and left.

He decided to wait up for Oggie to come home and fell asleep on the couch.

He woke as soon as the door opened. He rubbed his eyes and pushed himself up. "Og?"

Oggie yelped. "Sugar!"

"Sorry. I."

"Were you waiting up for me?" He turned on a dim light.

"I. You know, I didn't know where you were."

"Couldn't have looked that hard. I wasn't anywhere a safety officer wouldn't have found me."

"I didn't want to send an officer after you. It felt a little drastic. And I, uh, I know you get up to things you'd prefer to keep private."

Oggie laughed shakily. He came to sit beside Arden. He looked haggard and his clothes didn't sit correctly on his frame. The flush in his cheek and shake in his hands made Arden think he'd been arguing or even fighting. "I." He cleared his throat. "I haven't been honest with you."

"I'm not surprised."

"Stop flattering me, I'm trying to be serious," Oggie attempted to joke. He took a deep breath. His words didn't come out quite right, quick and slurred. "Morris, uh. He's paying me to do more than just spy on you. He, uh. He's." He pressed a hand to his mouth. "I got into trouble a while back, at the med center, like I told you. Morris was the one who got those charges dropped. And, I mean, they were serious charges and if, if he wanted, I'd be back in lockup in an instant."

"Oh."

"And so, he. Arden, he knows. He knows its fake. That we're not sleeping together, that you haven't relapsed. But, uh, the thing is, he wanted me to keep it going, seeing how deep you'd dig yourself, how far you'd let your reputation slip and then..." He spoke all in one confused rush.

Arden drew a blanket around his shoulders. He felt cold but knew it had nothing to do with the temperature. "Then what?"

Oggie reached into his pocket. He pulled out a small medicine bottle, clear glass with a sealed lid, the kind that had to be pierced by a needle. It had a label on it, the print too small for Arden to make out in the dim light.

They stared at the bottle.

"What is it?"

"Uh, I can't pronounce what it's really called, methy-something-di-fenty-something-or-other. Uh, in the Quarters we call it wish, cause, uh, you wish you'd never touched it. It's a heavy-duty pain killer."

"Knockout," Arden supplied. "At least, that's what we called it when I was in school. Kids probably have a different name for it now. Is that what you were stealing?"

Oggie nodded. "Stealing, cutting, and selling for a pretty good profit. But, uh. I didn't steal this one. Morris gave it to me."

"Why?"

"You are a drug addict, Arden."

Someone might imply he had a problem with formulas, but no one would dare to call the Autarch an addict to his face. Peers usually looked horrified if he applied the term to himself.

No one called formulas drugs, but that's all they were.

Wish, or knockout, or whatever it was, killed people with stunning regularity when not administered in the correct dosage. Even at his very worst, Arden hadn't touched the stuff. The amount Oggie had in that bottle could do in hundreds of adults.

Probably twice as many babies, Arden thought dully.

He licked his lips.

The dim light of the reading lamp made it glow golden and peachy in Oggie's hand.

In a flash, Oggie put the bottle on the table. He yanked his hand back like it had started to burn. "So, I haven't been honest with you."

"Are you...Are you going to try to kill me?" Arden asked.

"Morris wants me to. It makes sense. Dealer deals drugs. Addict takes drugs. The dose is super stupid easy to mess up. Bye-bye, addict. Hello, new Autarch, hello..." Oggie sighed. "Hello, lifetime of guilt and regret and probably getting blackmailed into killing more people."

"This is a really bad way to kill me."

"I'm not going to kill you!"

"Oh. Good. Way too suspicious."

"What's so suspicious about an overdose?"

"Nothing, but you should pick a drug I'm not allergic to."

Oggie glanced at the bottle.

"Throat closes up and everything." He'd almost died getting his wisdom teeth out. His mother had made very sure that no matter what Arden got up to, he knew which drugs had it as an ingredient.

"Fuck. That would have *terrified me*."

"Super good thing you changed your mind."

"I didn't...! Arden, I didn't change my mind, I was never going to kill you," Oggie insisted. "I wasn't even going to do any of this, but, shit, have you ever been in lockup?"

"No. Will you testify?"

"What?"

"Against Morris."

Oggie stared at him. "Is that it? I've...I've betrayed you."

"And now you've re-betrayed my uncle. Does that make you a quadruple agent? Put that on a resumé."

"Arden."

"Oggie."

"Are you mad at me?"

"No. But I would have been really mad if you'd sent me into anaphylactic shock."

"Why aren't you mad at me?" Oggie demanded. "You should be fucking livid."

"Because I've met my uncle, you idiot. I broke his favorite whiskey glass once and I thought he was going to skin me alive in front of Mama."

All the life seemed to drain out of Oggie. He pressed his lips together.

"Whatever Morris is holding over you, it won't matter once we get him convicted of conspiring to murder the Autarch," Arden assured.

Oggie didn't look soothed.

"What?"

"Why aren't you mad?"

Arden frowned.

"I pretended to be your friend, I took all your presents, and lived in your rooms and...and I used you."

"I know." He'd explicitly agreed to that arrangement.

"Just like he did. You were so hurt when he did it and I..." Oggie blinked furiously. "And I can't even hurt you at all," he mumbled wetly.

"What the fuck does that mean, Oggie?" Arden demanded. "Are you *trying* to hurt me?"

"No! But...but you should be hurt. I pretended to be your friend. If I was your friend, this would hurt," the younger man insisted tearily.

Arden squeezed his eyes shut. He thought, considered the options, then asked, "So...So you want me to be upset that you double-crossed me because you were being blackmailed by a sadistic psychopath?"

"No, I want you to...to be sad that I faked being your friend."

Arden wondered if Oggie was having a breakdown of some sort. "Walk me through it, Og."

"I faked it. I wasn't your friend and I pretended to be and it *doesn't even matter* to you."

"Oh." Arden took a minute to unravel the pieces there. "So...Oggie. Are you...Are you sad that we aren't friends?"

"Yes."

"You fucking...you're spare parts, you know that?" He grabbed Oggie by the shoulders a little more firmly than he'd meant to. "If we weren't friends, you wouldn't have told me any of this."

"I wouldn't have killed you!" the younger man nearly shrieked.

"No, I mean, about..." Arden sighed. "If we weren't friends, you wouldn't be so upset about us not being friends."

Sadly and into his hands, Oggie moaned, "I'm so fucking confused."

Arden couldn't explain something that didn't make any sense. He just dragged Oggie closer to him. "You should get help, Og. Real, professional, psychological help."

"I can't afford it."

Arden bit his tongue so he couldn't laugh. He squeezed Oggie tight. He looked at the glass bottle on the table. "Did anyone but you and him touch that?"

"No."

"Okay. And you'll testify in court?"

"Mhm." Oggie squirmed closer to Arden, deep into his embrace like he was frightened of something. "I'm sorry."

"It really would have hurt my feelings if you'd killed me."

"It's not funny."

"No, just, you know. I would have been thinking 'oh, no, my dear friend has murdered me!' as I was clawing at my throat."

"Arden, stop, it's not funny."

"Give it a year. I bet it will be really funny in a year."

Oggie knotted his hands in Arden's shirt. "I'm so sorry."

Arden kissed his hair. He'd always vaguely worried about Oggie, but those concerns felt a little more solid now. He'd never come home on anything before, or, at least, not this obviously. Arden knew he had to be on something right now. "Are you okay?"

"I don't know, sugar," he murmured.

He nodded off with his head on Arden's lap.

Without waking him, Arden managed to reach his tablet from the coffee table and sent a message to the chief safety officer. He asked them to bring Morris to lockup and to send someone here for the bottle.

They could tell who'd touched it and where it had come from; likely, Morris had taken it from one of the med centers he supervised.

The officer who arrived carefully packaged up the bottle for processing. She lingered and asked, "Uh. Chief says..." She cleared her throat.

Arden waited.

People didn't seem to know where they stood with him anymore.

"Your Eminence, the chief requests that we bring in thrall six eight—"

"Ogden Neilson," he suggested quietly. He stroked Oggie's cheek.

She quickly amended, "That we bring in Ogden Neilson to the Security Office for immediate questioning and safekeeping."

"Safekeeping?"

"People who testify against Mr. Torre often change their minds," she pointed out. "Have accidents, get sick..."

"He'll be safe with me," he said, but the longer he looked at Oggie, the more he considered that he had things to do in the following days. He wouldn't be home, and he couldn't make Oggie come everywhere with him.

"Yes, Your—"

"Wait." Arden touched Oggie's hair. "Oggie. Wake up."

"Hmm."

"Officer—"

"Officer!" Oggie sat right up.

"Julissa," the officer provided.

"Officer Julissa is going to bring you to the Security Office."

Oggie's eyes widened. He started to stand up. "Sugar, I can't."

"You're not in trouble."

"Sugar."

"You're not in trouble," Arden reminded gently.

Oggie shook his head. "No, I just, you know, sugar, they don't like me very much down there!" His voice jittered and got higher as he spoke. He backed away from the couch.

Arden followed. He put his hands on Oggie's shoulders. "You aren't in trouble."

"Can't I stay here? Can't I just stay inside? I won't go out, I promise, I..." He looked about ready to shake into pieces.

Arden glanced at Julissa. "Call for back up."

"Sugar, please!" Oggie shrunk away.

Arden didn't let him go. "Shh, stop. I won't make you go, I won't, I promise."

"Promise," he insisted.

"I promise. But someone has to come to keep you safe."

Oggie swallowed.

"You can stay here." He smoothed his hands over Oggie's arms, a gesture he hoped would soothe him.

"Maybe..."

"What?"

"Maybe Mara could come over."

"Yeah," Arden agreed. "You need to sleep off whatever this is."

Oggie nodded. "Nerves, I think."

Arden raised an eyebrow.

"And maybe a, a, uh, they make this drink at Vortex, it's scuff and Six and..." He glanced at Julissa. "I'll tell you about it later, sugar."

Arden maneuvered him toward his bedroom. "You'll feel better in the morning."

"Sugar, will you...? Will you indulge me terribly for tonight? I know I haven't got any right to ask...!"

"Ask."

"Could you stay for a bit? Just, just until I get back to sleep."

"Of course," Arden assured. He turned back the covers for Oggie, got him into bed, and made a reminder to thank every friend who'd ever gotten him through a night like this.

"Usually it takes the edge off but there's no taking the edge off your uncle."

"Morris," Arden corrected.

"I hate saying his name. I hate..." Oggie buried his face in the pillow.

Arden tucked him in and sat beside him until he fell asleep. He stayed long after that, actually, and conducted a hushed and uncomfortable conversation with the safety officer from the bed.

Julissa sent someone back with the bottle of wish and elected to stay with another officer as added security for Oggie and Arden himself. He hadn't seen why he'd needed protection until Julissa had kindly pointed out that he had a would-be assassin curled up next to him.

The most unfortunate officer of them all received the assignment to retrieve Mara.

She arrived, shoved several people out of her way, and grabbed Arden by the arm. She dragged him into the bathroom, which he intensely disliked, and poked him in the chest. "What did you do to him?"

He had the urge to climb into the tub and draw the curtain closed. "Nothing."

"Then why would he try to murder you!" she hissed. She had a practiced whispered shout, like she'd engaged in many clandestine fights.

"He didn't try to murder me. My uncle is blackmailing him to murder me."

Her pale eyes sliced into him. "That old man on deck two?"

He frowned. "How do you know Winnie?"

"He lives next to our mother."

Arden's frowned deepened. "Is your mother Eula Bowers?"

"No, shit, she's practically dust. Other side."

"Nolie Brownstone," he said.

"Doesn't fucking matter. That old guy wants to kill you?"

"No. My other uncle. Morris."

Her face contorted. "Oh. Him." She didn't ask why Morris wanted him dead. She did squint at him.

"What?" he asked.

She shrugged. "Your family try to murder you a lot?"

"No."

"You're taking it pretty well."

"Oh, well, Oggie was so worked up." He hadn't thought about it. He hadn't expected Morris to graduate to assassination, but it didn't shock him either. Maybe it should have. Maybe he'd think about it too much and cry in the shower later.

"Yeah." She glanced toward the bedroom. "Was he at Vortex?"

"Yeah. What is that, anyway?"

"If you needed to know, you'd know."

"Super fucking hate that answer."

She walked away and plopped herself on Oggie's bed. "I'll keep an eye on him. Go figure out your shit."

Figuring out his shit would have to wait until the morning. As soon as he lay down, he fell asleep.

Oggie refused to be alone with safety officers. He made Mara stay with him whenever he could and made the officers wait outside the door until Arden got home. Even with Arden at home, he became nearly hysterical if an officer got too close or looked at him too long.

He'd stayed inside for about a week straight now.

He'd tried working a shift at Crystal but between rumors about an actual assassination attempt, Morris's acquaintances, and the safety officers, he'd come home crying.

Arden had agreed to cover his and Mara's wages for any work missed between now and the trial.

"In a hurry?" Rhys asked.

Arden slowed his pace. "Oggie's been worked up."

Quietly, Rhys noted, "It's interesting he's still staying with you."

"Sorry?"

Rhys shrugged.

"Fucking don't. I'm sick of this insinuation shit. After everything you could at least be upfront," Arden said.

Rhys's face darkened. He cleared his throat. "Most people don't keep someone who tried to kill them as a roommate."

"He didn't try."

Rhys tilted his head and pulled in a breath. "Just, you know. Some of the evidence is...it's not favorable."

Safety officers had found the seal of the bottle pierced and a needle in the pocket of Oggie's coat. Arden didn't think that amounted to much in the way of murder charges. Maybe he'd sold a little on the side.

Oggie hadn't been exactly forthcoming. He'd only insisted, "I *wasn't* going to kill him," whenever questioned.

His answer satisfied Arden, even if it satisfied no one else.

He told Rhys, "I'm not worried about it."

"You're just..."

"I'm what?"

"You're..." Rhys sighed. "Arden, you're naïve."

Arden couldn't help but scowl at him. "Because I believed that people might like me?"

"Because you don't understand the economic and societal pressures that workers face to pretend to enjoy the company of a peer."

"I understand, and Oggie might too, that being my pet is a lot better than being my uncle's hired assassin."

"He understands a lot about being a pet," Rhys grumbled.

Arden stopped walking. They had neared his rooms and he didn't want to argue in front of the officers waiting outside his door. He didn't want to be in earshot of Oggie, either. "What the actual fuck does it matter to you?"

"Sorry?"

"You didn't want to be with me, so I know this isn't envy, so you better tell me what your actual problem with him is."

"Other than attempted murder."

"Absolutely other than that, since he never attempted to murder me."

Rhys pursed his lips. "And other than his ongoing criminal activities? And your formula use—"

"I'm *not* using."

Rhys met his eyes.

"I'm not! Not unless I really need something."

"Addicts always think they need something."

Arden swallowed. He'd really let Rhys get away with a lot if he was calling him an addict, too. "Is that all you think I am? What happened to I'm proud of you? Or, what? Is that as much bullshit as the rest of it?"

"If I didn't care about you, I wouldn't be worried that you've shacked up with a drug dealer who's using you and working for your nefarious uncle."

"Did you seriously just use the word nefarious?" Arden demanded.

"It doesn't feel like an understatement. I'm worried about you," Rhys insisted severely.

Arden crossed his arms and looked over Rhys. "You care about me?"

"Obviously."

Arden half-smiled. "Maybe not as obvious as you think. Maybe..."

"What?"

"Maybe I'm worried that...that you know, the game between classes, it's not much of a game at all for workers is it? Or, at least, it's one peers have made really hard to win. I know you said sorry for using me but...I mean.

Should that go both ways? Was I using you?" Arden asked. He'd thought about it a lot.

Rhys pressed his lips together and blinked a few times. He let out a breath, all through his nose.

"I never wanted to hurt you," Arden said, hoping Rhys would say he hadn't but unable to shake the feeling that he had.

"You didn't hurt me."

"No?"

"No," Rhys assured. "I care about you. Even if...if things didn't fit for us as lovers, I care. And I'm worried."

Arden grinned. "Well, you don't have to be worried."

"I'm not the only one who thinks Nielsen's a bad influence. Cole thinks—"

"Cole doesn't know him. Neither do you."

"He's not exactly the kind of the person I hang around with."

Arden blew a raspberry. "Times are changing, Mr. Malek. Come in and stay for a while."

Rhys rolled his eyes.

"Well?" Arden urged.

"I guess," Rhys agreed lifelessly.

Arden linked arms with him and dragged him inside.

The officers remained outside. Sometimes Arden sent one of them to take a walk out of nothing more than pity.

"Oggie!" he called.

Oggie practically burst out of the bedroom, mostly naked. He had a thin, slippery robe hanging off him, caught on his elbows and untied. "Sugar! Thank fuck, you're home, I was dying of boredom."

"You are allowed to leave."

"My nerves can't handle it." He gave Rhys a dirty look, then came over and kissed Arden on the cheek. "Did you bring work home?" he pouted.

"No."

"Oh." Oggie outright glared at Rhys.

"Stop it. You two need to play nice." He wrapped himself around Oggie. "Pretty please."

Oggie snuggled a little closer. "I'll get dressed." He headed toward the bedroom.

"You sure you two don't have other things you'd rather be doing?" Rhys asked.

Arden walked away.

Oggie had gotten a little...tense during his self-imposed seclusion. He'd always flirted but it had gotten a little less playful lately. Only his sister visited him, and Arden assumed Oggie craved something a sister couldn't give.

Oggie emerged in a pajama set that he had liberated from Arden's wardrobe. He draped himself on the couch. "So...what are we doing?"

"We could watch a movie," Arden suggested.

"What, all cuddle up in bed?" Rhys asked.

"I do have an actual screen."

"Oh, no, not a movie. Let's do something," Oggie insisted.

"I've got games."

Rhys said, "Get cards. We can play jack-a-darry."

"What's that?" Arden asked.

"You don't know jack-a-darry!" Oggie cried. He gave Arden a push. "Find some cards, we have to play. How don't you know?"

"It's a Quarters game," Rhys reminded him, somewhat sourly.

Oggie stroked Arden's cheek. "And here he is with two Quarters boys. We can teach him to play."

Arden stood to find a deck of cards and to escape the strange energy vibrating between the other two men.

"You aren't really *from* the Quarters, though," Rhys said. "That's what I've heard anyway."

Oggie scoffed. "From the Quarters. Fucking lived there for more than half my life, but I guess that's not really *from* somewhere."

Arden scrounged through the bar.

"I meant—" Rhys began.

"Yeah, yeah, you *meant* what everyone means. I grew up with new toys and clothes instead of hand-me-downs, fresh food instead of rations. We ended up in the same shithole, huh? Sucking back scuff and off the same guy."

Arden pretended he didn't hear that.

"Or, you know. Pretending to," Oggie added.

Arden returned with the deck of cards. He handed it over to Rhys. "How do we play?"

Rhys took some time shuffling the deck.

Arden tapped his fingers against his thigh, uncomfortable. This had been stupid.

Oggie twisted a bit of Arden's hair between his fingers. "At least one of us was honest about it."

"The last thing you are is honest," Rhys huffed.

"Let's not—" Arden started.

"Honest! Coming from you, fucking...that's amazing, you call yourself honest," Oggie said.

Arden gripped Oggie's forearm. "Let's not, boys," he managed.

Oggie stood. "I'm. Sugar, I'm sorry, I'm going to bed. Have fun." He went to his room.

Arden glanced at Rhys, still shuffling the cards, then followed Oggie.

He closed the door behind them. "Hey."

"No, sugar, I don't..." Oggie shook his head. He paced away from, and then back towards Arden. "You know they all hate me."

Arden put a hand on his shoulder. "That's because they don't understand. They don't know it was pretend."

Oggie stepped back. "It wasn't pretend, Arden. This was real, a real...an actual attempt on your life, over drug charges and...bad choices," Oggie admitted. He didn't cry or even sniffle. He'd probably done enough of that. Instead, his words came out flat, his face unmoved.

"You wouldn't have—"

"The whole time. It was the plan from the first minute. I've had that shit in my pocket for *months*. Do you know how many times I stuck that fucking needle in that bottle?" Oggie asked.

"Seven."

"What?"

"Just a guess. I know there were a couple punctures in the lid. I figured you were just selling on the side. You really carried it around with you?"

"I mean. Not all the time. That's not the point!"

"The point is, under duress, you agreed to do something, and then never went through with it."

Oggie gritted his teeth and let out a frustrated groan. "Why won't you be angry with me!"

"I can't."

"What the fuck does that mean?"

Arden licked his lips. He took Oggie's hand. "It means I want you to come play cards."

"What's the point?"

"You should get to know my friends."

"Why? I'm...once this is done—"

"What? The trial?" Arden asked. "You'll be cleared. Morris will go away."

"And I just keep pretending? I stay in your guestroom forever?"

"Do you want to stay?"

"I..." Oggie looked around the room. "Of course, I want to stay. It's really nice here. I'd be an idiot to give this up. But what happens to me when you meet someone? When it's time to turn the guestroom into a nursery?"

"That's a while off, Og."

"You never know. Sometimes things happen without any warning."

"Well," Arden said carefully, "I haven't been seeing anyone, *and* I generally don't sleep with the kind of people who can get pregnant, so I don't think any surprises will be on their way anytime soon."

"Still, you're the Autarch. You won't be single forever."

Arden didn't want to have this conversation. It could go in circles forever. He took Oggie's other hand and brought them both up to his mouth. He kissed his knuckles. "Will you come play cards and we can have this conversation when you haven't been day-drinking for a week straight?"

Oggie blushed. "Is it that obvious, sugar?"

"Super obvious."

"I'm sorry."

"Another week, you'll be cleared, free to roam *Eden* and go to whatever secret, illegal parties your heart desires. Come play cards."

Oggie nodded.

They returned to the couch.

Arden asked, "So how do I play this game?"

Rhys and Oggie bickered over the rules. Mara showed up a while later and threw a wrench into the whole thing. The three of them played and picked at each other, noting flaws in gameplay and rule violations so obscure Arden never actually picked up the basic rules.

He floundered through several games, though the other three focused so much on tearing each other apart that they left him alone.

He didn't know who won any of the rounds since none of them could agree.

He'd never seen Rhys get so vicious before. From Mara and Oggie he expected this kind of behavior, but Rhys gave back as good as he got, and even instigated sometimes.

Arden must have stumbled on some rift between factions in the Quarters.

After nearly an hour, Arden gathered up all the cards and said, "This game is stupid. Let's play kings."

The other three agreed.

A few rounds of kings lightened the mood. It was a silly game, meant more for children, though sometimes used as a drinking game.

Arden had considered asking Oggie to make a pitcher of something but actively feared what would happen with these three drunk together.

Before Arden could propose dinner, Oggie said, "I'm going to go lay down for a little while."

He ambled into his room.

Arden sniffed what he had claimed to be a glass of water and found it contained something undoubtedly alcoholic in nature. Hopefully not straight vodka, which was what it smelled like.

Mara looked like she wanted to strangle Rhys. She glared at him for a solid five minutes by Arden's estimate.

Arden asked, "Should I be worried about him?"

"He's spare parts, not worth worrying about," Rhys said.

"Shut the fuck up," Mara growled.

"You're being incredibly unkind," Arden pointed out.

Rhys rolled his eyes.

"It's not like you."

"It's *exactly* like him," Mara said.

"You don't even know me," Rhys shot back.

"But I know who you are. And who you hang out with."

"Are you two still in school?" Arden asked as casually as possible.

They both made faces at him.

"Cause you're acting like fucking children," he said.

They shifted.

"Yeah, that's right. A spoiled, piece-of-shit peer just said you're acting like children," he told them. "So...figure it out."

"I just. *Eden* needs stability and you've brought the exact opposite into your home," Rhys said. "That man is reckless and unpredictable. Arden, just because he doesn't want to kill you now doesn't mean he won't change his mind."

Reckless, maybe, but Arden found that Oggie had his own kind of predictability. He couldn't always guess what Oggie would do, but he could safely narrow it down to two or three options for most scenarios.

"Oggie's too spineless to hurt anyone. Not even to save his own ass," Mara pointed out.

Rhys shook his head. "He's—"

She dared, "Call him spare parts again."

"He's legitimately ill," Rhys said.

"You'd be ill too if you'd grown up like he had."

"What, with nice toys and—"

"Alone," she said. The word dropped out of her mouth like a weight. For once, she didn't sound angry, she sounded sad. "Mam never let Pop visit her during the day and she never let Oggie leave. And she sure as shit wasn't staying home with him. We're five fucking years apart. Five years and that boy was alone, you know, except maybe he wasn't all the time. Who knows who wandered in? A worker on cleaning duty. A friend of Mam's who dropped by. Who knows if they fed him and changed him, or if they hurt him? He doesn't remember." Mara looked toward Oggie's bedroom. "Trust me, the Quarters' nursery is better than that."

Arden felt sick.

Had one good thing ever happened on *Eden?*

Rhys had drawn in on himself.

"The other kids in the Quarters weren't nice to him, but at least we know what happened to him," Mara said. "So, yeah. Spare parts are all he is. But he's not bad."

Arden swallowed.

She stood up. "Tell him I'll be around tomorrow. If I spend another night here, I'll end up ripping out my hair. Or his."

When she'd left, Arden and Rhys sat wordlessly around the coffee table.

Arden picked up the cards and put them back in the box.

"I was going to say we should get dinner, but I don't think I could eat," Arden admitted softly.

"That can't be true," Rhys protested, his voice just as weak as Arden's. "No one would do that."

"People have done a lot worse."

"I'm a piece of shit."

Arden grimaced. "You were being uncharacteristically unkind."

Rhys sighed. He rubbed his face.

"What's your problem with him?"

"I." Rhys let out a long breath. "I hate that he's using you."

"He's not."

Rhys sighed.

"Maybe we're projecting a little bit?" Arden guessed. He wouldn't have fathomed to guess this before today, but now he better understood that Rhys saw him as someone who needed looking after. "Still feeling a little guilty about duping this poor naïve Autarch?"

"Maybe that's it."

"Maybe you both need professional psychological help."

"Can't afford it," Rhys said.

"Bullshit, I know how much you get paid. You can afford a therapist."

"Therapy is for peers."

"Therapy is for people who need therapy," Arden pointed out. "Let's give it a few days and then maybe you can try to treat Oggie like a person instead of the psychic manifestation of your own remorse."

"Yeah."

Rhys left, too. He gave Arden a long hug on his way out, which Arden would have really liked if it didn't feel so much like how he'd hugged Winslow, afraid he might not see him again. He hugged back hard and hoped, irrationally, that Rhys would be able to divine that he was truly alright through it.

Arden peeked into Oggie's room. He was making too much noise to be asleep, quiet moans and groans but no snores. He sat on his bed. "You awake?"

"Too drunk to sleep."

Arden put a hand on his arm. He understood that erratic wakefulness. He found a sour stomach tablet in the medicine cabinet and convinced Oggie to swallow it, then asked, "You want some Nine?"

"No."

"Okay."

"Shug, will you..." He let out a concerning, soft moan. "Fuck. Will you stay for a little while?"

"Sure thing." Arden made himself more comfortable on the bed.

Oggie nestled up to him, his head on his lap.

Half an hour later, he threw up without any warning. Apparently, one antacid wasn't enough to stave off an entire day of drinking.

Arden flinched from the onslaught of mostly liquid. "Fuck, Og, when was the last time you ate?" he asked without expecting an answer.

Oggie mumbled something.

Arden gagged on the smell and had to make a conscious effort not to vomit as well. He extracted himself from beneath Oggie, shed his soaked pants to avoid spreading the sick around, then escorted Oggie to the bathroom.

He managed to get the next wave of sick into the toilet.

Arden waited until he'd thoroughly emptied himself.

He spent about ten minutes just spitting into the toilet.

After that, Arden deposited him into the tub, stripped the sheets to save the mattress, and called for someone to come get the laundry.

He returned to find Oggie exactly where he'd left him. He wiped his mouth, threw a clean blanket over him, and went to take a shower.

On his way to the shower, he encountered the thrall he'd called to clean up. He stopped short. "Oh, hi, Peter."

"Your Eminence."

"Sorry about that." He nodded towards the mess.

"Bathroom too?" Peter asked.

"The toilet, yeah. Sorry."

Peter gave a charmingly resigned shrug. "It's the job."

Arden cleaned himself while Peter cleaned the room. He checked on Oggie one last time before he curled up in Oggie's newly made bed.

In the morning, he ordered the blandest breakfast he could think of, then went into the bathroom.

Oggie hadn't thrown up again, which was a relief.

He peeled back the blanket as gently as he could. "Og, time to get up."

Oggie groaned.

"Oh, come on, Oggie, you've got sick in your hair and you reek. And you're like...sweaty."

"Sugar, please go away."

"I can't, Og. You're really gross right now."

Oggie whined piteously.

"Come on, a bath, and then we can get back in bed and have a nice cuddle, and you can eat something," Arden wheedled.

"Mmm."

"Okay, well, I'm going to undress you," he warned before he started to unbutton Oggie's pajama shirt.

The other man neither protested nor resisted.

Once he had him undressed, Arden turned on the water, making sure to keep it tepid for a while. He turned up the heat little by little and added a lot of soap, not just to clean Oggie, but to cloud the water.

Oggie came to life slowly, stretching and sighing.

"Should I wash you or have you regained the barest shred of dignity?" Arden asked.

"Does that have to be an either-or question?"

Arden dumped water over Oggie's head. He'd liked the implication of that question a little too much. "Wash your hair."

"You're beastly."

Arden grabbed soap and a washcloth. He gave Oggie's back and shoulders a thorough scrubbing. "I ordered breakfast."

"Oh, I'm not hungry."

"You threw up pure liquid last night. You need to eat something."

"Nice coming from you."

Arden trailed his fingers down Oggie's spine. He stopped where skin met water, terribly tempted to go lower.

Oggie leaned forwards to expose more skin.

Arden took his hand back. "Good thing we're a fake couple. We'd be so fucking messy."

"Pet and peer aren't a couple," Oggie pointed out.

"Yeah, well, if it was real, you wouldn't be my pet." Arden ran the washcloth over his shoulder.

"You take a bath yet, sugar?"

A bath sounded nice, even nicer with Oggie. "I kind of had to shower last night."

"Ah." Oggie took the washcloth from him. "Be an absolute pearl and...and just, fuck, just go in the other room for a little while. I was going to try to be diplomatic about it, but I'm so fucking hungover."

Arden patted his shoulder. "Take your time."

A while later, Oggie came out of the bathroom, ate three bites of food, and cuddled up to Arden. He asked, "Haven't you got to be at work?"

"No, Og, I've got my tablet. I'll work from home."

"On my account?"

Arden glanced at him. He shifted. "You did throw up on me. Kind of interrupts a sound night's sleep," he pointed out.

Oggie whined. "You're so cruel to me."

Arden resumed going through his messages. Nothing interesting.

In fact, the only interesting thing he saw all day was a strange signal coming from Terra. Some kind of old-fashioned radio signal. He couldn't tune in to it, so he sent it along to someone who could interpret it better.

They'd found a few signals like that before. Usually songs or old news reports. One or two calls for help that had been too old to be worthwhile. Arden liked to have them sorted out anyway, even if they weren't helpful. He considered them part of *Eden*'s history, as much as part of Terra's.

Once they'd found a whole movie, back when Mama had been alive. She'd been so excited to have a new old movie to watch.

When his eyes started to hurt from staring at the tablet, he scooted down into the bed and wrapped his arms around Oggie. "Hey."

"Hmm?"

"Can I ask you something?"

"Sure."

"I mean, really ask you something, Oggie."

Soft and concerned, Oggie said, "Go ahead, sugar."

Arden couldn't ask what he really wanted to know. He couldn't ask any of the things he really wanted to know, about Oggie or the future, or the past, for that matter.

"What is it?" Oggie asked when Arden hadn't spoken for a while.

"Can you lay off the drinking for a while?"

"Oh."

"I'm worried about you."

"I don't drink." Oggie swallowed.

"Please."

"I can try."

"I'm, uh, I plan on taking a few days off, well, you know. As much as I can. To get ready for the trial and everything. We have a strong case and it's all a formality. I could throw Morris into the void if I wanted."

"You should."

"Hmm? Well, no one's ever done that."

"If anyone deserves it," Oggie mumbled.

Arden hated that. He scooched closer. "Can I promise you something?"

"Uh, I'm not good at keeping promises. If I was, you'd be dead," Oggie warned anxiously.

"No. Can I promise you something?" Arden repeated more clearly.

"Oh. I can't stop you. Can I?"

"I asked you if people had hurt you and you said no."

"So?"

"So you also told me you don't drink and that's super obviously a lie."

"I don't drink," Oggie said. "And people don't hurt me."

"Well. If you decide someone is, and if you want to tell me who, I promise I won't let them hurt you anymore."

Oggie stared at him, his eyes green and huge. "Why are you letting them hurt me now?"

Arden didn't know what to make of that.

"Do you like to hurt people, too, sugar? Just to see what happens?" Oggie asked. He touched Arden's ribs.

Arden flinched before he did anything.

Oggie dragged him closer, his fingers digging into Arden. He clung to him. "Or are you so used to it you can't tell the difference anymore?"

Puzzled, but mostly sad, Arden ran his fingers through Oggie's hair.

"Tell me I have nice hair," Oggie proposed. "Say it gives you something to hold on to."

"Just checking to see if you got all the barf out."

Oggie didn't huff or whine that time. He kept his grip on Arden and didn't let go, not even when Arden tried to pull back.

While he waited for the end of this captivity, Arden tried to think of ways to keep Oggie happy, distracted, and sober until the trial. A reliable witness did not show up hungover, or drunk, or high, and he didn't vomit on the stand.

He'd remember what happened, clearly and without hysterics.

Maybe this case wasn't as clear-cut as Arden had hoped.

They had Morris's fingerprints on the bottle, though, smudged on to the label in an as-yet unidentified bodily fluid. They'd tracked the batch to his supplies. It had never been reported stolen, which it should have been, given the value and potency of the drug. That alone implicated Morris.

It had to.

"Has Mara come by today?"

"No. I think she needed a little time to herself."

Oggie burrowed even closer to Arden.

Arden tried to shift but couldn't.

"It's been funny, living without her. We've been peas in a pod since she was born, you know."

Given what he'd learned last night that statement implied so much.

"She'd give me such a hard time when I got sick after a night out and I'd tell her she owed it to me after how many of her diapers I changed."

"That's what family's for," Arden guessed. Mama had never seen him get messy and Mother had never been the one to clean him up as a teenager.

What had she thought of him when he'd slunk back home on those nights? She'd told him he disappointed her, but what had she honestly thought?

What had anyone ever thought of him?

Had Mama loved him, had she loved Mother, or was she just as under their thumb as the rest of *Eden?* She had cuddled him and covered him in kisses, dressed him up and fed him morsels of her favorite snacks, and it had felt so warm and real.

Just as real as the way he'd felt about Rhys.

"Thanks for cleaning me up, sugar. I know it isn't what you signed up for."

"Don't be silly, Og. I signed up exactly for this."

"I don't remember that being part of our agreement," Oggie murmured.

Arden combed Oggie's hair away from his face. He wanted to tell him how beautiful he was, but he didn't need to hear that. He knew already. "No one gets involved with you without thinking they'll have to clean you up at some point."

"That's the second time you've called me messy today."

Arden told him, "You popped a blood vessel in your eye."

Oggie smacked him and rolled away. He wrapped himself in blankets and huffed periodically but wouldn't answer when Arden asked what was wrong.

Arden found that pretty amusing. "Tomorrow I want to go out."

Oggie huffed.

"We should walk around the Solar Deck."

"I couldn't bear everyone looking at me."

Arden rolled close to him and rested his chin on Oggie's shoulder. "So I'll close it."

"What?"

"Yeah, just you and me, Oggie. Anywhere you want to go on *Eden*, I'll close it to everyone else."

"That's..." Oggie turned over. His movement put him close enough to Arden that they nearly bumped faces. "Anywhere I want to go?"

Anything to keep him in a better mood, to stave off the day-drinking.

"Anywhere."

"So there's this book," Oggie began eagerly, "It's called *Mr. Murry Saves the Day*."

"I saw the movie."

Oggie sat up. "Well, you should read the book, because it's better, and because the ending is different."

"Sorry, I'll get right on it."

"In the movie, you know, they never show you who he picks, they just show him standing in the hallway, right, at the intersection. One way, left, to see Jeanette, and right, to see David."

"Well, yeah, but it's all set up, you know, the whole movie leads up to him picking Jeanette."

"That's why the book is better," Oggie told him. "In the book, you know, you're in his head, you know what he's feeling, not just what he's doing, and he, uh, he goes right. He goes to see David."

Arden smiled. "To the restaurant."

"To the bad match." Oggie smiled back.

"To the mess?" Arden guessed.

"It's the only book I've ever read where..." He trailed off. The smile faded from his face.

Arden urged, "Where what?"

"Where a boy like me gets the guy."

"Handsome young men always get the guy."

"No, pretty, messy bitches are a steppingstone. A moment of personal growth for someone else. A tragedy or something to pity. A funeral to attend, a wake-up call for someone else. An ex or a fling, or prostitute," Oggie explained with a serious intensity Arden had never seen before. "Disposable."

Arden took his hand.

"Let me pretend I'm not disposable. If you never ever give me anything else, give me that. One night of..." He blinked, his eyes wet, red-rimmed suddenly, and ten times greener because of it.

"Okay," Arden soothed. He hugged Oggie. "You need to sleep, I think, because you're getting morose, and usually that just means you're tired."

Oggie squeezed him back. "You're probably right."

Arden tucked him into bed and gave him space to recuperate.

He pulled up a copy of *Mr. Murray Saves the Day* on his tablet and read that instead of getting anything done.

He arranged for the Solar Deck to be empty for an hour tomorrow, then did his best to recreate the end of the book for Oggie.

No restaurant on *Eden* exactly matched the one from the book, but he did what he could. The whole thing was silly, a lighthearted Terran romance. Arden did his best impression of Terran manners from the time period and Oggie acted, well, exactly the way he always did, except with more exuberance.

He seemed, for a few days, genuinely happy, if one's happiness could be judged by how few drinks they had. One of those days coincided with Oggie's birthday, so Arden spoiled him particularly that day.

Getting Oggie to the courtroom had proven a trial. He had wanted a drink beforehand and Arden had desperately wanted a shot of Twelve, and it had taken every bit of will Arden possessed to keep them away from their respective vices.

"Tomorrow," he'd promised Oggie dozens of times. "We'll do whatever you want tomorrow."

He said it again now, before the trial started, before they'd have to separate and play their various parts. "Tomorrow."

Oggie had a death grip on Arden's hands. "Sugar."

"Fuck tomorrow. Tonight," Arden said. "We will get blackout drunk *tonight*."

Oggie nodded weakly.

"Okay?"

Oggie pressed his lips together.

Arden told him, "You're okay."

"Mr. Nielsen?" a safety officer asked. "This way, please."

Oggie shoved his hands in his pockets and went with her.

Arden went to sit beside his lawyer on the prosecution's side. He avoided looking at the defense.

He hadn't seen his uncle since Oggie had come clean.

He knew if he looked at him now, he'd come entirely undone.

Morris looked like his sister, the same full handsome mouth and stern jaw. The same cheekbones.

Arden had inherited those cheekbones from the Torres.

It would be like seeing his mother on trial for attempted assassination.

For his own assassination.

It seemed like half of *Eden* had turned out for the trial. He knew that live updates would go out to everyone.

For the most part, all Arden could do was sit and listen. His lawyer did most of the speaking.

This case should be open and shut.

Oggie, poor thing, took the stand first and revealed how Morris had come to him with his proposition. He kept it together through the prosecution's questioning, for which Arden and his lawyer had done their best to prepare him. What he explained made him seem like an awful person. He was a thief and a drug dealer, as well as a reckless, messy partier and he'd played pet to various peers, but nothing he said made him seem like a murderer.

At least there was that.

Morris's lawyer took his opportunity to question Oggie.

"Mr. Nielsen, tell us again how you know Mr. Torre?"

"Uh. Arden or...?"

"Morris," the lawyer confirmed.

"He helped clear up a few charges for me a little while back."

"Hmm. And what were those charges?" the lawyer asked.

Oggie looked at the judge. "Do I have to answer that again?"

"Mr. Nielsen has already given those details," the judge told the lawyer.

"I just wanted to confirm. You were stealing medical supplies and selling them for recreational use. Correct?"

Oggie shrugged. "Sure."

"Nothing else."

"No."

Morris's lawyer waited.

"No," Oggie insisted.

"And you don't have any other reason to collaborate with Morris Torre? No personal relation to him?"

"No."

"And he helped you 'clear up' those charges...for what reason?"

"I don't know."

The lawyer said, "We'd like to play a few videos."

Oggie blanched.

Arden's stomach clenched. "What videos?" he hissed to his lawyer.

The courtroom rustled.

"I don't know what they're talking about," Arden's lawyer admitted softly.

Arden twisted his shirt between his fingers. He tried not to stare at Oggie.

Oggie's eyes had gone wide and vacant.

The screen beside the judge had turned on.

"We do want to point out that these videos are freely available for anyone who searches on the right platforms," Morris's lawyer reminded smoothly.

Oggie hadn't moved.

The screen showed a series of pornographic scenes, not entire videos, but a compilation of shots from different videos. Thankfully, they turned the sound off and blurred the most sensitive parts of the films. Oggie featured in all of them and so did a different man. A pale-skinned man in a mask, the same one every time as far as Arden could tell.

"Mr. Nielsen, that is you, correct?" the lawyer asked.

"Just about all of me," Oggie whispered.

"What was that?" she asked.

"It's me."

"Anything you wanted to tell us about these videos?"

"Made them between the med center and Crystal," he mumbled.

"And these videos, were they produced by the Media Department?" she asked and clearly already knew the answer based on the look on her face.

"No."

"Ah. So, uh, Mr. Nielsen, are these personal videos? Or were you taking money for illegally filmed pornography?"

Oggie didn't say anything.

"Mr. Nielsen?"

"I guess they were personal then."

"Is this relevant somehow?" the judge asked.

"Mr. Neilson, one more time, you have no personal relationship with Morris Torre? Despite him clearing those charges for you?"

"No!"

"This is ridiculous!" Arden called. He got to his feet.

People looked at him.

"This is totally irrelevant. Are you going to let this keep going?" Arden demanded directly of the judge.

"Your Eminence, you did wish to have a trial," the judge reminded gently.

"A trial, not a circus. Get that off the screen."

Someone had paused the video on a particularly graphic moment.

The screen went black.

"May I continue?" the lawyer asked the judge.

"For now."

The lawyer gave a nod. "Mr. Nielsen, who was your partner in these videos?"

"I don't know."

"You don't know? I thought they were personal."

"I've done personal things with strangers before. Haven't you?" Oggie asked.

"You were not aware that Morris Torre was your partner in these videos?"

Arden stood up. He knew he'd gone red by how hot his face felt. "That's it."

"Your Eminence?" the judge asked.

"This is a joke. My uncle hired someone to assassinate me and we're watching porn," Arden told her.

"Those claims haven't been substantiated yet," Morris's lawyer pointed out. "In fact, no claims against my client have ever been substantiated."

Arden turned to look at him. "What's your name?"

"Bailey Spino."

"I'm two minutes away from having you disbarred." He finally looked at his uncle that much harder knowing his face had been behind the mask in the videos. Poor Oggie. "And you."

Morris smiled at him. "Yes, Arden?"

His mouth went dry. "You know I own this fucking station, right?"

Morris kept smiling. "I know."

Something, though, kept Arden from ending things.

He wanted proof. Proof that Morris had done this.

Public recognition that Oggie was innocent.

He needed that. In a hundred years, he wanted people to look up Morris Torre and see him listed as a criminal.

"This close," Arden warned the judge.

The court slowly and awkwardly resumed.

"We have audio, this time, Your Honor, Your Eminence, if it's allowed," Spino said.

"As long as it's not porn," Arden grumbled as he settled back into his seat.

They played the audio.

It wasn't porn.

It was a very friendly and flirty conversation between Oggie and Morris. Oggie relayed heaps of information about Arden to Morris, all of it framed in a perfectly bitchy way that made this seem more like a gossip session than an assassination plot.

"Just a little while longer, you know. Bye-bye, sugar daddy. You're going to have to set me up with someone again," Oggie's voice said.

Arden could imagine the face he would have made as he'd said it.

The audio ended.

They hadn't let Oggie down from the witness stand yet.

He stared at Arden.

Arden made what he hoped was a reassuring expression.

"Sounds like you two were friendly," Spino pointed out.

"I'm good at pretending."

"It seems that way, Mr. Nielsen. It seems like you and Morris Torre had more of an arrangement than—"

"He was making me do it and you know, being difficult with someone like him never made my life any better," Oggie snapped, "I don't know about yours."

"You want to know what I think?"

"No."

"I think this was as much your idea as anyone's. I think you planned this."

Arden cleared his throat.

The judge took the hint.

When dismissed, Oggie climbed down from the stand on shaky legs.

Morris came up and gave his side of things. It had been Oggie's scheme, he'd come to Morris with the idea, talked him into it.

Arden stared at a stain on the table while Morris spoke, his face burning hot. He had to clench his hands to hide their shaking.

No one in this court could believe that Oggie would independently come up with a plot to kill the Autarch. He had nothing to gain from that and no aspirations beyond fun and survival.

Arden pointed that out when it was his turn to talk and he immediately shot down the idea that Rhys and Oggie had somehow conspired to end Arden's reign.

"Any thrall with half a brain would rather have me in charge than Morris, and if you can find one thrall that says otherwise, I'll be on the first shuttle out of here."

And, if there had been shuttles that left *Eden*, Arden might have gotten on it anyway, just to be away from this debacle.

The ones they had still worked, they made sure of it in case of an emergency, but no one used them.

After a recess and a bit of debate, the judge gave her verdict: Morris Torre *and* Ogden Nielsen, guilty of conspiring to kill the Autarch.

Oggie squirmed out of the arms of the first officer that grabbed him and backed himself into a corner as people blocked his flight from the courtroom.

Arden hurried over to them and put himself in between the officers and Oggie. "Let him go, let him go," he insisted as he physically shoved himself between Oggie and the safety officer trying to wrangle him.

"Uh, Your Eminence?" the officer asked. He had a grip on Oggie's wrist.

Oggie twisted so hard Arden thought he'd break something.

"No, fuck off. He's pardoned," Arden said.

The officer stared at him.

"He's fucking pardoned. Go get Morris if you want to do something fucking useful," Arden snapped.

The officer left looking deeply perplexed.

He turned around and pulled Oggie into his arms before he could run away.

Oggie went stiff. "I'm so sorry, sugar."

"You did great." Arden held him tighter.

"I'm so sorry."

"Shhh, now, you were perfect."

Into Arden's shoulder, Oggie sobbed, "I don't want to go to lockup."

What the fuck had happened to him there? "Never. Not ever, ever again, Og, okay? I've got you. You're not in trouble."

Oggie lost it at that. He sagged against Arden and awful, ugly sobs wracked him.

Someone had the good sense to clear out the courtroom.

When Oggie had stopped crying, he dabbed his face clean and quietly asked, "Shouldn't we be blackout drunk about now?" He couldn't look at Arden.

"Yeah."

They'd earned it.

"I'm sorry, Og, I didn't know that they were going to do that."

"Oh, I can't! Arden, I can't talk about that right now!" Oggie cried.

"Okay."

As he'd promised, they got blackout drunk.

Arden didn't remember a lot.

He woke up with something congealed in his hair and Oggie sprawled across the foot of his bed.

Things more or less settled on *Eden* in the following days. The security officers stopped guarding his door, Council meetings resumed their normal tedium, and people stopped giving Arden such pitying looks.

Oggie stayed tense. He seemed nervous around Arden.

Finally, Arden sat him down and said, "We need to talk."

"What about, sugar?"

"Why are you being so weird?"

"Waiting for the other shoe to drop, I guess, shug. You've got to be about done with me by now," Oggie admitted. "This whole thing was about Morris and now he's in lockup."

"Oh." Given that confession, the next thing Arden had to say wouldn't likely go over well.

"That all you wanted to talk about?"

"I don't want you to go anywhere."

"But?"

"But I do want you to stay alive, Og. And I think you need to see someone. Get better settled. Talk about, well, talk about all the shit that's happened to you," Arden proposed.

"I don't like to talk about it."

"Oggie, this is...this is important."

Oggie nodded. "There's the other shoe, then."

"No," Arden insisted, "No. I just. Do whatever you want but I want you to be safe doing it. And Oggie, I'm worried about you."

"I'll bumble through. I always do."

Arden took him by his hands and looked into his eyes. "Oggie, I will never make you do anything, but please, think about it."

Oggie extracted his hands. "Oh, sugar, don't. This is all so much. Can't we have a little bit of fun? Go get one of the games. We can play a game."

"Alright."

Oggie played three abysmal rounds of jumble before he went to his room, claiming a headache.

Arden heard him go out late that night and come home early in the morning.

He needed space and time to process in his own way, Arden tried to tell himself. He would be okay.

He had to be okay.

About a week passed this way.

Finally, Arden got out of bed when he heard Oggie leaving.

The younger man froze when Arden emerged and turned the light on. "Oh, hi, sugar. Did I wake you up?"

"No, I."

Oggie looked him over. "Why are you dressed?" A hint of a smile turned up the corner of his mouth.

"You're going out, right?"

"I'd usually do."

"I, just. Og, we talked about..."

"No, *you* talked," Oggie pointed out quickly.

Arden twisted his hands. He never had trouble demanding anything from anyone, except, for some reason, from Oggie. "Can't we...I mean, if I. I know I asked before and you said your friends wouldn't like me..."

"Well, it's illegal and you're the Autarch, it's not about them liking you, sugar."

Arden blinked and rubbed his nose. "I just, sometimes it feels like we're only friends in this room. If there's other people, or if we go out, it's...it's not the way it is in here."

He couldn't exactly explain what he wanted to say. He didn't know how, and more than that, he didn't understand too well himself. Only that here, together, things felt tangible, and anywhere outside this room, life still felt like an act.

Oggie glanced around the space. "Sugar," he sighed. "I like you, and I like living here, I do."

"But."

"But," Oggie continued guiltily, "This room is the only place where we can be friends. Things between workers and peers, you know, they don't work out and I know, *I know* you think it will, that we'll be friends, but I've seen this before. You'll find a peer, Arden. I'm just a place holder."

"That's not true."

"When you decide you're done with me, I need something to go back to. Put your pajamas on. Go to sleep. You have places to be in the morning," Oggie suggested gently. He came over and gave Arden a kiss on the cheek. "Sleep tight, sugar."

Arden didn't know what else to do.

He went to bed. He lay in bed what felt like hours.

Then he got up.

He headed to Quarter Two and knocked on Rhys's door.

Someone else answered, which happened every time he did this. "Uh?" she asked disdainfully.

"Is Rhys home?"

"Yeah?"

"Can you get him?" Arden asked, trying not to lose his temper.

"Guesso."

From inside, another woman called, "Who is it, Lali?"

"The Autarch," she answered.

Gertie, who Arden recognized but had never formally met, came to the door. "We just got Darcy back to sleep."

Arden failed to see the point of that information. He waited for an explanation, which he didn't get. Finally, he asked, "Do you think you could go fucking get him or what?"

He'd have thought a middle of the night call from the Autarch would provoke a little more urgency.

Gertie nodded and left, closing the door on Arden.

Rhys came to the door a few minutes later. "Sorry about them. Come inside."

As he stepped inside the small apartment, he noted, "They're very rude, your roommates."

"It's the middle of the night."

Arden scowled.

"Is this a, uh, a business call?" Rhys asked.

Arden shook his head.

Rhys didn't look less worried. He gestured towards a worn couch. "Have a seat."

Arden sat. He started to fidget with a frayed patch on the cushion. "I."

He swallowed, then licked his lips. "I didn't know who else to talk to. And I need to talk to someone."

"About what?"

"About Oggie."

Rhys made a clear effort to remain neutral. He'd been better about things lately. Not exactly nice, but less outwardly and viciously disapproving than before. "Go ahead."

Arden didn't tell him everything, but he certainly overshared.

Rhys listened without a word.

Finally, Arden said, "I just, I wanted to throw up, you know!"

"Shh," Rhys urged. "Baby's sleeping." He looked pointedly towards the crib on the other side of the room.

"Sorry. Sorry, I am, and I'm sorry to bother you like this, but I can't talk to Cole or Cath or anyone about these things."

"Why not?" Rhys asked.

"Because they don't understand," Arden said. "They. You know, Cole, he's a good guy, he is, and he cares about workers, but he's not..."

"He's not personally involved with any."

"No."

Rhys made a face. "I suppose this is what friends are for..."

Arden gave a nervous smile.

"Knowing what you do about his parents, you can't be surprised Oggie feels that way," Rhys pointed out.

"No, but I just thought...I thought. I don't know. That things are different."

"You think being friends for months makes you stable, trustworthy. Reliable. His parents were together for eight or nine years, as far as I can tell," Rhys reminded.

"But I'm not like his mom. I'm...I care about him."

"Personally."

Arden nodded.

"What, exactly, do you want from Oggie?"

"Exactly?" Arden asked. "Nothing, uh, nothing specific? I don't know. He should probably drink less..."

Rhys pursed his lips. "Arden, I'm trying to ask if you have feelings for him."

"I told you, the whole sleeping together thing was fake."

"Oh, side note, was he sleeping with your uncle the whole time?"

Arden shrugged. "I didn't ask."

"No, no, I just, I mean. Shit! Those videos. Did he really not know?"

Arden's doubted that Oggie hadn't known. He might not have known at first, but at some point, the pieces must have come together for him. A mask only disguised so much about a person. "That's...that's not important.

That's not what I wanted to talk about."

"No, sorry, but no one saw that coming. I gasped. I really did. I've been meaning to ask but...it didn't seem like an appropriate workplace conversation."

"Not really," Arden agreed.

"Anyway. Do you have feelings for him?"

"I just said—"

"I'm not asking if you're sleeping with him."

Arden quieted. He hadn't considered it. "I don't know."

"Hmm."

"How am I supposed to know? I can't even spend time with him anymore. Whenever he's home, he's recovering and when he's out, I don't know where he goes or what he does. I'm *worried*, Rhys. I don't know what I would do if something bad happened to him."

"You can't help someone who doesn't want help," Rhys pointed out.

"So, what do I do?"

"I don't know."

"Aren't you supposed to be my Chamberlain?"

Rhys let out a bit of a laugh. "I don't have time to get into my track record on relationships, but let's just say you know how my last two turned out. I do better as a friend."

Arden whined.

"Oh, don't do that. I haven't heard you do that in forever."

He groaned.

Rhys rolled his eyes. "Why don't you go home and sleep on it?"

"I can't sleep, I'm worked up."

"Then at least go home."

Arden bit his lip.

"What?"

"I don't want to go home. I don't want to be waiting for him to get home," he confessed.

"We have to work in the morning."

Arden pouted and almost whined again.

"Fine," Rhys said. "Stay. But it's going to be awkward."

Arden grinned.

"It's not a sleepover, stop smiling."

"We haven't had a sleepover in *ages*," Arden said, still grinning.

"You can sleep on the couch or in my bed." Rhys stood.

Arden also stood. "Is...is that supposed to be a real question? And why do you even still live here anyway?"

"My friends live here."

"Well, duh, okay, but why not rent a less shitty apartment?"

"People have debts to pay off."

Arden frowned at him. "You could pay the rent?"

Rhys sighed.

"Are you paying off other people's debts?" he asked.

Rhys didn't answer.

"That's not exactly what I had in mind when I gave you a raise..." Arden murmured.

Rhys opened the door to a bedroom with several beds.

"Do you guys fuck in front of each other?" Arden asked immediately. He regretted it and, in that instant, knew he really did need to go bed.

Rhys turned around to look at him.

"I'm so sorry," Arden whispered.

"I'm so close to making you sleep head to feet."

"Well, you know I'm a cuddler, so you'd just end up with feet in your face," Arden pointed out. "Is this your bed?"

"Yes."

He made himself comfortable.

Rhys got into bed less enthusiastically.

"Does Gertie sleep in here?"

"Other people are trying to sleep. Shut up before I smother you."

Arden whispered, "Does Gertie sleep in here?"

"No."

"Rhys, I'm going to kill your friend," someone groaned.

Arden opened his mouth.

Before he could speak, Rhys pressed a hand over his mouth. "I'm so fucking serious, Arden, shut the fuck up and go to sleep."

Arden nodded.

Rhys nestled onto his side of the bed.

Arden breathed, "How come grown-ups never have sleepovers?"

"I will kill you," Rhys breathed back.

Arden didn't find anything funny after that. He quieted and snuggled into a pillow. It wasn't that he took Rhys seriously, it was being reminded of everything.

Quickly, Rhys whispered, "I didn't mean that. I'm sorry."

Arden shook his head.

Rhys put an arm around him. "I am. That was shitty of me."

"Could you two at least fuck so I can jerk off?" someone demanded.

Rhys sat halfway up and barked, "Shut the fuck up, Kile!"

No one said anything after that.

Rhys settled back down with Arden.

It took a while to fall asleep and Rhys had to wrest the covers off him in the morning.

He declined the offer to shower there and told Rhys they could meet up at the Public Chamber.

Before he left, he hugged Rhys. "Thank you."

"No, it's…"

"No, I needed someone to talk to."

Darcy started to fuss in her crib.

Arden pulled back. "I'll let you take care of her."

Rhys went to scoop up the girl. "Say bye to Arden."

The baby waved to him and said, "Buh."

Arden stared.

Shit.

Had he ever been this close to a baby before?

He waved back.

"You want to hold her?" Rhys offered.

"No!"

Rhys smiled. "Nothing bad will happen."

Arden eyed the baby. He stepped closer.

Rhys passed Darcy over without waiting.

Arden clasped her close instinctively, overwhelmed with the fear of dropping her.

She immediately started to fuss.

"Take her back," Arden demanded.

"Just bounce her."

Arden clumsily tried to bounce the baby.

She continued to fuss.

"Rhys, take her back."

"I'm actually going to jump in the shower quick," Rhys said and left Arden alone with the baby.

Arden stared at her.

She started to cry.

"Please stop," he begged, "Please, or I'll start too. Please please oh, ow, ouch."

She had grabbed a fistful of his hair.

He extracted his hair from her grip but had the feeling he'd lost a chunk somewhere in the process.

He tried putting her down, which turned her crying into screaming. He brought her back up close to his chest, shifted her around, bounced her and cooed to her.

She stopped crying before Rhys returned.

Arden had broken out in a nervous sweat.

"Oh, she likes you," Rhys noted as he toweled his hair.

"Please, take her back," Arden whispered.

Rhys took the baby. "See you soon."

"I hate you so much."

"Well, maybe next time you'll shut up when it's time for bed."

Arden took a step toward the door, stopped, and asked, "Did you use your own child as a tool for punishment?"

Rhys shrugged. "Yeah."

"And you thought I was a monster."

"I'll see you at Council."

Arden left and didn't realize he'd let Rhys dismiss him until halfway through his shower.

He checked on Oggie before he headed to Council.

At least he'd come home last night and made it all the way to his bed. He didn't even smell like vomit.

Not that Arden usually smelled him while he slept, but today he'd had the overwhelming urge to kiss his forehead.

He didn't like the urge, it felt weird and awkward and stupid, but he did it anyway.

He almost had to do it.

He kissed his forehead.

Oggie smelled clean and sweet. His skin was warm and smooth beneath Arden's lips.

He thought about that for the entirety of the Council meeting.

It sort of made him want to cry.

He sat through the Council meeting feeling weepy and strange.

"Your Eminence, are you alright?" Rhys leaned in to whisper.

He still didn't talk too openly at meetings.

Arden nodded. He handed his tablet over to Rhys. "Here, you basically wrote this anyway, why don't you present it?"

Rhys stared at him. "Are...If that's what you want, Your Eminence?"

He nodded.

Rhys smoothed out his clothes excessively, then turned toward the Council members. He cleared his throat. "Uh. I."

Arden touched his arm. "Go ahead."

Rhys cleared his throat again and then launched into the report they'd prepared on proposed adjustments to maintenance teams. It would, in theory, free up workers for more necessary jobs without compromising the safety of *Eden*.

Rhys did fine.

Better than Arden would have. No surprises there.

Arden couldn't sleep.

He'd had a lot of weirdly sleepless nights. Sometimes he went to bother Rhys, which Rhys claimed to absolutely hate but tolerated a little too well for that. Other nights, he stayed in bed watching shows or thinking stupid, useless thoughts about things he couldn't change.

He got up tonight.

Oggie had come home already.

Arden went to check on him. He sat on the side of Oggie's bed and watched him sleep for a while, like an absolute fucking creep.

He sighed.

A few days ago, they'd tried again to go out with Arden's friends. He'd had to beg, really beg, to get Oggie to agree.

Nothing bad had happened but his friends had been so cold toward Oggie.

Everyone thought Arden was still overusing formulas and that he'd only pardoned Oggie because of it, which had made everything awkward.

Oggie had turned into a shaky mess after about an hour. He'd said, "I'd rather be in lockup than have them look at me like that anymore!"

Arden had taken him home and asked, "What did they do to you in lockup anyway?"

Cheeks red, Oggie had admitted, "Nothing, just put me in a back cell and left me there for a few days."

"They didn't feed you?"

"No, no, they did, they just...all alone like that in the dark, sugar, I couldn't stand it."

Arden hadn't known what to say to that.

He felt like he never knew what to do anymore.

He knew what he wanted, which usually counted for something, but felt meaningless these days.

He stopped watching Oggie and went out to watch Terra.

He sat for a while in front of the window with his tablet on his lap.

Oggie found him there.

"You're up early," Arden noted.

"I turned in early last night."

"I saw."

Oggie sat next to him but leaned against the window and looked at Arden instead of at Terra. "Vortex is winding down."

"Hmm?"

"Places like that burn out quick. A new place will pop up in a few months, but I hate to be around when things fall apart. It gets ugly."

"Does that mean you're mine again?" Arden asked.

Oggie smiled. "We all are."

The sentence Arden meant to say faded as it got towards his lips. He glanced at his tablet. "Do you want breakfast?"

Oggie shrugged. "I don't know."

"You okay?"

"Getting there. Or, as close as I get. What about you, shug? You've been..." Oggie studied him. "Quiet."

"I keep wanting something I can't have. It's hard for a spoiled peer like me to deal with, not getting what I want all the time."

Oggie shook his head. "Are you two back at it?"

"Who?"

"You and Rhys. You've been going to see him in the middle of the night. I figured you were trying to keep it on the sly. Bad idea, going back to someone who left you, if you ask me. But then again, people do change..."

Arden shook his head. "No, I, uh." He shrugged. "We mostly just talk."

"About what?"

"What the fuck I'm doing with my life. Or about Darcy."

Arden spent more time with Darcy than he'd anticipated. The girl didn't sleep well and often woke during their late-night talks. He had even stopped being afraid of holding her. He saw her during the day, too, when Rhys stopped home for lunch and Arden followed him. She recognized him now.

Once, he'd tempted Rhys easily with a free meal, but he had food and a child he adored at home now. It made Arden wonder exactly how much of the time they'd spent together had been endured rather than enjoyed.

"He doesn't like me either," Oggie pointed out. "They all want me out of here."

"It's my home and I want you here," Arden said a little too forcefully.

Oggie looked away. After a bit, he said, "It's still early. You look tired. Maybe you should lay down for a bit."

"I'm okay."

Arden's tablet dinged.

"You look tired a lot these days, sugar."

"I need a vacation."

"A...what, like a trip? Where would you go?"

Arden's tablet dinged three times rapidly.

"Terra One."

"Uh." Oggie glanced toward the planet behind him. "Isn't everything dead down there?"

"Not everything. Just the things that make it possible for people to live there," Arden said. His tablet let out another flurry of dings. "People still live there, though. Barely hanging on. Sometimes they send out messages asking for help."

"Doesn't sound that great."

"It'd be better with company," Arden suggested. His tablet had practically broken into song and dance.

"Sugar, your, uh, your tablet is going wild over there?"

Arden turned off the sound and flipped it over so the screen faced down.

"Is something happening?"

"No."

"Arden."

"Nothing to worry about," Arden assured.

"Not some kind of asteroid heading our way?" Oggie asked nervously.

Arden smiled. "No. Do you want to go on vacation?"

"Uh."

"We could go, right now. The shuttles still work."

"Are you serious?"

Arden nodded.

"You can't...I mean, I have to work, you know, and you're, you're Autarch, you can't just pop down to Terra," Oggie reminded.

"You don't need to work."

"I sure fucking do."

Arden picked up his tablet, cleared all his notifications, and showed Oggie his account. "No, you don't."

Oggie stared. "What did you do?" he whispered.

Arden shrugged. "Cleared your debt."

"I! I didn't ask you to do that!"

"I know."

"I'm! This is an awful fucking come-on, you know! I never agreed to anything," Oggie nearly screeched. He scooted further toward the window, away from Arden and looking objectively terrified.

"Og, hey, shh. I'm not asking you for anything. I'm not. Take a breath."

Oggie pulled in a shaky breath. "I don't want to do this. Not like this!"

"You're not doing anything," Arden assured.

"Then why'd you do that?"

Arden swallowed. He took his tablet back. He hadn't expected Oggie to look so betrayed. He understood Oggie's misinterpretation of his actions, though. "I did it for everyone." He looked at the screen instead of at Oggie. He had literally a hundred messages waiting for him.

"You did what for everyone?"

"Every debt on *Eden* is cleared."

"Are you high?" Oggie demanded.

Arden sighed. "This system of labor isn't sustainable. Or ethical, for that matter, if you're worried about ethics. Which I guess I sort of am these days."

"That what you and Rhys have been talking about?"

"Uh. No. Mostly we talk about nothing. Which is nice."

After a long pause, Oggie asked, "Every debt?"

"It's a little rambunctious of me, isn't it?"

Oggie scooched in his direction. He took his hand. "It's absolutely wild of you, sugar. I'm sorry I got worked up."

"It's fine."

Oggie tightened his grip. "It's just...I do like to have a say in these things. To be asked first."

"I understand," Arden assured. He shifted his gaze to Terra. "The peers are going to riot."

"You all are too lazy to riot," Oggie pointed out. "What are you going to do?"

Arden shrugged. "Go on vacation."

"You can't throw *Eden* something like this then leave."

"I can if I leave Rhys and the Council in charge with some provisionary notes, then hop my ass on a shuttle."

"Arden!"

"I'm just saying."

Oggie's grip tightened on his hand even more, crushing his fingers. "Are you leaving?"

"Not for long. There's something I need to do on Terra." He looked at Oggie. "Come with me."

"I can't come with you."

"Oggie, come with me." Arden couldn't stop staring at him. "I don't want to be away from you."

"Sugar," he whined.

"I'm so scared but I have to go. Please, I need you."

Oggie sniffled, his eyes greener than they'd ever been with how red the whites had gotten. "People only talk to me like that when they're jonesing or horny."

"I'm neither," Arden assured.

"Then what do you need me for?"

Arden didn't know, exactly. He pressed his lips together and thought. "I..."

Oggie dug his fingers into Arden's wrist, his nails cutting into his skin. He gazed at Arden. "What do you really want from me?"

Arden didn't pull his wrist back. "I...I want to go away. I want to come back to a place where there aren't workers and peers anymore."

"Debt isn't what made us workers."

"Generations of systematic oppression is, yes, I know," Arden said. "Rhys likes to remind me."

"Why aren't you asking him to go with you?"

"Because I can't leave anyone else in charge while I'm gone."

Oggie took his hand back.

Arden rubbed his wrist.

"You haven't told me what you want."

He couldn't say it.

"Arden."

"What, Og? We're friends. I want us to be friends somewhere outside of this room. I want to go places with you and do something other than hide in here and play board games. I want..."

Oggie raised his eyebrows.

"I want you to know that you're not someone I'm going to throw away."

"And taking me to an empty planet proves that?"

"It's not empty. That's why I'm going there. Come with me. Be part of what helps save *Eden*," Arden insisted.

"Sugar, I'm still not sure I follow, but it seems important to you. Like...maybe too important," Oggie said, "And I'm a little worried what might happen if I say no. So I guess let's go."

Arden couldn't believe how thoroughly that had backfired. He'd turned an invitation into an obligation. "If you don't want to—"

"No, no, sugar, I might as well go, cause if you disappear and I'm still on *Eden*, they'll probably kill me."

Arden sighed.

"I'll go pack. How long do you think we'll be gone? I'll have to tell Mara, too, or she'll think we did some kind of suicide pact. She might anyway. She has a dark mind," he rambled.

Arden threw his arms around him and dragged him close. It shouldn't have gone this way.

Oggie squeaked. He gave Arden a pat on the back. "Alright, sugar. You go get packed, too."

Arden nodded.

He shoved a few things into a bag, unsure of what to bring.

Using service lifts and back stairways, he and Oggie snuck up to the shuttle bay on deck one. No one had come to work today.

Judging by what they'd heard on the way up, every worker on the station was celebrating. The peers seemed to have locked themselves inside.

Arden had never answered any of his messages. He'd sent a letter to Rhys and the Council members explaining what to do in his absence and his plans on Terra. He'd written another letter to Winslow to assure him he'd be back soon. He'd sent a third, very serious letter to the chief security officer about what to do if Morris Torre even mentioned that he should serve as Autarch in Arden's absence.

Once inside the shuttle, Arden sat at the controls and stared at them.

"Do you know how to fly this?"

"I read the manual."

"Sugar, this isn't how I wanted to die."

"How did you want to die?" Arden asked.

"Shug, I'm having serious reservations."

"No, it's...we have drills, it's fine, I can do this," Arden assured. He'd done this before, at least, he'd done dry runs where the shuttle never left the bay.

"Drills?"

"In case of emergency."

Oggie made a face. "I've never been to a drill."

Arden glanced up. "Uh. The workers generally are...not invited to participate in the evacuation drills."

"Oh, I super hate that."

Arden scanned the controls for the ignition. He found it and pressed it.

The shuttle vibrated.

Oggie grabbed onto Arden's shoulder.

"Go sit." That was the first thing the drills went over. Everyone seated and buckled in. Arden hoped that misstep wouldn't set the tone for their trip.

Oggie sat.

Arden, from the control panel, opened the shuttle bay airlock and managed to direct the shuttle out of it. It took much longer than it should have, but he did it without harming the bay or the shuttle.

He closed the airlock.

"What the fuck," Oggie breathed quietly and repeatedly for the entire first half-hour of their trip.

The shuttle had an autopilot function and all Arden needed to do was put in their destination. The craft would do everything itself unless something happened that the AI couldn't handle.

"Og, you okay over there?"

"Yeah, just...what the fuck?"

"It takes about eighteen hours to reach the upper atmosphere."

"Fuck."

Arden spun the pilot's chair around. "You sure you're alright?"

"Aren't you scared!"

Arden raised his hand to show that it shook. "I don't think I could even spit right now."

"Where are we going?"

"Someone asked for help. I figured, might as well help them."

"More mouths to feed?"

Arden shrugged. "More people to work. And who knows? It might just be a few people. Maybe only one."

Oggie unbuckled himself. He wandered around the cabin, reading the safety signs and looking out the window.

Arden turned back around and watched Terra.

He'd gone over this plan hypothetically with a few people.

He'd listened to the call over and over. A soft, high voice, probably a youth or a woman, asking for anyone to help.

All this time people had begged for help and *Eden* had ignored them. A day of travel and countless lives would have been saved.

What had they ignored them for?

"Og?"

"Hmm?"

"Thank you."

"Don't thank me yet. I'm about ready to have a fit," Oggie warned. "There's nothing to drink."

"There's water."

"No, Arden, there's nothing to drink."

"Oh. Well." He licked his lips. "Are we talking wants or needs when it comes to having a drink?"

Oggie swallowed. "I'll let you know if I get the shakes, I guess." He looked at his hands, which were indeed shaking. "Nerves, probably."

"I'm sorry."

"Ah, that's alright, sugar. I get through it fine. No seizures or anything."

Arden checked the first aid kit, as though it would help anything.

"I've been scaling back anyway, it's...I'll be fine. Come here."

Arden hesitated.

"Come here, get over here."

Arden went.

Oggie folded his arms around Arden. "You look so worried, shug, I hate that. Aren't we going on some big adventure?"

"Historic."

"Historic. Arden and Oggie, historic adventurers. Saving *Eden*, overthrowing the indenture system, surviving withdrawal." Oggie tightened his embrace. "Do you really think I'll be in the history books with you?"

"Yes."

"Not just as a terrible assassin, either."

"I'll make sure of it."

"I know you said you wanted to do more than play board games, but this is an awfully long trip."

"I packed jumble," Arden said.

"We should play, then. Get our minds off things."

At a small table behind the cockpit, they played for hours. They ate a fairly tolerable meal of rehydrated food and watched a movie. Oggie slowly grew quieter and crankier as time went on. He rubbed at his temples, drank an intense amount of water, then announced, "I give up."

"Give what up?"

Oggie rifled through his bags, then took a number of pills, which worried Arden, and said, "Wake me up when we get there."

"What did you just take?"

"Something to help me sleep."

"What am I supposed to do for twelve hours by myself?" Arden asked.

"Read a book, play solitaire, jerk off. I don't know. I do know that you'd probably rather I be asleep for the next leg of this." He settled onto the small Murphy bed across from the table where they'd sat together. His eyes flicked over Arden, something rotten and sultry in that glance. "I won't wake up unless you do something really awful to me."

Bile hit the back of Arden's throat. He swallowed. "Spare parts," he accused weakly.

He walked away, back to the pilot's chair, trying not to think of what Oggie had implied. He didn't go back there again except to use the bathroom and only when he couldn't hold it any longer.

Oggie didn't look peaceful in this sleep. He looked dead.

Arden wanted to shake him until he woke up.

Instead, he dozed in the pilot's chair, which reclined enough for a nap, and ate another rehydrated meal. He watched the planet grow slowly closer with one of the more intense senses of dread he'd felt in his lifetime.

He cried once, quietly and curled up, glad Oggie was asleep.

The shuttle passed through Terra's atmosphere shakily enough that Oggie stumbled out and asked, "Are we dying?"

"No."

He nodded, used the bathroom, and returned to hover awkwardly beside Arden. "I feel like shit."

"Food and water would probably help. You slept for thirteen hours straight."

"You look like shit, too."

"I'm just tired."

"Well, you go lay down. I'll wake you up if anything starts beeping or flashing. How long before we land?"

Arden glanced at the control panel. "About five hours until we get to the source of the signal."

Oggie smoothed his fingers through Arden's hair, his nails running over his scalp.

Arden's back straightened.

Oggie's grip on his hair tightened, pulling his hair.

Arden couldn't quite breathe. He stared up at Oggie, no choice with the way Oggie had angled his head.

Oggie shook his head, looking sad more than anything, then released Arden. "Get some sleep."

Arden went to lay down, his entire body tingling, but his scalp especially. He always felt empty in the places where Oggie had hurt him. He dropped into a dreamless sleep, exhausted physically and emotionally.

He awoke sometime later because something had jolted the shuttle.

Oggie appeared in the doorway. "Touch down," he announced softly.

Arden scrambled from under the covers. He hurried to a window and saw a flat, sparse expanse of land. Yellow grass and crooked trees. Crumbled remains of buildings.

Smoke in the distance and a crooked metal tower.

He couldn't breathe. He swallowed, or tried, but his mouth was too dry.

"There are people," Oggie told him softly. "I could see their tents as we came in."

A chill ran through his whole body.

"Arden, there's people," Oggie repeated.

He hurried over to the control panel and checked the environmental readings as he struggled into his shoes.

Oggie stood to the side, quiet, still.

"Are you coming?"

"I'd probably die if you left me on this thing alone."

Arden opened the shuttle door.

Hot, dusty air swept into the cool interior.

Oggie and Arden linked hands without a word or a glance.

They stepped out on to Terra, both shaky, their palms sweaty.

Arden checked three times to make sure he had the fob to open the shuttle doors before he closed them. He slipped the fob into a pocket on the inside of his vest, close to his ribs so he'd always be able to feel it.

They headed toward the smoke.

"What if they're vicious?" Oggie asked.

"I guess we'll run."

"Oh, easy enough for you, Mr. Handball. What about me?"

"I guess I'll have to pull you."

"I don't think you're strong enough."

Arden wiggled his fingers more firmly into Oggie's grip. "Then I guess we'll die."

"Sugar," he scolded.

It took them about half an hour to walk close enough to the tower to see the tents clearly. A dozen or so brown domes clustered protectively around the tower.

People stood in a huddle perpendicular to the path they had taken towards the settlement. More people than Arden anticipated based on the number of tents.

Women of many ages, and children. One or two people that might have been men, or masculine women, or without a binary gender. They all wore loose clothing in pale colors with little skin exposed. Some wore scarves around their heads. Many had dark makeup smudged around their eyes. They had little else in the way of decoration.

Arden felt silly wearing such tight, dark clothing. He'd started to sweat immediately, and the sun made his skin feel tight.

Oggie shimmered with sweat.

Arden and Oggie stopped about four yards away from the cluster of Terrans. Arden wiped his hand on his pants, then waved. He pointed to the tower. "That your tower?"

No one answered him.

They stood and stared a while longer.

One child, maybe thirteen, demanded, "What tribe?"

An older woman grabbed her shoulder and dragged her protectively back into the group.

It took Arden a minute to unravel the child's accent. The pronunciation of those two words revealed a languid drawl, all vowels and softened consonants. It made it seem like one long nonsense word.

He pointed skyward. "We came from a space station."

"What's that?" the child asked from the woman's grasp.

"It's a big, uh, big station. Up in space," Arden said.

"Brilliantly explained," Oggie whispered.

"*Eden* is a man-made structure outside Terra's orbit," Arden tried. "One of my ancestors built it before Terra..." He looked around. "Before the environment became so hostile."

A few people leaned close to whisper to each other.

Eventually, one woman with waist-length blonde hair stepped forward. She spoke in the same drawl, "Your tribe is peaceful?"

Arden and Oggie glanced at each other.

Arden shrugged. He hoped he'd understood her and replied, "Yeah. Pretty peaceful."

"I'd say so," Oggie agreed.

"Come in," the blonde said.

"Well, hang on," Arden said. "Are you peaceful?"

A giggle went through the group.

The blonde woman said, "We look like raiders to you? Or warlords?"

"Not particularly."

"Come in," she said again. "It's been years since we've come across another peaceful tribe."

Arden headed toward them.

Oggie trailed close behind.

People stared openly at them.

Children shied away when he looked at them.

One or two cried.

A woman with frizzy gray hair and deep brown skin joined Oggie, Arden, and the blonde on their walk deeper into the tents. She explained, "Don't mind the littles. Most of them never seen a man before, at least not up close."

"No?" Arden asked.

"Most men don't come in peace. Been about six years since we last met a tribe with men and didn't have to run."

"Really?" Arden's eyes swept over the gathered people again. Children seemed to come in three ages: five, twelve, and fifteen. The women's ages varied more normally.

"Really," the blonde confirmed.

"I, uh. My name's Arden, by the way. This is Oggie."

"Kineth," the blonde said.

"Tola," said the gray-haired woman.

"Where are we going?"

"To see my mother," Kineth said.

"She in charge or something?"

"No one's in charge," Tola said. "Mari tracks our lineages. She'll know the best matches for you."

Arden and Oggie stopped walking.

"Matches?" Oggie asked.

The women looked at them.

As though speaking to a child, Kineth said, "For the next generation."

"Oh, well, I wasn't on planning on staying here long term or anything,"

Oggie said.

"You'll leave your seed and go. That's the way of men," Tola reminded gently.

"I'd sort of hoped for a different kind of dialogue. Isn't there someone we can talk to? We got a distress call from here," Arden said.

"It must have been from the last tribe who settled here," Tola said.

"And where are they?"

Kineth shrugged. "All we found was bones."

"Fucking..." Arden breathed. "And you stayed here."

"Four old men picked clean by carrion birds and skin beetles. They traveled alone or got left behind," Tola said. "Come. Speak with Mari."

The women walked away.

Arden glanced at the crowd behind them, then followed the other two.

Oggie followed too. "Shug," he murmured.

"It seems like this Mari is important. We should talk to her."

"I'm sort of worried about skin beetles."

"Skin beetles eat the dead. Don't die and you don't have to worry about them," Kineth said.

"This is a lovely vacation," Oggie grumbled.

"Shh," Arden scolded.

Kineth stepped into a tent and announced, "Two men, Mama."

Arden stepped inside, blinking as his eyes adjusted to the dimmer light.

"Sit," said a woman with cropped blonde hair.

Arden sat where she gestured.

Oggie sat next to Arden.

Arden glanced back, but Kineth and Tola had left the tent without a farewell.

Mari asked, "Water?"

"Uh. Please."

"Yes, thanks," Oggie said.

Mari handed them cups of tepid water.

Arden slurped it down despite the temperature and stale taste. "We're from a space station."

"Travelers," Mari said. "That's good, the further the better."

"Listen, we didn't come here to—"

Mari held up her hand. "You're from far away. You don't know our customs. Listen first."

Arden nodded, shocked by how firmly she spoke with him. He didn't take offense, but he'd never been spoken to like that by anyone but Mother.

"When tribes meet in peace, we do no other business until the most important business has taken place. We do this first so that things don't go sour between tribes and prevent a new generation."

"It's just that..."

Mari quieted him with a look.

"Good matches spend the night together in a tent. Other business is conducted in the morning."

"I'm...That's. With strangers?" Arden asked nervously. He'd never hooked up with a worker and he more or less knew all the peers by sight if not by name, so he'd never had the chance to have sex with a stranger. Considering how much he hated new things, this sounded like a nightmare.

Mari gave him a gentle smile. "We burn jessa. It helps."

"And, uh." Arden glanced at Oggie, then looked back at Mara. "I don't...I really don't even know if I can have kids."

"You spend the night in the tent. Whatever happens...that's between those in the tent. No one will force anything. Other business is conducted in the morning," Mari told them. "I'm sure you have many interesting tales to tell, men from space. But first, we do what we can for the next generation."

Arden looked at Oggie.

"But we don't have to, like, get married or anything?" Oggie asked.

"No. Sometimes a deeper connection is found, and a man chooses to stay, but that hasn't happened in many years. Some may wish you to stay, though." She looked at Oggie appreciatively.

He gave her a nervous smile. "Lovely."

"You may leave, of course," Mari added quickly. "But no other business will be conducted otherwise."

Arden doubted he'd find any connection in the tribe's tent, no matter what they burned, but he had other things he wanted to talk about. He'd sit in a tent full of women for a night, no hardship there. It'd be like visiting one of Cathie's ladies' clubs. "Sure."

"Oh, been a while since I've been to an orgy," Oggie noted. "Where are all the men, by the way? You don't...like. Eat them after sex or anything?"

Mari looked concerned. "Famine, sickness, and violence claimed our men, slowly but surely over the years. We have some boys that will be men soon. That will be good. We do not kill our own. Is that common in your tribe?"

"No, not common, not really," Arden assured.

"We can talk more about our histories in the morning. Tell me about yourselves. Your family's bloodlines. I'll know better then who to match you with."

Arden provided the information he had somewhat uncomfortably. He didn't know his father's name, let alone his genetic information. He told her what he could about Mother's family.

Oggie rattled off a little information but admitted he didn't know much.

Mari listened, provided them with food and water, then left the tent.

She said, "Attendants will be by to bring you to the tent shortly."

"No mingling?" Oggie asked.

"Other business—"

"In the morning," Oggie finished.

She gave him a wry smile.

About an hour later, a pair of teenagers came by. They brought them to relieve themselves and wash up.

They didn't talk much, which Arden figured had to do with their tribe's ban on talking to strangers too much.

He understood it, in a way. Getting to know someone too much could make it hard to take them as a lover. First impressions mattered a lot.

He tried to prepare himself for an awkward, boring night. He didn't think he'd find anyone he wanted, no matter how much jessa they burned.

Whatever jessa was.

Their attendants brought them to a tent with sweet smoke trickling out of it.

"We can take your clothes," one offered.

"Oh, no thanks," Arden said.

He stepped into the tent.

The smoke made Arden immediately feel lightheaded and kind of silly.

Half a dozen women in their twenties or thirties sat inside, some dressed, some otherwise. Their eyes looked a little glassy.

Arden took a seat on one of the cushions.

When Oggie stepped in, undressed, every pair of eyes went to him. He smiled at Arden. "I do very well at orgies, sugar."

"I'm sure you do."

A pretty young woman gestured for Oggie to come sit next to her.

He went. "I'm Oggie."

She giggled. She immediately put her hand between his legs.

Without missing a beat, he took her hand back and kissed her palm. "What's the rush?"

"Jessa wears off in a couple hours," one of the women told him.

"Oh, I do just fine without it," he promised warmly.

Arden's cheeks had started to warm.

Four women had crowded around Oggie.

One woman lay on her back, having a good time on her own on at the far end of the tent.

Arden tried not to stare.

A woman, about thirty or maybe a little younger, came to sit next to Arden. "I'm Holly."

"Arden."

"I heard you're from space."

"A space station. We're not, you know, we're human."

She smiled. "You look pretty human."

"Are we allowed to talk about other stuff? I thought we were here to make babies."

She grimaced. "There's not enough jessa in the world to make me want to do it with a man."

"Yeah, I..." Arden glanced around the tent. He didn't have an issue with any of the women. His eyes landed on Oggie, though, who had his arms around two women.

They'd all cuddled up together.

"It's not that I don't like women. I mean, I did it with a woman once, and there have been others I wanted to be with but..." Arden shrugged. "I don't know. I guess I'm picky."

"Your friend seems to have, uh, shouldered that burden for you."

Arden snorted.

He looked at Oggie again.

"I bet you could pick off that one with the freckles," Arden told Holly.

A freckled woman with golden skin seemed more interested in the girl beside her, who focused fully on Oggie.

No one had done anything more than cuddle, or kiss, or purr yet, but Arden felt hot all over. He was glad he'd left his clothes on.

"Ah, Sher wants a baby so bad, I'm not going to ruin it for her. You think he can handle four, though? That's a tall order."

"I guess we'll find out."

He and Holly had a bit of a running commentary on the actions of the others, postulations, and guesses as to how things would go.

Oggie snuggled and squirmed, he caressed and kissed, but that was about it.

He had his mouth on someone's throat when he made eye contact with Arden.

Arden swallowed. His mouth had filled with saliva, which he disliked as much as he disliked the tense, hot discomfort between his legs.

It got worse the longer Oggie looked at him.

He dropped his eyes, then glanced back to find Oggie still looking in his direction.

Holly said, "You should probably just go over."

Arden shook his head.

Oggie shrugged his way out of the pile of women. He crawled across the cushions to Arden.

Arden licked his lips and swallowed. He tried not to squirm but desperately wanted some kind of stimulation. He'd be fondling himself in a corner in a few minutes.

"You don't want to come over, sugar?" Oggie asked, kneeling in front of Arden. Fuzzy, golden hair on his thighs glowed in the low light of the tent.

"Not...not really into orgies, I guess."

"Drugs not helping?"

Arden swallowed and thought of all the things he'd rather be doing with his mouth. "Go on back, you looked like you were having fun."

Oggie glanced over his shoulder.

The women had surged together in his absence.

"They won't miss me." His eyes shone and his lips had gone ruddy. He had color in his cheeks and a flush all over his body.

Arden tried, and failed, not to glance between his legs.

Beautiful all over, but Arden had known that.

"Go on, shug," he encouraged gently.

"I. I don't know."

"Don't you want me?"

Arden stared at his mouth. "Not, not as an obligation, or a *quid pro quo*."

Oggie grinned. "You'll regret it either way."

"Og, I don't want to be another person who hurt you."

"Arden, you've already hurt me so badly," Oggie said. His eyes shone in the light.

Holly quietly moved away from them.

"You hurt me every day. You smile while you do it." A few tears slipped down his cheek leaving perfect trails on his skin.

Arden's throat tightened and his heart twisted, which conflicted awfully with the vicious hardness between his legs. He tried to swallow. "It's warm in here, don't you think?"

Oggie dragged his fingers over the fly of Arden's pants.

Arden gasped.

"Get undressed." He kept his hand over Arden's cock.

"Oggie, I don't want to hurt you," he pleaded.

Oggie took his hand back and grabbed Arden's jaw. "Then stop pretending to be my friend."

Arden wanted to weep.

The sounds of pleasure from the other side of the tent turned his stomach and heated his guts all at once.

"Which is it, Arden, you want to go jerk off alone or do you want to finally fuck me?" His fingers dug into Arden's jaw.

"Why are you being so mean?"

"Because I hate you so fucking much. I hate that you don't get mad at me, or look at me, or...Or...!"

"Oggie," he begged.

"I plotted to fucking kill you, Arden, and you didn't even care, it didn't even bother you. I don't understand why you keep pretending to like me, but I can't...You know, I'd rather keep playing this stupid fucking game than not see you anymore," Oggie growled.

Arden didn't understand.

Oggie needed professional help, and a stint in rehab, and maybe medication. But maybe, Arden realized, more than any of those things, he needed something he'd probably never had in his entire life.

Not from a distant mother, disillusioned father, or angry sister, or from any of the people who only saw how beautiful he was.

He put his hand on Oggie's wrist and pulled his hand away from his jaw. "Oggie, I love you."

"Shut up."

"I do, I love you. I love you so much that it doesn't matter what you do to me. Kill me or hurt me or take everything I have. I don't care."

Oggie grabbed him.

Arden took in a sharp breath. "Please."

Oggie kissed him, hard, almost too hard, and desperately. He clambered into Arden's lap and wrapped his arms around Arden so tightly he could barely move. He pulled back and stared down at Arden. "You don't mean it." He practically vibrated against Arden.

"I love you."

Oggie pulled Arden's hair hard and put his other hand around Arden's throat. He squeezed dangerously hard. "You don't." His voice shook.

Arden couldn't breathe well enough to protest. He put his hand over Oggie's wrist again and leaned into his hold. He kissed him, softly.

Oggie went slack. He started to pull back. "Sugar, I'm sorry, that was...I don't..."

Arden didn't let him go.

"What the fuck," Oggie whispered.

Arden held on to him.

Despite the emotional turmoil, he was still urgently aroused. He kissed Oggie's bare skin, his throat and shoulders.

Oggie sighed and leaned in.

"Tell me it's okay," Arden requested. It hurt a little to swallow or talk. He wondered if he'd have bruises in the morning.

Oggie nodded.

Arden kissed him, slower than before.

The others in the tent had abandoned the idea of making a new generation entirely, writhing together with increasing frenzy.

Oggie pulled Arden's shirt over his head, worked at the fly on his pants. "Let me see you, sugar," he breathed.

Arden thrust up against his hand as soon as Oggie freed him.

Oggie pushed him back, straddled him, then spit into his palm and wrapped his hand around both of them.

Arden arched up and still wanted him to be closer. He drew him down so he could kiss him, so he could taste his skin, smell it. He wanted as much of Oggie in as many of his senses as possible.

The others in the tent had reached their crescendo and quieted, and now seemed amused by something.

Probably whatever herb they'd burned to create this atmosphere.

Arden didn't care.

He cared about Oggie.

They rolled their bodies together more frantically than Arden had imagined.

Not that he'd imagined this much. He hadn't let himself. He'd known as soon as he did, he'd start pursuing it.

He came, a hot rush of pleasure that faded and left him feeling sweaty and hollow, and rather sticky.

Oggie gave a few last rolls of his hips before he finished, too. He buried his face in Arden's throat. He started to pull back.

Arden didn't let him go. "Stay."

"No foreplay at all, I was right."

Arden snorted. "Next time I'll rim you for an hour beforehand."

"I will hold you to that, sugar."

Arden, less distracted now, became more aware of the giggles and whispers around them.

He and Oggie pulled apart to find they'd earned an audience.

Holly, looking ruffled and pleased, said, "Anything left for the next generation?" with a ridiculous smile on her face.

Arden glanced at Oggie.

"You can just scoop some up," Oggie said with a gesture toward his belly. "That's how they made Arden, anyway."

"My mother most certainly did not scoop cum off someone's stomach at an orgy," Arden protested stiffly. "I was made in a lab."

Oggie shrugged. To the women, he said, "Offer stands." He examined his hand, then glanced around the tent. He made a face.

Arden said, "Listen, don't bother. There's tons of men on *Eden*, you won't have to have weird tent orgies anymore." He couldn't quite believe he had to interact with people so soon after orgasm. He needed a cuddle and a shower, not a chat.

"It's not weird!" one woman protested.

"It's definitely weird," Holly said.

"Wait, what's *Eden*?" someone asked.

"It's his kingdom," Oggie said. He rested his hand carefully on his thigh, apparently resigned to its state.

"I'm not a king."

"It's his autarky," Oggie amended snottily. "It's a fuck-off big space station."

The women stared at him.

"No one wanted to mention that beforehand?" Holly asked.

"I tried! That woman, Mari? She said all business had to wait until after this!" He gestured around the tent. He wiped his hand on his thigh when he caught a glisten of cum on his palm.

One of the women pointed to a bowl of water and a pile of cloths by the fire.

Arden wet one for himself and Oggie.

"Oh, you're a doll," Oggie said and immediately went for his hand.

They wiped up and answered the barrage of questions the women had about *Eden*.

Oggie didn't talk much. He sat a little way away from Arden, sort of curled in on himself.

Arden reached out and offered him his hand. Some people wanted space after sex, but Arden had always liked to cuddle.

Oggie didn't noticed he'd held out his hand. Or he'd ignored it.

Arden started to worry.

"We should go tell everyone," someone said.

"Wait until morning," another advised. "They'll freak out if we leave the tent. Mari gets all worked up!"

"Oh, do you remember that time with that moldy jessa? What a fucking mess!"

Someone brought out thin sheets.

They made up the cushions and sheets into makeshift beds on folding cots the women had retrieved from the sides of the tent.

The whole affair took on the air of a sleepover.

People dropped off to sleep. They'd all exhausted themselves after all.

Arden draped a sheet over Oggie's shoulders. He hadn't made himself comfortable like the others. "You okay?" Arden asked quietly.

He shouldn't have had sex with him. He'd known going into it that this wouldn't pan out. There was no way he could sleep with Oggie without doing damage.

Oggie said, "Most days I only feel sort of like an unstable piece of shit but it's really making itself known to me right now. It's not a feeling I like to sit with either, but since the only available drug seems to be an aphrodisiac, I guess I don't have a lot of options."

"You could talk about it."

Oggie shook his head.

Arden leaned against him. "Or we can go to sleep and worry about it in the morning."

"There's no way I can sleep."

"Why not?"

"I practically strangled you."

Arden rested his head on Oggie's arm. "You'd have to be a lot stronger to strangle me with one hand."

"Doesn't make me feel better."

"I love you."

Oggie sighed.

"Unless you don't want me to. We can pretend it was just the herbs." That might have ruined Arden, but he'd do it if Oggie wanted.

"It's one thing at an orgy. It's another thing on *Eden*."

"It doesn't have to be."

Oggie snorted.

"I'm not saying it will be easy! But we can do it."

"I don't know."

Arden yawned. "Lay down with me?"

They lay down.

Oggie skated a finger over Arden's throat. "This is going to look awful in the morning."

"Yeah, you're going to need to see a therapist."

"You should be pissed."

Arden recognized the flaws in his emotional response. "I just want you to touch me."

"That's so fucked up."

"I'm really tired of being single."

"Arden, fuck," Oggie said.

"You feel something about me. Something strong. No one's ever felt that way about me. Not once. In thirty-six years."

"I thought you were thirty-five.

"I was. Now I'm thirty-six."

Oggie lamented, "I missed your birthday."

"You had other plans that night," Arden said. He draped an arm over Oggie's waist and scooted closed enough to nestle against his chest.

"If you'd told me it was your birthday...!"

"Next time," Arden said. "You didn't say it back."

"This is a really bad idea."

"Awful idea."

Oggie combed his fingers through Arden's hair. He kissed the top of his head. "I love you, sugar, and it hurts so much."

Arden kissed his chest. "I'll fix that," he wanted to say, but it felt arrogant and dismissive. Instead, he said, "I'm sorry."

In the morning, every person in the settlement asked a thousand questions.

At least, Arden felt that way.

Oggie had gone quiet again.

Arden was desperate for a shower, which he voiced to the nearest available Terran.

"A what?"

"A shower. To clean myself?"

"Oh. Uh. There should have been a wash bin in the tent."

Arden had already availed himself of that and done his best to look presentable. His hair needed a comb like nobody's business. He'd braided it and pinned it up as best he could. "Oh, right. Slipped my mind I guess."

Four more people came up to ask him questions.

"Come eat," Holly said.

He glanced at those who'd approached him.

"They'll follow, don't worry."

Over a rather sparse communal breakfast, Arden explained *Eden* and his offer to bring people there repeatedly.

Oggie didn't chime in even once.

"How do we know it's even real?" one woman asked.

Holly said, "Didn't you see that big *thing* that landed over there?"

"The shuttle," Arden supplied.

"The shuttle. We all watched them land it."

The woman shook her head. "No, I was out foraging. I didn't see anything."

"Everyone can come see," Arden offered. "I can show you a picture of

Eden, too."

"A picture," one woman scoffed. "Anyone can draw a picture."

Arden protested, "I didn't draw it. It's a photograph."

"A what?"

He spent fifteen minutes trying to explain photographs, and then movies, got nowhere, and said, "Just come to the shuttle. I can show you a movie."

The women all exchanged suspicious glances.

He looked at Holly, who'd become something of a liaison for him.

"Girls learn early on not to go with strangers who want to show them something," she explained.

"Oh." Arden hadn't anticipated this level of mistrust.

"Rapists, kidnappers," she began to recite, "Cannibals."

"Oh, no, that's alright, I get the picture," he said before she could say anything else.

She shrugged.

"I, uh." He glanced at Oggie, who'd barely eaten. "You know what, I think we can bring a few things back."

"We aren't going anywhere," Holly said amiably.

Arden tapped Oggie's arm. "Come on, before it gets too hot." His skin had gone tight and red on the shoulders and arms, which the women assured him was normal enough for someone of his complexion.

Holly walked out with them and offered Arden her shawl. "Sunburn will get worse, like as not. You'll want to cover up."

"Thanks." He arranged it to protect his head and shoulders. If he kept his arms tucked in, it would save them, too.

She shrugged. "I'm interested in all this." She gestured toward the shuttle in the distance. "You need a hand carrying anything?"

"I think Oggie and I can handle it." He wanted a chance to talk without anyone around. In this settlement, someone else was always within earshot.

Oggie trailed behind Arden as they walked.

Arden lagged and tried to take his hand. The stiff way Oggie's hand sat in his reminded him of when he'd touched Mother's hand to see if she'd passed. "Og, what's wrong?"

Oggie shook his head.

Arden leaned in close and kissed his cheek. "Come on, you can talk to me."

"I can't right now. Please." Flat. No pouting or whining, no teasing. Just quiet and even.

"Okay." Arden let go of his hand.

The next fifteen minutes of their walk passed in silence.

Arden headed to the bathroom so he could at least brush his hair.

What he saw in the small mirror above the sink surprised him.

Livid bruises on his throat, clearly in the shape of a hand, and small, round ones on his face where Oggie had grabbed him.

No wonder everyone had been staring at him.

He touched the marks, stretched his neck so he could see better. A weird smile settled onto his lips.

He glimpsed Oggie's face in the mirror, too, watching over his shoulder with the absolute worst expression on his face.

Oggie ducked away when he realized Arden had seen him.

Arden followed and caught up with him.

Oggie had backed himself into a corner and had a cagey look on his face.

Arden didn't get too close. He knew that look and how close Oggie was to hysterics. "Can we talk?"

"There's nothing to talk about."

"Well. I mean. There kind of is, Oggie."

"What's there to say! You...you *saw* what I did to you."

Arden smiled and licked his lips. "I did. Can I come over to you?"

"You should stay away from me."

Arden came over anyway. He took Oggie's hand and tugged gently to urge him closer. "I don't *want* to."

Oggie yanked his hand back and moved away again. "You said it yourself, you know, if we were really a couple, we'd be messy. And everyone on *Eden* already hates me enough as it is, I don't need...imagine if your friends could see you!"

Arden touched his throat, which did hurt. His friends would have had something to say about it for sure and nothing good.

Winslow would be appalled.

"Then what do you want to do about it?" Arden asked.

"I don't know."

Arden watched him with his hands on his hips, thinking. "Listen, if I come over there, are you going to get worked up?"

"No," Oggie sulked.

Arden approached slowly. "Would it be terribly unwelcome if I gave you a hug?"

"Arden, I really can't do this!" he protested shakily. "I can't."

Arden touched his arm. If he'd thought Oggie meant it instead of just being frightened, he'd have started crying. He nearly had on the walk over. "Hey. Og. Look at me."

Oggie fixed his eyes on Arden. "What?"

"Don't tell me if you can't, alright? Tell me what you want."

Oggie swallowed.

"Go on," Arden urged. "Even if it's telling me to never touch you again."

"I..." He licked his lips and swallowed. "I want you. I want it to be real. I don't want to be spare parts. I want people to look at us and think that I'm good for you. I don't want to worry that you're going to get sick of me. But I know you will and it's all going to come apart and your friends all—"

"Hey."

Oggie pressed his lips together.

"Give me half a chance."

Oggie sniffled.

"If you want to."

"In the worst way," Oggie confessed. "I'm sorry I said you hurt me. It's not...You haven't done anything, you know. You've been sweet, honestly."

Arden waited.

"But...I don't know. It hurts so much to want what I can't have."

"I understand what you mean."

Oggie rubbed his face.

"How long do you think it will take for me to get sick of you?"

"A month."

"Og, come on, we've been living together for months already."

Oggie shook his head. "That's different."

"Okay, alright. A month." Arden leaned against the wall. "A month is not a long time to convince anyone of anything. How about...how about you give me a month and we'll revisit this conversation?"

"And then what?"

"And I'll obviously not be sick of you by then, so you can say..."

"You'll be sick of me in a week," Oggie supplied.

"And in a week, I'll come to you and say, 'I'm not sick of you yet'," Arden said.

"And I'll say, 'give it a day'."

"Oggie, by the end of this, you'll have me telling you on the hour," Arden pointed out.

"What if I need that?"

Arden absorbed the enormity of that question. He couldn't keep up with a schedule like that. It wasn't possible, let alone healthy.

Oggie touched the bruises on Arden's throat. Gently, with concern and confusion in his eyes, like he wasn't the one who'd made them.

Arden took his hand and kissed his fingers. "Did you like hurting me?"

Oggie flinched from the question. He yanked his hand back.

"I didn't mind it, but it was...it was a little too much."

"You didn't mind it."

Arden smiled. "I mean, there's a few details to work out! Like, uh, how hard. When to stop."

"Are you fucking with me?"

Arden shrugged. "No."

Oggie sulked, "I hate it when people do things like that to me."

"Hmm." Arden pursed his lips. "You liked doing it to me, though?"

"I didn't mean to go that far. I wouldn't...I...I don't want to *hurt* you. Not...Not for real. I just, I..."

"Need therapy. And we're going to need a safe word, huh? Or like...a gesture. I couldn't really breathe."

Oggie stared. "You're frustratingly calm about this."

Arden shrugged. "I've been trying to keep thousands of people alive for...thirteen years. This is like a little baby problem. I can handle lagging productivity, nefarious plots, unhappy peers, and frustrated workers, so I think I can handle a, uh." He looked over Oggie. "A guy who needs a little work. Especially cause I think he'll *really* be worth it."

Oggie shook his head.

"Not to mention, I'm already in love with you, so we might as well do it. Right?"

Oggie sighed.

He prompted, "Right?"

"Fine."

"Just fine?"

"We can try."

Arden grinned. He threw his arms around Oggie. "You're supposed to say that you're in love with me, too."

"I thought about killing you so I wouldn't have to feel like this anymore."

"Am I that fucking unpleasant to care about?" Arden asked.

"It's absolute torture, sugar," Oggie confessed.

Arden hugged him tighter. He kissed Oggie's cheek, then nuzzled against his throat. His head filled up with dozens of ways to make things easier for Oggie. He said, "I don't want this to be...to be an obligation. Don't feel like you owe me anything or I'll make things awful for you if you don't sleep with me."

"I don't."

"I mean it, though. If you...if you feel like you want to leave and you can't, you always can. I'd rather have you smother me than feel trapped with me."

"That's so grim, sugar," Oggie whispered.

"I don't want to hurt you, either."

Oggie didn't let him go for a while.

They pulled apart eventually. They scrubbed up in the cramped shower in the shuttle's bathroom.

Arden riffled through his clothing to find something lighter and looser. He ended up in baggy gray trousers and a thin tunic, an outfit he usually reserved for walks on the Solar Deck or trips to the more humid farming bays.

He unscrewed the projector from the wall in the passenger seating area and dug around for the right cables to connect his tablet to the projector in case it wouldn't connect wirelessly. The projector was several generations older than his tablet, from what he could tell, which wasn't usually a problem. He took the cables anyways, since they both had standard cable inputs. It wouldn't do to lug everything there and not be able to use it. He found extra batteries and packed those, too. He didn't think these people had anything in the way of electricity.

He wondered about the voice he'd heard on the radio signal. It had been a young voice, and maybe female, and he didn't think it had belonged to the old men they'd found.

Maybe those old men had gotten left behind.

Maybe something bad had happened to the owner of that voice.

He packed the things he'd gathered into a backpack.

"Shug?" Oggie called from the doorway between the pilot's breakroom and the passenger seating area.

"Careful on the stairs," Arden warned.

"Just making sure you're down here."

"Where else would I be?"

Oggie picked his way down the stairs. He crouched next to Arden. "I don't know, running away from me."

Arden twisted and kissed him. "Nope."

Oggie pulled back, evaluated Arden's face, and made some internal judgment that rearranged his expression into one of acceptance, almost resignation. He leaned in and kissed him.

Soft, and sad, too. Like a kiss goodbye.

Arden urged him in closer and did what he could to change the tenor of the kiss, to make it warmer. He fumbled to move aside the bag he'd packed and pulled him onto his lap.

No audience this time, no aphrodisiacs, and none of that emotional tension.

It was nice, having him close like this.

Arden kissed him over and over. He could do it forever.

Oggie cupped his face, gently this time. Everything about him had become careful and appreciative.

It made Arden feel delicate. The most he'd weighed in years, on the floor of an old shuttle, totally sober, and he felt *delicate*.

After a while, Oggie whispered, "Didn't you come down here for something?"

Arden kissed him one more time. "Yeah."

Oggie tucked a few pieces of Arden's hair behind his ear. "Shouldn't we get back to our friends in the tents?"

"If you're ready to go back."

Oggie nodded.

Arden kissed him again. "Then you should get up."

"I'm finding it pretty difficult to leave," he purred.

"Yeah?"

Wiggling a little, he said, "Sugar, you have no idea."

"Enlighten me."

"My legs are numb from sitting like this, for one—"

Arden scowled. He tried to stand.

Oggie pushed him back and gave him another kiss. "*And* you're really just so handsome."

Arden rolled his eyes.

Oggie kissed him, then stood. He helped Arden to his feet. "What's that look on your face?"

"My looks are not what anyone likes me for. Usually, it's just money or influence."

Oggie skimmed his fingers over Arden's jaw. "Sugar, you're to die for."

Arden blushed. He stepped away and scooped up the bag he'd packed. "I, uh."

"Someone's told you that before, haven't they?"

"Sure, but no one means it."

Oggie gestured between himself and Arden. "This makes a lot more sense now."

Arden clutched the bag to his chest. "Do you think we should bring some food with us! Doesn't seem like they have a lot to share and I don't want to be rude, you know." He started upstairs.

Oggie followed. "It would probably be good manners."

"I think so. Don't you think so?" He didn't know why he'd gotten so nervous all of a sudden. Not over a single compliment and a half-hour of rather tame kissing.

"Have we got food to spare?"

"Sure. I mean. We keep this stocked just in case we ever have to leave *Eden*, you know, if there was an emergency, so there's rations for like...days." Arden dragged out the box of dehydrated food.

Oggie inspected one of the thin, foil packages closely.

"What?"

"You passed these out on Giving Day one year."

"They were close to expiring."

Oggie gave him a push. "Some gift!"

"No one's perfect." He shoved a dozen packets into his bag.

"You need me to carry anything?"

"I've got it." He adjusted the shawl Holly had lent him, then shouldered the bag.

Oggie took his hand as they walked, his fingers twisting around Arden's. He seemed happier than he had before.

Holly and a handful of kids waited for them when they made it back. "No one thought you were coming back."

"Oh. I, uh, I brought a movie. And some food."

"What's a movie?" one of the children asked.

"A bunch of moving pictures that tell a story."

"What kind of food?" another child asked.

"Uh. I don't know." He took his backpack off and opened it up.

The children descended like gremlins, taking the foil packets, and studying the pictures printed on them.

"What is this?" one demanded as she shoved a picture of spaghetti in his face.

Other kids had scattered.

"Spaghetti. Uh." Arden glanced at Holly.

"Have we been robbed?" Oggie asked.

"No, they're just showing their moms."

"Mm," Oggie hummed.

"No one steals food, don't worry. Our tribe isn't like that," she assured.

"What's peg-heady?" the child asked.

"Uh. Like. It's a type of pasta?"

"Why's it *red*? Is it *blood*?" the girl demanded.

Holly grimaced at the child. She took the food packet back. "Go play."

The girl ran away and emitted a hideous shriek of laughter as she went.

"That one's, uh...She's a little funny," Holly explained as she watched the child run.

Arden didn't know what to say to that.

"Good at finding lizards, though," Holly noted. She nodded toward the bag. "What's the rest of that?"

Arden scanned the tents. "Do you have a big white sheet I can use?"

"Probably." She headed off and gestured for him to follow.

They found the settlement mostly empty.

"Where is everyone?"

"Foraging."

"Oh."

"We're stopped here for a while, then we'll head up north a little more. There's usually good water up there and not too many other people around this time of year."

"Ah."

"People are riled up about what you said. Taking us all somewhere."

"It's optional," Arden assured.

"Those men from space, they keep saying, and talking about how your space station doesn't seem big enough for all of us to live on."

"Well...Wait, hang on. No one's seen *Eden* yet."

"We all saw you fly in on it."

Arden stopped walking. "That's just a shuttle. It's not the space station."

Holly turned and folded her arms across her chest. "So how big is this place of yours?"

Arden glanced around. He saw ruins only. He pointed to the tallest building he saw, a crumbled skyscraper in the distance. "Bigger than that."

Oggie shaded his eyes to peer at the building. "Much bigger. Why do you all live in tents, anyway?"

"Tents are easier to move around. We go where the food is."

"Hmm." He turned to Arden. "Shug, you ever been inside a Terran building before?"

"You know I haven't."

"I've always wondered what they looked like. I mean, not like in the movies. In real life. You know, those sets your Entertainment Minister dreams up are not convincing."

"It's propaganda."

"Obviously, but it's inaccurate to the life we know which kind of diminishes the effect. Good propaganda appeals to people."

"You want the job?"

"Arden, you can't keep giving your lovers cushy government jobs. It's pure nepotism," Oggie scolded, "And also, no, I don't want to make propaganda."

"Technically, the title is Entertainment Minister of the Media Department."

"You know if you'd told Mari you two were involved, she might not have made you take matches," Holly informed them.

"We aren't...I mean, we weren't, then," Arden said.

Holly made a face. "Alright. Jessa's like that for some people. Anyway. Sheet's in here."

They followed her into a tent and waited as she searched through for a large, white sheet. She handed them one.

Arden set down his bag. "We can't do anything until it's dark, anyway. Are those buildings safe to go in?"

"Depends on by what you mean by safe," Holly said.

"How likely are we to die or suffer serious bodily harm?"

"Uh." She stopped to think. "The older kids are always sneaking off to play there. They usually come back. Go with a friend, bring water, and run if something seems off."

He glanced at Oggie. "You want to do something that will possibly end in tragedy?"

"If you'd ever witnessed half the things I've done, you wouldn't even bother to ask me that. But what about you? *Eden* can't afford to lose its Autarch."

Arden shrugged. "I left Rhys in charge. He'll figure it out if I don't come back."

Oggie borrowed a scarf from Holly and she found them a canteen.

"We'll be back before dark," Arden said. "If not, uh. Well, maybe someone will come look for us?"

"I don't know, can we get into your shuttle to loot it?"

He reached to check for the fob in his vest pocket. The vest didn't exactly go with his outfit, but he liked having the fob close to his heart. "Not without me."

Oggie had pushed his hand down before he could touch the fob.

"So, someone would come looking for you. I might. I like those pants. Do you think they'd fit me?"

"They would look cute on you," Oggie agreed, his eyes skimming over Holly. "Totally different look on your body type, but I think it would work."

"I'm mostly interested in the pockets."

"Practical," Oggie agreed. He placed a few fingers in the middle of Arden's back. "Let's go for a walk."

Arden went where Oggie steered him.

Once they'd made it outside of the settlement, Oggie advised, "You shouldn't touch items of value you've hidden on your person."

"Oh."

"I know on *Eden* no one would lay a finger on you, but that doesn't mean anything here."

Arden felt stupid.

Oggie took his hand and pecked his cheek. "What do you want to explore?"

Arden glanced at the sun. It hadn't made it halfway across the sky yet. He scanned the buildings.

One of them looked *exactly* the way he imagined when he'd stared down at Terra. A short building with several floors mostly crumbled away. Made of brick with a crooked tree growing through it, it looked like a residence, not a store.

He brought them in that direction.

"You know what I was thinking about?" Oggie said.

"Hmm?"

"When I was seventeen, I got this nasty infection from one of the people I was seeing."

"Okay..."

"It's probably better we didn't, you know, *participate* in that orgy. You know. Cause who knows what they've got. Or what we might have."

Arden gave Oggie a concerned look.

"No, not that I've got anything actively, but I swear I read about, uh..." Oggie closed his eyes. "Fuck, I've done too many drugs, I can't think when I'm sober anymore. Immunities! That's the one. Like, we've got stuff in us that we're immune to. But other people won't be."

Arden started to worry.

"And the same for them. Like they think they're healthy but we're going to be covered in sores...Sugar, I'm not saying for sure!" Oggie smoothed the pad of his thumb over Arden's cheek. "Just something to think about."

The knowledge that the stupidest Autarch in history now ran *Eden* settled over him. His mother never would have done this. Bex Torre might come to haunt him at this point. He was about to get the whole station infected with some horrible Terran disease.

Or wipe out the scraps of human life on Terra by letting Oggie give them some strain of sexual infection.

His throat tightened.

He stopped walking.

He needed a shot of Twelve.

The closest one was more than a day away.

If *Eden* hadn't ripped itself apart by now.

What had they done to poor Rhys?

A baby at home and now the whole space station to take care of without even a day's notice.

"Sugar?" Oggie asked.

Despite his nearness, Arden could barely hear him. He flinched when Oggie touched him.

"Hey, uh..."

"I'm so fucking stupid."

"Oh, sugar, *no*," Oggie insisted.

"I am, I am, I'm so stupid."

Oggie wrapped his arms around him. "No, shug, come here, you're not." He kissed the side of Arden's head.

"I didn't," Arden began, but couldn't finish because he started crying.

His mother would hate who he'd become. Every choice he'd made would have had her frowning, looking at him the way she had when he'd thrown a tantrum. The way she'd looked at him when he'd outgrown something or asked for a second helping of dessert.

Oggie expertly coddled him through this, shushing him and rubbing his back. He kept his arms around Arden so he couldn't run, even when he wanted to. Oggie's voice never rose above a murmur. Over and over, he told Arden, "You're okay. I've got you."

At one point, Arden sagged, ready to curl up.

Oggie caught his slack and cradled him close against his chest. "Oh, good thing you're skinny, shug. I might have dropped you," he scolded tenderly.

"I'm about to commit genocide," Arden rasped.

"Now you're just being silly," Oggie admonished. He stepped back from Arden and used his sleeve to wipe his face. He lifted his face by the chin. He looked at him critically. "You're okay."

Arden tried to shake his head but Oggie had a firm grip on his chin. He kept a hold of Oggie's arms, afraid Oggie would step farther away. "I'm not."

"Oh, you certainly are okay." Oggie tightened his grip a little more, then pressed a soft kiss to Arden's lips. He let go of Arden and smoothed the back of one finger over Arden's cheek. "Nothing hurts, does it?"

"No," Arden had to admit.

"Has anything bad happened?"

"I—"

"Yet," Oggie added.

"Not yet," Arden sulked. He felt jittery and couldn't let go of Oggie.

"So you're okay. Right now, in this moment, you're okay."

"I'd kill for some Twelve."

"I would lap scuff off the floor given the smallest opportunity."

Arden let out a shaky chuckle. He tightened his grip on Oggie.

"Now, come on. We're going exploring, aren't we?"

Arden couldn't quite move. He glanced back toward the tents.

His instinct was to find some corner and turn into something small. Wrap himself in blankets, take some Twelve, and cancel his appointments for the day.

No one had ever asked him to continue on with what he'd been doing after he'd cried like that.

He frowned at Oggie.

"Come on." Oggie tugged his hand. "You wanted to see this sad pile of bricks, right?"

One step at a time, Oggie coaxed him on their original path like nothing had happened. Maybe a little gentler, but no longer fussing over him.

Arden didn't quite know what to do with that.

Oggie led him inside the building. "Watch your step."

Rubbish littered the floor. Bits of brick, sundry broken items, and smaller debris that turned into generic, brown dirt and clutter.

Arden had never seen anything so filthy in his life. He wanted to touch it. He also felt afraid to breathe too deeply.

"Don't touch anything, I see you looking," Oggie warned.

Arden put his hands in his pockets to lessen the temptation. He kicked over bits of rubble and desperately wanted to pick up the items he could see on the counters. He wanted to clean the dirt off them and figure out what purposed they'd served.

"What do you think this was?"

"A florist," Oggie guessed, his eyes on the tree.

One branch grew awkwardly out a window. The rest created a sort of ceiling over them.

Arden nudged open a door with the toe of his shoe. Inside he saw a hollowed-out metal box that must have been an oven, a refrigerator with no door, and ransacked cabinets.

He moved deeper inside. The remains of a table, broken and layered with years and years of dust and grime, a cracked and collapsed screen that had fallen from its wall mount, and then, in the last room he entered, a bed.

Mostly made of moldered fabric and clumps of mattress foam, a large rotted rectangle remained in the right spot for a bed.

"People lived here."

The Torre family had left *Eden* before Terra One had become fully ruined. When Bex and her first wave of citizens had boarded the space station, people had remained on Terra living as normally as they could.

Insecure and frightened lives, but not scavenging nomads in tents by any means.

When had this building last had residents? A hundred years ago? Fifty? How long did it take a society to collapse?

He went to touch something.

Oggie said, "Don't touch anything!"

He shoved his hands back in his pockets.

Oggie linked arms with him.

They wandered through the other accessible apartments.

Some doors he couldn't open. Other rooms had bulkier litter that made the rooms impassable. Cabinets had fallen from the walls, or appliances had gotten tipped over. One room had broken furnishings piled up against the door.

Finally, Oggie said, "Sugar, I could use a bit of fresh air."

"On Terra?" Arden asked. "That's a tall order."

"There might be less dust outside, though." He sounded congested and a glance revealed that his eyes had gone red.

"Are you okay?"

"Just allergies, I think."

On their way out, something small darted across their path and up a wall.

Oggie outright screeched.

Arden dragged him away from whatever they'd seen.

"Fuck, fuck, where'd it go?" they demanded of each other.

It took them about five minutes to calm themselves enough to spot the small creature watching them from the wall.

It licked its eyeball.

"Oh, fuck. Fuck. Shit. Is that an animal?" Oggie demanded, his grip on Arden's arm impossibly tight.

Arden stared. "I think it's a lizard."

"That's fucking disgusting. Ugh. You didn't tell me there'd be *animals* down here."

Arden's skin crawled at the sight of the thing.

No animals lived on *Eden*. No pets, no livestock, not even pests.

He'd seen animals in movies and read about them for school, but he never thought he'd see one.

"Sugar, can we go? That thing is looking at us!"

He and Oggie edged out of the room, eyeing the lizard the whole time.

Once outside, Oggie shuddered. "Ugh, I'm about ready to go back! Aren't you? Enough exploring for one day."

"It was only one building."

"A small one. What if the other buildings have bigger animals?"

Arden hadn't considered that.

He never considered anything.

He looked up at the sky and momentarily lost himself in it's hot, grayish-blue expanse. He couldn't see the sun, panicked, then remembered that clouds existed down here.

He didn't like that he couldn't see *Eden* from Terra the way he could see Terra from *Eden*.

"Do you think Rhys is doing okay?"

"I'm sure he's fine."

"That was rotten of me, wasn't it? To take off like that?"

Oggie made a face that suggested agreement. "You at least told people where you were going?"

"I made sure to do that."

"Maybe when we get back, they'll be so glad to see you they'll forget everything else that happened."

"Fingers crossed."

Fingers crossed they had anything to go back to.

They headed back to the settlement with the agreement they'd ask someone to show them around more another day.

About a dozen people gathered to watch Arden set up the sheet and the projector. He'd done this with Mama, but he didn't remember exactly the right steps. He managed to get it done before they lost daylight entirely.

Over dinner, he played them informational clips about *Eden* that he'd found on the shuttle.

"Who are these people?" Tola asked about the actors in the

commercials.

"Actors."

"Hmm."

When he ran out of clips and the Terrans ran out of questions, he played a movie. The first one he saw, really, a simple family drama about a girl who didn't want to go into the same career as her family.

About the father's character, Mira asked, "He lives on *Eden*?"

"No, he's...he's just an actor. This movie's old. He's probably dead."

"An actor, you keep saying that. What's an actor?"

"Someone who plays a role in movies. Pretends to be someone else."

"And everyone on your spaceship, they look like the people in these movies? So clean and..."

"Handsome," Tola filled in.

Arden tried not to wrinkle his nose at how desperate these women were to see a man. "No, we don't all look like that."

Mira looked at Oggie, who had his knees pulled up to his chest and his chin on his knees. He'd devoted his full attention to the screen.

"Is he an actor?"

Arden almost laughed, then felt awful when he remembered those films they'd shown during the trial. "Oggie's whatever he wants to be."

"You should have told me," Mira said, "That you didn't go for women, by the way. Waste of jessa. Got everyone's hopes up."

"I don't think it was a waste," Holly chimed.

Mira scowled at Holly.

Arden looked at Oggie again. He didn't think it was a waste either.

Oggie caught him looking. "What?"

Arden scooted closer to him and leaned against him. "Be my Entertainment Minister."

"Arden, I already said I don't want to make propaganda."

"Then don't make propaganda. Take over the Media Department. Do whatever you want with it."

Oggie looked back at the movie. "I said no."

Arden nudged him. "Why not?"

"I'm not qualified, for one."

"Neither is Frakes."

Oggie gave him a sharp look.

"Most people aren't. I didn't get my job based on qualifications. And unless the qualification to be a bartender is day-drinking, neither did you. You're either quasi-randomly assigned to a work crew or you inherit a position."

"Fucking excuse you, I make *excellent* drinks."

"And you were good at PT, too, weren't you?" Arden asked.

"Yes..."

"Good reports, except for the missing supplies and workplace affairs. 'Picks up things quickly.' You get that comment a lot. 'Sharp', 'quick', 'detail-oriented'. Those are in a lot of your reviews."

Oggie frowned at him. "You went through my reports?"

"Oh, like you wouldn't have?" Arden asked. "And 'pretends not to work all day.' That came up a couple times."

Oggie continued to frown and narrowed his eyes. "What's your point?"

"There are no more peers, and no more thralls, and if that power structure is to change in a meaningful way, then emancipated workers are going to need to take powerful positions. I'd like those positions to go to competent people with the ability to learn quickly on the job."

"Absolutely not. I have no intention of working, not if I'm going to be sleeping with you," Oggie declared.

Arden didn't protest. He turned his eyes back to the movie.

When it finished, they packed up everything and started to head back toward the shuttle.

Kineth advised, "You shouldn't leave camp right now."

"Why not?"

"Never know what's out in the dark."

Arden looked to the horizon and couldn't see the shuttle.

"Bring a light, people see you're alone. Go without light, you get lost, fall down a hole..." she trailed off and shrugged.

"I've got room," Holly offered.

As they walked back, she nudged Arden and said, "And I'm a heavy sleeper, so don't worry about waking me up."

Arden forced a smile. Though he considered himself by no means sexually repressed, he disliked that other people had witnessed something so personal. Part of him liked the public declaration of his feelings for Oggie, to bring something that made him so happy out of the shadows.

They'd kept themselves cloistered too long, but a smoky, dark orgy was not how he'd imagined declaring his intentions.

Not too salacious, either, as far as orgies went. As far as Arden knew. He'd imagined them differently.

He and Oggie both lay away for a while at night.

He knew Oggie was awake because he hadn't started snoring.

Oggie had the pleasantest snores Arden had encountered. Little huffy wheezes that sometimes turned into snorts if he rolled on his back.

He rolled over on his cot. "Og."

Oggie ignored him.

"Oggie," he said.

"Hm?"

"Would you ever have said anything?"

"About what, Arden?"

Arden wanted to be closer to him. He scooted to the edge of his cot. "About, uh. About how you felt."

Oggie rolled over. "No."

Arden could barely seem him and just caught the glint of his eyes. "Oh."

"Would you have ever said anything?"

Arden folded his arm under his head. "I didn't think you'd have wanted me to."

"No?"

"You made it pretty clear that people used you and went after you for your looks. I didn't want to do that."

"There's a big difference between using someone and pursuing a relationship."

Arden admitted, "I'm sure there is, but when you own everything, the lines of consent get blurry."

"Rhys like to remind you of that?"

"He's not wrong."

"No," Oggie agreed. "He's not wrong. But this isn't how I imagined us. I imagined, probably, what Rhys imagines when he reminds you about consent."

"And that's that?"

"That you'd fuck me some night, get tired of me a few weeks later, kick me out a few weeks after that."

"Awful."

"What did you imagine, then?"

Arden let out a breath. "I didn't. I did my best not to think about how desperately I wanted you to be my friend, let alone more than my friend."

"But you did think about it," Oggie pointed out.

"How could I not? You were gorgeous and basically naked all the time and you'd…You were playing around but you were flirting and, just, half-dressed and just…"

"Just what?"

"So hard to beat at board games!"

Oggie grinned so broadly Arden saw it even in the low light of the tent. "I had to play myself most of the time growing up. It makes you sort of good at it."

"I would have been your friend forever and that would be just as good, Og, if you change your mind."

"Yes, alright, but I am sort of wildly in love with you and hideously stunned that there's any chance you might have feelings for me, too."

Arden rolled off the cot and crossed the foot and half to Oggie on his knees. He threw his arms around him and snuggled his cheek up against his neck. He squeezed him and kissed his jaw.

Oggie went rigid, then relaxed. He curled up against Arden, then hauled Arden onto his cot, even though there wasn't room for two people.

Arden didn't sleep soundly through the night, but he and Oggie didn't talk anymore either. They lay there, though, quiet and relaxed.

Arden, with extreme care, had moved the shuttle closer to the tents, so they wouldn't have to sleep in Holly's tent anymore if they stayed too late.

Plus, the bed behind the cockpit had more space for them to share.

They'd spent a little more than a week among the Terrans. All the adults had infinite questions about *Eden*. Some of them didn't even believe it existed.

He did what he could to provide proof and assurance of a better life.

The Terrans who considered leaving a possibility concerned themselves with the impact their departure would have on the others, as well as on themselves. If too many people left, it would compromise the safety of those left behind.

Arden sat in the shade of a layered canopy of gauzy sheets and watched someone climb the radio tower.

At least twice a day, someone nimble shimmied up the tower, checked in all directions, and declared the area still safe. As far as he'd seen, that was all they used it for. Part of him wanted to give it a try, but he also valued his life and dignity.

He wondered what they had thought while watching the shuttle approach. Too fast to pack up and move, too fast to even flee.

Nothing to do but watch and hope the shuttle didn't bring something awful for them all. No wonder people had stood there like that, watching them walk over.

Three young children and two youths sat with Arden beneath the canopy. The youngest children stayed in the camp under the watchful eye of older women or those who couldn't disperse throughout the landscape to find food, water, or other resources.

One of the youths had a twisted leg that stopped him from going too far from the camp. The other, a quick-eyed, nervous girl, knew the position of every child in the camp but seemed much too rigid and routine-oriented to wander through the grasslands with ease.

Arden wondered how they both did when the camp changed locations.

He more than wondered, he sort of worried. He imagined the girl's panic, the boy lagging behind. He hoped someone walked with him.

The three children flicked through pictures on Arden's tablet.

They talked more to each other than with Arden. Sometimes they'd toss him a question, but mostly they ran through wild speculations about *Eden*.

"Is that you?" a little girl asked.

Arden looked at the picture. Him, a dozen years ago, with shorter hair, dressed up for a special occasion.

His inauguration.

He looked awful. Gaunt and pinched, with bags under his eyes even makeup couldn't conceal.

"That's me." He took the tablet and stared down at the old picture.

He looked ill. He'd sobbed for hours before the ceremony. Hadn't eaten in days, except when people had watched him, and only the tiniest, slowest bites. He'd barely eaten then, and he'd taken far too many formulas. Enough that a doctor had given him a few dire warnings and sent him to therapy.

The little girl who'd held the tablet crawled uninvited onto his lap to get a better look. "Why do you wear such ugly clothes?" she asked.

He didn't know what to say. He didn't mind the question or her intrusion into his personal space, but he didn't know how to handle them. No one on *Eden* treated him like this.

"I don't usually dress up that much," he provided.

A lot of people here didn't like his clothes. Too tight, too heavy, too dark. They didn't like the shine or glimmer, either. They said it made him too easy to see and too easily overheated.

"Don't you get too hot?" she asked.

"It's cold on *Eden*."

He'd traded water and food for clothes more suited to the environment. He didn't look too out of place in them.

Oggie looked like a glorious savannah prince in these loose, pale clothes, his hair glowing in the sun, his skin bronzing easily beneath its rays.

Right now, about seven women of various ages, recently returned from foraging, had circled around him.

Oggie had gone out with the women and they'd come back laughing.

The girl asked, "How cold?"

"Colder than it gets at night," he answered, not sure what frame of reference she'd have. He placed his hands on the back of her neck. "Colder than that."

She yelped at the coldness of his touch and squirmed away, though she smiled while she did it. She grabbed his fingers. "Are you dead?"

He made a face and hoped he misunderstood her question. The blurred drawl of the Terrans still tripped him up sometimes. In a hundred years, it would border on its own language.

"Mammy says dead people go cold. Gran wasn't *that* cold when we found her."

"Not dead yet."

She returned her attention to the tablet.

The women around Oggie used their scarves to cover their mouths and giggled at almost everything he said. They played with their hair and batted their eyelashes. They showed off what they'd found to him and found every excuse to touch him.

It was like watching a nature documentary.

Oggie had lots of offers to stay somewhere other than the shuttle.

They'd reached the hottest part of the day, which meant everyone trickled back to camp for a small meal and to take shelter. They would reemerge for the cooler, dimmer hours of the evening.

Mothers started to call their children.

Arden lost most of his company.

The youth with the twisted leg, Arden thought his name was Gideon, must have seen Arden watching Oggie and his suitors, because he said, "Mari says one father with too many women might be dangerous. Makes too many half-siblings."

"Sound thinking."

Oggie must have felt their stares because he turned and waved to Arden.

Arden waved back.

"You're the king in space, right?" Gideon asked.

Arden didn't nitpick, just nodded. "Sure am."

Gideon looked at Oggie again. "So up there you can have anyone you want?"

"That's sort of an ethics, thing, though, isn't it?" Arden said.

"A what?"

"Ethics. It's a...A philosophy of moral behavior. You know, right and wrong."

"Oh."

"Like, just because I'm in charge doesn't mean I should make people do things."

Gideon asked, "But that's the point of being in charge, isn't it?"

"I mean, for personal gain."

The point seemed lost on the youth.

Arden didn't press the conversation.

Oggie beckoned Arden over.

Arden went with little desire to do so.

The women saw him as competition for Oggie, which he understood. None of them had done much to indicate they considered Arden a potential mate. Somehow, without asking either of them, the Terrans had decided Oggie would go for men and women, and that Arden's interests rested exclusively with men.

It sort of rankled him.

Many of them also thought his story about *Eden* was an elaborate kidnapping ruse.

He didn't know why they didn't suspect Oggie was in on it.

"Sugar, Farah was telling me the most interesting story about…what was it?"

Farah said, "How I escaped a cult," in a flat voice. She scowled subtly at Arden when Oggie wasn't looking.

"No, tell him what kind of cult," Oggie insisted lightly.

"They worshiped beetles. The leader carried a big one around in a little woven basket all day long."

"Oh. Uh."

"We had to do whatever the beetle said, or they'd tie you out for the skin beetles to eat."

Arden's eyes widened.

"They didn't tie me tight enough," Farah said with a shrug.

"Isn't that so interesting?" Oggie asked.

"Fascinating," Arden agreed.

Oggie glanced up at the sky. "Let's get you out of the sun, shug, before you boil." He put a hand on Arden's shoulder and steered him toward the shuttle. He absently rubbed the back of his fingers against the fabric of Arden's shirt. "I could use a nap!"

"Long walk?"

"Mmm. You should have come."

"No. They invited you out because they're courting you. I'm not exactly welcome."

Oggie stepped into the shuttle and glanced back at Arden. "You don't mind them courting me?"

Arden stepped inside. "It's not for me to say."

Oggie artfully collapsed into the pilot's seat. "So, you wouldn't care if I slept with one of them? Or all of them?"

Arden tried to tread carefully, saying, "I don't think expecting you to be exclusive would end anywhere good."

"Expecting *me?*" Oggie asked.

Arden fidgeted. He'd put his foot in it. "Well. You like to have fun."

Oggie pulled in on himself.

"What?" Arden asked nervously.

He shrugged. "I knew it."

"Knew what, Og?"

"That you thought of me like that."

Arden approached and knelt by the seat. He put a hand on Oggie's thigh. "I don't...I don't want us to get ahead of ourselves. I love you, but..."

"But you don't think it will go anywhere," Oggie supplied sullenly.

"Mostly I'm scared that I'll ask you for too much, or something you're not comfortable with."

"You think I wouldn't be *comfortable* sleeping with just one person?"

Arden held in a sigh. "I think you're a person who doesn't like rules, or being told what to do, or being expected at home. And if that's not how you are, then I'm not sure who I've been living with."

Oggie wrinkled his nose. When he stood and walked away, he looked more hurt than offended.

Arden thought, then followed. He caught Oggie in his arms.

"No, Arden, I'm not in the mood for you right now."

"Okay, can I say one thing?"

"No."

Arden let go.

Oggie turned to face him, arms crossed. "Well?"

"You said no."

"For fuck's sake."

"If you honestly and definitely want us to stop seeing other people—"

"What other people have you been seeing?" Oggie scoffed.

"Don't be rude!" Oggie's expression grew petulant and Arden immediately scolded, "Don't. Stop. Get that look off your face. If you want to be exclusive, *fine*."

"No, it's not...I'm just mad you think I wouldn't want to be."

"Do you want to be?"

"I don't know!" Oggie even stomped his foot.

Arden tried to hold back a smile.

Quieter, more sad than pouty, Oggie asked, "You really think I can't be exclusive?"

Arden saw things a little better now. "Why's it matter what I think?"

"It doesn't."

"You're ridiculous."

"It isn't ridiculous to want to be treated like I'm respectable for once."

"I respect you."

Oggie shook his head. "No one does."

"I do!" Arden insisted. He brought Oggie in for a hug. "Have I made you think I don't?"

Oggie didn't answer. He sighed and relaxed against Arden.

"I respect you, Oggie. I'd respect you if you slept with a thousand people. I'd respect you if you came home with a different person every night."

"Oh, I don't bring my lays home. Sex is strictly on locale, or *maybe* at someone else's place."

"On locale?"

"Where I met them," Oggie clarified.

"Then who were those people you brought home?"

Oggie shifted. "Just a few people who needed something."

"Hmmm." Arden rested his head against Oggie's shoulder. He swayed them slightly, his hands on Oggie's waist. Dancing without music. "Have I made you feel like I don't respect you?"

Oggie sighed. "No. But I wish you had. I wish you didn't treat me well, then I wouldn't feel bad about what I did."

"For such a smart person, you're pretty stupid."

Oggie started to say, "Spare parts," Arden could tell just by the look in his eyes, the twist of his lips before he opened his mouth.

He kissed him before he could get more than the initial sound out.

Oggie leaned into the kiss, sighing against Arden's lips and touching foreheads with him. He pulled him in close and pressed his face against Arden's shoulder, drawing in a deep breath, then letting it out slowly.

He stood close to Arden.

Arden could feel the heat of his skin through the thin fabric of their clothes. He liked to be close to him and Oggie, he thought, liked to be close to him too, but like this. Clothes on, no heat or hardness; warmth and quiet and peace.

They had kissed and cuddled a lot, but nothing more.

Oggie hadn't hurt him again, either, not even a poke or a pinch.

Arden started to hum, an old-fashioned tune, a favorite of Winslow's. Slow, sweet, made for dancing. He swayed again, moving Oggie with him.

"What are you doing, shug?"

Arden stopped. Oggie didn't like to dance as far as Arden could tell. At least, not with Arden anyway. "Sorry."

"I don't know that song."

"It's old."

Oggie gave him a funny look. Not bad, but funny. He rested his thumb on Arden's lips, hardly there at all.

"Are we still fighting?" Arden asked.

"Was that a fight?"

He didn't give Arden a chance to answer before he pushed his thumb past Arden's lips. The slightest pressure on his teeth to open his mouth and then the mild sting of salt on his tongue.

Arden couldn't breathe in the best possible way.

His mouth filled up with spit, the taste surprisingly sweet.

He could smell sweat on Oggie's hand, and dust, and something else. Something green. Whatever he'd gathered with the women.

His heartbeat thudded softly through his whole body. His lips absently closed around Oggie's thumb.

Oggie pulled back his thumb and sucked it clean like he'd been eating with his fingers.

Arden swallowed. His mouth felt empty. He made himself close his mouth instead of standing there slack-jawed and staring at Oggie.

"I could use a nap. The heat makes me sleepy." Oggie walked away.

Arden could only follow him.

The shuttle stayed cooler than Terra One. It had various life support systems meant to make space travel not just feasible but comfortable. As long as Arden kept the solar panels on, those systems ran constantly. A small haven of coolness and clean air in the vast yellow and brown wasteland.

Despite this, few of the Terrans elected to visit the shuttle, let alone take advantage of its comforts.

They didn't trust it.

Arden couldn't get the taste of Oggie's skin out of his mouth.

He dreamed about it while they napped and woke up disoriented. Not only that, though. Nervous for some reason. His dream drained away as soon as he woke.

He woke alone.

He pushed himself up and looked around.

Oggie sat at the table, his eyes on Arden's tablet. Moving back and forth. Reading. He looked up when Arden sat up all the way. "You got a message."

"I read it this morning."

It had taken a long time for a message to travel from *Eden*. Rhys had sent it three days ago.

"Didn't want to mention it?"

"I didn't want to worry you." Arden had written back to assure Rhys and the Council that he hadn't died and that he planned on returning. He'd tried to send a few pictures, but they likely wouldn't send through the shuttle's communication channels over this distance. "It's probably good you came with me."

"I'd be in lockup for sure. *Eden* is in quite a state. You sure we shouldn't go back?"

"Rhys can handle things. And I'd feel like an idiot if I went back empty-handed."

"Then you're going to have to get people to trust you before you try to whisk them away to a place that they have no reason to believe in," Oggie advised.

"I don't know, I can think of a handful that would come if you told them you thought they were pretty."

Oggie set down the tablet and leaned back in his seat. "That's your plan." He didn't ask. He stated, flatly, his eyes as dead as they'd ever been.

Arden wanted to pull the sheets around himself. "You're charismatic and beautiful and *Eden* needs help."

"Could have asked me."

Arden gave a guilty smile. "You're doing it anyway. Why ask and make it disingenuous?"

"I thought you didn't want to use me."

He couldn't answer. He wanted to cry.

The serious look on Oggie's face thawed into a smile. He came over to the bed. "You're so sensitive, shug. I always forget you're easier to prick than the rest of us." He draped an arm over Arden's shoulders and rested his head against Arden's. "I have to tell you, though, eighty percent of what I do is disingenuous."

"Should I be worried?"

"No, you're a good fifteen percent of my honest emotional output." He kissed Arden's cheek.

"What's the other five?"

"Drinking and nervous breakdowns."

Arden shouldn't have laughed, but a chuckle escaped.

"I spent so long on my own, you know, or with only Mara, or my parents, that once I moved to the Quarters I had to learn how to act like a person. I'm never sure if I'm faking the right things."

"That's why I think you'd be a good Entertainment Minister."

"Because I'm fake?"

"You're good at manipulating people. You pick up on cues other people don't see and know how to twist them. You watch, even when you look like you aren't. You influence people while acting like you don't care what they do."

Oggie moved away from him. He pushed himself into the corner of the bed and drew his knees close to his chest. He eyed Arden.

"I don't mean it like a bad thing."

"That's a little too honest of you."

Arden shrugged. "I was never good at acting like a person either."

Oggie stayed in the corner.

Arden turned to face him and crisscrossed his legs. He rested his elbows on his thighs. "I don't feel like I'm acting around you."

"No, me neither," Oggie admitted quietly.

"I think I dreamed about you."

"What'd you dream?"

"I don't remember."

"Oh."

Slowly, Oggie unfurled from his corner. After a while of quiet, he asked, "Was it a dirty dream?"

"Might have been."

"I've left you rather unattended when it comes to those things." He had such a discrete way of saying things sometimes, subtly seductive but restrained.

"I don't think so."

"Liar."

"No," Arden insisted.

Oggie looked at Arden's neck, surely evaluating the yellowed bruises. "Then I scared you off."

"Also no." Arden slid himself closer. "Maybe taking things easy after a drug-fueled orgy is normal."

"Wouldn't know. I usually don't see people after an orgy."

"You go to a lot?"

Oggie shook his head. "A handful. I'm usually too drunk, which gets unpleasant. They last a while, you know, and I have this awful tendency to pass out and someone has to haul me off the pile. I've thrown up a few times, which ruins things for everyone."

"Ah."

"All the cravings and side effects aside, though, I think maybe I'm a little better for having dried out down here," Oggie admitted.

"You seem steadier."

"I've got this feeling that once I'm back there, though, it will all come back. One wrong look..."

Arden understood. He took Oggie's hand and gave it a squeeze. "You'll have to be careful if you've lost your tolerance."

"Spoken like someone who's been there."

"Once or twice."

"Sobriety doesn't stick to you?"

"I've never tried to be sober. Just less dependent."

"Never thought about it like that."

Arden kissed his palm. "Therapy."

Oggie let out a shaky breath. "Do that again."

Arden kissed his palm, then traced the tip of his tongue over his palm up toward his inner wrist.

Oggie squirmed like it tickled but his cheeks flushed like Arden had done something much more intimate. He pulled his hand away.

Arden skimmed his fingers up Oggie's calf, under the loose leg of his pants. Barely touching, just enough to feel the hair on his legs. "I can be gentle with you."

Oggie practically yanked his leg back. He looked unsure, almost frightened.

"I'll be so careful."

"Shug."

They had hurried the first time, acted with desperation rather than care. Not bad, and desperation had its place, but Arden wanted to be tender with him. He assured, "I'll always stop if you say no, or if you look like you want to say no."

The look of mistrust on his face made Arden's stomach twist.

Arden wanted to touch him, but he kept his hands still. "You take care of the things you want to keep."

"I've held up without."

"Have you?"

Oggie didn't answer. He spread out from his corner and rested his head on Arden's thigh. Tentative, but not forced.

Arden played with his hair.

Eventually, they ate, and spoke of lighter things. The incessant dust, their shared and newfound fear of birds and snakes, their horror that on Terra people ate animals, and a love for the sun.

Something about the sun felt right. Not filtered through a pane of glass or simulated by a bulb.

Voices began to carry inside, the sign that the heat had faded enough to resume their day.

They washed up, then rejoined the Terrans. More work waited for them, though Arden tended to get left alone. They assumed his incompetence and disinterest, and, from what Holly said, didn't want to piss him off and lose their closest source of water.

He'd shown a few of them the wastewater recyclers, which they'd liked, and explained how the shuttles could, in theory, bring people anywhere in the system if they'd provisioned properly. The shuttle could run forever as long as it had fuel or an alternate power source like a star.

The pilot manual had mentioned something about harvesting water from comets and generating nutrient paste from algae cultures if provisions did run out.

He didn't think they'd need that.

When it grew too dark, or all the work was done, people socialized. Some nights they watched a movie. Other times, the women sat around and told stories. Either way, the children sat raptly. So did Oggie. He soaked up stories like a sponge.

It solidified two things: that he had to replace Lazlo Frakes and that Arden had fallen in love with him.

Arden steeped himself in these moments. They'd never happen again.

He'd never see Oggie drenched in sunlight or bathed in the flicker of a fire again. He took pictures for historical documentation as well as for personal reasons.

Someday he wanted to be able to show someone these. He wanted to point out exact moments and say, "This is when I hoped we would last. This is when I knew we would."

Holly sat beside him. "You stay in camp a lot for someone who wanted to go exploring."

He looked up at her, almost groggy. He'd lost himself in the future. "Uh."

"Come with me tomorrow."

"Sure."

"Rumor has it there's a ruin full of books. Might be useful."

Arden tried to hide his surprise. "You guys read a lot?"

"No, none of us can read. Our last reader died twenty years ago. But I thought you might want to find a few to bring when you go home."

"That's kind of you."

"It might be all you leave with."

"I don't understand that," he admitted.

"Terra might be a dry, hot, hostile ball of dirt, but it's all we know. We aren't brave space explorers."

He grinned in disbelief. "No one's left *Eden* in two lifetimes at least. You've seen and done more things than I can imagine."

Holly glanced around. "If we wanted to come back...You know, if we didn't like it up there."

"I'm not in the habit of keeping people hostage."

She sighed. "Do you ever feel like you were meant for something different?"

"Frequently."

"There's something in me that just doesn't belong here. I don't fit. I never have. My tent is the only tent that isn't shared."

"Come to *Eden*."

"I'm honestly considering it," she said. She glanced at the other Terrans. "A few of them are so desperate to get laid they might go just for that. If this was a tribe of men, they'd have gotten on your spaceship as soon as you told them you had women waiting for them in the sky."

He snorted. If they thought of his offer in those terms alone, no wonder they didn't buy in. "It's not just about finding partners, you know. We have food and healthcare—"

"What?"

"Medicine. Doctors. Running water. *Clean* water. No raiders or warlords. An outdated and oppressive class system, yeah, but I'm working on that. And having new citizens would probably really help...Bex Torre built

Eden to give humanity a safe haven, a place to wait out the troubles on Terra One. Not everyone got the chance. I want to fix that."

"Like I said, I'm considering it. Better than staying here. It gets dryer every year. There used to be a river a few miles east. It hasn't run in a decade."

Arden sighed.

Eden never could have saved everyone, but he wanted to help those who'd scraped this long by before there was no one left to help.

Bringing this group of relatively healthy, civil, and peaceful Terrans provided an ideal test run. He'd never get every human, but he could do better than the previous Autarchs.

After a few minutes, Holly confided, "Teo tells this story wrong every time. She always fucks up the middle."

"How's it supposed to go?"

Under her breath, Holly provided a running commentary of corrections to Teo's narration.

Arden thought she and Cathie would get on wonderfully.

He turned in early.

He brushed his fingers over the back of Oggie's neck as he went.

Oggie glanced his way, a question in his eyes.

Arden shook his head.

He shook out his clothes and hung them up to air out overnight. Laundry happened less frequently on Terra. He nestled into bed, the coolness of the sheets bliss after the heat of the fire and the air. He dropped off to sleep.

He woke when Oggie slipped into bed. He rolled over.

"Sorry, sugar, I didn't mean to wake you."

Arden rolled over.

"Go back to sleep."

Arden slung an arm over his waist before Oggie had a chance to tuck a sheet around himself. He'd done that every night they'd shared a bed. Arden hadn't noticed it at first. He didn't mind it, but skin against skin came as a shock at this point.

"Any good stories after I left?"

"Mmm, a few. One about a, uh, a snake and fox. I nodded off halfway through, though." He stretched and yawned.

He smelled like dried sweat, salty and a little musky.

Arden kissed his collar bone.

Oggie tensed up.

Arden drew back.

The sheet had been intentional, a deliberate barrier.

He tucked a sheet around Oggie.

"No, sugar, if you want something, that's fine. We can do something."

A decline would upset him, pressing on would be dicey. Arden thought about making something up, but he didn't want to start lying to him, even to save his feelings. "You didn't seem interested."

"No?"

"You kind of flinched."

Oggie rolled onto his back and folded his hands over his stomach. "I kind of did."

"And you've kind of been, like, wrapping yourself up in a sheet."

"Oh, what? Yeah. My thighs stick together if I don't put one between."

Arden propped himself up. "What?"

"Don't you get hot when you sleep?"

"No."

Oggie made a face. "Probably cause you're made of fucking ice."

Arden pressed a hand against his ribs.

He flinched. "Yeah, that. Fuck, Arden, have you seen a doctor about that?"

"I have cold hands, it's not a medical issue."

"Maybe you can slide your hands between my legs, so I don't get all sweaty."

Arden chuckled. He wedged one hand under Oggie's body to warm it up. "So you kind of flinched," he said again.

"Listen, I don't want you to think I'm...traumatized or anything. It's not like that. I'm..." Oggie paused. "Adjusting."

"To?"

"I'm not sure. I keep expecting something bad to happen and it keeps not happening. It's making me jumpy."

"Hmm." Arden rolled close to him again.

"You should have at least yelled at me by now."

He traced a finger over Oggie's collarbone.

Oggie didn't tense this time. He turned aside the sheet and tapped Arden's flank. "Come here."

"I'm right here."

"No, come *here*," Oggie said. "Don't make me pat my lap like a creepy uncle."

Arden slid on top of him as smoothly as he could. "What are we looking at in terms of options?"

"Very sensual question."

"Tell me again about the time—"

Oggie covered Arden's mouth. "Really, now."

Arden pulled back. "We don't have extra sheets. And I didn't expect...You know, this wasn't what I planned on doing. I didn't pack anything!"

Oggie ran his hands up Arden's back, drawing him down. "What if I said no?"

"I'd leave you alone."

"What if I didn't want you to leave me alone when I said no?"

"I guess we'd have to think of something else for you to say when you really mean no," Arden said, but the idea of doing anything to someone who'd said no made his stomach turn. He hadn't ever before, not even the way Oggie meant it.

"Really?" Oggie asked, not hopeful but surprised.

Arden swallowed past the lump in his throat. "No."

"I didn't think so."

They lay there, chest to chest.

Oggie brushed one hand up and down Arden's back. "I'll have to learn not to do that," he mused, "Or we'll never get anywhere with each other."

"I couldn't even pretend to hurt you."

Oggie pushed his thumb against the vein in Arden's neck, then slowly wrapped his fingers around Arden's throat. He tightened his grip slightly.

Not enough to restrict Arden's breathing or hurt, but definitely enough to create a sensation of restriction and powerlessness.

"You like this?" Oggie asked.

"I do."

Oggie's eyes narrowed. "Honestly."

"I've never minded a little roughness."

The smile reached Oggie's eyes. "Oh, so you're kinky." He gripped a little harder. "Could have said something, sugar. Here I was thinking you meant it when you said you were just desperate and touch-starved."

Arden pressed against him. He wanted to kiss him but Oggie didn't let him get close enough. "I didn't say that."

"I just want you to touch me, those were your words." Oggie released him.

"What about straps? Buckles?" Arden reminded. "Don't pretend it's just me wanting this."

Oggie dug his fingers into Arden's side. "Count the notches in your spine."

A breathy whine escaped Arden.

Oggie dug his nails in.

Arden squirmed.

Oggie let go. Wide-eyed and unsmiling, he looked frightened.

"It isn't a bad thing," Arden offered.

"It *feels* bad. Wanting to hurt people? It feels...perverse."

"If you like it and I like it, what can be bad about it?" Arden asked. "Anyway. We don't have to unpack this right now. We can wait until we're home, until we know each other a little better."

"Might be smart."

"Not either of our strong suits."

Oggie smiled. He kissed him. "No." He rolled them on to their sides and turned himself to be the little spoon. He wiggled his ass against Arden.

Arden kissed his shoulder. He kissed the back of his neck, then right behind his ear.

Oggie molded against him. He drew Arden's arm around him and kissed his fingertips. He clasped Arden's hand close to his chest and didn't let go.

Arden wanted to stay in this moment forever and it hurt that he couldn't. He pressed closer to Oggie. "Og?"

"What, shug?"

"I like this."

"Me too."

Arden kissed the crook of his neck. "I want things to stay like this when we go back."

Oggie stayed quiet.

"I know that's stupid."

"It's not stupid," Oggie said softly. He kissed Arden's fingers again. "It's not stupid at all."

A few tears eked out of Arden's eyes, no matter how hard he tried to hold them back. He managed not to outright cry or even sniffle. He fell asleep holding on to Oggie and woke up the same way.

Oggie hadn't moved away in the night.

"You up?" Arden asked.

Oggie stirred.

"Og."

"Mmm."

Arden gave him a squeeze. "Time to get up."

Oggie rolled away and stretched. He groaned, "Do I have to?"

Arden climbed over him and headed to the bathroom. He'd started his shower by the time Oggie came in to relieve himself.

When Arden heard him start to leave, he requested, "Come in."

"What?"

Arden pulled back the curtain to the stall. "Come in the shower."

"It'll be awfully cramped."

"That's kind of why I'm asking."

"Oh." Oggie looked somewhere between surprised and flattered. He tucked a piece of hair behind his ear. "Sure."

He stepped into the shower and practically had to stand nose-to-nose with Arden.

Arden splayed a soapy hand over his stomach, which was somehow soft and firm at the same time, lightly muscled beneath a thin, smooth layer of fat. He thought about moving his hand lower but moved up instead. He took time to marvel at his perfection, and to discover a few things that an artist would have omitted if he'd really been the beautiful painting come to life that he resembled. A mole on his side, a few scars scattered about, an odd-shaped birthmark on his lower back, things that made him lovelier.

He drew Oggie in for a kiss.

Oggie leaned into it, but too much, and moved their faces beneath the shower spray so they had to move apart to breathe.

A few more kisses, and then Arden started to wash him all over. He saved the most intimate parts for last.

Oggie melted beneath his hands, resting against the wall with his eyes fluttered shut. He let out a small, tender moan when Arden finally slipped a hand between his legs.

The narrowness of the shower prohibited a lot in the way of movement; Arden couldn't, for example, drop to his knees comfortably in front of him. He had to practically press him into the wall to have the room to move his arm enough.

The whole thing felt mildly juvenile in an excitable way, not in an immature one. Of course, Arden had done this a few times in the locker room, hands pressed over each other's mouths so the other kids wouldn't hear.

Oggie giggled afterward, then covered his mouth. "Sorry, sugar, I am, I wasn't laughing at you," he hurried to assure.

Arden pecked him on the mouth. "If we can't laugh at each other, we probably shouldn't be having sex."

A small, unsure smile flitted across Oggie's face.

Arden kissed him once more then cleaned his hands. He stepped out of the shower.

"Uh." Oggie half-stepped out after him.

"No, go ahead, finish up. I washed my hair yesterday."

"You're sure?"

Arden nodded gamely and grabbed a towel.

Oggie regarded him warily then retreated into the shower. That wariness lingered as they moved through the rest of their morning, dressing and eating.

Finally, Oggie accused, "I didn't get you off."

Arden had a mouthful of toast and jam. He made himself keep chewing. When he'd swallowed, he said, "I know."

"Didn't you want me to?"

"Not really."

Oggie practically glared at him.

Arden gently assured, "Sometimes it's enough to do something for someone else."

"Not with me," Oggie said, then amended, "I mean, people...People don't do that for me. It's the other way around."

Arden took another bite of toast and chewed, using the time to think. "Does this represent a problematic change in expectations?"

"Not problematic, as such."

Arden set down his toast and brushed off his fingers. Rehydrated bread had an unseemly texture and toasting helped make it tolerable. He hadn't added enough water to the jam, either, leaving it slightly too sweet and sticky. He couldn't tell if he wanted to eat or have this conversation less. "Unwelcome?"

"I." Oggie drew his knees up to his chest and put his chin in his knee. He watched for him an uncomfortably long time. Finally, he sighed. "The lows of addiction do come with some amount of self-reflection. I'm sure you're aware. I have spent many mornings-after thinking about *why* I let people treat me the way I do."

Arden waited as Oggie paused, gathering himself. He knew those moments.

"Part of me knows that I don't deserve nice things. I want them, but I don't deserve them. When I have them, I always ruin them. You're turning out to be something nice, Arden. I don't deserve it, I shouldn't have it, and I will definitely ruin it."

A deep concern and one Arden understood. "Do you want to talk about it?"

"No. Kind of. I don't know. I don't."

"Okay."

Oggie sighed.

"I'm always here to listen."

"I know. But..." Oggie stared at the wall. "Somethings are harder to say than they are to listen to."

Arden considered that and understood what he meant. He stood up and kissed the top of Oggie's head. "Love you."

"Mhm."

Arden didn't take offense to the lukewarm response. Oggie had a lot of things to work through. He probably would for years. Maybe the rest of his life. Arden found Oggie's company easy and pleasant, but he knew ugly things lurked somewhere in the future for him.

Going back to *Eden* would challenge them both.

It could make quick work of their relationship.

He kissed Oggie's hair again, for good measure.

Arden had never seen so many books in his life.

Pages littered the floor, torn and dirt-crusted. Shelves had tumbled on to their sides, spilling tomes over the floor like vomit in front of a toilet.

Arden didn't want to take a step deeper into the room for fear of treading on the already-ruined books. It felt perverse.

Eden had few printed books. A thousand or so in possession of various peer families. Winslow had a good collection. He tended more toward books than his sister. Mother had possessed a sizeable collection. She'd used them as decoration instead of as books. Not that she hadn't read, but she'd preferred tablets.

Arden wanted to pick up every page.

Oggie stared at the room with a sort of wonder.

Holly walked inside, stepping on the pages. "All the useful books have probably been picked already. But who knows? There aren't a lot of readers left."

Even workers knew how to read.

Arden took a few careful steps, avoiding as many pages as he could.

The dirt and dust, along with the heat, made it hard to breathe. He covered his mouth and nose with his scarf.

Soon enough, though, curiosity overcame reverence. He started inspecting covers. A few things crumbled and cracked at his touch.

He recognized a lot of titles, common enough entries in the literary canon that digital copies existed on *Eden*.

A glance at Oggie showed his eyes had gone red, though if the blame lie with dust or emotion Arden couldn't guess. He sneezed several times in a row and scowled at Arden when he caught him staring. That tipped the odds in favor of the dust.

Holly listlessly poked around. Every so often she found a book and would call something to the effect of, "Look at this one."

Arden would go over, read her the title, then she would either throw it on the ground or place it in her bag.

He pushed deeper into the library, climbing over a splintered shelf and ducking under another one wedged in a doorway.

High up, untouched, he saw a book, decrepit with age but otherwise intact. It leaned against one corner of its shelf with a thick layer of dust. Undisturbed for years.

He couldn't reach it even when he stretched on his tiptoes. He put a tentative foot on a lower shelf. It creaked and then, when he put more weight on it, cracked. He stared up at the book. He could make out a smudge of color on the cover.

He gave a careful hop but still couldn't reach.

He wished his mother had designed him to be taller. She'd picked a good height, tall enough to be stately and somewhat imposing, but not enough to intimidate or seem ungainly. Then again, she'd planned for a daughter.

It left Arden at a perfectly reasonably height but by no means tall.

He hopped once more, less carefully.

Pages slipped and slid under his feet when he landed.

He managed to catch himself before he fell but felt a sharp strain in his leg. Not a snap. He hadn't pulled anything, but he'd made himself sore.

He straightened up and rubbed his inner thigh.

Faintly, Oggie called, "Shug?"

"I'm fine."

"Where are you?"

"Over here."

Oggie's voice came from closer that time. "That doesn't tell me anything."

"This way," Arden called back.

He heard Oggie climbing over a few things.

"There you are," Oggie said when he set eyes on Arden. He came over to look where Arden stared. Without asking, he came up behind Arden and lifted him.

Arden squeaked but snagged the book when he could reach it.

"Got it?" Oggie asked.

"Mhm."

Oggie set him down. "So much for not touching anything."

Arden shrugged. "If anything's going to kill us, it would probably be eating their food."

Oggie nodded his agreement. "What'd you find?"

Arden brushed away the grit to show a generic fiction cover. "*A Beautiful Lie.*" He cleaned off the back to find it was a thriller about infidelity and maybe also corporate espionage. "You find anything?"

Oggie coughed into his elbow. "My childhood dust allergy."

"Oh. Let's get some air, then."

"Please."

They regrouped with Holly and found some shade under a tree.

They had stayed too long in the library.

The sun sat directly above them and heat radiated up from the ground wherever they looked.

"Better not walking back," Holly advised.

Arden agreed.

He longed for the cool, dim interior of the shuttle. He took another sip of water. Tepid. Always tepid.

He wanted ice.

He wanted a lemon slush.

He nudged Oggie. "Did your mom ever take you to Thimble and Thyme?"

"Hmm?"

"It's off Goshawk. They had all kinds of desserts and they'd do these frozen lemon slushes...Mama would bring me sometimes after shopping." He could practically taste it. The little dish and the small, flat spoon. Mama would always get something decadent, but Arden had loved the way the lemons made his mouth pucker.

She'd always given him a bite of hers if he'd asked anyway.

"Uh. No. Mam didn't take me out much."

Much, or not at all? Arden wondered. "First thing when we get back, we have to go."

Oggie wrinkled his nose.

"That sounds amazing," Holly admitted.

"We can all go," Arden immediately offered. "Everyone who comes back."

Oggie coughed into his arm and cleared his throat. The dust hadn't done him any good.

Arden passed him the water.

His eyes had swollen.

"We have antihistamines in the shuttle, I think."

"I hope so."

"I didn't know you were so allergic to dust."

"I thought I grew out of it. It hasn't happened in years. Then again..." He trailed off.

"Hmm?"

"I spent a lot more time in dusty places when I was little."

Arden didn't think he wanted the details. He scooched over closer to Oggie and rested his head on his shoulder. The past had unpleasant things and he wanted to imagine a pleasant future. Delude himself of one, at least until they went back to *Eden*. "You like sour things; you'd like a lemon slush. You can get whatever you want though. I don't make the rules."

"Yes, you do."

"I'm thinking about changing that," Arden said. He hadn't shopped the idea out to anyone, not even Rhys or Cole, yet.

"What do you mean?"

"I mean, like...it's one thing to be in charge, it's another thing to be a despot."

"You're not a despot," Oggie assured with a degree of concern.

"Not right now. There were times in the past that I've danced with that occupation, though, and I don't know that I won't again in the future. And the Autarchs that came before me? Some of them were, no doubt, and I don't know who will come after me."

"Your kids will come after you," Oggie reminded.

"If I have kids. And if I have kids, well, who knows if I'll be a good father? What if I raise a horrible tyrant?"

"Depends who you raise 'em with, I guess."

"Depends," Arden agreed.

"Is that normal?" Holly asked.

"Hmm?"

"People choosing not to have kids," she clarified. "Down here it's...it's not a choice. You do whatever you can to get one."

"Not you."

"No fucking way, not me," Holly agreed. "But try telling anyone else that."

"It's a choice on *Eden*," Arden said.

Oggie huffed. "Is it?"

"We don't *make* anyone have kids."

"No, but you sure do a lot of convincing," Oggie pointed out.

Arden felt like he didn't have the right to lean against Oggie anymore. "I'm working on things."

Oggie sat up and jostled Arden off his shoulder. He sneezed several times. "Sorry, shug. Come back over."

Arden returned his head to his shoulder. "I'm changing things."

"Sure are," Oggie agreed. "You don't want to be Autarch?"

"I think...I think *Eden* needs a new kind of leader."

Oggie checked his forehead as if checking for a fever.

Arden pushed his hand away.

Oggie smiled.

Holly asked, "So you're not gonna be king anymore?"

"I don't know. That's a big change and I've thrown enough changes at *Eden* for now," he said.

And, not to mention, if he wasn't Autarch, he didn't know who he would be or what he would do or how he would cope with anyone having the audacity to tell him what to do.

"People already don't trust you, Arden," she said, "You might not want to tell them you're king then change that as soon as they follow you to your kingdom."

Arden pressed his lips together. "I thought people weren't going to come with me."

Holly shrugged. "No one's sure what to do. It's a big choice. Everything would change for us."

Arden crushed his instinct to say, "Not everything," because Holly was right.

Their environment, way of life, form of government, culture, and maybe even their life expectancy would change.

"The question is..." Holly stared out over the yellow grass. "Is this a way of life we want to hang on to? Even if it wasn't getting dryer every year, who wants to live like this? There's never enough food or water, half the kids that get born end up dead, we end up running from raiders at least three times a year."

"The sharing is really nice," Oggie said.

"You don't share in space?" Holly asked.

Oggie giggled.

"We're getting there," Arden said.

She raised her eyebrows and returned her attention to the grass.

Arden pulled his bag over. He took out the book he'd found, set it next to him, then found the food he'd packed. He offered a bit of lunch to the other two and picked at the energy bar he'd chosen for himself. He ripped it into tiny bites and chewed each one thoroughly before he swallowed.

Old habit.

Still, he'd gained weight in the past months. Not much. Maybe ten pounds. Probably most of it from drinking. It smoothed out some of the sharpness of his bones.

He couldn't see the bones of his wrist so well and didn't know how he felt about it. He knew that he needed to be careful with his weight, that if he got too thin his friends would start worrying, that his doctor would start worrying, that he'd end up back in therapy because of it.

He'd struck a careful balance the past five years or so. Not too thin, but never out of control. Sometimes the things that entered his body had been the only things he could regulate. His therapist liked to point that out.

Then Oggie had come along, making him drinks, and before that, it had been Rhys, always hungry and sighing over the meals Arden had ordered him.

He sighed. He opened the book and started reading so he had something else to think about.

"Read it," Oggie requested.

"Hm?"

"If you're going to ignore me—"

"I wasn't ignoring you!"

"Then you should at least read out loud."

Arden flipped back a page. "On the first of the month, every month, I bring my rent check downstairs to Mrs. Ludlow. My girlfriend finds it strange that I pay with a check, but I always have as long as I'd rented from her..."

Oggie settled back against the tree and rested his hands on his stomach. After about twenty minutes, he started to snore, louder than normal.

Arden stopped reading.

"Keep going," Holly said.

He glanced at her. He thought she'd fallen asleep too. She had her eyes closed and hadn't moved since he'd started reading. He cleared his throat, took a sip of water, and returned to reading.

After a while, he put aside the book.

He wanted to take a nap, too. He'd grown accustomed to an afternoon rest. Something stopped him from closing his eyes. He couldn't have expressed exactly what.

On Terra, he never felt exactly safe unless he was at the settlement. Maybe it was all the talk of raiders and warlords, the ritual of climbing the tower to check the horizons, the fact that they'd settled in an area where they'd found four skeletons.

He thought often about the quiet, soft voice he'd heard in the distress call.

A bird careened in the sky.

Arden watched it make circles across the infinite blueness of the sky. Not a cloud in sight today.

He wondered what other parts of Terra looked like. It couldn't be all this hot and yellow. Oceans still covered huge parts of the surface.

When the sun had sunk low enough, they walked back. He asked, "Have you ever been to the ocean?"

Holly shook her head. "Worse there."

"Worse how?"

"More likely to come across people."

"Isn't that better?"

"Not the kind of people you want to come across. More animals, too, the kind that wouldn't think twice about a human snack."

He nodded.

"Didn't you want to go to the beach?" Oggie asked.

"Just to see it."

"Maybe we can stop by."

"Maybe."

"You thinking of heading out?" Holly asked.

"I don't know how much longer we can stay," Arden admitted.

Holly nodded.

"Especially with no answer from anyone."

"I..." Holly cleared her throat. "I'll come with you."

Arden stopped walking for a moment, then hurried to catch up. "Really?"

"What's here for me?" she asked.

Arden couldn't answer. He smiled. He wanted to hug her but didn't know if she'd want that.

Oggie started chatting immediately, telling her all the things she'd like about *Eden*. It made it seem like he didn't care for Terra at all.

At camp, Arden helped shell sunflower seeds.

Oggie sat beside him, his narrow fingers making quick work of the shells.

Women crowded around him.

Holly sat next to Arden, whispering quick bits of gossip about the others to him. She didn't speak unkindly, but as though she'd gleaned her knowledge through careful observation. He wondered what kind of life she'd lived.

No one treated her poorly or excluded her, but she always hung just on the fringes of activities.

Before Arden had come over to help with the seeds, she'd sat about a foot away from the others. Maybe that had to do with Oggie, though. Most of the women flocked to him, sometimes acting as if they couldn't help it.

Sher put her hand on Oggie's thigh. She leaned in to tell him something. Her dark eyes remained fixed on his face as though he were something other than a mortal man.

Oggie giggled at whatever she said.

Arden watched it happen without any sense of envy or jealousy. Still, a strong current of dislike ran through him. He couldn't put a finger on the exact feeling.

He and Oggie acted like a couple. They spent every night in the same bed. They showed public affection towards each other. They *acted* like a couple and even though they hadn't agreed to exclusivity, no one else knew that.

They shouldn't have assumed it, either, but no one gave Arden a second thought when it came to Oggie.

They saw him as competition, but only in a specific way. One he couldn't put his finger on.

Arden shelled a few more seeds. He kept thinking.

He didn't like, he decided, that they acted as if Arden didn't mean anything to Oggie. He wasn't looking for deference, but he wanted some kind of...

He glanced at Oggie and forced his fingers to find another shell.

"What are we making with these?" he asked.

Holly nodded towards several loaves of dough. "Gonna mix em in."

He nodded.

Sher had wiggled closer to Oggie.

He stood up.

He didn't want to watch this. He thought about heading to the shuttle, but he wanted to move.

He circled the camp, staying close to its perimeter. It hadn't gotten dark yet, but he didn't like to go too far on his own.

Oggie stepped out from between two tents and said, "Boo!"

Arden flinched and scowled at him.

Oggie grinned. "Scared you," he announced proudly.

"Of course, you did, jumping out like that."

"You want to tell me why you took off?"

"I needed to think."

Oggie took his hand.

They walked quietly around the perimeter together.

They'd made two loops when Oggie finally asked, "What did you need to think about?"

Arden shook his head. He didn't want to come off as jealous. He wasn't jealous, either, that was the thing. He didn't mind these women drooling over Oggie. He found it amusing at times. He wouldn't care if Oggie slept with them. He almost wished he would, just so they'd stop acting so desperate.

"Not gonna answer?" Oggie prompted.

"It's...Everyone acts like..." He sighed. "Everyone acts like we aren't together. I mean. Like. They know we're sleeping together but...But they act like that's all it is."

"Hmm."

"Or am I too sensitive?"

"No, that's pretty spot-on," Oggie agreed.

"You should sleep with them and get it over with."

"I don't want to sleep with them."

"No?"

"No."

"Oh," Arden said.

"But no one takes me seriously when I say that. They think 'no' means 'try harder.' You know, like I think that I'm so good-looking that they should prove something to me."

Arden frowned.

"And, you know, they're right. I usually give up and let people fuck me after a while."

They walked a little longer.

"I get the impression," Oggie began out of nowhere, "That they're not used to the idea that this sort of thing *is* a permanent thing. Or, you know, less than casual. I mean, most of them have never had anyone to be more than casual with."

"Maybe."

"I mean, guys come around twice a decade, maybe, it seems, and don't stay long. I think they don't get it. What we're doing."

Arden leaned his head on his shoulder as they walked. "You're probably right."

"Does it matter to you a lot?"

"No," Arden sighed.

"Sugar, if it matters," Oggie began.

"No, no. Don't ruffle any feathers."

"That'll be harder for me than being exclusive. I think I was born to ruffle feathers. I don't know that I was born to sleep around. That's more of a hobby than a lifestyle."

Arden put an arm around Oggie's shoulders. "Then you do whatever you were born to do, Oggie."

He pulled away and sneezed. He looked better since they'd found him allergy pills, but his eyes still had a hint of irritation. He sneezed once more, then came back to Arden's side. He kissed Arden's temple. "What if I was born to—"

Arden kissed him. "Then do it. If it makes you happy, Oggie, do it."

Oggie blinked.

Arden kissed him again.

"What if it's something bad?"

"Do bad things make you happy?"

Oggie shrugged. "I end up doing them anyway."

He spilled his arms around Oggie's neck and pulled him close. "You're all out of reasons to do things because you *have* to, Oggie. From now on, you can do things because you want to."

"It's not that easy, Arden."

"I'm making it that easy."

Oggie pulled away. "Not everyone gets to do whatever they want all the time."

"You do."

"Only *you* get to do that."

Arden pointed out, "And what I want is for you to do what you want. Does it work like that?"

Oggie let out a frustrated groan. "This is stupid. I didn't come over here to talk about stupid shit like this."

Arden hugged him. "I'm sorry."

It took Oggie a moment to hug him back. He pulled in slow, deep breaths. "You know," he began but didn't say anything else.

"Go on," Arden said after a while.

"I." He kept breathing, slow and steady. Maybe that was all he could do. "Let's keep walking."

Arden nodded.

They finished their loop and returned to the sunflower seeds.

This time, though, Oggie sat right next to him. He didn't resume his light and flirty conversations with the women, even when they tried to talk to him. He hooked his leg over Arden's and folded his hands on Arden's shoulder. He kissed his cheek.

Arden started shelling seeds.

They still had half to go.

Oggie didn't help anymore, he stayed wrapped around Arden.

"You two have a nice walk?" Holly asked.

"Not really," Oggie answered.

Arden kept shelling.

Oggie loosened his grip but kept the proximity. He lay down with his head in Arden's lap.

"Are you feeling okay?" Kineth asked.

"I'm thinking."

"Can't think and work?"

"Arden will do my share."

Arden glanced his way. He didn't protest.

Oggie went to bed early.

Arden checked on him and got told to go back outside. He went and tried to mingle with the Terrans. He set up a movie for everyone. He stayed until it had finished. He took down the projector, packed it up, and brought it into the shuttle, the same as he did every time that he used it.

He hesitated before getting into bed. "You awake?" he asked softly.

Oggie didn't answer, didn't move, but he wasn't snoring.

"Oggie?" he whispered.

He stayed still.

Arden put a hand on him. He should have gotten into bed or found somewhere else to sleep. Something stopped him. He gave Oggie a shake.

It felt like shaking a person who'd passed out.

No.

It felt like...Bile hit the back of his throat. He rolled Oggie over and checked his pulse, his fingers shaking as he pressed them against the tepid flesh of Oggie's throat.

A pulse.

He had a pulse.

Slow, but there.

He turned on the lights above the bed. He checked Oggie's eyes.

Oggie jerked away from him with a gasp. "What the fuck," he slurred.

Arden whispered, "I'm sorry."

Oggie rubbed his eyes.

"I couldn't wake you up."

"I couldn't sleep. I took a pill."

"I'm so sorry," Arden said. "I'm sorry, I, I got worried."

Oggie sighed. His eyes closed. He rolled over. "Lights."

Arden turned off the lights. He got into bed but couldn't sleep for hours. He pressed as close to Oggie as he could get.

He woke before Oggie, too, and made breakfast to have something else to think about.

Oggie rolled out of bed, gloriously rumpled and well-rested. The irritation from his eyes had gone altogether. He stretched, then shrugged on a robe. "You made breakfast?"

"I mean, I added water..."

"Figured you can't cook."

"You figured right."

Oggie sat beside him. "Did you wake me up last night?"

Arden nodded. "Sorry."

"I didn't know if I dreamed it or not." He pulled a plate in front of himself. "Do you know what day it is?"

"No." Arden checked his tablet and relayed the date, which Oggie didn't seem to care about. He continued, "Rhys says they'll have to quarantine us when we get back."

Oggie nodded. "Makes sense."

"Morris made a bid for my position."

"And?"

Arden licked his lips. He didn't know how he felt about what had happened. Yes, they'd followed his orders, but he didn't know that he'd expected them to.

"And?" Oggie asked.

"You and him, the two of you, I mean. I know about the videos."

"You and everyone else. What's your point?"

"You said they weren't personal. I mean, you meant that, right?" Arden asked.

Oggie licked jam off his finger. "Morris got me out of lockup, told me I'd lost my job, said he'd gotten me reassigned to a new job. He said he'd pulled strings to do it, that thieves didn't have a lot of options. This or waste refinement. I took the job he offered me. I. The mask freaked me out at first. Your uncle talks a lot when he fucks. You know, that obnoxious kind of dirty talk. You like that, huh, you little bitch?" Oggie mimicked the last line in a parody of Morris's voice. "If he'd kept his fucking mouth shut, I probably wouldn't have figured out it was him."

Arden's mouth opened a little. He'd guessed as much but he didn't like the details. Oggie deserved to talk about it and Arden owed it to him to listen.

"Six months later, I got a notification from the Labor Department that I was significantly derelict in submitting my paperwork for my new assignment. I was barely twenty and I cried a lot. I think I scared the lady I tried to bring my paperwork to, like...I think she thought I was having a breakdown. Which I fully was."

Arden took a sip of water. His mouth had gone sticky. He hated thinking of Oggie, who was still young, but that much younger and so scared.

Oggie picked up his toast, then set it down without taking a bite. "Funny enough, I only got that notification after I started asking why it was taking so long for my wages from this new job to come through. I didn't see Morris after that for a few years. I mean, I saw him around. I see everyone at Crystal. But he pretended he didn't know me until you started talking to me and Mara."

"I'm sorry."

"Does that answer whether our involvement was personal?" Oggie asked.

Arden nodded. "Mhm."

"He made a bid for your position?"

"I, uh. I left orders that if he did, they should strip his funds and personal property. And, uh. Move him from a private peer lockup to the general worker lockup."

"That's..."

"A death sentence," Arden finished for him. He swept up crumbs from the table.

"How long did it take?"

"They found the body after eight hours. They think he was killed after about two, though," Arden admitted. He cleared the plates and threw away the remains of breakfast. He started to wash the dishes, something he barely knew how to do. Crumbs and jam he could handle, but half the time he missed spots or left the plates either greasy or soapy.

Thirty-six and he couldn't wash a plate.

He could orchestrate a murder, though.

It would have been more honest to throw Morris into space.

Oggie leaned beside the counter that housed the tiny sink where Arden labored over their two small plates. "I think they're clean."

Arden dropped them onto the drainboard. They clattered. A chip pinged off one.

"You can't be sad to see him go."

"Not...I didn't." Arden forced a breath. He kept staring into the sink. "I thought it would teach him a lesson. A hard one. Hopefully a painful one. I didn't think they'd kill him."

"You didn't think putting Morris Torre with a bunch of workers would kill him?" Oggie clarified.

"No."

"Sugar, you're his nephew and the most powerful man on *Eden* and he tried to have you killed. What he did to me was...pretty kind in comparison to what a lot of people got."

Arden picked up the scrub brush from the sink and pushed crumbs toward the drain. "I know. I just...I *know* I just didn't *know*. I didn't *understand*. I'm too stupid to think anything through that much."

"I wouldn't lose sleep over it."

"I didn't want to be a murderer."

"It's murder if it's on purpose," Oggie pointed out, "Otherwise, it's manslaughter."

"I didn't want to do that either."

Oggie blew a raspberry. "Nothing to do about it now. You stripped his funds? I guess that means you can really spoil me now. What if I wanted my own apartment? Just so I have somewhere to go when you get sick of me."

Arden unstuck his tongue from the roof of his mouth. He had a drink of water. He wanted Oggie to chastise him or shout, or something to make Arden feel awful. Right now, he didn't feel anything except discomfort at his lack of guilt. "I'll get you an apartment if it will make you feel better, but I didn't take his money."

"Oh. Cause he's got kids, doesn't he? I think he mentioned them a few times," Oggie recalled.

"Uh. No. I added to the Public Health Fund."

"The what?"

"It's new. It's...sort of. You know, money for public health. I need to sort it out better when I get back...Or, you know, I need to put people in charge of sorting it out." He took another sip of water. He seized on this new topic to keep his mind off Morris. "Have you ever been to rehab?"

Oggie's eyes narrowed.

"No, no, not like that, I'm not trying to send you to rehab. Peers with addiction problems go to rehab, peers who get hurt at work file for compensation. Peers go to therapy and the doctor and...I mean. How many of your addict friends every got any kind of treatment?"

"None."

"None? Not even overdoses?"

"You know how much it costs to treat an overdose? Cheaper to die."

A grim outlook if Arden had ever heard one.

"So that's the thing," Arden said. He retrieved his tablet. "Have you ever heard of a Form Fifty-Eight B?"

"No."

Arden pulled up the form.

"I didn't even know there were fifty-eight kinds of form to fill out."

"There's actually about a hundred, excluding the sub-forms." He handed the tablet over to Oggie. "Form Fifty-Eight B, Request for Public Health Assistance in the Treatment of an Alcohol or Narcotics Overdose."

"What the fuck is Public Health Assistance?"

Arden flicked to another form. "Fifty-Six C, Request for Public Health Assistance in the Treatment of Chronic Illness. There are two dozen forms for different kinds of medical problems. These forms date back to the first generation of citizens. Bex Torre signed off on these."

Oggie squinted at the tablet. "I've never fucking heard of this."

"Yeah, so I checked the records for people who worked in a Public Health Office. The last one died two hundred years ago. The offices are all closed. They're storage closets in med centers."

"Say it like I'm stupid."

"*Eden*, in theory, provides healthcare to workers. Anyone who makes less than a certain hourly wage can fill out one of these forms, bring it to a Public Health Office and have their care paid for, as long as there is available funding."

"Except they can't."

"Because no money ever got put into the Public Health Fund. A little bit, at first, you know, cause this was...Oggie, this was done with mind-blowingly systematic effort. The first generation of workers had rights. Step by step, Councils and Autarchs picked away those rights. Stopped replenishing public funds. Stagnated wages. Stopped upkeep on the Quarters. Reduced ration quality. *Turned down the heat.*"

Oggie stared at him.

Arden felt like he'd lost his mind.

He'd dug himself further and further down this rabbit hole since Rhys had gotten hurt in Hydroponics Three. All those nights staring down at Terra One, staring at his tablet, putting together these discrete pieces of information to realize what all his ancestors had done.

Bex Torre had not just created a narcissistic monument to herself, she had planned this for her indentured citizens. Extreme backlash to the Terran political state she'd left behind.

He shook the tablet. "My mother kept a journal. Most Autarchs do.

She...She knew. She knew what she was doing. She knew what her predecessors had done."

"She never told you?" Oggie asked.

Arden sighed. He tossed the tablet on the table. "She knew I wasn't ready. I was younger than you are now when she died. She got sick and her mind went so quick. Her body lasted longer than her mind did. She never got the chance. If she'd lived another twenty years, I'm sure she would have...She would have told me. Planned the next steps with me."

Oggie sat down. "How long have you known?"

"I've been putting the pieces together for more than a year at this point." Had that long passed since Rhys's injury? A bump on the head had set all this in motion. "I realized my mother was in on it...twelve days ago," he said.

Oggie glanced at the date. "Twelve days ago, you cleared our debts."

"Funny timing, huh?"

"Arden."

"What was I supposed to do? Keep taking money from thousands of people that my family has systematically abused and enslaved for generations? I mean...What the fuck am I supposed to do? I can't...I can't *fathom* the evil it takes to do this to people or that I would have been part of it, and an active part, not just a passively awful piece of shit like I've been, if not for the fact that my mother's mind rotted before she could show me how."

Oggie clucked his tongue.

Arden barreled on, "I would have been just like them. Just as fucking awful..." He swallowed. Licked his lips.

"Don't you think you're being dramatic?"

"About how fucking terrible this all is? Absolutely not."

"No, it's...it's awful. Immoral. Disgusting," Oggie agreed easily. "I don't think you get much out of thinking about who you would have been instead of working on who you are."

Arden frowned.

"My father told me that. He pulled out a few gems every once in a while. I think...I think he would have been a good dad if he'd, you know, gotten the chance to be our dad. He tried, at least, when he was sober enough to talk." Oggie waved a hand. "Anyway. Why are you telling me all this?"

"I have to tell someone."

"Hard secret to keep," Oggie agreed.

"And I need someone to help me figure out how to tell everyone else without starting a riot."

"Fuck, Arden, you can't tell people that! They'll *kill you*."

"People deserve to know."

Oggie shook his head. "People in the Quarters kind of like you right now, Arden. They might fucking love you, actually, since you cleared their debts. Do *not* ruin that. Clearing your conscience is not worth destroying the first chance these people have ever had to trust their leader."

Arden didn't know what to say.

"Sugar, listen, this might be the first time you've heard this and it's...Listen, look at me, okay?"

Arden looked at Oggie.

Oggie put a hand on his shoulder. "Not everything is about you. Your feelings don't matter."

"My mother actually told me that a lot."

"Your job is to fix how hard your family fucked us."

"I'm trying."

Oggie cradled his face. "Try harder."

Arden had to ask, "You used to hate me, didn't you?"

"I did agree to fucking assassinate you."

Arden's eyes went painfully wide of their own accord.

Oggie grinned. He assured teasingly, "I never hated you *that* much. You should never listen to anything I say. I have no idea how to act like a person."

"Up until right now, you did a pretty good job."

"But would you even want me if I wasn't damaged enough for you to fuck without feeling like you were ruining someone's life?"

"What the fuck, Oggie?" Arden breathed.

Oggie leaned in and kissed his face, then released him. "Come on, let's go give those dusty idiots one more chance to hurdle themselves into space based on promises from strangers."

"Uh."

"What?"

"Can..." He swallowed and couldn't believe himself. "Can I blow you?"

Oggie tilted his head. "What about our conversation turned you on?"

"I don't want to think about it, I want you to cum in my mouth."

"When you put it like that..." Oggie untied the front of his robe and let it slip over his shoulders.

Arden knelt in front of him. He rested his forehead against Oggie's hip. He had so many uncomfortable emotions and wished he hadn't stirred them up. He wanted Twelve. He didn't want to feel anything or think about anything. He didn't want to have to work this hard to fix *Eden*.

He kissed Oggie's stomach and glanced up at him.

Oggie smiled.

This had never felt like work. People had told him he gave good head. He'd never trusted them, of course; who'd tell the Autarch, or the Autarch's heir, that he was a bad partner? He liked doing it though. He hoped people liked receiving it.

They always came, if that counted for anything.

He took Oggie into his mouth, semi-soft, but not for long.

The uncomplicated slide of tongue and lips. Warmth, the salt of someone else's skin, and later their cum. A hand on his shoulder, or fingers in his hair. Whimpers, or groans, sometimes words or shouts. One thing he'd never managed to fuck up that badly.

Oggie let out a silly little gasping cry when he came, pushing deeper into Arden's mouth and tightening his fingers in his hair.

Arden glanced up to see he had a hand pressed to his mouth.

A giggle escaped through his fingers.

Arden licked his lips and smiled. He held in a chuckle.

Oggie giggled a little more and then they were both laughing.

"Get up, fuck, get up," Oggie said through his laughter. He pulled Arden up and into his arms.

Arden sank into his embrace. "Thanks."

Oggie really lost it at that. He laughed so hard he cried. He laughed through getting dressed and throughout the day, sometimes he'd look over at Arden and start laughing.

Arden announced their intended departure and the Terrans stared at him like they didn't understand why he'd told them.

Holly broke down her tent and stowed it in the cargo hold beneath the passenger seats.

He didn't have the heart to tell her she wouldn't need her tent.

A few more people followed suit, which surprised Arden. A slow trickle of people began to store things in the hold, more people than Arden had ever anticipated based on the lukewarm reaction he'd gotten to his tales of home.

People joined in so slowly and took so long that it was two days before everyone had begrudgingly stored their things in the hold.

He confided to Holly, "I didn't think it'd be more than you."

"We've been together for decades. I guess if one of us is going..." She rubbed the back of her neck.

"More friends than you thought?"

She shrugged. "That or we're all more desperate to get out of the dusty shithole than we ever talked about openly."

"It would have made it hard to be hopeful," Arden guessed.

"Everyone on *Eden* is going to shit their pants," Oggie noted.

"The Council is going to fucking kill me."

Oggie kissed his cheek.

Once everyone settled into their seats in the passenger area and he checked to make sure just under one hundred people had buckled in, Arden turned on the shuttle engine.

Oggie scrambled to sit. Holly had made herself at home in another of the seats in the cockpit.

Arden didn't breathe until they'd made it off the ground.

Slowly rising, then picking up speed, the shuttle hurtled upwards.

With the coordinates for *Eden* in the autopilot, Arden had nothing to do.

He tried to ignore the sounds of children in distress.

"Do you think they're all right back there?" Oggie asked.

Arden got up but only to close the cockpit door. "They're fine."

"That's a little concerning," Oggie admitted.

"I'm overall very concerned right now so at least we're on the same page," Arden said. He returned to the pilot's seat and stared out the window. He could see the ground grow further and further away.

He took a few minutes to compose himself. He checked his appearance as best he could in the mirror. He'd traded his Terran clothes for what he'd brought from *Eden*. He couldn't go back looking like a prairie nomad.

He smoothed down his hair.

Little brown dots had cropped up over his cheeks and nose.

He took a breath, then another, then he headed back to the passenger area. He roamed the aisles, checking on people, assuring those who looked the most concerned. He played the flight safety video, then put on a cartoon for the kids so at least the adults didn't have to worry about their children's anxiety as well as their own.

He couldn't believe all these people had decided to come to *Eden*. He'd expected half a dozen, maybe, and just the ones who wanted to have sex with Oggie.

He announced, "I'm up front if anyone needs anything."

He'd sent Rhys a message a few days before he'd intended to leave. It would take a while to transmit, so the message and the shuttle would arrive fairly close together.

It had taken so long to get everyone on board, though, that maybe Rhys would have a better head start on setting things up.

He paced between the cockpit and the passenger area about ten times in two hours before Oggie grabbed his arm. He dragged him over. "Come sit. I'm trying to teach Holly to play jumble."

"Something about 'I can't read' isn't translating for your man," Holly said.

"I know you can't read, but these are letters," Oggie insisted. He held up a tile. "This is the first letter—"

She smacked the tile out of his hand. "I can't read. I told you four times already."

Oggie flinched like she'd struck a much harder blow. "I was trying to teach you," he growled. He rubbed his hand.

Arden eyed Holly. He'd never gotten a hint of this sort of behavior from her before. Her cheeks had gone red.

She picked up the tile from where it had landed. She set it back among the other tiles. "Sorry."

"Yeah, well, don't do it again," Oggie sulked.

Arden took his hand and kissed the red mark. "Let's find another game."

"I'm gonna go sit in the back," Holly said.

"You don't have to—" Oggie began.

"No, I." She sighed.

"Holly, come on, we'll find a game with no reading. What about numbers? Deck of cards has pictures, too."

"I can't see up close," she admitted. "My gran was a reader. She tried so hard to teach me before she passed but I just, I can't *see*. She taught my brother instead, but he died when we were still kids. Our last reader."

"You need glasses."

She swiveled her head towards Arden. "I need *what?*"

"Glasses. They adjust your vision, so things aren't blurry." He'd never noticed the golden-hazel hue of her eyes before. He'd known her eyes were brown, but he'd never looked into her eyes like this. Or maybe he'd never thought about her eyes before.

She frowned.

Arden promised, "We'll get you glasses first thing. It'll be great. Mace used to have glasses when he was little...Made them a little easier to tell apart."

"They aren't identical, are they?" Oggie asked.

"They're not twins."

Oggie's eyebrows raised. "Hm. Could have fooled me."

"Everyone thinks they are."

Holly shuffled around a few tiles. She sighed.

"Which one's older?"

Arden stopped to think. "Mason...I think. I'm pretty sure Mace is older."

"And he's the one on Council?"

"No, he's a supervisor in Hydroponics. Cole is a Council member. He won the—"

"The worker vote, you're right. I remember now. Honestly, I feel bad, but I've only ever seen them together."

"You'll get used to it."

Oggie let out a snort, dry and bitter. "I can't think straight around your friends. They scare the shit out of me."

Arden took his hand. "It will be different."

"It won't be. You'll never make them think I'm not using you. We could be married for fifty years with six kids and people would still think I was—"

"Six! I don't think I could manage one," Arden interrupted, half-serious but mostly to get Oggie's mind off what Arden's friends thought of him.

"I can barely manage myself."

"That's because you're twenty-six, you've got like two decades before you should think about having kids."

Holly stopped shuffling the tiles. She gave Arden a critical look.

Arden explained, "I think...uh. Life expectancy might be a little longer on *Eden* than on Terra. People tend to wait until they're ready."

"*Peers* tend to wait until they're ready," Oggie reminded. "People keep asking Mara why she doesn't have any kids yet. I think people assume I have a gaggle somewhere."

Holly pushed the tiles into a pile in the center of the table. "Can I ask you something personal?"

"Might as well."

"You said you were made in a lab. What does that *mean?*"

"Oh. Uh. Well." He decided not to delve into the extent to which his mother had used designer genetics and explained instead, "My mother was older when she decided to have kids. A lot older. She found a sperm donor and a surrogate, and you know..." He waved his hand.

Holly shook her head. "No. I don't."

"She'd had some of her eggs preserved when she was younger. She'd never been interested in dating or families or anything like that. But, uh, you know, someone had to be Autarch after her so she picked a man to donate his half and she found another woman to carry the baby...to carry me once the doctors had put her half and his half together." Arden smiled. He wondered if Mother had been excited to have him. He didn't know how lonely his childhood would have been without Mama. "It worked out that she fell for her surrogate."

"She fell for her?"

"You know, they fell in love," Arden clarified.

"So, your mother. She was the queen before you were king. And she had a woman?"

Arden pointed out, "You aren't unfamiliar with the concept of two women getting together."

Holly said, "No one in our tribe has paired up in a long time. All the pairs I can remember were never like that. Or you two."

"We'd have a hard time making that next generation you all want so much," Oggie pointed out. He had his chin tilted up and a smug little smile on his lips. "You're going to have a great time on *Eden.*"

Holly flushed.

Arden chided, "Og, be nice."

"I am being nice!"

"Be *civil*, how about that?"

"Utterly impossible, I was raised by dust bunnies, screens, and wandering visitors. You're lucky I even know how to use a fork."

Holly looked horrified.

Oggie casually waved his hand. "Listen, it doesn't sound as bad after a few drinks."

Arden held his tongue. What he wanted to say didn't need an audience.

He drafted a few people into rehydrating food, struggled to figure out how to recline the seats into a more comfortable sleeping position, and checked the control panel six or seven times before bed.

Not that he'd wanted anything bad to happen to himself or Oggie, but the stakes had skyrocketed.

Holly kept him company when Oggie slept, then slept on the couch when Oggie took his turn to watch the control panel.

About thirty minutes after Arden laid down, someone crept past him up toward the cockpit. He remained perfectly still until he heard a woman greet Oggie.

He nearly went back to the cockpit.

"Where's your little friend?" she asked.

Arden sat up.

Oggie answered, "Sleeping. You didn't see him on your way in?"

"Guess not," she said. "You didn't want to get in bed with him?"

"Someone's got to keep an eye on things."

She purred, "I can think of a few things for you to keep an eye on."

Oggie sighed loud enough that Arden could hear it from beside the bed. He'd climbed out and started toward the door. "Can I be really upfront with you, Tyl?"

"Sure."

"I've spent almost half of my life fucking people I don't really want to fuck. Or trying to impress people I did want to fuck by doing whatever they wanted. I mean, it was fun, I guess, when I got off, but I'm trying really hard not to ruin this."

"Ruin what?"

Arden retreated to the bed, ducking out of Oggie's line of sight just in time.

"I don't think you can understand. I don't think you have any frame of reference for who he is and what I am and how fucking impossible what I want is."

Tyl said, "Well, you're gorgeous and he's...I mean. I guess he's king, right? That must count for something."

Oggie groaned. Arden imagined him slumped in his seat. "I'm trying to tell you I'm not interested."

"Oh."

"Sorry."

"Could have said something sooner," she grumbled.

"You're about to meet more guys than you've ever seen in your life. You'll get over it," he assured dismissively.

She stomped back through the cockpit.

Oggie groaned again.

Holly stirred on the couch. She pulled the blanket tighter around herself. She yawned, then went still again.

Arden wondered if he should check on him. He wondered about it for too long and fell asleep.

He woke to the sensation of a hand on his arm and Oggie softly saying, "Shug, it's time to get up."

"Hmm?"

"We'll be home in a few hours."

"Ten more minutes."

"How could I say no to that?" Oggie asked. He took a seat on the bed.

Arden rested his head on his lap. "I'm not ready."

"I know."

"I don't want to go."

"I know." Oggie smoothed his fingers through Arden's hair.

"I mean. I certainly didn't want to stay on Terra."

"I understand."

The enormity of what lay before him terrified him. He'd done the unthinkable, something wildly reckless not once but twice in hardly any time at all. They'd spent a month or so on Terra and he'd only received three updates from Rhys.

He couldn't guess the true state of *Eden*.

The idea that he should not have trusted Rhys hovered on the edge of his fears. He'd always made his loyalties clear. Maybe he wouldn't return power as easily as Arden had given it.

Maybe they'd killed all the peers.

Fuck.

"I really understand," Oggie said.

Arden rolled onto his back and gazed up at Oggie. "Do you think I'm doing the right thing?"

"I wouldn't know the right thing if it crawled down my throat and lived in my small intestine."

Arden took a moment to process that. "That's not true."

"You have no idea who I am, Arden. Not a single clue."

"That's not true, either." They hadn't known each other for years and he still had things to learn, of course, but he felt safe saying, "I see you, Ogden Nielsen."

"About as well as Holly saw those jumble tiles."

"You know we never really see ourselves, right? You *can't* physically. Mirrors and photos aren't the same."

Oggie rolled his eyes.

"You're hiding things, I'm not saying you aren't. Everyone does that. Unless you have some deep ulterior motives, though, I think I get it."

"What are you hiding?"

"Incompetence, shame, insecurity, gallons of anxiety..." Arden tried to think of something else.

"Oh, they make it in gallons now?"

Arden remained on his back for more than the ten minutes he'd originally requested. The idea of facing anyone on *Eden* immobilized him.

Oggie didn't push him. He made a few gentle suggestions for the better part of an hour. Finally, he said, "If you don't get up soon, sugar, we're going to fly right into *Eden*."

Briefly, he thought of letting it happen.

Briefly.

Suicide was one thing. He had no intention of becoming a mass murderer.

He dragged himself out of bed and pulled on the first clothes he found. No time for a shower, he'd dallied too long.

His heart in his throat, he directed the shuttle through the open door of the bay. The entire time he worried the shuttle wouldn't fit through the door. He knew it would, he'd flown the thing out, but the question of *what if* wouldn't stop circling his mind.

Oggie barely made a sound.

A din of voices rolled forward from the passenger area. They had windows, they could see *Eden* and their reactions created a mélange of wonder and terror.

He wanted to cover his ears.

The shuttle landed less softly than he'd hoped. His teeth clacked together with the force of it. He'd probably done it wrong because there was no way someone had designed it to land like that.

A green light blinked on the console. An incoming transmission.

He touched the button to open the channel. "Hi."

Rhys said, "Don't open the shuttle doors."

"Okay."

"We're sending in a medical team, then sealing the bay until we know for sure what you brought back."

Past the tightness in his throat, Arden said, "I brought back people."

A rush of familiar voices came over the channel all at once.

"Arden!" Cole shouted, louder than the rest, preceded by the sound of a shuffle. "Arden, fuck, are you okay?"

"I'm...Yeah. I'm fine. I am. How's *Eden*?"

Cole began, "*Eden* is..."

Six or seven different voices provided an answer.

"Adjusting."

"Getting used to things."

"A little tense."

"In shambles," said one voice, one Arden recognized as a Council member who usually opposed his plans.

Another shuffle, more forceful this time.

"Is, uh," Cole began, "You're really alright, Ardi?"

"Of course, I am."

"And...Nielsen? He's with you?"

"Where else would he be?"

"Ah," Cole sounded disappointed.

Arden glanced at Oggie. "Uh. Anyway. How long are we holding for?"

"The team will be in soon," Rhys assured.

"How are you!" Arden remembered to ask, too late as usual.

"Me personally?" Rhys asked.

"Yes."

"I'm fine, Your Eminence."

Arden didn't like that answer. He asked, "How's Darcy?"

"Darcy is well."

"Good, good. She learn any new words while I was gone?"

"Shoes. Except she says it 'shus' and it melts my heart every time."

Arden smiled. "Did she stop saying 'fuck' yet?"

"No."

Arden grinned. He shouldn't have. Accidentally teaching a child to swear added nothing to his reign as Autarch or his personal achievements. It did make him giggle every time she said it. He liked that she paid enough attention to him that his vocabulary had made it into her babble.

He had to ask, "Gertie still mad about it?"

"Pissed," Rhys confirmed, then added, "Your Eminence."

He smiled even wider.

"The team is in and the bay is sealed. You can open the doors."

"Did you get my last message? About setting up a few decks in the Quarters?"

"No."

"I'll resend it! Takes forever to get anything from here to Terra..." He grabbed his tablet and resent his last set of requests.

Then he opened the doors.

Eight people in breathing masks, scrubs, and gloves stood just outside the shuttle.

A ninth stepped forward. "Your Eminence, my name is Margaret

Steyer."

"Oh. Hi, Maggie. I didn't know you were a doctor."

"It's been six years."

He gave a sheepish smile. "I am terribly self-absorbed..."

"Oh, no one would ever say that to your face, Your Eminence," she joked.

Arden ignored her.

Behind the medical team, a short, chubby little man hurried his way toward the shuttle. He wore not protective gear but a lush purple smoking jacket and navy trousers. The tassels on his loafers swung as he hustled.

"Winnie!" His heart clenched. "Winnie, what are you doing?" He climbed down the shuttle steps, past the team, and said, "You shouldn't be in here."

Winslow hugged him hard enough to knock the air out of him. "Oh, you're such an awful boy, Arden, making me *worry* like that, all these things...! Everything you did and you just *go*. You're such a horrid child sometimes."

Arden hugged him back. "Winnie, it wasn't that bad."

His uncle stepped back. "Not that bad!"

"Don't yell at me, I can't come back to you yelling at me," Arden pouted.

"You are *spoiled*—"

Arden hugged him again. "Winnie, don't, don't yell at me. I can't stand it!"

Winslow sighed. "Stealing a shuttle—"

"You can't steal something if you own it," Arden reminded. He took his uncle's hand and pulled him along. "Come meet my friend."

Winslow narrowed his eyes. "What friend?"

"His name's Oggie."

"The Nielsen boy. I know all about you and him."

Arden nodded. "It's not the way the news says it is between us, it was just...it was a setup. Honestly. Look at me, do I look like an addict that went through withdrawal on a planet with no medical facilities?"

Winslow looked him over.

"No," Arden answered for him. "I look like I went on vacation. Look, I have a *tan*. When has anyone from *Eden* ever had a real tan?"

Sadness flitted over Winslow's face. "We were neighbors when he was just a little thing...Arden, that boy—"

"Don't tell me he's spare parts or a bad influence, I get that enough from everyone else."

Winslow stopped walking. "Nothing that's happened to him has ever been right. His life has been full of ugly things. Don't be another one."

Arden swallowed. His only family, his only *real* family in the entire world, and that's what Winslow thought of him?

Oggie stood in the door of the shuttle. He watched the medical team as well as Arden and his uncle. His face stayed smooth, unreadable, his eyes most of all.

Arden had never met anyone with eyes like his. Dead, hollow eyes that looked like someone had plucked them off a doll.

Instead of saying anything meaningful, Arden resumed his walk back to the shuttle and said, "That's a little rude, Winnie, I don't think I'm *that* unattractive. I suppose I could lose a few pounds though. I have let myself go..." He paused in front of the medical team. "Maggie, do you want them to come out to you or do you want to go to them?"

"Can you send them out a few at a time, Your Eminence?" she requested.

He nodded. He climbed back into the cockpit. "Og, why don't you go get checked out? I'm sure you're dying to get out of here."

"I'll wait with you."

Winnie puffed his way up the stairs. "Arden, I wasn't done with you!"

"Winnie, I've got work to do! You can scold me later." He made his way back to the passengers and gave them a rundown of what would happen next.

It took longer than anticipated since he had to explain everything from doctors to vaccines, including the purpose of drawing blood and letting strangers take urine samples.

He did his best to assure them, then finally decided he'd go first to put them more at ease.

The Terrans watched as he got a full medical workup. He'd gone to the doctor a lot and the process had acquired a soothing familiarity.

Oggie went second. He flinched so much Arden wondered if he'd even gone to the doctor before.

Those in the Quarters didn't go often, but surely his mother had taken him for checkups as a child.

The Terrans finally agreed, though not without suspicion and bellyaching.

Arden examined the makeshift lab they'd set up in the bay.

Good thing he hadn't driven the shuttle into it.

A few workers hovered uncomfortably in a small, portable kitchen.

He hadn't considered how long this quarantine could last.

They'd probably have to sleep on the shuttle.

He stopped caring about sleeping on the shuttle when he got his first bite of real food in a month. Not rehydrated, not scavenged from the wastes of Terra, but an honest bite of warm, rich mushroom barley soup, thick with vegetables.

The Terrans devoured what the cooks provided.

Winslow remained quiet. Not a thoughtful kind of quiet, either. He was brooding, still mad at Arden.

Every so often, Winslow eyed Oggie, too.

Oggie looked away each time. He looked away any time someone from *Eden* looked at him. Oh, he made it seem like everyone else bored him, like he thought no one could come close to holding his interest.

Arden saw through it. Or he saw what he wanted. He'd never know.

Arden took Winslow's bowl when he'd emptied it and reached his hand out for Oggie's.

Oggie rolled his eyes and handed it over like it was the most pedestrian come-on he'd ever endured.

Arden collected as many bowls as he could carry. He deposited them in the vat of soapy water awaiting their arrival.

The worker standing in front of it did not look at him.

Arden thought he looked familiar. "Do I know you?"

The man gave him a sour look. "Kile."

"Oh. Rhys's friend. Right?"

"No one else was stupid enough to come into a bay full of people that might be contaminated with a bunch of unknown diseases."

"Oh."

Kile shook his head. "He talks you into things. But you knew that."

"He's certainly persuasive." Arden stared into the water. "Uh. How are things out there?"

"Peers aren't happy."

"And the workers?"

Kile hesitated. "Overwhelmed."

Arden appreciated that. "We'll get there."

"No offense, Your Eminence, but I don't really need platitudes."

Arden sucked in a breath. He didn't know what to say. He made an awkward gesture. "Well. You know. I'm not good at those either..."

He walked away to get more bowls.

He didn't stop moving until he'd gathered every last bowl.

As long as he kept moving, he felt okay. Whenever he paused to talk with someone, he grew uncomfortable.

He felt every set of eyes in the room. Every time someone spoke, he thought he caught his name on their lips.

Looking at him, laughing at him, waiting for him to fuck up.

He eyed the small lab.

The medical team clustered together on one side, running tests. They hadn't stopped moving either.

He edged over, taking in the supplies they'd brought. He saw everything needed for first aid, bottles of vaccines...and formulas, their bottles all lined up on a single shelf, adorned with plain numbers, one through twenty.

He stared at the bottle of Twelve and the little shot glasses stacked beside the formulas.

It made sense to bring these. It made sense for them to be here.

So why had the sight of them shocked him?

Why had it felt like water after a brutal practice?

One of the medics noticed him lurking. "Did you need something, Your Eminence?"

That title felt like soap on a cut. "Uh. I." He glanced back toward the Terrans, spread out through the bay, talking and taking things in. "Making sure everything's going well?"

"So far so good."

He nodded and walked away.

He retreated to the shuttle.

He nearly got into bed before he remembered that Winslow needed somewhere to sleep now.

Stupid old fool. He shouldn't have come here.

He scavenged through the shuttle for another set of pillows and blankets. He made up the bed for his uncle and the couch for Oggie. He piled a few pillows and blankets on the pilot's chair. It didn't recline but he'd dozed off in it before.

He'd wanted to go to bed so badly, to curl up and hide from everything again.

With that option thwarted, he went back out and sat next to Winslow. "Aren't you even going to ask me how my trip was?"

Winslow didn't answer him.

The silent treatment. He must have been truly pissed off.

Arden pulled up the pictures on his tablet and slid it onto his uncle's lap. The first was a sweeping panorama he'd asked someone to take from the radio tower. He'd thought about climbing it himself and had chickened out. The woman who'd scaled it had been happy enough to do him the favor.

She'd liked that she could take the picture and zoom in on the more distant parts.

"I got a distress call from that radio tower. They said they didn't send it, that they didn't even know how to work it. I couldn't figure out how anyone had gotten it to work but Holly told me some tribes have these old generators. They drag them around on sleds."

Winslow turned toward him.

"I guess having generators is more dangerous, though. They make noise, which means raiders know you're there *and* they know you have something worth stealing." Arden flicked to the next picture. A tree with twisted branches. He'd begged Oggie to stand next to it for scale. "Holly says up north the trees are tall and straight. I didn't get any pictures of those; we didn't move around."

He continued this scrolling narration until he came upon a picture that he hadn't meant to show anyone. He quickly flicked past it.

Winslow flicked back.

Arden tried to pull the tablet back. Not that it was anything bad. He even looked nice in it. Something about the picture of him showing a child how to set up the projector had an intimate quality to it.

He didn't have any pictures like that anymore.

Winslow didn't let go. "Who's this young man?"

Arden squinted at the picture. "His name is Yunis."

"No, *this* one," Winslow said. "He looks just like my nephew except he knows how to smile."

Arden took the tablet. He cleared his throat. "This, uh, this is a building, a bookstore or a library."

Winslow didn't look at the picture. He looked at the Terrans milling around. "Why did you bring them here?"

"Because you shouldn't have to pay for a seat on a lifeboat."

"You've upset a lot of people."

"Does that mean you don't support me anymore?" Arden asked. "Or does it mean you finally want to hear about what I'm doing?"

"You were such a spoiled little boy. Your mama and I both did that to you. I never." Winslow touched his own face. "I never thought you'd be anything else."

"Oh."

"When your mother passed and you had such a hard time with it, people worried, you know. I always told them you were too spoiled to do anything that took effort."

"You told people that!"

"Better than letting them think you'd turn out like Morris. And speaking of him—"

"I can't, Winnie, I absolutely can't talk about that. Not now."

Winslow put a hand on Arden's arm. "Tell me you didn't mean for it to end like that."

"I didn't. I promise."

Winslow didn't look reassured.

"Want a tour of the shuttle?" Arden asked. He stood and walked away.

His uncle followed him inside.

Arden showed him the bathroom and the bed, then said, "You look tired. We can talk more in the morning."

"Tired! I haven't slept through the night in a month, thanks to you. I've never worried like that in my life."

Arden swept Winslow into a hug. "I love you."

"I love you, too."

Arden kissed his fluffy curls and wondered if hair like that lurked in his genes. He remembered then that he bore no genetic relation to Winslow. "Get some sleep."

Winslow patted his back.

Everyone else had gone to bed, every Terran, medic, and worker.

Oggie and Arden sat in the cockpit, the door closed to the rest of the shuttle, not talking to each other.

Arden had offered him the couch to sleep on, to which Oggie had responded, "I'm not sharing a room alone with your uncle."

They hadn't spoken after that.

Arden didn't feel right leaving him to go to bed. "We can share the couch," he offered after too many quiet minutes.

Oggie shot him a dirty look.

"I had to give him the bed, Og, he's so old!"

"I'm not mad you let an old man sleep in a bed," Oggie hissed.

"Then what's wrong?"

"Why does something have to be wrong?"

"You seem distant."

"I'm not trying to blow you, so something has to be wrong?"

Arden snapped, "That's not what I said."

Oggie didn't answer.

Arden gave it a few minutes. He was tired, though, and he didn't know what to do. "I'm going to get some sleep. There's room for you if you want it."

Oggie stayed quiet.

Arden lay on the couch. He hadn't realized how much colder it got on *Eden*. The Terrans had talked about it almost exclusively. That and the food.

He hoped he'd done the right thing.

He tightened the blankets around himself and pressed his face into the pillow.

He woke up alone.

Winslow still slept.

He eased off the couch and into the shower. He needed it, for his nerves as much as hygiene. He washed his hair.

That always made him feel better.

He left it loose to dry.

People from Terra had started to stir and ask about breakfast.

He went to the workers and asked them to start cooking.

Kile said, "It'll be a way off. More people to cook for than anyone figured."

Arden nodded.

"What needs to get done?" Kineth asked.

Arden glanced over his shoulder. He hadn't expected her to be so close.

Kile frowned.

"We aren't used to being..." She frowned too, as if searching for the right words. "Treated like babies."

Arden tilted his head.

"Littles help out with what they can. Only babies get a free meal," Mira explained. "Show us how to help."

Kile pointed to a knife block. "Could probably cut up the peppers and onions."

The Terrans descended on the kitchen.

Arden stepped back. He scanned the bay for Oggie and couldn't find him. He approached the medical team. "Any news?"

"You're in good health."

"Huh."

Maggie said, "Surprised?"

"Normally I get told off for a few things."

"You could use more iron," she offered almost as a consolation.

"What about the Terrans?"

"No heinous diseases so far, but we have more people to examine and rather incomplete knowledge of existing diseases on Terra One."

"So even if they all get clean bills of health...?"

"Something could still pop up," she confirmed.

He crossed his arms.

"And we don't know what our germs will do to them."

He uncrossed his arms and settled his hands on his hips. "Fuck."

Maggie shrugged. "Worse care scenario we all die. Best case scenario...We all live, I guess."

"Is that your professional opinion?" he asked.

"It's my hopeful-for-the-future opinion," she answered.

"Great."

She pointed out, "Most doctors wouldn't come into this bay unless you threatened to strip their funds. Cole Baker personally asked me to do this when the Council couldn't get anyone else."

"Oh. Well. I appreciate it."

"Ah. I needed a reason to get out and work since Dad passed. Keep busy, you know?"

"Yeah."

She looked at the Terrans. "None of them are getting clean bills of health. They all need dental work and like...six kinds of vitamin boosters. A few of them need serious health care, too, like...bones that need to be reset and chronic diseases. At least seven of them probably have melanoma and that's just the ones we looked at so far."

"That's grim."

Maggie shrugged. "From what they've told me, they're lucky to be alive."

Arden looked around the lab. His eyes lighted on the line of formula containers. He pushed his hands into his pockets. "Well. Thanks."

He walked away without waiting for an answer. A quick peek inside the shuttle found Winnie still sleeping. He did tend to sleep in. Arden watched him long enough to make sure he still breathed.

He went to the glass window of the bay. An operations room lay on the other side. Currently, a handful of people sat inside.

He rapped on the glass.

A trio of heads swiveled toward him. Cole, Xio, and a worker he didn't recognize.

He waved.

Cole scrambled over and pushed a button. "Ardi! Morning!"

"Morning."

"I swear as soon as I can get my hands on you, I'm going to strangle you!"

"That's not nice."

"Nice! You threw the station into chaos and went on vacation with an assassin! How's that for nice?"

"I don't know, I guess you can look at it as righting generations of systematic wrongs and oppression, then putting my life at risk to rescue the people we abandoned."

"No one's putting it like that."

Arden smiled. "I'm going to make sure the history books do."

"We were worried about you! You can't—"

"Oh, yell at me later. My tablet finally updated with all the reports. Do you have time to talk?"

"You want to talk about reports?"

"I've been gone for a month."

Xio approached the window. "You look well, Your Eminence."

"So do you."

"I wrote up a summary of Engineering if you want to go over it. I thought a month might be a lot to go over all at once."

He appreciated the effort and didn't tell her a month's reports meant nothing compared to all the numbers he'd seen in the past years. "Sure, let's go over it."

He found a chair and they conversed for the better part of an hour. Given all the changes that had come from releasing the workers from their debts and putting Rhys in charge, he welcomed her summary. He didn't know if every department had undergone such changes.

Holly brought him breakfast. "You almost didn't get any."

"Thanks."

She stared at the people on the other side of the window. "They can hear us?"

He nodded.

"Hi there."

Cole and Xio looked at each other.

Cole asked, "What?"

"She said hi!" Arden clarified. "You'll get used to the accent."

"What accent?" Holly asked.

"You talk slow."

"You talk fast!" she accused.

Xio said, "Hi."

Holly jabbed her thumb toward Arden. "He really king up here?"

"He's Autarch," Xio answered.

"Yeah, they don't seem to get what that means," Arden said.

"He's the king," Cole confirmed.

"What about you?" Holly asked.

"No."

To Arden, she said, "He dresses even worse than you."

"Don't be rude. Cole, you look very handsome."

"How can you move in that much clothes?"

Arden grinned at Cole. "Oh, you should see what he wears when he's not at work."

Cole's olive cheeks darkened. "Arden, don't make fun of me in front of the Terrans. You'll make them think I'm a joke."

"No, they're all going to try to fuck you," Holly said. "Joke or not."

"All their men died. It's...it's kind of had an impact on their collective psyche."

"Huh."

"Anyway. Oh! Have you talked to Oggie at all?"

"I haven't seen him."

"Me neither. If you do, tell him it's a good idea for him to be Entertainment Minister."

"You can't keep giving government jobs to your friends and lovers."

"*You* were elected."

"I haven't seen Oggie either," Holly said.

Arden turned around and scanned the bay. "He literally *has* to be in here somewhere. What do you think, Xio? Wouldn't he be a good Entertainment Minister?"

Xio shifted and didn't look exactly at Arden when she answered. "Isn't he the one who tried to kill you?"

"It wasn't like that. He didn't *try*."

"And I thought you two weren't even really sleeping together," Cole said.

Holly covered her mouth and turned away.

Arden didn't know if they could hear her snorting on the other side of the glass, but he certainly could. "Sleeping with me is not a job. Entertainment Minister is. And Frakes is terrible."

"Oh, no, I don't know," Xio protested, "I kind of liked *From Never to Forever*."

Arden wrinkled his nose instinctually. Frakes had gotten that movie approved in the deepest days of Arden's troubles. "It's *awful* and not even the fun kind."

She pressed her lips together and lowered her eyes. "I think it's kind of sweet."

Arden raised a hand and waved her opinion away. "Anyway. We need to replace him."

"You think Nielsen can make movies that promote what we're doing?" Cole asked. "He doesn't seem...He doesn't seem like he does *that* kind of work."

Arden walked away before he started a fight. He didn't need to argue over this in front of Xio or the Terrans.

He spied Winnie talking to Tola and decided not to interrupt.

He checked the far side of the bay. He made sure to check behind the fuel containers. He found a pillow and a blanket in a small storage alcove.

No Oggie, though.

Arden sat down and waited.

It only took about twenty minutes before Oggie showed up with a packet of rehydrated food.

"You miss breakfast?" Arden asked.

Oggie scowled.

"Can we talk?"

"I'm sure you're going to anyway."

"Come sit with me."

"Is that an order, Your Eminence?"

"Yes."

Oggie sat.

"What's wrong?"

"Nothing."

"Oh, so you hide in corners and sleep on the floor when you're in a good mood?" Arden asked.

"Fuck off."

Arden had seen him get hysterical, morose, and flighty. He'd seen him become erratic. He'd never seen him so sour before. "What happened?"

"Why did something have to happen?"

"The other night you were telling Tyl you didn't want to mess anything up and now you're avoiding me."

"You were eavesdropping?"

"I overheard. It's not the same."

Oggie grunted. He shoved a gummy piece of bread in his mouth.

"Oggie. Please."

"It's..." Oggie threw the food packet away from himself. He put his head on his knees. "It's not just one thing. It's a thousand fucking things. Like...Like Rhys!"

"What about Rhys?"

"He fucking hates me, first, and you still like him, second, and—"

"Hang on. I still like him?"

"Obviously. I saw the way you looked when you were talking to him. And you were always going out to see him in the middle of the night."

"If you'd like to be exclusive—"

"That's not the point!"

"Care to let me in on the point then?"

Oggie sighed. "I'll always be a stand-in for what you couldn't have until you find something better."

"Fuck, Og, I..." Arden sighed. "You think that's the kind of person I am?"

"I think that's the kind of person you all are."

Nothing in the world could make this conversation better. Arden thought about asking to postpone it, but a larger part wanted this resolved now. And, quarantined as they were, they had nothing else to do and no way to avoid each other that didn't involve Oggie hiding.

Arden told him, "I still want you with me."

"For now."

"Yes, for now. Now is all we have. What? Did you want me to fucking propose? It's barely been a month."

Oggie glared at him.

Arden half-smiled. He scooted closer. "Oggie."

"I didn't! I'm not stupid. I'm not. I know it will never be like that."

"I wouldn't say never."

"I'm not talking about *marriage*, Arden, but I don't..."

After a heavy pause, Arden urged, "Go on."

"You said if we were together it wouldn't be how we pretended it was. Pet and peer."

"It isn't."

"It wasn't on Terra because it couldn't be. The same social structures didn't exist. But I just." Oggie pulled in a nervous breath. "I just. I heard their voices and then your uncle showed up and I just. I can't. You *said* it wouldn't be like that, but you didn't even...You didn't even ask or anything."

The idea of formally asking Oggie to be his partner had never occurred to him. Weakly, he pointed out, "We agreed to give it a month. You're supposed to ask if I'm sick of you yet."

"Are you?"

"No."

"Give it a week."

Arden scooched closer. He put his hand over Oggie's. "Is that what you want? A commitment?"

"I..." Oggie sighed. "I don't know. No one will take me seriously anyway."

"I take you seriously. Doesn't that count?"

"Arden."

"Alright, you're right, I'm sorry. Do you want to keep living in my rooms?"

"Yes."

"And sleeping together?"

"Yes."

"I'd like things to be...to be a little more romantic than just that. Than just sleeping together. I'd like us to be a couple. Go out together. Share a bed if you want."

Oggie agreed, "I could do that."

"And we'll check back in with each other in another month?"

Oggie nodded.

Arden kissed his knuckles. "I love you."

Oggie nodded again.

"One down. How about the other nine hundred and ninety-nine?"

"What?"

"You said it was a thousand things. What are the other—"

Oggie pushed him. Playful, not aggressive.

Arden looped his arms around Oggie and dragged him close. He nuzzled against him. "Tell me what else."

Oggie sighed, then launched into an hour-long monologue about everything that could, and he believed would, go wrong.

Arden couldn't get a word in edgewise, not to confirm or reassure.

Eventually, Oggie ran out of possible tragedies to list. He sank further into Arden's arms and went quiet.

"I didn't know you worried so much," Arden said.

"I don't. Usually I don't give two shits about anything. Or anyone. I mean. Not like that, I'm not a monster. But I haven't..." Oggie sighed. "I feel so rotten and shriveled inside and you don't make me feel that way. I don't like it."

"I'm sorry."

"Not your fault I'm fucked up."

"Still..."

Oggie continued, "I hate it and I need it all at the same time. Even when you make me feel something bad at least it's different than the kind of shitty I usually feel."

"Don't you ever feel good?"

"Yeah, for about ten seconds when I cum."

"Oggie, come on."

"Or in that golden glow between drinks three and seven."

"Og."

Oggie smiled. "And like this. When you hold me. Or when I make you laugh."

That made Arden's stomach flutter.

"You make me laugh, too, and smile and..." Oggie licked his lips. "And I want to keep that so bad."

Arden tightened his arms.

"Arden!" called Winslow from some distance.

Oggie attempted to sit up.

Arden kept him close. "Should I say something?" he asked quietly.

"He's going to keep looking," Oggie said.

"I'd like you to meet him."

"I've met him. He lived right next to my mother," Oggie reminded. "He always had candy..."

"He's my only real family."

"Arden! You awful thing, where are you!" Winslow called, closer now.

"Please." Arden nosed Oggie's throat. "Pretty please."

"Fine."

Arden rolled away from him to poke his head out of the alcove. "Over here, Winnie!"

The old man swiveled toward Arden's voice. "What in the world are you doing over there?"

"Come here!"

Winslow made his way over. He put his hands on his hips and frowned at them on the floor. "What is this, some kind of love nest?"

"I'm not that desperate," Arden said. "Come sit."

"I'm much too old to sit on the floor!" Winslow scolded.

Arden patted the top of a storage crate.

Winslow sat but he took his time about it. "What are you doing?"

"Talking. I know you two already are acquainted but uh, Oggie, Winnie. Winnie, Oggie," Arden said.

Oggie gave a small wave but didn't look at Winslow.

Winslow looked at the blanket and pillow, the question written on his face.

Arden asked, "Did you need something? Or did you just want to say hi?"

"No one could find you. You made us worry."

Arden made himself smile.

"Always making someone worry about you," his uncle scolded.

"Win! How long are you going to stay mad at me for?"

His uncle huffed.

Oggie fidgeted.

Arden took his hand.

Winslow stared at their linked fingers.

Arden studied his uncle, trying to read his face, daring him to say something. "How's your month been? And don't give me anything about worrying or sleepless nights. I'm asking about your social life."

"I suppose once things settled, everything went more or less back to normal."

"How bad was it?"

"It would have been smoother if you hadn't taken off."

Arden shrugged. "Am I going back to a warzone?"

"You know I don't follow those things," Winslow said. "Although."

"Hmm?"

"That Keats boy and his friends are displeased."

Arden grunted. Bull. He'd hoped not to hear from him again.

Winslow looked between Arden and Oggie on the floor again. "What are you two *doing* over here?"

"Talking, I told you already. Nowhere is exactly private in here," Arden said.

Oggie tugged his hand back. "I, uh. Your Eminence. I need to...I'll. May I be excused?"

"Of course."

Oggie scrambled to his feet.

Winslow frowned at Arden. "What are you doing to that boy?"

"Nothing."

"Arden, it isn't my business to tell you this but the way that boy grew up—"

"I know."

"He's *frightened* of you. Can't you see that?"

Arden swallowed. "I think it's you, actually."

"Me? What have I done?"

Arden smoothed the seam of his pants. He sighed and debated what to say. "Nothing personally, I'm sure. He's right to worry, though. No one will make it easy for us."

"I don't follow."

"Being in a relationship," Arden clarified. "He's a worker. I'm...Well. I'm Autarch. And there was his business with Morris. It's unsteady ground we're on. Has a peer ever publicly taken a worker as a partner? Not a pet, or a tryst. A publicly recognized partner."

"Not to my knowledge."

"Then you understand."

Winslow fiddled with a candy wrapper. "No, Arden. I don't."

Arden sat up straighter.

"I don't understand what you're doing at all. Not with that boy, not with the space station..." The candy wrapper slipped from his fingers. "I'm worried."

Arden picked up the wrapper and offered it to his uncle. Winslow didn't take it, so Arden slipped it into his pocket. "Do you think I'm doing the wrong thing?"

"Sometimes."

"Oh." He stood up. "Did you get breakfast? Holly said it went fast."

"No."

"Let's see about that."

Winslow didn't stand right away.

Arden turned to look at him. "Win, are you coming?"

"I tell you I'm worried and that's all you can say?" Winslow asked.

Arden crouched beside him. He put his hand over his uncle's, too aware of the papery texture of his skin, the thinness of his hair, the veins around his eyes. He didn't have many years left. Not more than twenty, which felt like absolutely nothing when Arden thought about how long he'd have to live without Winslow.

Without a single real family member. His grandparents had all passed, and he didn't love any of Mother's family the way he loved Winslow. His cousins ranged from awful to boring with a few exceptions.

"I've never given you any reason to believe in me but I'm going to ask you to do it anyway, Winnie. I am trying my best and I am trying to do what I think is right. I..." Arden drew in a breath. "I inherited so much and not all of it is nice. If I tell you I think what I'm doing is the right thing to do, do you believe me?"

"I don't know."

"I guess first you'd have to believe I want to do the right thing." He tightened his grip on Winslow's hand. "It's a big thing to ask."

"Be a good boy."

"I'm trying," he promised.

A good boy.

Sometimes he wondered if Winslow knew that Arden wasn't twenty-three anymore.

He kept a hold of Winslow's hand as he stood.

They went to find him breakfast.

"He looks like his mother," Winslow noted as they watched Oggie and Holly.

The women who'd been so interested in Oggie now gave him cold looks.

"Hmmm?"

"Lighter, of course, both of them. From their father...Nolie tried to keep it under wraps, but we saw him sneaking out in the morning. But tan like that? He looks just like Nolie," Winslow shared. "I did always wonder what had happened to them once the parents broke things off. It doesn't seem like things have gotten much better."

"Well, fuck, Win, I am nice to him. Is there some kind of rumor going around about how I treat my boyfriends?"

"I always thought..."

"What?" Arden prompted.

"I always thought keeping a pet was a little tasteless."

"He's *not* my pet."

"No, but that trial made it pretty clear he'd done it for other people."

Arden sighed and returned to watching Oggie.

Oggie noticed after a while and returned his gaze, one eyebrow raised. "What?" he mouthed.

Arden shook his head.

"He is a handsome young man. I see why you picked him."

Arden had to say, "I didn't *pick* him."

Oggie came over. "You stare at someone like that and a fellow starts to get ideas."

"Deepest apologies, Mr. Nielsen."

"I suppose I could forgive you."

Oggie looked steadier than he had when he'd fled.

Arden gestured for him to sit. "Tell Winnie I didn't pick you."

"No, Morris picked me."

Arden blanched.

Oggie grinned at him. He took Arden's hand, then looked at Winslow and thought better of it. "But really, if Mara hadn't decked that girl, I don't think you ever would have noticed me. You only looked at your drinks unless she was talking to you."

"I do genuinely like her."

"She hates you."

"She hates everyone."

Oggie shrugged. "True enough. Including me, I guess, since she hasn't shown up to make sure I'm alive."

Winslow cleared his throat.

"What?"

"I don't want to be the bearer of bad news..."

Oggie's face went ashen. "What happened to her?"

"She...She did seem to think something untoward had happened to you. No one believed that you two had taken a shuttle. Quite a few rumors flew. Awful things, I won't repeat them," Winslow said. "She took it quite hard and…made a nuisance of herself for the Chamberlain and Council. She's been confined to quarters since."

Oggie breathed, "Oh, she's probably ripped her hair out by now." Some color had come back to his face.

"They actually confined her to your quarters, given that they were empty," Winslow told Arden.

Arden couldn't imagine she'd taken that in stride. "She's alright, though?"

Winslow nodded. "As far as I know."

Arden told Oggie, "I'm sure she's alright."

"She's always alright. Strong Nielsen trait, being alright."

Arden took his hand.

Oggie stared at their linked fingers, sneaking glances toward Winslow.

Winslow lightly cleared his throat and addressed Oggie, "So I hear you two had quite the adventure on Terra. Something about a building full of books?"

"We only found one we could read," Oggie said then realized Winslow wanted more. He told the story in more detail, his face polite and his eyes empty. He perked up a little when Winslow asked what the book was about.

Oggie had devoured it in a few days and had refused to tell Arden how it ended.

The two fell into a conversation about books. Oggie carried himself well throughout the conversation and by the end of it, he had Winslow chuckling and telling stories about all the times he'd snuck out under the guise of going to a book club.

Arden really liked this story.

Winslow told it like he'd done something salacious instead of just sneaking on to the Solar Deck to read.

Oggie had the good grace to act like Winslow's story shocked him. "Weren't you worried about getting caught?"

"Oh, no, I never worried about anything when I had Marcus with me."

"Marcus sounds like a catch."

"He was a very good friend to me."

Without looking at Arden, Oggie's fingers tightened.

After a little while longer, Winslow excused himself for a nap.

Oggie's eyes followed him as he walked away. "I was supposed to live that life. Naps and books all day long?"

"You can do whatever you want."

"Stop saying that."

"You can."

"I have a job…Maybe. Who knows, actually? I either have a job or need to find a new job."

"Only if you want to."

Oggie scowled.

Arden scooted closer and rested his chin on Oggie's shoulder. He held off on making any promises. "What if you took a little time off?"

"I've taken loads of time off between the trial and Terra."

"Just to sort out a few things. Settle in. Ease back into working."

"Is that what you plan on doing? Ease back into being King of Space?"

"What if I left Rhys in charge? What if I did nothing all day? Not a care between the two of us..."

"You'd get sick of me even faster."

Arden pecked his cheek. "I can think of dozens of things to do."

"They better not be different positions cause that's still all one thing."

"You're so *suspicious*, Oggie."

"There are only two reasons people keep me around."

"I kept you around for months without having sex," Arden reminded. "And I'm allergic to the drugs you deal."

Oggie didn't accept or reject the point he'd made. He went still and quiet for a while. Finally, he murmured, "I've dealt other drugs. I can probably get you whatever you want."

Arden kissed his temple. He meant to offer comfort, but as the words came out, he knew they sounded cruel. "There's nothing you can give me that I can't get from anyone."

Oggie started to stand.

Arden put a hand on his arm. "Hang on, wait, I didn't mean it like—"

"It doesn't matter how you meant it. It matters that it's true."

"Wait."

Oggie shook his head. He retreated to the shuttle.

Arden watched him go, then headed in the opposite direction. He made a nuisance of himself in the lab and the kitchen. He didn't help any of the various processes in either location but stayed there anyway.

Maggie tolerated him better than Kile.

After dinner, Rhys called him over to the bay window. He stood alone in the operation room.

Arden got so close to the window he probably left marks on it. He wanted to jump through the glass and grab the other man. Instead, he demanded, "What happened to your face?"

Rhys's fingers found a shiny, pink scar on his cheekbone. "Mara didn't like my answers about where she could look for her brother if she didn't believe he'd gone to Terra One."

Arden touched the glass.

Rhys lined up his fingers with Arden's. "I'm so mad at you."

"I'm sorry."

"I can't believe you took off like that."

"Don't yell at me, I'll cry."

"You look really good."

A few hot tears slid down Arden's cheeks. "Can't do body checks when the only mirror is the size of your face." He felt immediately ashamed of himself.

Rhys stared at him, his hand pressed flat against the window. "Hang on, I'm going to come in there."

"No!" Arden said, too loud. "No, no, don't you fucking dare."

"Then stop crying."

"I'm not crying." Arden scrubbed his face dry. "What would Darcy do if you were trapped in here with us?"

Rhys let out a hard breath through his nose.

"How's *Eden?*"

"It's a shit show. People thought you were dead."

"I'm really sorry." He wiped his face again. He let a slow, controlled breath through his nose.

"I..." Rhys swallowed hard. "I can't do this, I can't, what the fuck, Arden? I'll come back when I can see you. I mean. When I can...I."

Arden nodded. He understood. "Soon."

"Soon," Rhys agreed.

"Say hi to Darcy."

Rhys walked out of the room.

Arden sat down and pressed his back to the wall. He hugged his knees tight to his chest and couldn't let go. He couldn't cry, either. He had nowhere to hide and couldn't lose his shit in front of over a hundred people.

He made himself stand.

He had to keep it together.

He walked to the lab. His fingers shook as he picked up a shot glass. Twelve lapped over the sides of the glass and over his fingers when he poured. The shot nearly gagged him, the slippery bitter taste unfamiliar after so long without one.

Immediately, it became clear he couldn't handle a full shot anymore.

He made it inside the shuttle before his legs gave out.

He spent hours on the floor beside the couch, motionless. Numb inside and out, sick to his stomach from skipping dinner, warm and too high to care who saw him or what they'd think. He stared at the ceiling, his hands folded on his chest. All he could do was breathe. In and out, slow and shallow.

Sometimes he forgot to breathe. His head would spin and he would gasp.

People walked past him but didn't interact.

He heard voices, so many voices, outside the shuttle. Laughing.

He turned his head to the side.

The carpet, stiff and rough, dug into his cheek. He barely felt it.

A mouthful of stomach acid worked its way up his throat and trickled through his parted lips.

He closed his eyes.

Arden hadn't had a clear thought in four days.

He'd made it off the shuttle floor and kept himself more responsibly numb. Winslow disapproved and Oggie wouldn't talk to him.

Arden didn't care.

That was the point.

In six hours, barring any unfortunate test results, they'd be free to leave the bay.

He couldn't be like this when that time came.

He found Maggie.

Twelve made it easy to tell her, "Dump the rest of it."

She frowned at him. "Your Eminence, I don't follow."

"The rest of the Twelve. I can't have it in here."

He'd taken a shot right before breakfast. He'd be desperate for another one by lunch. Not physically, he hadn't gotten back into bodily addiction that quickly, but he liked being empty more than the way broken glass ground in his throat whenever Oggie walked away from him.

"You're sure?"

"I can't be like this out there."

Maggie made a face he interpreted as agreement. "I'll take care of it."

He nodded and walked away.

He melted into the couch for as long as he could.

The Twelve wore off.

Anxiety clawed its way up his throat and lived in his mouth. He swallowed it back down constantly as he went over what would happen with the Terrans.

An hour before the end of quarantine, six people from the Transition

Committee came in. They acquainted themselves with the Terrans and presented the orientation program developed during the quarantine. A few weeks meant to help them adjust and familiarize themselves with *Eden*.

The Terrans grew quieter and quieter.

Their silence rang in his ears.

He'd sent out a speech for Rhys to read in his stead a few days ago. Apparently, the citizens of *Eden* had taken to the idea of newcomers better than the upheaval to the class system. After all, who hadn't stared down at Terra One and wondered what still lived there?

Whether they could come together to make a common people would take time to figure out, but Arden felt some small degree of hope about that at least.

Productivity would dip initially, with new mouths to feed and new workers to train, but projections looked good as long as the Terrans took well to work crews.

He hoped they would.

Their return had quieted the idea that the workers had conspired to kill Arden and throw a coup. Rhys reported people had settled a lot during the quarantine. A few holdouts maintained they kept Arden in quarantine because he was a dupe and his plastic surgery still needed to settle.

Despite how numb he'd kept himself, he found that conspiracy thoroughly amusing.

Oggie wouldn't look at him when he approached, so he left him alone and walked out of the bay on his own.

Rhys stood about ten yards away.

Mara came over and punched Oggie in the arm. She immediately laid into him.

Arden wanted to intervene but Oggie turned his back to him when their eyes met.

The Transition Committee moved the Terrans away in a noisy rush of directions and reassurances.

Arden announced, "I'll be in my rooms until this evening. Should anything arise, please, come to me as you would have before. I'll see you all at the Welcome Dinner."

He walked away.

Rhys trailed behind him, wordless and light-footed, but so familiar that Arden sensed his presence.

As soon as the door to Arden's room closed, Rhys grabbed him.

Arden flinched.

"What the fuck is *wrong with you?*" Rhys demanded.

"I'm sorry."

"You can't do things like that!"

"I'm sorry."

Rhys crushed him close. "I worried about you."

"I'm sorry."

"Stop saying that."

Arden swallowed. He twisted his hands in Rhys's shirt. "I'm so sorry don't be mad anymore I'm sorry."

Rhys sniffled. "Tell me you're okay."

He couldn't make himself say it. He started to cry.

Rhys wrapped an arm around him, the palm of his hand cradling the side of Arden's head. He kissed his temple. "I hate it so much when you cry."

"*I'm sorry*," he sobbed.

"What the fuck happened?"

"Everyone's mad at me."

Softly, Rhys assured, "I'm not really mad at you."

Arden kept crying, useless as ever.

Rhys rubbed his back. "I'm glad you're back. That's all. I'm glad you're home safe."

It felt so nice to be held.

The sound of Rhys's heart steadied him almost as well as a shot would have. It made it a little easier not to ask for one. It reassured him that he hadn't completely undone the progress he'd made.

Four days wasn't enough to fall into a full-blown addiction.

He could get back on track, go back to taking a shot when he needed it, not to lock out the world.

Compared to where he'd been, this was a slip-up, not a relapse.

He settled down. He squeezed Rhys. "I..."

"You can tell me," Rhys said.

"I fuck everything up."

Rhys brought him over to the couch. He kept an arm around him and their hands together. "What, specifically, did you fuck up this time?"

"You're supposed to tell me I don't fuck everything up."

"So what did you fuck up?"

Arden sighed. "Oggie's mad at me."

Rhys huffed. "Good."

"Rhys!"

"Arden, he's—"

Arden pulled away from Rhys. He wiped his face one last time. "Can I really talk to you about this?"

Rhys nodded. "Sorry. Yes."

"I love him."

Rhys made a face.

Arden smacked him. "Don't!"

"Fine."

Arden crossed his arms.

"Well?" Rhys prompted. "I promise, I'll be good."

Arden gave him a doubtful look.

"I swear."

"Fine." Arden huffed, sighed, then related what had happened between him and Oggie on Terra as best he could. He tried to explain his feelings, his suspicions about Oggie's feelings, and what Oggie had outright admitted.

Rhys didn't say much. He listened and nodded. When Arden had exhausted the topic, he only said, "I'm not good at stuff like this."

"That's not helpful."

"I told you, I'm better as a friend. I always have been. I don't..."

Arden raised his eyebrows.

"I love people, but I don't fall *in* love like other people do. I don't know if it's because I'm too cynical or if I was just born a little...off. But I don't. I don't understand these things."

"Hmm."

"But maybe drugging yourself senseless and avoiding him wasn't the right thing to do."

"Maybe," Arden admitted.

"You should find him before the Dinner cause after tonight we've got about a hundred things to talk about more important than your personal life."

Arden looked around the room. He'd imagined this differently. He'd imagined coming home with Oggie and finally kissing each other silly in the privacy of their rooms. Dressing up for the Dinner like Mama and Mother had. He remembered them standing in front of the bathroom mirror together, smiling at each other, helping each other button things, fastening necklaces, and Mama insisting the Autarch let her put on just a *hint* of color on her lips.

He stood up.

Rhys said, "Uh. Maybe bring him flowers."

"What?"

"I like flowers. He might, too. I bet no one's ever brought him flowers."

Arden bought flowers. He went to check Mara's apartment since he couldn't think of anywhere else Oggie could be.

He wasn't there, but someone pointed him in the direction of someone they'd seen Oggie with earlier.

Arden followed the breadcrumb trail of Oggie sightings through most of deck eight. No one he talked to seemed at all surprised to find a peer tracing Oggie through the Quarters. A few people even mentioned the flowers were a nice touch.

Finally, he reached a door that someone swore they'd just seen him go through just a few minutes ago. "Have you seen Oggie Nielsen?" he asked for the thirteenth time in forty-five minutes.

The woman who answered the door looked at Arden and the flowers he carried. Her face twisted between worried and apologetic, but not at all surprised. "He's..."

"Can you ask him to come talk to me?"

"You, uh. You want me to interrupt him, Your Eminence?"

"Is..." Arden didn't know how to answer that. "What's he doing?"

"They *just* closed the door, they're probably not...you know. Yet."

"If you don't mind."

The woman nodded. "I'll...Just. I'll be right back. Unless you want to wait inside?"

"No, thank you." Arden didn't like being inside the homes of workers. He hadn't visited many, but they all shared the same shabby cleanliness. Cluttered and crowded, but scrubbed spotless, the same as the workers themselves. Workers prided themselves on how well they could do a load of laundry, how long they could keep a set of clothing wearable, or how sturdily they could mend a pair of shoes.

The woman stepped back inside and gingerly closed the door.

About five minutes later, Oggie came outside with his shirt half-tucked in and buttoned crookedly.

Arden held out the flowers.

Oggie stared at them like he'd never seen flowers before and didn't understand what they meant.

"I'll be really busy soon. I didn't want to leave things however they are right now."

Oggie kept staring at the flowers.

Arden held them out a little further. He almost said, "Rhys told me to bring them," but caught himself in time. "They're for you."

Oggie took them.

"Can we please talk?"

"Are you asking me or is this an order?"

"I'm asking."

"I don't want to talk to you."

Arden pressed his lips together. He nodded. He couldn't leave yet. His feet wouldn't move.

"Fucking say it, whatever you came down here to say if you're not going to leave," Oggie snarled.

"What I said to you was wrong."

Oggie frowned.

"There are so many things you give me that I couldn't find anywhere else. I know I hurt your feelings. I understand why you're upset."

"No, you don't."

"I said I loved you and then I said something that sounded an awful lot like I could replace you with anyone who'd sleep with me and bring me drugs. That would hurt my feelings too. Especially..."

"If drugs and sex were all you brought to a relationship?" Oggie guessed.

"Especially if people treated me like that's all I had to offer," Arden corrected gently. "What I wanted to say was that...was that *literally* any item you'd procure for me I could get without you so you didn't have to worry about me using you for things, like tangible things. But I shouldn't have said it and especially not the way I did."

The paper of the bouquet crinkled as Oggie moved.

"When...If." Arden tried to think of what he wanted to say. "Come home. When you're ready. And no matter how busy I am, I'll make time if you change your mind about talking."

"You didn't talk to me," Oggie reminded. "You wandered around that stupid bay for days and days and you didn't say a single word until now."

"...I was high," Arden offered weakly. "Like. Like I missed the toilet when I went to sit on it high. And you kept walking away from me."

"Lost your tolerance?" Oggie guessed.

Arden nodded.

Oggie glanced over his shoulder toward the apartment. "Funny how old habits come right back."

"Is that what you want?"

"Not really."

"Me neither."

Oggie examined the flowers. He crushed a few petals between his fingers. The scent flooded the air between them.

"Come home," Arden offered again. "Please."

Oggie sighed.

"If you're ready."

Oggie ripped the bloom off a flower and crushed it in his fist. He systematically destroyed the entire bouquet with a calm focus. He stopped when one remained. He extracted it from the remains of the others, his fingers dyed and sticky with the fluids from its brethren. "The guy inside, he, uh. He treats me like shit. Every time. I can't think of a single nice thing to say about him, not one fucking thing, and if you hadn't come down here, he'd probably already have fucked me. I fucking hate him. I mean, I really do, and somehow, within five minutes of seeing him, I'm getting undressed."

Arden didn't know what to say.

"And you're actually really nice to me and I wouldn't talk to you because you misspoke. I knew what you meant. And I knew you wanted to talk to me, and I *watched you* take those shots. Left you on the floor when I wasn't even sure you were breathing."

Half a word slipped past Arden's lips, meaningless and unconnected from his thoughts.

"I don't think anything can fix me. I think I'm going to be like this forever. Fucking people I hate and intentionally hurting people I love."

"I still want you to come home."

"I shouldn't."

"It's your home, too, Oggie."

Oggie looked at the ruined flowers around his feet. "You should probably get me into therapy sooner rather than later."

"In the morning."

Oggie sighed.

"And really, Og, no one can fix you if you don't put the work in."

Oggie started walking.

Arden followed him, not sure of their destination or if he was meant to follow.

On the stairs, Oggie said, "I should actually probably say thank you."

"For?"

"Coming to look for me."

"I thought if I left you alone for too long..."

Oggie glanced back.

"If I didn't tell you now, I don't know when I'd have gotten the chance and then it would have been too long and you'd probably really not have wanted to talk to me. You would have taken it as confirmation that I'd gotten bored of being with you."

Oggie paused and turned around. He leaned against the railing.

Arden came to stand on the step below him. "Which isn't true. I think we'll be together for a hundred years before I'd think of getting bored of you. And not because you're salacious or wild or anything like that. Because you're smart and funny."

Oggie pressed his lips together. He blinked and started walking again.

"And you're a liar. Liars always keep you on your toes."

He spun around.

"Someone checked on me that night on the floor. Winnie can't bend down like that and a Terran probably would have freaked out. A medic would have brought me for treatment. That kind of only leaves you."

"You were high. You probably imagined it," Oggie sniffed. He marched up the stairs and all the way to their rooms without looking back.

Noisily, he prepared a bath.

In Arden's bathroom, not in his.

He brought his clothes from his closet and laid them out on Arden's bed.

"What did you plan on wearing?" Oggie asked.

Arden hadn't thought about it. He shrugged.

"I need to know so I know what to wear."

Arden searched his closet for something that would satisfy workers, peers, and Terrans. Elegant and eye-catching, but not too showy, and now apparently, not too dark or shiny.

He found a pair of gray trousers and paired it with a muted lavender top, and a dark silver-gray jacket with a hint of metallic shimmer. Formal and functional.

He laid it out on the bed.

Oggie put his hands on his hips.

"You don't like it?"

"I like it."

Oggie nodded toward the bathroom and walked away.

Arden followed him. He watched as Oggie slipped out of his clothes. His hair had grown a little shaggy over the past few months, curling around his face.

"Are you going to stare at me or get in the tub?"

"Is both an option?"

"No."

Arden started to peel off his clothes. He tried not to look at himself in the mirror. He'd only seen photos or caught glimpses in the small shuttle mirror.

Oggie came up behind him and draped his arms around Arden's shoulders. He kissed the side of his head.

The sudden sensation of skin against skin made Arden close his eyes. The tenderness of his touch melted him.

"Look at yourself."

Arden opened his eyes.

Oggie turned him toward the mirror, still wrapped around him. "Look," he urged gently. He put a finger under Arden's chin to lift his gaze. "Look at how beautiful you are, sugar."

Arden didn't see it. He couldn't.

No matter what he weighed, thin or fat, he never saw beauty.

He looked okay, sometimes even pretty good, but never beautiful.

Now he looked ungainly. Tan in some places, pallid in others. Thin through his limbs with a new accumulation of fat on his upper thighs, his hips, his stomach. Not enough to really get pinched by his clothes, but they wouldn't hang off him, they wouldn't skim so nicely over him now. His ribs, if he stood up straight, still showed a little. He touched his collar bones. Still there but not pronounced.

He straightened his posture and held his breath. Better.

Oggie kissed the crook of his neck and folded his arms around him, bearing down so he couldn't stand up straight enough. "Why do you do that? Anytime you think someone's looking at you, you suck in like you've got anything to suck in."

"I do."

"So what if you did? You'd still be beautiful."

Arden shook his head. "I can't do this."

"One thing."

"What?"

"Look in the mirror," Oggie said, "And tell yourself you're beautiful."

Arden started to pull away.

Oggie didn't let go. "Listen, I'm not saying you have to say it out loud. Think it."

Arden stared at his reflection.

"Cause you really are."

Arden finally had to step away. "*You're* beautiful."

"No. I'm practically flawless. I'm a marvelously lucky roll of the genetic dice. I am as the sun, blinding in my magnificence."

Arden raised his eyebrows.

Oggie gave him a crooked smile. "But you don't have to look like me to be good-looking. Come on. I've been dying for a soak. I think I have dust from that place embedded in my skin." He skated his fingers from Arden's shoulder to wrist, then pulled him toward the tub.

Once they'd both settled in, Oggie kissed Arden's shoulder and proposed, "Let's pretend those things didn't happen."

"Which ones?"

"You dosing yourself with enough Twelve to make you drool and me ignoring you and almost screwing that guy."

"You can't always pretend—"

"I'm not saying always. I'm saying this time. We had a really good talk, sugar, and I got mad cause I'm scared. I've never done this. And you did those shots cause you're scared too. Let's go back to our talk and start over from there again."

Arden pulled away and turned to face him. "Are you being sensible?"

"I am capable of it."

"So you choose not to be?" Arden asked.

"Now you're getting it. What do you say? Our month starts now."

"Okay."

Oggie kissed his cheek. "Good. Now you're being sensible, too."

"How's your sister?"

"Ripping pissed."

"She did look upset."

"She'll get over it," Oggie said. He stretched and sank up to his shoulders. "She gets mad fast, but it burns out quick. I mean, she gets above her base level of pissed off fast. How's Rhys?"

Arden settled against the opposite side of the tube and sank into the water. "I shouldn't have left like I did."

"He survived."

"It was thoughtless."

Rather coolly, Oggie noted, "That's you all over, sugar."

"You're going to give me whiplash, I swear."

"I can start drinking. That tends to keep my mood more consistent."

Arden opened his mouth to protest.

Oggie winked.

Arden splashed him.

Neither of them bathed in any meaningful way. They lounged, legs touching, the water lapping against their chests. They didn't talk much.

"So you're cozy with Rhys's kid, huh?"

"What?"

"You asked about her first thing."

"Oh."

"It's not a bad thing. I didn't figure you as someone who likes kids."

"She's about the only kid I know. I can safely say I like Darcy. I don't know about the rest of them."

"You were nice to the kids on Terra, too," Oggie reminded.

Arden hadn't considered anything he'd done as particularly nice. "I just asked myself 'what would Winnie do?' if I wasn't sure. He was...He *is* a great uncle."

"He wasn't a bad neighbor, either."

Arden trailed his fingers through the water. "Win was..."

"Go on."

"Win was the first grown-up who believed me."

"About what?"

He lifted his hand. Water dripped from his fingertips. He watched the ripples. He lowered his hand and repeated the process. "Mama loved having a little dress-up doll. Mother planned for a female heir. Winnie...Winnie let me be who I was. He didn't have an agenda for me, so when I said, 'I'm a boy' he could accept it without compromising any of his own hopes or dreams."

A soft, quiet sort of affection reached those green eyes. "You never talk about that."

All the ripples and drops of water in the world couldn't distract him. He looked at Oggie, whose face was patient and reassuringly neutral. "I feel like I'm not supposed to."

Oggie remained thankfully even. No rush of sympathy, no reassurances that Oggie believed he was a man, no discomfort with the admission.

"A lot of people don't like me to talk about it, either. It makes them uncomfortable. Everyone knows. I mean, my transition is a clear part of the public record. But I'm not supposed to talk about it. I'm supposed to pretend the first eight years of my life...well. Ten, if we talk about how long it took people to believe me. Pretend a decade of my life didn't happen, pretend I didn't get treated like a girl."

"I'm listening," was all Oggie said when Arden paused.

"I didn't hate it, being treated like that way. There were parts I liked. But...I *am* a boy. I like being a boy. A boy. I supposed at my age I should be a man, but even Winnie still thinks of me as a child. Being considered a girl didn't make me miserable but living as I am. As a boy. That made me so *happy*. It was...This...this wonderful realization. That I could be more than alright, that I could feel ecstatic about who I was instead of trying to figure out why the pieces didn't quite fit."

"Shug." A gentle smile settled on Oggie's lips.

"Everyone thinks that I did all this to make myself less miserable, but I *wasn't* miserable. I might have been when I got older or if it had taken too long to get where I needed to be. But I did it to be me, not to be...not miserable. People expect me to have been miserable. To have been ashamed. They don't understand why I don't cut my hair short. If I'd always been considered a boy, it wouldn't make a difference how I did my hair. Or they think that my gender is why I use formulas or why...why I want to be thin so badly. They tie all my problems into something that never bothered me to begin with...Does that make sense?"

"The most sense you've ever made."

Arden chuckled. "I guess I think about it a lot."

"I'm glad you told me."

"Not everyone who transitions feels the same way I do but...but it's how *I* feel. That counts for something, doesn't it?"

"You're the Autarch. Doesn't it count the most?" Oggie teased.

"Oh, stop. I don't want to be that kind of Autarch."

Oggie rested his leg against Arden's leg. He applied a little pressure, then let up.

"Thanks for listening," Arden said.

"Anytime, sugar. Honestly."

"You know I'll listen to you, too. If you want."

Oggie smiled, less gentle, more nervous. "Maybe if I can think of something that isn't depressing."

"I'll listen to the things that are hard to say, too."

"I'll scare you away."

Arden shook his head. "Not likely."

His leg pressed against Arden's again. This time he didn't let up. He kept his leg there, lightly holding Arden's in place against the tub. "I hope not."

Arden pushed his leg back, not enough to give resistance, but enough that he hoped it acted as a gesture of comfort.

After a while, Oggie cleared his throat. "So. This big dinner tonight. What should I expect?"

As they finished soaking and started getting dressed, Arden provided an extensive rundown of the night's itinerary complete with his hopes for the event. A simple state function, dinner and drinks. The drinks in moderation, of course. He hadn't seen alcohol on Terra and didn't want to get all the Terrans blind drunk their first night among the general populace of *Eden*. The dinner would serve as a mixer for everyone who called the station home now. He hoped the Terrans would provide lubricant between the workers and peers.

He voiced that exact sentiment to Oggie who grinned and said, "Might not be the only lubricant you'll need tonight if you play your cards right."

Arden snorted and resumed dressing. He tucked in his shirt, then checked in the mirror. He untucked it, then tucked it back in.

"Leave it like that."

"You think?" Arden asked.

"Or better yet take it off."

"You don't like it?"

"I'd like it better on the floor."

"Oggie, if you wanted to fuck, you could have said something earlier! We've got to go soon."

Oggie laughed at him. "I've waited this long. Another night won't kill me."

"How long?"

"I've been expecting it since I came here that first night. I've been wanting it since you beat me at jumble but that was on a purely physical level."

Arden pressed his lips together to stop an unabashed, delighted smile from taking over his face.

Oggie took his hand and started walking.

They did have places to be, after all.

"One more absolute bastard that I'd fuck for whatever abominable reason I end up fucking them for...it's like...even *while* I'm doing it I know it's going to be shitty, but I do it anyway. It's like I'm...I'm so desperately broken that I'm attracted to people who will treat me badly and fuck me even worse," Oggie continued as they moved into the hall.

Other people headed in the same direction, peers all of them and dressed in various states of peacocking.

Arden frowned at them. He had explicitly called the Welcome Dinner a semi-casual event. Absently, he told Oggie, "You shouldn't fuck people you don't want to."

"But I do want to. That's the problem. I *want* to be treated badly."

Arden returned his attention to Oggie. "Do you actually want it or are you accustomed to it? Sometimes we acclimate to things without liking them at all. I ate carrots for six years after Mother passed before I realized I didn't actually like them."

"You don't like carrots?"

"That's not the takeaway I intended."

Oggie's fingers tightened on his. "But it's the only thing I can address without a lot of introspection."

"Oh. Is..."

"Go on, shug."

"Is that the only reason you like me?" Arden asked. He didn't think so but wanted confirmation.

"No, no, I gave up on that. I think I'll have to like you for normal, perhaps even healthy reasons. I might have to fuck you cause you're usually nice to me and try to do the right thing most of the time."

"I think that's better."

Oggie shrugged. He leaned against Arden to confide, "We still have to sort out that thing about how rough you like it."

His throat tightened. He had to remind himself to breathe normally and that they'd be in public soon. No sense in getting excited.

Previous lovers had played at roughness with him for the sake of humoring his preferences. He'd never delved in too deep to those preferences because no one had ever shown an interest in such things. He functioned fine without it but the idea of having someone who wanted to find out with him...His mouth watered.

"My mother would be ashamed if she knew what I'd done with *Eden,* but I think that would piss her off most. Letting a worker..."

"Letting a worker," Oggie prompted, his breath huffing against Arden's ear.

"I don't know, what are you going to do to me?"

Oggie nuzzled the side of his face and kissed his cheek. "I don't know but I can't wait to find out."

"I..."

"Hmm?"

"I wish we'd found each other sooner."

"How much sooner? Like...when you were twenty-six and I was sixteen sooner? Or when I was twelve and you were twenty-two? Nine and nineteen..." Oggie gestured vaguely to indicate the increasingly terrible trend in their age gap.

"Og, fuck, do you have to make everything *awful!* Really!"

"What's the youngest you would have had me?"

"I. That's...Oggie, that's a *reprehensible* question."

With a flutter of eyelashes, Oggie reminded, "I am a little young for a man of your age, Your Eminence."

"If you keep this up, I'm letting go of your hand," Arden warned.

"Ten years isn't bad at our respective ages. Better than I've done with a lot of people anyway...And imagine, when you're fifty and I'm forty, it will be fine, and when you're ninety and I'm eighty, it will be like nothing at all."

Arden accepted the change in tone, recommitted to his decision to find Oggie a therapist as soon as possible, and made a few quiet decisions about his future. Things could change, of course. Things he'd planned had gone wildly astray before. A year ago he never would have imagined his life being anything like it was now.

Oggie smoothed a hand over Arden's sleeve. "Would it be terrible if I got blind drunk tonight?

"I don't think the Terrans have ever drank before. I'd appreciate it if you could be a good role model."

"For once."

"Please."

The most dramatic, wistful sigh escaped him. "I could try. Five?"

"Three."

"Four, then," Oggie decided, his nose in the air. He peeked at Arden. "Right?"

"Of course."

They entered the Big Room together. Arden thought about changing the name. He'd have to at this point.

The Terrans stood together in a tight cluster off to one side of the Big Room. In the center, he saw the children trying to peek around their mothers. The members of the Transition Committee stood with them. They looked more like guards or captors than liaisons.

Arden approached.

A dozen voices greeted him with questions.

He held up a hand, which did nothing to quiet them.

Oggie sniggered.

"Please, really, I can't answer if you're all talking at once."

They kept talking.

Finally, he crossed his arms and gave a sour look.

They quieted down after that.

"How do you like it so far?"

"Everyone is staring at us," one said.

"Of course, they are. We've spent our whole lives never meeting anyone new."

Holly pushed her way through. "How can you never meet anyone new? There's *hundreds of you*."

"Thousands, actually," Arden corrected.

"And he just means the peers, there are less of them and they're very much in each other's business," Oggie added.

"Go mingle," Arden suggested.

"I don't want to," Holly said.

Arden offered her his arm.

She squinted at him.

Oggie took hold of Arden's other arm. "Like this."

Holly placed her hand on Arden's arm.

"Come meet my friend Cathie. You'll really like her," Arden said.

"You said that a dozen times already."

"Well, I happen to think you'll like her!" Arden escorted Oggie and Holly through the room, his eyes peeled for his friends.

Cathie found him first. She wrapped him up and lifted him off his feet. "Ardi! Oh, I was so worried about you."

"Oh, Cath, I'm fine. I'm always fine."

"Like a roach," Holly provided.

Cathie set Arden down but kept her arms around him.

"Cath, this is Holly, she's, uh," he began.

"From Terra One!" Cathie supplied. She let go of Arden and turned to take in Holly.

"Holly was a great help to me on Terra."

Holly elbowed him in the side. "Ah, I showed him around a little, that's all. Taught him how to find onion shoots, too."

Cathie made a face. She looked over Arden. "Sounds just like you..."

Arden blushed.

"Picking onions. What else?" Cathie asked.

Arden shrugged. "Whatever needed to get done, I guess."

"You wouldn't help pluck those birds we caught," Holly reminded.

"Oh, I couldn't! I almost threw up just watching. Oh, their poor little feathers..."

Holly rolled her eyes.

Arden scanned the crowd for the others he wanted Holly to meet. He spotted Rhys and almost immediately forgot about introducing Holly to anyone. He left behind the other three and approached Rhys. "The baby!"

Darcy kicked her legs and grinned at Arden. She leaned out of Rhys's grip.

Rhys tightened his arms. "Darcy, you're gonna fall."

"She just wants to see me!" He hadn't anticipated how happy her chubby little face would make him.

Rhys handed over the baby.

Arden immediately hoisted her up into the air. "Hi, booger."

"Don't call her that."

"Little booger baby," Arden continued. He feigned dropping her.

Darcy giggled.

Arden settled her on his hip. "I'm gonna keep this for now," he told

Rhys.

Rhys glanced around the Big Room.

"What?"

"Gertie doesn't like you."

"Still?"

Rhys shrugged. "She thinks you're a bad influence."

"It was one swear."

"No, it's more the extensive formula use, capitalist ideologies, and authoritarian power structure."

Arden shifted the baby, then glanced around to see if Gertie lurked somewhere nearby. "Who would teach that to a baby?"

Rhys began to answer.

"Especially one as cute as this!"

Rhys sighed.

"I know, I know, I'm a piece of shit, I *know*, but you know...I'm not that bad, am I?"

"People don't know you as well as I do."

Arden grinned. "A few people might."

"Don't flirt with me in front of the baby," Rhys admonished.

"Or in front of your date, how about that?" Oggie asked from behind Arden.

Arden turned and grinned at him, too. "Oggie, this is Darcy."

Oggie gave the baby a thin smile.

"Dar, say hi, Oggie."

Darcy waved. "Hi, Goggie."

Arden's grin widened.

"Nice to meet you," Oggie told the baby.

Arden kept the baby with him as he made the rounds, which forced Rhys to stay nearby.

He returned Darcy when he had to give his speech. He didn't want to let her go. He hadn't realized how much he'd missed her until he'd seen her.

"Hello, everyone. It's good to see you all again. I hope you're as pleased to have me back as I am to be back. I am still alive despite anything you might have heard."

A nervous chuckle rippled through the crowd.

"First of all, I have to thank the Council members and my First Chamberlain for doing their best work while I was gone. I have to thank all of you for bearing with us in this transition. I have to thank our new friends from Terra One for trusting that we could build a home together here."

He looked out over the crowd. Every soul on *Eden*, save for the ones who had stayed home in protest. He could see the clusters of people. The peers clumped near the front of the room, shining; the workers crowded in the back, a sea of neutral colors. Light and flowy, Terrans studded both crowds.

He'd never seen the room at capacity before.

"I hope that I have given you sufficient reason to believe in me and my vision for the future. For years, we tried to make *Eden* thrive under a system where most of her population could barely live. It's time to heal that rift and heal our home. A while ago, I asked my peers to be kind and...And now I stand in front of *all* my peers and ask for that same thing. Please, be kind. Trust us. Welcome our new friends."

He took a breath.

Someone clapped.

One person, then a few more, then dozens.

He couldn't keep from smiling.

It lasted for half a minute, maybe less.

A glass hurtled on to the stage.

He threw up his hands in time to block his face. It clipped off his arm, then shattered on the floor.

"Fuck you!" roared a familiar voice.

He saw Bull shoving through the first few rows of the crowd.

Fuck.

Arden glanced around for safety officers.

Movement fluttered through the crowd.

"You're *ruining* everything." Bull had made his way through everyone and climbed onto the stage. "Destroying our home."

Arden shrunk back.

Fuck.

To the crowd, Bull demanded, "Don't let this fucker trick you. He's handing *Eden* over to the thralls."

"No, I—"

Bull grabbed Arden by the front of his shirt and dragged him forward. "If you let him get away with this, we'll be starving in a year."

Arden started pulling back Bull's thumb, trying to free his shirt. Once he got his shirt free, Bull grabbed his hair.

"Look around you, look at those fucking thralls, look at how they're *watching you.*"

Arden fought to get Bull's hand out of his hair but couldn't do anything to untangle his fingers.

Bull yanked him forward.

Arden moved himself to where Bull wanted him to avoid hurting his neck.

"This is our fucking chance to show them *we are not going quietly.*"

"Don't!" Arden shouted.

A handful of safety officers climbed onto the stage.

The crowd shoved and surged. People shouted.

"Don't listen to him. This is not the time for—" Arden grunted when Bull punched him in the back. He hit the floor. Thankfully, Bull had let go of his hair.

Arden could see other fights in the crowd, more verbal than physical.

He couldn't see Oggie or Rhys.

They had been right in the front row.

He tried to stand.

Bull put a foot on his back and shoved him back down.

Not too long later, six safety officers tackled Bull in the middle of his speech about the right to rule and natural class divisions.

Arden pushed himself up, dusted off his knees. He stared out over the crowd, not sure what to say, or do. How could he recoup from this?

He made himself smile. "Sorry about that! For those of you who don't know Bull...Well. Now you do. He's not exactly the best *Eden* has to offer, is he?"

The crowd quieted. At least he had done that.

"If we're honest, I think he's still mad at me for doing that to his eye. I don't know what the fuss is, I hear the eyes they make up in the lab are just as good as the real thing. They did a pretty good job with a few things for me."

A few people tittered.

Arden straightened his clothes and brushed himself off. "Anyway, dinner will be out soon. Make sure you visit the bar and get a drink before we sit."

He stepped off the stage trying not to let it show how much his legs shook. He felt like he'd done a thousand squats.

Cole grabbed his hand.

He yelped.

"Sorry, sorry, Ardi, I...Are you okay?" Cole slid his arms around Arden.

Arden nodded. "Probably a few bruises but you know how easy I mark up. Fucking Bull! Leave it to him to ruin this." He glanced around. "Where are Rhys and Oggie?"

"Oh, they...Some of Bull's friends were in the crowd trying to rile people up and Mason...Well. With Bull on the stage and everything. He needed air. They went with him. And I think Rhys was nervous for the baby." Cole pulled back and straightened Arden's shirt for him.

"Right, of course. Is...is Mace okay?"

"He just needed air. He...Well. You know. You're really okay?"

"Yes, yes, now get the Council members and help me get people settled. Fucking Bull. Do I look okay?"

"You actually look great. Like. You look healthy."

Arden laughed. "People keep saying that and I'm starting to suspect that healthy is a polite way of saying fat."

Cole abruptly pulled him into another, fiercer hug. "Ardi, you look *amazing*."

Arden wanted to cry. He sniffed. "Go get people settled."

The Council members dispersed through the peers.

Arden went to talk to the Terrans and assure him Bull was just an idiot with a personal agenda, not a serious political threat.

He approached the workers.

He found Mara's pale cloud of hair.

She shook her head when she saw him.

"Don't punch me. I saw what you did to Rhys."

"I thought you'd had Oggie killed."

"He said he told you."

"Oh, yeah, that sounds very credible. Heading to Terra for a vacation?"

He understood the misgivings. "So now that you know he's alive, are we good?"

"No."

Arden sighed. He glanced around the workers. "How are they doing?"

"I don't fucking know."

"Well, can you help me find out? We're supposed to be mingling."

She rolled her eyes. "Then go mingle." She walked away from him.

He stared at the throng of people, wished he had some Twelve in him, and took a breath before he immersed himself in the crowd. He had spent his whole life pretending to want to talk to people.

He engaged in pleasantries with as many people as he could. He reassured everyone who looked to him for reassurance. He fielded suspicions with the answer, "Don't worry, Rhys would never let me get away with that." A few people thanked him for clearing their debts, which he hadn't expected.

One woman about Winslow's age hugged him, her gnarled fingers grasping on to his jacket.

At first, he felt quite concerned. He'd been manhandled not too recently, but he didn't think this old lady could do as much damage as Bull.

He hugged her back.

"It was the only thing to be done," Arden told all the people who thanked him.

A voice on the speakers announced that dinner would begin soon, so Arden had a reason to leave the workers and go back to his friends.

At his table, he'd arranged for a select handful of people to sit with him. He tried to get an even spread of people. All the Council members had arranged similar tables.

Someone had to set a good example.

Cathie and Holly arrived at the table together. Cathie looked upset and Arden couldn't think of a reason for her not to be after Bull's display.

Holly seemed overall amused by all of it. "You took that like a champ."

"I was too startled to cry."

Oggie, Mace, and Rhys found their way to the table, too. Mace looked twice as upset as Cathie and Arden quietly asked if he'd rather be at home.

"No, it's better to be distracted. I...I've got to go find Lourdes. I'll see you tomorrow?"

"I'll make time," Arden promised.

Nothing else of interest happened for the rest of the dinner. A few Terrans drank too much, despite everyone's warnings, and a worker and a Terran got caught screwing in a backroom when a waiter went to get more plates.

Arden honestly felt surprised that hadn't happened sooner.

He stayed until everyone else had left.

Rhys took Darcy home but not before Arden gave her a squeeze and a kiss.

Rhys gave him a funny sort of look, not upset or disturbed, but a warm kind of puzzlement.

Oggie drank more than he'd said he would, but not too much. He fell asleep, his arms folded on the table.

Arden rubbed his back once the last civilian had cleared out. "Wake up, hon."

"Mmm."

"Come on, it's time to go home."

Oggie stretched and yawned and made a general production of getting to his feet. He rubbed his eyes and stumbled the whole time they walked home.

In their apartment, he started to head to his room.

Arden didn't let go of his hand. He nodded toward the master bedroom. "What do you think?"

Oggie nodded. He threw his clothes on the floor and burrowed into the blankets.

Arden settled in beside him. He kissed his shoulder, the skin warm and smooth. He still smelled faintly of soap.

Arden didn't use Twelve except in the cases of real emotional emergencies, but months passed in a blur like he had steeped himself in the stuff. He couldn't remember when he'd done what or who he'd done it with. Moment-to-moment, of course, he remained lucid. He hadn't lost his mind, he was just busy beyond belief.

It turned out bringing dozens of illiterate, uneducated workers with skills specific to Terra to *Eden* required more managing and training than he'd anticipated.

Setting up people to manage the Public Health Fund and Public Health Office also proved to be a larger undertaking than he'd anticipated. Not because no one could run it, or because there wasn't enough money, he made sure the money was there, but because at least twelve workers came in a week seeking treatment for addiction alone.

More needed mental health services and at least half the active workers had chronic but mild injuries.

On top of that, there was managing public perceptions and the peers who had a hard time understanding why the workers deserved decent treatment.

Oggie looked over Arden's shoulder as he looked through another report.

Arden had promised him an uninterrupted breakfast, but he hadn't delivered.

"Looks like it's a good time to be a physical therapist..." Oggie noted.

"You thinking of going back?"

"No."

Oggie hadn't worked since he'd come back to *Eden*. That wasn't to say he'd done nothing. He read a lot. He spent time with Holly and his sister. He went to have lunch with Winslow when Arden really couldn't find the time to check on him and came home with candy wrappers in his pockets.

He'd started seeing a therapist, too. Once a week, unless he felt like he didn't want to go, which happened sometimes. Usually, he came back from sessions and told Arden he didn't see the point. More than once, he'd said, "I don't need some overeducated peer to tell me my habits are unhealthy."

Oggie took the tablet from Arden and seated himself on the other side of the table. "I went to see a movie with the girls last night."

"I'm sorry I got home so late."

"It was horrifically bad. Like...Just terrible. Do you read the scripts Frakes sends you or what?"

"I haven't had time."

Oggie put the tablet face down on the table. "I've been thinking."

"I'm sorry I got home—"

"Sugar, I'm not mad."

"You should be."

Oggie took his hand. "Is it too late to take that job you offered?"

Arden frowned.

"The Entertainment Minister?"

"Oh. Oh! No, no, of course not, not at all."

"Good."

They stared at each other.

"I accept, then," Oggie told him.

Arden didn't know what to do. He looked at his breakfast, his tablet, and Oggie. "Uh. Good. Great. That's...Oh, that's such a relief. I can't tell you how many people I've interviewed for that position. Half of them don't know the difference between metaphor and cliché."

"I do have terms to accepting of course."

"We'll get a contract."

"No, terms for us. I'll be busy too so you won't be able to just fit me into your schedule whenever you can."

Arden's stomach turned. He and Oggie hadn't done much more than sleep in the same bed since they'd gotten back. There hadn't been time for anything. Sometimes they got to eat together or have a whole conversation. Most of the time, though, Arden came home and went to bed, too burnt out to do more than cuddle.

Sometimes Oggie tagged along but there was too much to do to pay him any attention.

Oggie squeezed his fingers. "I want you to start taking time off. Sleep in once in a while. Or come home early."

"I—"

"You can. I want dinner together, at least once a week. I want one day a month that's just for us."

"Oggie, things are so busy—"

"Things have been busy for *months*, shug. You need to start delegating or you're going to fall apart. *We're* going to fall apart. I miss you."

Arden pressed his lips together. He'd lived in such a blur of activity that he'd barely had time to eat or sleep, let alone miss anyone for more than five minutes.

"That time on Terra spoiled me. Is it so bad that I want a little bit of that back?"

"No."

"You have a solid Council and a very capable Chamberlain. You can ask people to do more."

Arden shook his head. "They have families..." He trailed off and looked up at Oggie, realizing what he'd said.

Oggie didn't take his hand back or look hurt. "I know I'm not as important—"

"You are."

"Then stay home once in a while. Make time for me."

Arden nodded.

Oggie came over and seated himself on Arden's lap. He cradled Arden's head against his chest. "I'm really starting to worry that you don't want to see me."

"I do. It's just..."

Oggie had to urge, "Go on, shug."

"My family did this to *Eden*. I've got to fix it."

"They didn't do it alone. You can't fix it alone, either."

Arden tightened his arms around Oggie's waist. He sighed.

They stayed like that for a while. It was the longest Arden had spent conscious with him in weeks.

"Give me two weeks," Arden said. "Two weeks to figure out how to make this work. Hire some people, get them up to date."

"Only if you stay at home with me tomorrow."

"I—"

"No one will blame you. *Eden* is not falling apart, she's just a little messy right now. One day doesn't hurt anything. Take it from someone who's also a little messy right now."

Oggie spoke with such soft insistence that Arden agreed.

He came home late again that night and found Oggie already sleeping. He thought about those nights he'd waited up for him, how uncertain and lonely he'd been. And that had been before they'd been more than friends. He crawled into bed beside him and Oggie immediately rolled over and nuzzled up to him.

They stayed in bed most of the morning. Arden woke hours later than usual to find Oggie reading next to him.

"Good book?"

"Mhm. New one out by Jensen Jackson. Decent so far. A little predictable but her stuff always is, don't you think?"

"I never got into her work much."

"I'll just finish this chapter..."

Arden scooted closer and rested his head on Oggie's thighs, curled up against his legs. He hadn't gotten this much rest in months. He burrowed further into Oggie's thighs. "Hi."

Oggie set down his reading. "Hi."

Arden slid one of his arms under Oggie's leg. "Hi."

"Are we going to do this all morning?"

"I feel like I owe you a lot of 'hellos.'" Arden hugged Oggie's thigh. "Did you have a plan for this day off?"

"Many months ago, on a hot, dusty planet, beneath a crooked tree, you promised me a lemon slush."

Arden had never made good on that promise. He'd meant to, but so many things had slipped his mind. "You can get whatever dessert you want. It doesn't have to be a lemon slush."

"Aw, thanks, shug," Oggie said. "I can get whatever I want?"

"Don't make fun of me."

Oggie lightly walked his fingers along Arden's side.

Arden squealed and wiggled away when he started tickling him. "No, no, no, Oggie, don't. Oh...Stop!" He twisted and grabbed Oggie's wrist to hold him still.

Oggie crawled on top of him. He stilled Arden's movement with his thighs. He didn't give up tickling, though.

"Oggie, stop!"

Oggie's stopped. He wet his lips.

"You're gonna make me pee," Arden panted.

Oggie waggled his eyebrows.

"Ew."

"Hey, some people like it," Oggie reminded. "I mean...it's not my preference but I'm pretty adaptable."

"Not mine either."

"That's another thing we were supposed to do..." Oggie brushed his fingertips over Arden's throat.

"We'll probably have time to get a lemon slush and have sex. Maybe even a few things in between."

"I'd also like to go for a walk together. Very public. I want you to absolutely *spoil* me in public. People have been spreading the most awful rumors."

"Such as?"

"That you only liked me when I was the only man around."

"Oh."

"Which is stupid, because then they go and follow it up saying they think you're sleeping with Xio Benevides."

"I'm not."

"I don't care if you are, I just don't want anyone thinking you like her better than me."

"I like you better than a lot of people, Xio included."

Oggie settled back, seated on Arden's legs. "You like Darcy better than me."

"Darcy is a baby, that's different."

"But if we were both dying and you could only sa—"

Arden shook his head. "That's a ridiculous question."

"But if you *had to*."

"I never have to. I'm Autarch. I can have whatever I want. And you're a grown man, so stop being jealous of a literal child."

"Maybe I'm just jealous you see her more than me."

"Well, if you can convince Rhys to carry you around in a little backpack, that might solve the problem."

Oggie narrowed his eyes.

Arden took his hands. "Come here."

Oggie didn't.

Arden tugged on the front of his pajamas. "Come here, Oggie."

Oggie settled against him. He placed his cheek against Arden's chest.

"I'm glad you told me what was wrong. I'll do better. We can do whatever you want today."

Hands knotted in Arden's shirt. His chest muffled the ugly whimper that pushed out from Oggie's mouth.

"Hey."

Oggie sat up and pulled away. He sat at the edge of the bed, facing away from Arden. "No, sorry." He wiped his eyes.

Arden pushed himself up. "No, it's…"

"I'm fine," Oggie insisted. He wiped his eyes again, then his nose.

"What's the matter?"

Oggie shook his head.

Arden scooted closer.

"It's nothing, it's really stupid. Just never mind." Oggie sniffled once more then forced a smile. "Let's get ready, hmm? I want you to show me off like I'm the prettiest boy in *Eden*."

Arden slid over to him. He put a leg on either side of Oggie and wrapped his arms around his shoulders. He nuzzled against his throat. "What if I showed you off like you're the most beautiful boy on *Eden* and I'm madly in love with you?"

Oggie didn't smile or laugh. He pulled one of Arden's arms across his chest and hugged it tightly. He swallowed.

"You can tell me what's wrong."

"Just promise you like me, shug."

"I promise."

"Really promise."

Arden squeezed him with his arms and legs. He kissed his cheek. "I really promise."

"I love you."

"I love you, too."

Oggie sniffed. "I didn't...You know. I."

"Go ahead."

"When I was little and waiting for someone to come home, you know, I thought. I thought I'd grow up and someone would love me enough to come home. And I grew up and I realized that's not how it works. It's not. I *know* that. I'm not a little kid anymore."

Arden hadn't considered that. Burying himself in work to sate his guilt and he hadn't bothered to think about Oggie, one of the truest examples of what the peers had done to the people of *Eden*.

"I try so hard to wait up for you and I try to make sure I get up to say goodbye in the morning, but I can't." Oggie's voice thickened. "I'm just waiting again."

"It won't be like that anymore."

Oggie leaned against him.

Arden squeezed him.

They stayed like that for a while. Until Arden's throat loosened and Oggie stopped sniffling.

When Oggie finally pulled away to use the bathroom, Arden fetched his tablet and hurried to set a series of alarms and reminders for himself. No more leaving without saying goodbye, no more falling asleep after five minutes of conversation.

Oggie deserved better.

They did everything Oggie wanted that day. Arden didn't even have to make a show of doting on him publicly, he did it naturally. He couldn't take his eyes off the other man, he didn't want to talk to anyone else, and he'd have given him the entire space station if he'd mentioned wanting it.

Oggie had circles under his eyes that Arden hadn't noticed before.

They walked the Solar Deck and Goshawk Alley together. They didn't actually buy anything at any of the stores.

In fact, Arden didn't buy anything other than a pair of lemon slushes.

Oggie seemed content to have nothing but Arden's attention. He made a particular show of having Arden wrapped around his finger to certain people, including Xio Benevides.

Arden assumed he had a list of people who thought Arden no longer enchanted with Oggie's company. Arden played along. He wondered if he hadn't given enough consideration to people's casual comments about him finding someone to settle down with eventually. He hadn't paid attention to anything anyone had said unless it had to do with work.

Over dinner with a group that Oggie had picked out, Arden tuned into a hushed conversation at another table.

More peers complaining.

He tried not to look at them.

He couldn't make everyone happy and he wasn't foolish enough to try. At least three people a week petitioned him to have Bull released from lockup. Arden had charged him with assault, as well as inciting violence.

Workers went everywhere in pairs these days.

So did peers.

The Terrans traveled in clusters, but that had more to do with their culture than class tension.

A few people had gotten into fights, although according to Rhys and his other sources among the workers, almost all the incidents represented escalations of long-standing personal tensions between certain peers and workers.

Three peer-worker couples had stepped out together officially. These, too, were long-standing affairs.

It had shocked Winslow to find out one of his oldest friends had carried on an affair with a worker for over forty years. The class differences hadn't worried him, but it had hurt his feelings to know his friend hadn't told him sooner.

Arden grabbed Oggie's hand, seized with a new concern.

"Oh!" Oggie startled. "Shug, what?"

"Can we make a stop on the way home?"

"Sure. Course. Where?"

"I should check on Winnie."

Oggie nodded. He returned to the person he'd been talking to. "Uh. What was I saying?"

Riley Hmong said, "You said you'd gotten a new job?"

"Oh! Right. Yes," Oggie said. "They'd been interviewing people left and right but couldn't find anyone they liked. Arden practically begged me to take the position."

Arden knew better than to contradict him. He took his hand, kissed his knuckles, and added, "You know how I get when I want something."

"Oh, who knows what would happen if you ever heard the word no?"

"I'd probably die of shock."

Oggie grinned and it looked genuine enough, making the corner of his eyes crinkle like most of his smiles didn't. He gave Arden a kiss and that felt genuine as well. Gentle and not as showy as the kisses he usually doled out in public.

Hands linked, they walked to Winslow's after dinner.

Halfway there, Oggie started to grow less genuine and act like more of the vapid trophy he played in front of other people.

Arden had thought that the façade would drop but he hadn't taken Oggie out enough for that to happen.

When they stepped off the lift to Winslow's hall, Oggie stopped. "What if I met you at home, shug?"

Arden, a few steps ahead, looked back. "What do you mean?"

"I." Oggie glanced down the hall. He stared directly at the door of apartment 207. "I haven't been here in years."

When he checked on Winslow for Arden, they always met somewhere public.

Arden came to stand beside him. "You don't have to come."

"It isn't anything about your uncle."

"No, of course not."

"Last time I was here I ran from here all the way to deck eight. This girl had paid me to...well...anyway, she brought me up here, to uh. To do it. And I just...once I saw that door. That fucking door..." Oggie sighed. "Booked it. Had to give that girl back her money, too."

"If you need to go, that's fine."

"I'm sorry."

"Don't be. I'll see you soon."

Oggie pressed the lift button. Then he grabbed Arden's sleeve. "Maybe. Maybe go get him. Bring him back for a nightcap or something. I do like him!"

"Alright."

Oggie nodded. He stepped onto the lift.

As the doors closed, Arden saw him pull his jacket close around himself. He hurried to Winslow's apartment and let himself inside. "Win!"

A small yelp indicated Winslow's location within the apartment.

Arden went to find him. "Win, hi, get your shoes."

"What?"

"Get your shoes."

"I haven't seen you in months."

"I know, that's why I'm here now."

Winslow shook his head. "Has it ever occurred to you that I might have other plans?"

"Have you got other plans?"

"Of course, I haven't got plans, it's nearly bedtime."

Arden looked him over. "No pajamas yet. Come on. Come back for a drink."

"A drink."

"A nightcap. Please. We were going to come say hi, but Oggie...Please, Winnie."

Winslow sighed. He sat on the bed. "Get me the brown ones."

Arden went to his closet. He saw two pairs of brown shoes, then another three at the back. "Which brown ones?"

"Oh, any brown ones, I suppose."

Arden grabbed the first pair.

"Oh, no, not those."

"Winnie."

"They're not brown, they're butterscotch. Brown, Arden."

Arden went in and got the pair of shoes that could only be called brown and never by any other color. He unlaced them and placed them in front of his uncle. He sat cross-legged on the bed and waited.

"You're still living with that boy?"

"You know I am. You saw him last week for lunch," Arden reminded tartly. He had to add, "He's not a *boy*. He's twenty-six."

"Practically a child," Winslow scolded.

"He's older than I was when I became Autarch."

Winslow huffed but that had more to do with bending over to put on his shoes.

Arden sighed. He looked at his hands. "Win, do you really think I'm doing something bad with him?"

"I think..." Winslow placed his hands on his knees and pushed himself up. He puffed.

Arden climbed off the bed and knelt in front of his uncle. He tied the laces for him.

"Oh, you don't..." Winslow sighed. "Thank you."

Arden stood. He offered his hand to Winslow to help him stand. "You didn't answer. You think I shouldn't be with Oggie."

"I'm concerned. You're not...Arden. You. You have your struggles. And he has his. I don't see how it would work out."

"Well. It will be work. I think that's usually how things work out."

Winslow shook his head at him.

"I know you think I'm such a spoiled little boy..."

"It's not just that. What would your mothers think of this?"

Arden kept his hold on his uncle's hand as they walked to the lift. He took his time to think, too. "Mama...I think Mama would like Oggie. Don't you? I think she'd finally have someone she could dress up. I think she would have *loved* to buy him the glitteriest, frilliest things and I think he would have loved to try them on for her."

Winslow made a wet, sniffling noise.

"I think they'd have gone to the movies together and he would have made her these fruity, fancy drinks and they would have just *ripped* those movies apart. I think she would have loved him. I think she would have been really happy for me."

Winslow's bent, knobby fingers tightened on Arden's. "Maybe you're right."

Arden surreptitiously dabbed his eyes with his sleeve. "I hope so. But I didn't come here to talk about me! What have you been up to? I haven't seen you in ages."

That provoked a rambling recap of the last few months, complete with all the best society gossip, toned down to be a little politer than how Winslow had heard it, of course.

Oggie greeted them with steaming mugs. "I made hot toddies. I think they're so nice to finish off a night. Nobody ever wants one, so I don't get to make them that often. They should be alright, though."

"I'm sure they're perfect."

Winslow took a seat on the couch.

Arden and Oggie sat on the loveseat but kept themselves apart from each other.

They all sat with drinks clasped in their hands, now and then checking if they had cooled enough to sip.

"Uncle Winnie was telling me that he didn't like that last movie either. What was it?"

"*Together in Time*," Winslow said.

"Oh, I haven't seen that one yet. Was it atrocious?" Oggie asked.

"Absolute drivel," Winslow confirmed. "No plot at all to speak of." He sipped his drink and his eyes lit up. "Oh, that's good!"

Oggie gave a tight, nervous smile. His cheeks darkened.

"Oggie makes the best drinks on *Eden*," Arden bragged.

"Chas Markson is better," Oggie said. "And Delia St. Clair."

"Never heard of them," Arden said.

"They work the popup circuit, so you..." Oggie trailed off. He sipped his drink and didn't look at Arden.

"One of these days you're going to have to actually tell me what that means."

"Doesn't matter, I haven't been in ages. You haven't tried that yet." Oggie pointed to his drink.

Arden looked at his glass, which he'd already half-emptied.

"You'll have to tell me if it's any good."

"Try it yourself."

"You know I don't drink," Oggie reminded with a sulk.

Arden made a show of taking a sip. "It's delicious."

"Feels genuine when you do it like that."

Winslow glanced between them.

Oggie tittered awkwardly, set down his drink, and paced over to the bar. He touched a lot of things and made noise doing it, but as far as Arden could see, he didn't actually do anything. He went from the bar to the bathroom.

"Is he alright?" Winslow asked.

"Not usually," Arden answered. "Cole's writing a new book of poems."

The change of topics effectively distracted Winslow until Oggie returned.

When he came back, he'd washed his face and changed into a pajama set. He maintained a polite quiet for the rest of Winslow's visit. He also refilled his drink twice.

Arden knew better than to say anything in front of Winslow. When he came home from walking Winslow to his apartment, he found Oggie curled up in bed, nested in the covers.

Too still and quiet to be asleep.

The room had a faint sour smell.

Arden scooted next to him. "You feeling okay?"

"I threw up."

"You call for someone to clean up already?"

"No."

Arden got out of bed, stripped off his clothes, and mopped up the small puddle of vomit next to the bed with a towel. He tossed it in the hamper, then brought Oggie a glass of water and made him rinse his mouth when he refused to get up and brush his teeth. Finally, he scooted under the covers next to him.

He couldn't think of anything to say that didn't feel patronizing or to ask that wasn't invasive.

He put an arm around Oggie's waist, separated by what felt like six inches of blankets and sheets.

He woke two hours later than he usually did the next morning. He'd already informed Rhys of his intentions. The response he'd received from his Chamberlain seemed relieved rather than disappointed, which he hadn't expected.

Maybe he'd been working everyone too hard, not just himself.

He gently poked and prodded at Oggie until he woke up.

Oggie scowled up at him. "What time is it?"

"Time for breakfast."

Oggie groaned.

"I've got to be showered and fed in the next hour, so if you plan on seeing me before dinner, you'd better get up."

Oggie rolled deeper into the blankets.

Ten minutes into Arden's shower, he pulled back the shower curtain.

On instinct, Arden moved to cover himself. "Oh." He relaxed and resumed washing. "What?"

"You're supposed to be at work right now."

"I did some rearranging."

"You said it would take two weeks."

Arden shrugged. "Brush your teeth before you come in, I couldn't get you to do it last night."

"I remember."

Arden drew the curtain.

Oggie joined him after a few minutes. He stood, arms crossed, at the end of the shower.

Arden flicked a bit of water at him. "Stop pouting."

"I'm not pouting. I'm angry."

"Because...?"

"I don't know."

Arden offered him the bar of soap.

He took it and made a show of huffing and sighing while he washed.

"So, I don't think you have plans, I made an appointment for us to go meet with Frakes tomorrow afternoon. He knows I've been trying to replace him anyway, so this won't surprise him. I'm going to try to sell him on a, uh...six-month transition period for you to take over. I'll agree to keep him on for a year after that, too, as a sort of...consultant to the Media Department."

Oggie switched with Arden to stand beneath the water and rinse.

"Assuming you meant it about taking that position?"

"I did."

"Perfect. I'm going to get new staff hired and trained, but that will...well, if I'm going in later like this, and if I want to train quality people, I'll have to take longer than two weeks. I hope you don't mind."

"I guess not."

"But I'll still be home for dinner."

Oggie glowered at him as he washed his hair.

"What?"

"I'm still mad."

"Really mad?"

"I don't know!" Oggie snapped. He immediately looked reticent. Hair still sudsy, he put his arms around Arden and dragged him close. "I don't."

Arden's hair immediately got soaked. He held in the complaint. "Are we okay, Oggie?"

Begrudgingly, Oggie answered, "Yes."

"*Eden* is okay, too. I needed someone to point that out."

Oggie stayed quiet.

"I need you."

Oggie snorted. He let go of Arden and went back to washing his hair.

"I need you and I'm sorry I didn't do better. I will do better."

"Great. Can't wait to see how it goes."

Arden touched Oggie's arm. "I love you."

The irritation and haughtiness on Oggie's face softened. "I love you, too, shug."

"I'm gonna go order breakfast."

"Toast," Oggie requested.

Arden stepped out of the shower. He had to find an extra towel for his hair. "You know, you play your cards right and uh..." What he'd wanted to say felt silly and presumptuous.

"And what? You'll finally fuck me?" Oggie guessed.

"Well, that."

"I'll feel so privileged to have your cock in my ass, Your Eminence."

"Absolutely not," Arden said. "You're going to fuck me into the mattress if we're going to do anything."

Oggie chuckled.

"You want anything other than toast?"

"Oh, just a big heaping helping of that ass."

Arden grinned. "You know, with a mouth like that you're never going to find a gentleman to marry you."

Oggie poked his head out of the shower. "I thought my mouth was *exactly* why you were going to marry me." He said in such an exactly right way, holding Arden's gaze, that even disheveled from the water and blotchy from the heat of the shower, something in Arden quickened.

Arden tossed aside his towel and climbed back into the shower. He slid his arms around Oggie and kissed him. He'd have to skip breakfast, or eat on the go, or just plain be late, but he couldn't go now.

Oggie twined around him.

They fumbled with each other, soap-slicked hands slid between each other's legs, their mouths practically sealed together.

Oggie shoved him back against the wall, his fingers comfortably firm around Arden's throat.

He fumbled his hand out of the shower and found the lube Arden kept in the counter drawers. "Turn around."

Arden almost protested. He wanted to see Oggie, to keep kissing him.

Oggie bit his shoulder and slid slicked fingers inside of him. "Turn around."

Arden whimpered. There was an art to his brutality.

"Go ahead, shug, I'll make you scream," he promised. He took his hands back and kissed Arden's throat. "Okay?"

"Okay," Arden managed. He turned without protest.

Oggie kissed the back of his neck. He wrapped an arm around Arden's throat, wedging him between the shower wall and Oggie's body. "Is this what you wanted?" he asked, finding an odd blend of menace and warmth.

"Yes."

Oggie pushed inside of him, the movement deliberate and forceful.

Arden squeaked, mostly in surprise. He hadn't meant to, and he hated that he'd done it.

"Too much?" Oggie asked.

"Been a while," Arden answered, his cheeks warm.

Oggie kissed the back of his head. He moved more subtly this time.

Arden pressed back against him.

"Harder," he asked after a few of those more careful movements. He kept asking until they were nothing but thrusts and grunts, one seamless thing jerking its way towards a quick and desperate climax.

And a blissful one, one that drained Arden of doubt for the moment. He breathed slowly after Oggie released him, his forehead against the wall.

How had he not made time for this?

Oggie sighed against his throat.

Arden twisted so he could see him again.

Oggie skimmed his thumb over Arden's lips. He tilted up Arden's chin and pushed aside Arden's hair to reveal the places where he'd bitten him, checking for marks. "Everything okay, sugar?"

"Perfect."

Oggie bit his lip. "I could have gone a little...a little harder. If you'd wanted." Quickly, he added, "Or easier. Whatever you want."

"We have to see."

Oggie took the washcloth and started to wipe away what they'd spilled from Arden's skin. He did it so gently that when he offered, "I'll still fuck you into the mattress later if you want," it took Arden by surprise.

He would never get to work at this point. "I'll marry you. If you want."

Oggie pulled back, a half-smile on his face. He tilted his head. His smile widened, soft and tentative.

Arden grinned. He raised his eyebrows. "Don't pretend you weren't serious."

Oggie let out a chuckle, then had to cover his mouth. "Shug, really," he said between giggles.

Arden's smile only widened. He kissed Oggie, who couldn't stop laughing enough to kiss him back. "I'm not saying right now..."

"No, of course not. I don't even know if I like you anymore, I haven't seen you in months. And *this* is definitely not how you're going to propose to me, either," Oggie sniffed. But he smiled while he said it, a broad, goofy smile. "Although I did like that little squeak...!"

Arden blushed.

"I'm not teasing!" Oggie insisted with a kiss. "Very becoming. Did you ever make that noise for Rhys?"

"Oh, let's not do the jealous thing!" Arden insisted.

"Who says I'm jealous? Maybe I just need something to think about when you're gone again all day," Oggie said. "I bet watching him hate-fuck would really do something for me."

"You might actually be a menace to society."

Oggie beamed and climbed out of the shower.

Arden went to work with a piece of toast in his hand and his hair still damp. He also went with a settled sort of calm that he hadn't felt in years if he'd ever felt it at all.

Eden wouldn't fail.

It couldn't. He and Oggie had a whole life to spend together. Darcy had to grow up and Rhys had to give his daughter everything he'd never had. Winslow needed peace in his final years.

The autarky would fail. The peers would disappear. The workers and Terrans would surely have the run of the station before Arden took his final breath.

Eden would thrive.

ABOUT THE AUTHOR

Dan is an author and educator who has lived in Connecticut for their entire life. They received a degree in education and later wrote their Master's thesis on representation of women in same-sex relationships in contemporary Spanish literature and cinema.

More from Dan Ackerman

What Everyone Deserves
2017 Rainbow Awards Honorable Mention
"Although the story deal with some real 1950s issues – discrimination, homophobia, interracial couples and hate crimes – it did it in a way that perfectly suited the characters and the story." - Divine Magazine

In this 1950s period drama, Junius is a New York City fertility demon with a crush. Ever since falling from heaven he's been alone. Except for the mothers and children he watches over.

James Kelly Rosenburg, a black soldier with snowflakes in his hair, walks right into his life with a big problem. James Kelly, turned vampire during the war, is new to New York and its prohibition against vampire killing in city limits.

Junius offers to teach him to overcome his bloodthirsty instincts and live a proper Manhattan life. Their growing friendship leaves them both conflicted as they explore a city both welcoming and alienated by their kind.

That Doesn't Belong Here
2018-2019 Rainbow Awards Honerable Mention
"I liked the ... atmosphere that he created, alongside the paranormal creatures that roam the street. I liked that he wrote characters I could emotionally care for. If Ackerman writes another LGBT fiction, I will give it a try for sure." - Ami, The Blogger Girls

That Doesn't Belong Here begins when Levi and his friend Emily discover an impossible creature in an abandoned pick up. The thing is wounded, frightened and the two friends cannot leave him to the mercy of rubberneckers and tourists. This novel explores what it means to be a person, as the creature, Kato, begins to display not mere intelligence or friendliness but what can only be explained as humanity. The question of who we are allowed to love arises for Levi and Kato, as they are not just crossing the boundaries of gender or sexuality, but of species.